SONG OF THE CAGED WARRIOR

THE CURSE OF SOTKARI TA: PREQUEL

MARIA A. PEREZ

Published by: Maria A. Perez

Editor: Stephanie Hoogstad

Cover Design: Christian Bentulan

ISBN: 978-1-7351133-9-5

Ebook ISBN: 978-1-7351133-8-8

Disclosure: This book contains violent situations including violence against children and teenagers. There are also depictions of trauma and claustrophobia, and explicit consensual sexual scenes.

DEDICATION

I wrote this book during a particularly difficult time in my life. To Sylvia, Wilma, and TP, beautiful, strong, admirable women who help me keep steady when the world gets shaky.

BOOKS BY THIS AUTHOR

The Curse of Sotkari Ta: Book One

Broken Bonds, The Curse of Sotkari Ta: Book Two

Rising From The Curse, The Curse of Sotkari Ta: Book Three

Song of the Caged Warrior, The Curse of Sotkari Ta: Prequel

Montor's Secret Stash of Poems (A companion book to The Curse of Sotkari Ta series)

SONG OF THE CAGED WARRIOR

My life I fear has ended
Before the starting line
Son of the Great Warrior
Brother of a fallen hero
Now lost among the Lostai

I want to soar to the heavens
Embrace my ancestors
Trade this shield tainted
With the crest of Xixsted
For a battle axe of yore

But, lo, I cannot travel
Not to a future that has passed
Nor to a past lost in my present
I sing an old Arandan melody
In the whisper of a caged beast

It is a lullaby of sorts
Sung to myself in the crate

Where I was trapped like goods
In the cargo bay of this
Prison of humiliation

I can only dream of fresh *bomar*
As I chew the gristle
Of enemy meat, so tough
Bitter as day-old *yomoso*
With the sting of a *zirem* rod

I stashed my *bendorai* amulet
From my first revolution on Aranda
A talisman of my tribe
I clutch it with a fist of vengeance
It is cracked like my young heart

I live, and that is something
But better to die with honor
Than survive in shame
So my goal is set for me
Live now to die later, with glory

I carry always an Arandan torch
It ever burns in me
My heart is heavy but strong
I still sing a warrior song
I aim to be a *vimor*—loaded, deadly

PART I

YOMABAR LABOR CAMP

1

—————

At the first sound of thunder, Mother called us in. A few weeks before, my older brothers had finally taught me how to play *moros*, and we were in the middle of a spirited match with the boys from next door. It was a physical sport, but I was tall for my age. Father always said that I would grow up to be the tallest of my brothers.

Frequent thunder had rumbled through our area for several weeks, but it had not rained much. At night, even the ground vibrated, keeping me awake.

"Mother, there is not a cloud in the sky. Why did you interrupt our game? We were beating them," I said, stomping my feet.

I found it odd she did not deal sternly with my defiant behavior, as usual. Instead, ignoring me, she addressed my two older brothers and older sister.

"We are leaving. Each of you, pack a quick bag of essentials while I do the same for Montor and Arixa."

Arixa was my twin sister.

"What is going on?" asked my older sister, Lorma.

"No time for questions. As soon as your father arrives, we are leaving."

I peered out the window, searching for the source of the explosive sounds that were becoming louder by the second. Mother tugged me by the arm.

"Stay away from there," she scolded. "Go to the back of the house until I call you. Take Arixa with you."

I sensed fear in Mother's tone, and even though we were the same age, I was protective of my twin sister. She was much shorter than me. I took my assignment to heart and led Arixa to the storage area in the back and waited. When Father arrived, he gathered us together in the kitchen.

"Children, remember how we have talked about what is happening on our planet?"

Father was referring to stories he had shared with us that I clearly had not paid enough attention to. At my young age, I was not so concerned with Aranda's current events.

"Aliens are meddling in our affairs and trying to turn the tide in our planet's clan wars. I learned this morning that they are aiding the Morant clan. Our province is being bombarded by weapons beyond our known technology. It is not safe here anymore. I have rented a mobile home vehicle for us and Foxor's family. We will have to hide out in the wilderness until the danger passes. Follow me."

"What kind of cowards are we? Why are we so ready to let those bastards take our home and land?" said Drator, my eldest brother.

All our jaws dropped in unison. Drator was the only one of us who would dare to speak to Father in such a tone. He had been home for a few weeks on a break from his off-world business school. No one else in our neighborhood had ever traveled to another planet, even within our star system. He was kind of a celebrity in our small village.

Everyone froze. My other older brother, Rimax, and I looked away when Father glared at Drator.

"I am no coward, but I have a family to take care of."

"Well, I am unattached and ready to fight for my freedom. This is as good a time as any to let you know I have joined a militia."

Another explosion outside, even closer this time, reverberated through our home.

"Sounds like the invaders will arrive any moment now," said Drator. "You should leave. I will slip out the back door to meet my militia friends."

"No, son," said Mother. She looked at Father, tears running down her cheeks. "Do not let him do this. What about his studies?"

Drator gulped and rolled his shoulders.

"Mother, please do not insist. I have made up my mind. I was looking for the right time to tell you."

Father inhaled deeply and met my brother's eyes. He walked over to him and placed his hands on Drator's shoulders.

"Drator, you are almost an adult. I understand your warrior spirit." Father turned to Arixa and me. "Truthfully, if it were not for these young ones, I would have done the same. Good luck, son. May the High Spirit accompany you in battle."

Mother whimpered, but she knew there was nothing else to say. We took turns caressing Drator's cheeks with the backs of our hands to show him our affection and wish him well. He walked out the back door as we walked out the front one.

Foxor and Lasarta—my parents' best friends—and their two teenage sons waited for us outside. Father was the last to board the vehicle. I looked out the window. Down the street, several families were getting ready to leave in their vehicles, too. I was about to ask where we were heading when a blast sent us careening across the street. My sisters shrieked. I stopped short of doing the same. That would have been too embarrassing.

"Hold on!" shouted Father.

We would have suffered much more than the jarring movement had we not been strapped in. Our vehicle crashed against a neighbor's house. Smoke obscured our window views. Father rushed us out of the vehicle.

"Everyone out!"

I unstrapped my safety belt first, next Arixa's, and, grabbing her hand, led her outside. I could barely see through the thick smoke, and everyone was coughing. The commotion ahead of us struck fear in my heart. Father led us away from our vehicle now engulfed in flames. Some of the neighbors' homes and vehicles were on fire, too.

After Mother checked each of us and confirmed we were all OK, we ran towards the woods behind our neighborhood. A flash of light struck the ground, followed by another thunderous sound. We stopped in our tracks. I rubbed my eyes to make sure I could see clearly. Trees and bushes were converted to ashes, leaving a flattened area of ground. A shiny structure the size of our town's sports stadium descended in slow motion. Fascinated, I laid eyes on a real spaceship for the first time. Other neighbors gathered around as the craft touched the ground.

A hatch opened and a bunch of short people without hair who looked like nothing I had seen before marched towards us. They wore uniforms. Remembering my father's earlier words, I concluded they must be the alien race he spoke to us about. Mother gathered Arixa and me and moved us behind her. Lasarta and my older sister stood next to Mother. Father, Rimax, Foxor, and Foxor's sons stood farther ahead.

I stepped sideways to sneak a peek at what was going on. One of the aliens made a hand gesture, bringing the bunch behind him to a halt.

He must be their leader.

They carried weapons similar to those depicted on televised Arandan science fiction serials. The eldest male of each family on our block joined Father and Foxor to face the aliens. Rimax and Foxor's sons took a step back. I counted fifteen Arandan elder males. Other crafts were landing in the distance.

The alien leader spoke into a device, broadcasting his words loudly in Arandan.

"I know you must be concerned, but there is no need for alarm if you follow instructions. As you must know, much blood has been shed on your planet because of your civil wars. We Lostai have come to serve as intermediaries between your clans and restore peace."

We were close enough to Father to hear him reply, "What do you want?"

"This territory is in contention. For your safety, we will transfer you to a neutral zone."

Some of the Arandan males laughed. Father turned around to look at Mother, his expression graver than I had ever seen in my life.

"And what if we decide to stay?" said one of our neighbors.

"Your government has given us authority over this region." The alien leader made a hand signal, and the soldiers aimed their weapons at us. "You have no choice."

Another of the Arandan elder males spoke up.

"We will leave of our own accord. I will not put my family's safety in your hands."

The next moments were etched in my memory. Our neighbor turned his back on the alien leader and walked back to his family. The alien leader made another hand gesture.

Father shouted, "No!"

The first line of soldiers aimed their weapons at our neighbor and his family. Instead of projectiles, the weapons emitted beams of light. My mother and sister cried out and covered their faces. I heard others gasping and wailing. Our neighbor, his wife, and four children lay on the ground. The large circular wounds carved in their chests did not bleed but were bordered by red jagged edges and blackened flesh.

My whole body shook. I had never witnessed death in person before other than when I went on a hunt with Father and my brothers. I hated the fear that consumed me and the sobbing I could not contain. That was inappropriate behavior for a strong Arandan warrior and my little sister's protector. I immediately hated the aliens who had reduced me to a sniffling coward and hung my head in shame. Words emitted from the device made me look up.

"I regret this unfortunate lesson. Please do not make us teach you more. All of you will board our ship now. My soldiers will guide you."

Father turned to look at us again, his face like stone. He signaled to Mother and Lasarta to bring us forward. We took slow, careful steps to join him and Foxor. Some of the alien soldiers gathered around us as the others opened a path to guide us into their spacecraft. Arixa squeezed my hand. Tears streamed down her face.

"Do not cry, little one," I whispered. "I will take care of you."

2

My heart pounded as Lostai soldiers herded us into the craft and down corridors lined with strobing blue lights. At first, the futuristic environment enthralled me, but I was soon overwhelmed by the blaring alarms sounding off everywhere around us. Amazed, I took in the view of the consoles, screens, and computerized equipment. Charts and images hovered in midair. Later, I learned these were called holographic displays.

"Father, why is it so cold in here?" I whispered.

He signaled that I should remain quiet while he and Mother kept my siblings and me between them. I rubbed my hands over my arms, trying to warm myself. No one said much until we arrived at an area comprised of several large rooms without doors. Other Lostai soldiers met us there.

One of the soldiers tapped a hand-held device, and I heard a buzzing sound. Something like green electricity flashed in the front of each room for a second. Another Lostai soldier sent each one of us into the room, counting as we walked in. Once the soldier arrived at a certain count, they moved to the next room.

My family and Foxor's were among the first in, but another family was separated. The soldier placed the parents and older siblings with us and ordered their two toddlers to the next room. When the children clung to their mother, the Lostai soldier pulled them away and shoved them into the next room. Mother covered her mouth at the sounds of the children's wailing. Their father's eyes blazed as he rushed forward to face the Lostai soldier.

Father warned him, "Use caution and self-control, my friend."

The father's voice trembled as he spoke to the Lostai soldier.

"Please, can you switch my children with someone in this room so our family can be together? My children are upset with being separated from their mother."

Foxor's two sons chimed in.

"You can switch them with us."

The Lostai poked the children's father hard with a long rod. A sound like lightning and an odor of scorched flesh filled the area. The male's wife screamed, and the children cried even louder as they watched him double over in pain. The soldier used the same translation device as the Lostai leader had done earlier.

"Be quiet and tell your children to shut up, or we will punish them also!"

The soldiers dragged their father into our room to join his wife and older children and stepped back from the entrance. The green electricity flashed again. Foxor's sons charged forward to tackle the soldier, but some invisible force knocked them back. I looked at Father. His jaw clenched.

"It is a force field. They have fenced us in like cattle."

We all heard the toddlers call out to their mother.

"Shut them up, or we will do it for you!" ordered the Lostai.

The children's mother, named Saroti, encouraged them to calm down.

Some females from the other room shouted back, "Saroti, do not worry. We will watch over them."

Sobs bubbled up in my chest again, but I controlled myself. Arixa was already weeping. Mother pulled her close to muffle the sounds. Soon, all the children in both rooms were crying and sniffling.

After all our neighbors were placed in rooms, the Lostai leader entered the area and addressed us using his device. This was the first time I could see his facial features more clearly. His face was eerily round, as opposed to the angles of our high cheekbones, regal wide noses, and strong jaws. Our skin was covered in a tawny soft fuzz, while the Lostai's skin seemed gross to me in its smooth paleness. His eyes appeared dark compared to our yellow eyes. Father always told us you could learn a lot about a person by looking into their eyes. The Lostai leader's browbone protruded so much that his eyes appeared sunken in his face. I could not even tell what color they were.

"We will lift off shortly and travel to another planet in this sector called Tormix. I realize probably very few of you have ever experienced space travel, but you need not worry. This craft is equipped with gravitational and environmental controls that will make the trip feel uneventful for you."

"I would hardly call this uneventful," whispered one of the older males in our room.

"There is an area in the back of each cell for your biological waste and cleansing. We will provide you with a meal in the morning. I suggest you try to rest."

As time passed, my eyelids grew heavy. Mother and the other females sat on the bare floor, their backs resting against the walls. The males remained standing, huddled on the other side of the room. Arixa fell asleep, stretched out with her head in Mother's lap. My older brother, Father, Foxor, and his sons spoke to each other in murmurs. My older sister, Lorma, took my hand and coaxed me to the floor so I could sit beside her. She placed an arm around my shoulder, pulling me close.

"I should be with Father and my brother planning our escape," I said.

She smiled and caressed my cheek.

"Shhhh. Get some rest, little warrior. I think we will have plenty of battles to deal with in the days ahead."

They kept us in those rooms throughout the entire fifteen-day trip to Tormix. I later learned the rooms were actually prison cells. Father encouraged us to stretch, walk around, and exercise. We were never given blankets or pillows for sleeping. There was no way to get comfortable on the hard floor, and the chilly temperature kept me shivering. The Lostai provided us with soap for bathing but no change of clothing. The water was icy, too. Each family took turns washing their undergarments and setting them to dry on some shelving in the bathroom.

Besides being cold all the time, the food was the next worst thing we had to endure. The morning meal bar looked and tasted like a rectangular piece of dirt. I gagged the first few times Father forced me to eat it.

"I know it does not compare to your mother's excellent cooking, but we need everyone to stay nourished to face whatever challenges await us," said Father.

I assumed he meant we would fight these Lostai, who had incarcerated us for no reason. That was all the motivation I needed. At midday, they would bring in a large pot, small bowls, spoons, and a ladle. I stood first in line to get my portion and pinched my nose as I swallowed the cloudy liquid. It was impossible to figure out what substance the pasty brown balls floating in the soup were made of. The evening meal was better because the vegetables came with a slice of bread, although everything smelled foul to me. Besides the unpleasant taste and odor, the portions were tiny. My stomach never stopped growling.

At first, Mother wanted me to stay close to her, but as the days passed, she allowed me to spend time with Father, my brother, and the other males. Sometimes, they engaged in idle chit-chat, pondering on topics such as how our local sports teams were faring or whether games were being played at all. At other times, the conversation became a bit complicated for me to follow.

"The Morant clan has made a foolish mistake allying themselves with the Lostai. I cannot believe how they have allowed these aliens to meddle in our affairs," said Father.

"Is it really that surprising, Josher? The Lostai gave the Morant clan advanced technology and helped them gain an advantage against the other clans. Perhaps any of the other clans would have done exactly the same if given the opportunity," replied another male.

"It is obvious these people do not have our best interests at heart," continued Father.

"I agree with Josher," said Foxor, placing his hand on Father's shoulder. "I fear that soon these Lostai scum will be the ones ruling over our planet."

"Father?"

Everyone turned to look down at me. Tension squeezed my neck, and suddenly I wished I had kept quiet.

"Yes, son?"

"What is Tormix?"

"Montor, it is a planet on the other edge of this sector."

"I do not remember it mentioned in my science class."

"Yes, until these aliens arrived, we were not aware of what existed outside of our own quadrant."

"Why are they forcing us to go there?"

They all looked at each other, a shared uneasiness at my father's reply.

"We do not know, but I must be honest with you, Montor. You are old enough not to be coddled. I do not think it is anything good."

My father was muscular and a skilled fighter. One time, three members of another clan interrupted our hunt. They threatened to steal our kill from us. Father challenged them to a fight, facing them one by one. He defeated the three of them, and they were required to give us part of their bounty in recompense.

"Father, you should challenge their leader to a duel. You are so much taller and stronger-looking than he is. I am sure you could defeat him. Then we could go back home."

Father took a long, hard look towards the section of the room where the females congregated with their younger children before replying to me.

"I wish it were that simple, son. I fear these people do not have our sense of honor. They do not play by our rules, but do not worry. We will figure out a way."

I did not like this version of my father. It was the first time I saw him shy away from a fight. Anger boiled up in me.

"When I am older, I will escape and join Drator in the militia. You have taught us we should never cower from a bully."

Foxor patted me on the head, which irritated me. I was not joking.

"Josher, looks like you have another warrior in the works with this one. Look how tall he is at only four revolutions. He will one day be a force to be reckoned with."

"Yes, and he is also smart for his age, but he needs to remember his place," replied Father. I dared not look up at him to avoid facing his stern eyes. "The time will come when we chase these alien invaders off our planet, but we need to proceed carefully. Right now, they have the advantage."

"Yes, Father."

3

———

As soon as we disembarked, I noticed the bright light blue heavens were nothing like the mustard skies of home. The warmer temperature was a welcome relief from the frigid spaceship, but I worried about how different everything looked.

"Montor, what is this place?" shouted Arixa. "Why are the clouds white? I am scared."

Mother shushed her with a look. We were quickly learning to speak in hushed tones.

The Lostai soldiers led us from where we landed to a clearing by a mountainous area. A forest bordered the camp on one side, and several rows of shacks constructed of sheet metal lined the opposite side. They kept us walking until we were right in front of the shacks.

"These are your dwellings, one per family," said one of the lieutenants.

For a moment, I thought their translation device might have been in error. The entire shack was no larger than my old bedroom.

"How will we all fit in there?" I whispered to Lorma. She shushed me, too.

The Lostai leader launched into an impassioned speech, waving his arms and smiling at us. While he spoke, an oval metallic object the size of our family's land vehicle zoomed in from behind the mountains and hovered over us. Soon, several more arrived.

What are those?

Not wanting to be reprimanded again, I kept my thoughts to myself.

"Your homeland is currently a war zone. We have done you a favor by moving you to a safe location. You can repay us for our kindness in a small way by earning your keep until the conflict on your planet is resolved."

Father's facial expression stiffened further with each word emitted by the device.

"The caves in these mountains contain crystals we convert into an energy source for our spacecrafts. We ask you to help us extract this material. The warden here will fill you in on the details."

With no further gesture or explanation, the Lostai leader walked away. Most of the soldiers who had led us there also dispersed, leaving the warden flanked by only five soldiers to address us. The warden was also Lostai, but his body language differed from that of the Lostai leader. He paced back and forth as he delivered his instructions. When he stopped walking, he squinted at us and poked his fingers in the air. The oval crafts continued to hover above us as he spoke into his translation device.

"This is a new labor camp, and I oversee this place. I have experience with you people, so I will start things off in an ordered manner and keep it that way. Disobedience will not be tolerated here."

I looked around and wondered if everyone's breathing had sped up the same as mine.

"An energized force field surrounds the mountains and woods. You will not survive even touching it with a finger. The borders are clearly marked. Each family will get one bucket of drinking water per day regardless of how many people there are in a family. You are welcome to barter among yourselves."

Several of the elder males clenched their fists, and one whispered, "They have weapons but are only six, and we are many. Let us jump them now."

Father turned around and said, "If we do that, what makes you think they will not summon more soldiers and kill us all, starting with our females and children? Self-control is key. Our time will come."

Father was well-respected within our community. We remained motionless as the warden, whom I disliked from the start, continued speaking.

"Your offspring grow at an accelerated rate different from Lostai children, so we will not use age to determine who is old enough to work in the mines. I understand that until the age of puberty, Arandan children develop at twice the rate of Lostai and many other species in this sector. Therefore, appearance and size will guide us on who is required to work and which older siblings take care of the younger children."

Will they send me to work? Everyone says I am tall for my age.

"Each person will receive three sets of clothing. After twelve days of work, everyone gets one day off. You can do on that day as you please as long as it does not violate any rule. After every twelve-day cycle, each worker earns one credit, which allows you to use the reproducer on your day off. One order per person."

I had heard that fancy homes in big cities on Aranda were equipped with reproducers, but I had never seen one.

Suddenly, the warden chuckled and wagged his finger at us, reminding me of when my older brothers mocked me.

"Now, do not start getting any funny ideas. You cannot get luxury items and weapons since the reproducer is programmed to only provide necessary items. We know you primitive people still like to engage in hunting. You are welcome to create traps in the woods to capture small animals and birds that might be to your liking. The forest is relatively safe. You may also set up gardens in the area behind your dwellings. We can only provide basic nutritional bars and soup as meals. I hear you already received a meal on the spacecraft, so I suggest you get settled in your dwellings and rest. Soldiers will come by later with your labor uniforms and drinking water. Work starts tomorrow."

He walked away but then whipped around, laughed to himself, and tapped his forehead.

"Oh, I almost forgot. There is a stream in the woods safe for bathing. You Arandans tend to get a repulsive body odor. Each one of you must bathe there once a day. I suggest first thing in the morning. Failure to comply will result in punishment."

One male in our group had heard enough, and before anyone could stop him, he lunged at the warden. Others followed, despite Father shouting for them to get back. I heard a loud vibrating sound above and looked up to see the oval objects change color from grey to neon red. Beams of light rained on the Arandan males who had charged forward. Someone covered my eyes, but the shrieking and gasps let me know something horrible had occurred. I did not like being shielded from trouble, as if I were a delicate female, and pulled away from whoever was holding me. It turned out to be my older brother, Rimax. Mother scooped Arixa in her arms. I ran up to Father.

"Son, *shermont*! What are you doing here? Get back there with your mother."

His voice sounded frantic. I wanted to see for myself what everyone was screaming about. It took my mind a moment to piece together the scene in front of me. Instead of bodies, faces, and limbs, only scorched clothing and oozing mounds of flesh remained of the males who had rushed forward.

Father grabbed me by an arm and took me back to my mother, scolding me, "Montor, next time you ignore my orders, you will earn a severe punishment."

His harsh words did not match his expression. He appeared more worried than angry. Still, he shouted at Mother, Rimax, and Lorma.

"What is wrong with all of you? Can you not control him and keep him back here?"

Embarrassed, I stared at the ground. Even though at times I was impulsive, I hated causing trouble for Mother or my siblings. Tears flowed down Mother's cheeks as she pulled me close to her. The warden's translator device boomed.

"I hope you learned that lesson well. Every time one of you gets out of line, all of you will bear the consequences. No meals will be distributed tomorrow to anyone."

Father stepped forward to face the warden, and Mother's face crumpled in worry.

"Warden, I regret the poor judgment of my friends. Please consider this has been stressful for all of us. Allow us to hunt or forage the woods for something to eat this afternoon. We will not be in a good mental or physical state to work tomorrow on an empty stomach."

The warden considered the request. He rolled his eyes.

"So, are you the leader of these people?"

"No, warden, but I am trying to help make things better for all of us."

"Fine, but if anyone else gets out of line, your family specifically will lose another day of meal rations. The workday starts at dawn, so I suggest you not stay out too late."

Father sighed deeply.

"I understand. Warden, we cremate our dead. Can you accommodate this?"

"No. People who do not follow orders and cause problems are trash and will be treated as such."

The warden looked up at Father with cold eyes. Father's jaw clenched, but he maintained control.

"OK, give us a moment to say a prayer before you dispose of them."

The warden waved his hand dismissively, turned around, and as he walked away, replied, "Make it quick. By the way, what is your name, Arandan?"

"My name is Josher."

"Welcome to the Yomabar Labor Camp, Josher. I am Warden Nerimat. The less your people get on my nerves, the better."

Father turned his back to the warden and addressed us.

"Time to pray for these souls."

There was no priestess in our group, so the eldest female took on that role. She recited a prayer, after which she guided us in the sacred death chant.

"Let us cement the names of our friends in our history."

In chorus, we repeated several times the names of the ten males we lost. While we were still chanting, a different type of beam emanated from one of the oval objects. The contraption levitated the remains of the dead and took them away. Except for some females sobbing, we were silent. Father distracted us from our grief.

"As we are not familiar with this planet, we do not know how soon night will fall. Let us go investigate whether there is anything edible in the woods. I suggest the mothers stay here with the children and find out what these people have supplied us with in these so-called dwellings. Everyone else should remain in one large group and come with me."

Rimax patted me on the head as he walked past me towards Father.

"Go with the females, baby."

I silently seethed and was about to follow Mother when Father called me.

"Montor, come with us."

Mother turned and made eye contact with Father. Some unknown message was transmitted between them.

"Montor, be careful," she said before I ran off to Father's side.

One step into the woods made it clear, once again, how different this place was from home. I had never seen plants or trees with green leaves and stems. Aranda's vegetation boasted various shades of orange, instead. The trees in the woods by our home had brownish green trunks, compared to the dark browns I saw in this forest.

"Father, the colors of the trees and leaves are so strange. Do you think we will find something to eat here?"

"Keep your eyes open. Something should turn up."

The forest was thick with vegetation. The sounds of hooting birds, chirping insects, and even small animal squeaks and grunts filled the air. Although we found fruit-bearing trees, tubers, and nuts on the forest floor, I did not recognize anything. Despite my consternation, the beauty of a shrub caught my attention. The petals on its star-shaped flowers alternated in dark purple and light blue with bright red pistils shooting out of its center. The fresh, herbal fragrance reminded me of the sudsy soap we used at home to bathe. I decided to bring a bunch for Arixa, who loved girly things like flowers and perfume.

Rimax and the other teenage boys climbed the trees and found eggs in bird nests. We took off our shirts and tied them in a way that allowed us to better carry the items we found.

"Everyone, forget trying to capture animals and eggs for the time being, as we do not have a way yet to cook them. Also, do not eat anything. Remember, we have no idea if this stuff is toxic for us," warned Father.

At twilight, we placed everything gathered in a pile. Father and other males smelled and inspected the fruits and nuts, but there was only one definite test. Someone would have to eat them. The three eldest males stepped forward.

"We have lived enough and will probably not survive for long the rigors of working in those mines. Let us be your testers."

One tester tried the round green fruit and the small orange berries. He tolerated them fine. Another of the elders cracked open the nuts with a rock. After placing one in his mouth, he wheezed, and his lips inflamed. They tossed those away. The third tester bit into a tuber with no noticeable effect.

"I suggest we wait until we are hungry before we eat any of these items. It will give us time to observe any other effects. Let us go back and try to get some rest. Who knows what new challenges face us tomorrow?" said Father.

Everyone agreed. We carried as much as we could, and the elder female divided everything as fairly as possible. Confusion reigned when we first arrived back at the shacks as we tried to sort out which ones each of our mothers had settled in. We found Mother. She wisely had selected a corner shack bordering another wooded area.

"It seems we will need to relieve ourselves in the forest," she said. "I figured it would be better if we were near an area that provides some privacy."

I offered Arixa the bouquet of flowers I had gathered for her. They brought a smile to her frightened little face.

"Thank you, Montor. They are beautiful," she whispered after placing one behind her ear. "Are the woods scary? Mother says we need to do *lae-ley* out there."

I caressed her cheek. "It is different but not scary. I am sure Mother or Lorma will accompany you when you have to go."

Her expression was a mix of discomfort and disgust.

"It is kind of gross, though." She grabbed my hand and pulled me into the shack. "This is our home now." A pained look crossed her face.

Inside the tiny shack, a third of the space was occupied by the four chairs and square table that made up the only furniture. The remaining space would barely be enough for our family of six to lie down and have some standing room. Soldiers had delivered folded stacks of uniforms and set them on the table. We placed the fruits and tubers the elder female had assigned to us on the chairs.

"Let us wait before trying these items," said Father. "I would like to be sure the elders do not show any delayed adverse reaction before we eat them."

The soldiers had also brought a bucket of water and one glass. We each drank a half glass. Father said we should be careful how much we consumed for the time being. There was no door, flooring, illumination, or windows. As night fell, the temperature dropped. The six of us huddled together on the dirt floor and tried to get some sleep. My parents positioned themselves in the center. Arixa and Lorma lay next to Mother; Rimax and I, next to Father.

Pebbles on the rough, uneven ground made it impossible to get comfortable. The earlier images of mutilated bodies came to me. If at least they had appeared like normal fallen warriors with spear or bullet wounds, perhaps I would have been less horrified. Instead, they had been reduced to unrecognizable, bloody, burnt pieces of flesh. The sounds of the females screaming filled my ears. I pressed my forehead against my father's side.

"Father, why has this happened to us? Did we do something wrong to deserve this?"

"No, son. Sometimes, evil comes knocking at the door. That is when we tap into our mental and physical strength to face the challenge."

"It is not fair. How can we fight against their weapons that can melt bodies?"

I probably should not have said that. Arixa whimpered, signaling she was listening to us.

"Do not be made to feel a victim. We are proud warriors. With careful thought and planning, we will pull ourselves out of this situation. Now, everyone, we must try to rest."

I shifted my legs and moved around, attempting to shake the fear that kept me wide awake. Finally, Mother's whispered prayers helped me to drift to sleep.

4

For a moment, I thought the loud noises were nightmares. I awoke with a start and peeked out of the shack's entrance.

"Get back here, Montor!" shouted Mother.

In an instant, Father was outside scoping out the situation. The Lostai soldiers were banging the sides of the shacks with their weapons. It was not yet dawn.

The now-familiar sound of the translation device boomed in my ears.

"Arandans, this is your warden. It is time for your morning bath. Take your uniforms with you and return here dressed by dawn, ready to start your workday." He pointed his weapon diagonally towards the forest. "You will find the stream about a fifteen-minute walk in that direction. Since it is your first day, I have given you extra time, but you should plan on spending no more than ten minutes there. My supervisors will be here waiting to assign you to your duties. Do not make them wait."

Father told us to grab our clothing and rush out. He looked up. The oval contraptions were hovering over us again. The warden pointed them out to us.

"Our surveillance devices will turn a green color to alert you that it is time to finish up at the stream and head back here."

"Hurry," Father said as he led us into the woods.

Foxor, his wife, Lasarta, and their sons caught up with us.

"Josher, I admire your self-control and leadership, but I fear many of the males here will not tolerate this for much longer. They are treating us like animals," said Foxor.

"I know, but not only our lives are at stake. We need to protect our females and young children. I do not intend to tolerate this situation forever either, but we must put our rage and passion aside for a moment and take time to strategize. In the meantime, we must obey if we want our families to survive. I will emphasize this with our friends, and I suggest you do the same."

Although the stream was wide, its flow was calm and safe, even for children younger than me. I felt queasy at first getting into water that was mostly lacking in color. Our seas and rivers were red. These waters were translucent with some greyish-green spots. I could see little fish swimming about and small creatures crawling on the bottom. The females and the young children stayed in the shallow water while the males went deeper. As far back as I could remember, I knew how to swim. Father must have taught me at an early age. He allowed me to go in the deep with him. I was the only child among the adult males. We all kept our clothes on while in the water and used them to scrub our bodies.

One male named Foranti spoke in an aggressive tone.

"The first chance I have, I will get my hands on a weapon and kill that piece of crap warden."

"Then you better kill your wife and children first, for they will suffer the consequences of your rash behavior," replied Father.

"You must be getting old, Josher. The man I fought with is not who I see before me."

Before marrying our mother, Father had fought in the clan wars. My older brothers told me stories about this phase of his life. He was known across several clans for his bravery and military prowess.

"You are correct. I am now a father and a husband. I will be smart about how I defend my wife and children."

"Fine, Josher. Cower behind them and stay out of my way."

"Unfortunately, I cannot allow that. Your actions will also affect the rest of us. I ask you to be patient. You saw what happened yesterday. These things hovering over us are observing our every move. The moment you grab a weapon, you will be pulverized, and the rest of us will be punished."

Foxor chimed in.

"Josher is right, Foranti. We are all angry, but we need to put up with this for now and get settled into a routine before we can come up with a plan. Have you forgotten we are on a foreign planet and enclosed within a force field?"

Foranti waved his hands in the air and looked around at the other males as if summoning support.

"You and Josher are just like the rest of us. Neither of you is our mayor or lieutenant. Why should we follow your orders? You do not speak for all of us."

Father approached Foranti, and Foxor grimaced. I had seen that expression on Father's face before. It scared me to death. Father raised his voice even louder than Foranti's and poked him hard in the chest.

"I will kill you or anyone else with my bare hands if I think you will cause us to be punished again. I claim leadership of our group unless someone else wants to challenge me for that position." Father looked around. "I am waiting. Anyone?"

Silence.

Father glanced at the surveillance device hovering overhead and lowered his voice.

"Good. Then listen carefully. We will conform to the rules here for the time being. Once we are familiar enough with the routine, we can discuss what options we have. Does anyone disagree?"

Foranti looked around. No one said a word.

"OK. As a team, we will impart our own justice on any of us who causes problems. Agreed?"

Knowing we had less than ten minutes, Father rushed to each of the thirty-two males in our group and ensured that they supported him as leader. Rimax and I swam swiftly beside him.

"Thank you for the confidence you have placed in me. I have no desire for power or anything like that. I am only trying to protect my friends and family. We will decide things as a team and ask the elder female to help keep things fair between us." Father looked up again at the hovering objects. He clenched his fist but kept his arm down and slightly splashed the water.

"Together, we will defeat this enemy," he said, keeping his voice low.

Everyone replied "Yes" and mimicked his tone and gesture. We exited the stream, and each family dispersed within the woods to change into their uniforms. Foxor and his family joined us, so our group could create a circle around the person changing clothes while facing away to provide some privacy. Arixa's uniform was too large, so Mother helped her roll up the sleeves and the cuffs of the pants. Once we were all dressed, we squeezed the excess water from the old clothes and raced back to the shacks.

Soldiers and the warden awaited us. As soon as we arrived, he ordered us to organize into family units. The warden inspected the families, deciding each person's role. He assigned Mother, Father, and Rimax as mine workers. Lorma was designated a child caregiver, with Arixa and me in her care. Foxor, Lasarta, and his sons were also mine workers. I could not believe even the fragile elderly female was assigned to work.

"Everyone, take a drink of water and follow the soldiers into the caves. Your shift lasts until dusk. Normally, you would get a nutritional bar at midday and soup at the end of the shift, but your meal rations have been forfeited because of yesterday's behavior. You will get a bit of water at midday. If there is anything you found in the forest last night that you would like to eat, you may bring it in your pocket and have it at the midday break."

The elder males who had tasted the fruit the night before had shown no adverse reaction, so Father said we should each take one with us.

It took us longer to get to the cave than it did to get to the stream. Across from the mountain range stood gleaming white triangular buildings with large windows. It reminded me of futuristic cities depicted on televised, fictional serials. Shiny vehicles without wheels magically zipped back and forth between the cave and the white buildings. The large cave's ceiling was as high as the theater in our old neighborhood. The inside of the cave looked like the Lostai spaceship, with electronic equipment and holographic displays of star charts and other unfamiliar images. Lostai soldiers walked about everywhere or were seated in cubicles or around larger tables.

Once we were all inside the cave, the warden stood before us. Several armed soldiers stood behind him.

"Attention, Arandans. The workers will be led down one of those tunnels to be separated into groups and trained. I suggest you follow your supervisors' instructions. They have the power to reward and punish you based on your performance. The children and caregivers will go into the rooms over there." He pointed to what appeared to be prison cells, like the ones on the spaceship. "At midday, my supervisors will distribute water.

At the end of the day, we will all assemble here, and you will return to your dwellings. Is that clear?"

No one answered.

"By the way, you will need to learn Lostai. This is how you pronounce 'Yes, sir' in my language."

He made a hand gesture, and the soldiers behind him pointed their weapons at us.

"Do you understand?"

He made us repeat "Yes, sir" in Lostai several times until we pronounced it to his liking. Something worse than anger brewed inside me. I looked around and saw it in the eyes of every single Arandan. With a quick gesture, the warden signaled to the soldiers to get each group moving in the right direction.

"Montor, Arixa, come with me," said Lorma, taking each of us by the hand.

After herding us into the prison cell, they activated a force field. The warden did not post any soldier to guard the cell, but every so often, one came around to peer at us. At one point, two soldiers came by and joked among themselves in their language, pointing at us and laughing.

In our prison cell, we found eight other caregivers around or just over the age of puberty, six female and two male. Lorma was assigned three more children besides Arixa and me who did not have an older sibling. Each caregiver was responsible for five children, except one who only had three. Two female adolescents had babies assigned to their group who kept them occupied. The rest of us sat on the floor, bored and dejected. I hated seeing Arixa's watery eyes and puckered lips and started singing some of her favorite songs to distract her. Lorma and some others joined in. For a while, we forgot where we were until we heard the babies crying. They were hungry, and there was no consoling them. Soon, the warden came by with his translation device.

"Why are you not keeping the babies quiet? We cannot concentrate on our work with that incessant howling."

The tone of his voice, his body language, and his scowl transmitted the anger that the audio on his device could not. Terrified, we all looked at each other, not knowing what to say or do. There was a male about Lorma's age in the room, so it was not her place to speak up, but he seemed petrified. She took a deep breath, stood, and approached the force field.

She looks so much like Father.

"Sir, the babies need to be suckled by their mothers. There is nothing we can do to stop their crying. Please, can your soldiers find them and bring them here briefly to feed their babies? I am sure they will quiet down after they are full."

The warden regarded Lorma for a moment.

"Who is your father?"

I could see Lorma gulp from where I was sitting.

"Josher."

"Ah, yes, I should have guessed. What are the names of the mothers?"

Lorma consulted with the others and found out the names.

"Reminta, Salema, and Lirta."

"Very well. We will put out a call for them, but after the babies are fed, you better make sure they stay quiet. I cannot control my soldiers if they get cranky from all that noise."

As if on cue, a nearby soldier hit the force field with his weapon in a menacing way, causing it to spark. I jumped in fear and grew angry at his cruel chuckle.

"Sir, the mothers will need to be brought back at least two more times before dusk. And you probably need to do the same for the babies in the other cells," added Lorma.

The warden rolled his eyes but nodded.

Lorma sat back down next to us.

"You are so brave," I said to her.

Arixa buried her face in her hands. I heard her sobbing. Lorma pulled us both close.

"Do not worry. Everything will be fine."

The mothers arrived. As the females suckled their babies, the older adolescents bombarded them with questions about the mines. One of the mothers who had a bloody gash on one of her hands was the most talkative.

"They organized us in groups of twenty. Two supervisors are assigned to each group. The tunnels are dank and narrow. They took us up to a certain point and then sent us down to areas that we can only reach by crawling on our hands and knees." She wiped the blood off on her shirt. "The rocks that line the floors and walls are as sharp as razors. I smelled a strange odor like gas that gave me a fit of coughing. I doubt our elders will be able to endure much of this."

"What do they have you looking for?" asked a girl.

"Bright green crystals that are embedded in the rock. They look like jewels but are warm to the touch. We are given a small laser tool that allows us to carve the crystals out of the rock."

"Maybe the males can use those tools as weapons against the supervisor," said an older boy.

"I do not think so. When I came back here, one supervisor collected the tool from me while the other had his weapon ready to fire if I resisted."

After the babies were fed and rocked to sleep, their mothers were escorted back to the tunnels. We were told to remain quiet to avoid waking the babies.

"Maybe now is a good time for you to take a nap," said Lorma.

Arixa quickly accepted the suggestion and curled up on the floor. I did the opposite, standing to stretch my legs and wanting to be brave like my sister. Mesmerized, I tiptoed to the front of the force field and took in the activities going on in the cave. Symbols and maps flickered and floated in the air in bright colors. Images of Lostai and other beings that I had not seen before appeared and disappeared in a fog of light. When my legs tired, I sat and watched the soldiers pointing at the holographic charts and working with the equipment on their stations.

My stomach rumbled. I pulled out the green fruit from my pocket and sniffed it. The pleasant aroma and thin skin invited me to take a bite, only to be disappointed by the hard flesh and sour taste. It needed some more time to ripen, but hunger pangs helped me imagine it as a tasty snack. I munched on it while observing the area outside the cave entrance. Soldiers were engaged in some sort of drill, practicing with their weapons and sparring with each other.

I will learn by watching. One day, I will join Drator and fight against these people who have taken us away from our home.

5

Father, Mother, and Rimax spoke little on the walk back to the shack and appeared exhausted. Their soiled uniforms stuck to their sweaty bodies. Mother's pants were ripped in the knee area, and Rimax held his hands against his chest, obviously in pain. Father's expression made it clear he was not in the mood to answer questions about how the day had gone for them. Night fell by the time we arrived back at the shack. Inside, we each drank a glass of water. Mother stepped outside again and called Rimax out, asking to see the palms of his hands. The moonlight provided enough illumination. Arixa, Lorma, and I watched from inside the shack in silence. Whatever Mother saw caused her to cover her mouth, while Rimax jutted his chin stoically.

"Lorma, bring me the shirt I was wearing yesterday and a glass of water," Mother said, trying to hide the tremor in her voice.

Mother moistened the cloth and dabbed at Rimax's hands. She took her time and was ever so careful. Rimax winced but did not utter a sound. Father stepped outside also and paced like a caged animal. Inside the shack, Arixa tucked her chin and looked up at me with eyes that seemed to get sadder by the day. It was well accepted in our family that Rimax, with his mild nature and obedient behavior, was Mother's favorite. I remembered how Lorma and Drator often teased him, saying he was so good he should study to be a priestess even though only females entered the priesthood. It was good-natured sibling ribbing. In all honesty, we admired his kind heart. I needed a distraction to avoid getting teary-eyed, too, so I signaled to Lorma to come back inside.

"Lorma," I whispered, "I wonder what happened."

"Shh. Obviously, they had a rough time. I am sure we will hear about it eventually. You will find out Father's thoughts soon enough, since he takes you with him to bathe with the older males."

She was right. The next morning, in the stream, everyone spoke of their experience in the mines.

"I am sure my wife has several fingers broken. Some heavy rocks fell on her hand. She is in extreme pain. The supervisor offered no treatment or pain medication," said one of Father's friends.

"Those tunnels are hazardous. I am sure these people have the advanced technology to mechanize these tasks, yet they are risking our lives," said another.

"We are cheap labor. As Josher has pointed out many times already, these Lostai do not care about our well-being at all," said Foxor.

Father was unusually quiet until Foranti said, "Your son was in my group, Josher. I saw what they did to him. He was punished for slowing us down. They used a rod they call a *zirem* on his hands. I would have defended him, but you said we should adhere to their rules. What will they do to him next if he cannot work with his hands so badly burned?"

I saw no sympathy in Foranti's eyes as Rimax lowered his. Father put his hand on Rimax's shoulder and glared at Foranti.

"I said we needed to be smart about how we deal with them. We still should defend ourselves. I will speak with the warden about this treatment."

No one said anything about Rimax being barely above the age of puberty. There were adolescents his age in the children's group. Lorma was older than him and had not been sent to work. The males in our family were among the tallest in our community. Father once told us we inherited this trait from his maternal grandfather. Rimax's height worked against him, and the Lostai considered him an adult. It made me wonder how long they would hold us here. Although I was still three revolutions away from puberty, everyone in our family always made a big deal about how I was taller than any of my brothers had been at my age.

Maybe I will be the first child sent to work with adults.

I shuddered at the thought. On our way to the stream, Rimax secretly had shown me the ugly red welts covering the palms of his hands.

The warden did not meet us at the shacks when it was time to head to the caves. Instead, he sent his supervisors to group the workers according to their assignments and lead the kids and their caregivers to the prison cell.

I overheard Father say to his supervisor, "I need to speak to the warden."

"And I need a vacation, but I am stuck here dealing with you people," answered the supervisor, his words laced with sarcasm.

Father's voice remained calm, but his eyes could have burned holes in the Lostai's skull.

"If you do not take me to the warden, we will refuse to work. You will have to kill us all, and your military will have wasted time, energy, and resources bringing us here. These people have accepted me as their leader, and they will follow my instructions. Many are waiting for an excuse to rebel against you. My son, Rimax, will walk with me when I speak to the warden. I will not waiver on this request, either."

The supervisor smirked but replied, "Fine, I will take you to him."

When we arrived at the caves, my eyes followed the supervisor, Father, and Rimax as they separated from the group. I caught sight of Mother's worried expression as she continued with the rest of her group down the tunnel. My stomach twisted and turned with apprehension, but as soon as we entered the prison cell, Lorma distracted us with clapping and chanting games.

Later that evening, Father shared with us how the conversation went with the warden.

"The supervisor took me to the warden's office and told the warden I had threatened to disobey orders. He expected it to be a quick conversation and lingered. Perhaps he thought the warden would have me punished. Instead, the warden dismissed him. Once the supervisor left, I told the warden he needed to agree to some basic concessions to ensure productivity. I said these should include medical treatment for any illness or injury."

"What was his reaction?" asked Mother.

"He started off by saying this would increase his operational cost. I countered with the same thing I told the supervisor. There would be a much higher loss if they were forced to kill us all and find and transport a new workforce. I tried to approach our conversation like a business transaction."

Father accomplished a lot in that negotiation. The warden agreed to give medical treatment to the injured. Lostai medical technology was far more advanced than what we possessed on Aranda. Rimax described being taken to an infirmary where a physician placed a pliable metallic pad on each of his hands. We gaped in disbelief at his palms. They showed no signs of being burned, not even scars. Mother kept inspecting his hands, turning them over and over. The warden also conceded to have Rimax reassigned to Father's group. Lorma had also mentioned to Father what happened with the babies the day before. Father's last request to the warden was to exempt pregnant females and mothers with nursing babies from work. They were allowed to remain in the shacks where they at least had chairs to sit on.

On the way to the stream the next morning, Father tried to downplay the events of the previous day, but he could not avoid everyone's praise. Even Foranti said, "Well, Josher, I must admit, we were right in letting you do your smooth-talking."

The following lunar cycles were difficult, but we fell into a routine. After the first twelve days, Rimax, Father, and Mother earned a credit each. Everyone agreed to let our family be the first to use the reproducer on our day off. Father said we had to be frugal and strategic about how we would use the credits. We first acquired a pot, a heater, and a set of spoons. This allowed us to boil the tubers and eggs we harvested from the forest to supplement our diet. Mother found herbs that helped add some flavor.

Father requested special permission to program the reproducer to make basic carving knives available. The warden said if any of us attacked his personnel with a knife, he would kill ten of us, randomly selected, including females and children. Everyone promised Father they would take care not to make such a mistake. We spent the next set of credits on a knife, seeds, and a blanket.

Basic tools and materials that aided us in hunting and fishing and rudimentary comfort items made our lives as prisoners a bit more bearable. We also reproduced large quantities of salt and an insulated receptacle to preserve meat, fish, and produce. Large leaves were gathered and placed on the ground to create a softer floor for sleeping. As we earned more credits, we acquired a mattress. On our off days, we explored the woods, and in the evenings, the entire community shared meals, singing and chatting as a group. It was our only down-time from the drudgery of our daily routine and created cama-raderie. The teenagers constructed primitive drums and flutes to accompany the singing.

Father's supervisor, named Horaz, did not like that Father seemed to have the warden's ear, so he worked his group extra hard. The elderly Arandans quickly succumbed to the rigors of laboring for long hours in tunnels with poor ventilation. Cave-ins, explosions of naturally occurring gas, flash flooding, and toxic fumes made working in the mines a hazardous process. It was only a matter of time before we lost more Arandans to mining accidents. There were also incidents where some super-visors were quick to punish what they deemed as insubordina-tion or lazy behavior. Through Father's intercession with the warden, these were kept to a minimum. Father convinced the warden that spurring Arandan rebellious sentiment would only cause problems for everyone.

We were all caught by surprise when a new group of Arandan prisoners arrived at the camp. By then, the first seedlings of Mother's garden had sprouted. Luckily, these Aran-dans were from a friendly neighboring clan. The warden stopped mining for a few days and shifted work to the construction of shacks for the new arrivals.

Soon, the new workers got accustomed to the established routine. One male from the new group was a doctor named Serinth. During morning bath time, Serinth told stories of how our region back home had become a brutal battle zone. He said he had tended many wounded Arandan militia soldiers and remembered some of their names. Everyone was curious, so he rattled off names he recalled. When he said "Drator," Rimax and I looked at Father. His face turned to stone.

"Drator?" Father asked. "Of what clan?"

Arandan clan names are only spoken or written on the most solemn occasions. The doctor would not have said the person's clan name without a specific request. I held my breath, waiting for his reply.

"He told me he was from the Ventamu clan." Serinth lowered his eyes as he realized who he was talking to. "He said his Father's name was Josher and that he had four siblings."

"That is my son," said Father. I could tell he was trying to maintain composure, but he was breathing heavier than normal. "How is he?"

Serinth did not look up or answer.

"What happened to him?" insisted Father.

The doctor finally spoke.

"I am afraid he died of his injuries. By the time they brought him to me, there was not much I could do. It is a shame how many young Arandans have been lost."

That was the first time I saw Father's face so crumpled in grief. Rimax ran to Father and pressed his face against his chest. I just stood there and bawled. It seemed I had been holding in the need to cry for a long time, but the news of Drator's death was too much for me.

If Rimax was Mother's favorite, Father favored Drator, and the rest of us looked up to him. He was the eldest male sibling, the one destined to replace Father as the patriarch of our family. We were in awe of him. His excellent grades in school had earned him a scholarship that, supplemented with Father's savings, allowed him to attend an off-world business school only the wealthy could afford. A competitive athlete, he taught me sports and welcomed me into his games when most other boys my age still played with their sisters. And despite it being an act of rebellion, it was clear Father was proud he had joined the militia.

Now, I will never be able to join Drator to fight against these filthy Lostai.

Father waited until the evening after work to tell Mother. She cried for a long time before leading us in the death chant ritual. During the evenings that followed, she sobbed after she thought we were all asleep. Sometimes, she and Father would walk out of the shack in the middle of the night and stand outside of the entrance. Father embraced her, rubbed her back, and caressed her cheek. Mother never regained her smile after that day.

6

———————

Soon after we learned of Drator's death, Horaz, Father's supervisor, gathered the entire community to deliver some news. The warden had returned to his home world to deal with family issues and left Horaz in charge.

The work environment changed for the worse. Horaz forgot about the concessions Father had negotiated with the warden. The supervisors were now encouraged to control us with an iron hand. More Arandan prisoners were arriving at the labor camp, so there was little motivation to tend to the injured. Members of the community disappeared mysteriously. Rather than receiving medical treatment, the injured were executed.

It became increasingly difficult for Father to control the resentment building up among the Arandan workers. To make matters worse, some of the new workers belonged to rival clans. The resulting fights among prisoners created even more instability. A vicious circle of insubordination and punishment became the norm. Father and Mother did their best to shelter us from the surrounding violence.

After four lunar cycles, seasons changed, and temperatures dropped. Ice fell from the sky in cold, hard chunks. I had never seen such a thing. Our home province was a seaside tropical paradise. We were not made for this kind of weather. Horaz insisted we continue our morning baths in the stream even amid the winter storms.

Arixa's sniffles and difficulty breathing were the first signs that she was sick. Doctor Serinth helped Mother reproduce the right ingredients to create an ointment. I watched night after night as Mother rubbed Arixa's throat, chest, and back. It provided some relief, but soon the hacking cough returned. A cold fear pierced my chest like the icy winds outside.

I often stayed awake caressing Arixa's head and singing songs to her long after everyone else fell asleep. They were all exhausted from their daily grind, but I had energy to spare. One night, I felt the heat coming off her skin.

"Mother, Mother, something is not right!" I shouted.

Mother checked Arixa, and her eyes filled with tears.

"Josher, she has a fever."

Father walked outside and dampened a cloth with icy rain. With a gentle touch, he applied the cloth to her fore-head and chased the fever away. We went to sleep, but in the morning, Arixa awoke us with her moans, and she was warm again. Father found Doctor Serinth and brought him to our shack.

"Josher, I am sure she has an upper respiratory bacterial infection. I do not think it is viral because none of you are sick. A basic antibiotic might do the trick."

"I will ask Horaz for it," said Father.

Father requested an audience with Horaz, but his new supervisor said Horaz did not have time for him. Two days later, as luck would have it, Horaz came to inspect the workers lining up in front of the shacks. Arixa had stopped eating, barely spoke a word, and could no longer make the walk from the shack to the caves. Lorma carried her.

As Horaz walked past our shack, Father called out to him,

"Horaz, please, I would like to speak to you. I have asked my supervisor several times to allow me to see you."

Horaz cocked his head. The rest of us watched from our respective spots. I did not like the look on his face.

"I think I hear an insect buzzing," Horaz mused in a condescending tone.

My heart jumped as Father fell out of line and walked up to Horaz in long, quick strides. Father lost the deference in his voice and replaced it with a growl he used with enemies.

"You will hear me now. My young daughter needs a basic antibiotic I am sure you have in your infirmary. I am respectfully asking you for some and will work during my next few off days to cover the cost."

Horaz's cruel smile was cemented in my memory.

"I do not need the extra hours of one lone Arandan worker. We are bringing thousands more of you people here. If you continue to get out of line, you may lose more than one member of your family," replied Horaz, pointing at the surveillance devices hovering over us. "Get back in line, Arandan."

Horaz turned and continued on his way. I looked around. Everyone shared Father's feelings of rage and impotence. That evening, after a long day of work, Father snuck into the woods and brought back a bird. Other than to relieve ourselves, we were not allowed to go into the woods at night. He and Mother quickly worked to remove the feathers and butcher the bird. She boiled it and added some vegetables and herbs. I cried as she tried to coax Arixa to eat, but by now, she could not even hold her head up.

"Stop crying, Montor," ordered Father. "You will only upset her more."

That night, no one slept. We watched as Arixa's breathing became even more labored. I wanted to cover my face and not see what was happening, but I also hoped the few spoons of broth Mother coaxed Arixa to swallow might bring back her strength. Many family members used to joke that Mother's soup could raise a person from the dead. Maybe there was some truth to it. Nothing could have prepared me to watch Arixa take her last breath and the color drain from her face.

No!

I thought I would stop breathing too. My stomach pulled in like I was about to vomit. Mother burst into loud wailing while she cradled Arixa's body against her chest. Between her sobs, Mother repeated over and over, "No, please do not take my little one."

Father shouted a string of curse words before he slid his hand across his face in grief. He walked out of the shack, doubled over, and howled as if in pain. Foxor and Lasarta came running out from the shack next door and tried to console him. Now, we were all crying. I could not make sense of what was happening.

Why did the bacteria get her? I am so much stronger. I could have survived it. Why her?

Lasarta came into the shack and hugged Mother while she still held Arixa. Mother looked unsteady, as if she were about to fall.

"I am so sorry, so sorry," said Lasarta, as she tried to pry Arixa's body from Mother's arms.

"No, no. Do not take her from me."

"Do not worry. I am only laying her down. You look dizzy. Let me help you," pleaded Lasarta.

Finally, Mother allowed Lasarta to place Arixa's body on the mattress. Lasarta guided Mother to a chair. Soon, Mother's bawling attracted the attention of many more neighbors. They gathered outside our shack. Some females came in to help Mother, who appeared like she would fall out of the chair. I wanted to be with Father and walked out of the shack towards him but kept my distance. I had never seen him openly cry. Foxor spoke to Father in a soothing but firm voice.

"Josher, I cannot imagine your pain. I am so sorry, but you know they will not allow us time in the morning to honor her body and soul. We must rush to do it now. I will take care of everything," said Foxor.

Father inclined his head. No words came out of his mouth. Foxor saw me and pulled me over.

"Stay with your father. I need to take care of some things."

I was not tall enough to reach Father's shoulder as Foxor did, so I held his hand. Soon, Rimax arrived, and the three of us held each other up.

The elderly female who had taken on the role of priestess when we first arrived at the labor camp died sometime before. Foxor came back with her daughter, named Tomaxa, who had since replaced her.

"Josher, my mother explained to me our basic rituals. Do you want me to help take care of your daughter's passage into the spirit world?" asked Tomaxa.

Father acknowledged her only with a nod. Now, everything was moving too fast for me. The acting priestess brought out Arixa's body wrapped in one of our hard-earned blankets and headed towards the woods. Everyone who had come out of their shacks followed her. No one mentioned anything about the fact that it was against the rules. Someone carried a bucket of water. Lasarta and Lorma held Mother's hands. Rimax, Foxor, his sons, and I walked beside Father.

Tomaxa gently placed Arixa's body on the ground and summoned our attention. She recited a prayer and said, "This child is on the way to the spirit world. We need to add her name to her clan's history. Let us chant her beautiful name so she may be received with love."

"Arixa, Arixa, Arixa..." Everyone joined in the chanting, but I could not stop crying.

Tomaxa asked the teenage boys to come forth and dig a shallow grave. She laid Arixa's body in the tomb. I covered my eyes.

"As our ancestors taught us, we will burn this body. It is now but a shell, and the smoke will carry her soul to the spirit world."

I knew our dead were cremated, but I had never seen a body burned. Normally, that was handled by professionals in a crematorium prior to the death ritual.

"Wait!" shouted Father.

He ran up to where Arixa's body lay and fell to his knees.

"Montor, come here."

I could not believe my ears.

What is he going to do?

Father called me a second time, and I inched my way to him. He caressed Arixa's cheek and reached over to remove the cord around her neck. Our clan followed a tradition of wearing cords with amulets. These were gifted to us at life milestones such as marriage or to celebrate certain accomplishments. At a minimum, everyone wore the amulet given to them upon reaching their first birthday. The dead were cremated with their amulets. Removing Arixa's cord was highly unusual.

"Come here, son," he said, caressing my cheek. "You and Arixa are twins. You grew together in your mother's womb, so a part of her remains alive in you. Are you willing to wear her amulet with honor?"

I hunched my shoulders and blurted out the first thing that came to my mind.

"But it is a female amulet. It has a feminine virtue."

I was referring to the fact that parents requested from the High Spirit a virtue for their child and engraved the word in the child's first amulet. Male children's amulets usually were engraved with words such as WARRIOR, STRENGTH, and COURAGE. Mine was engraved with the word VALOR. The female amulets contained words relating more to their roles as wives and mothers.

"Arixa's virtue is LOYALTY. This is an important quality to possess, regardless of gender."

Father wiped away the tear making its way down his cheek.

"OK, Father. I would like to wear it. Thank you."

"Tuck your amulets under your shirt to keep them hidden, so no one is tempted to take them from you. You are a good brother, Montor...and a good son."

Father placed the cord around my neck and embraced me. New sobs bubbled up in my chest. Our bodies swayed. Tomaxa cleared her throat and asked if any family or friends wanted to get closer to Arixa's body for any last prayers. Our people did not believe in saying goodbye to a cadaver, but that was how it felt to me. Lasarta helped Mother forward. Foxor, Rimax, and Lorma followed. My vibrant family was broken, and anger replaced my grief.

Goodbye, little Arixa. I promise, one day, I will make the Lostai pay.

Lasarta led us in another prayer.

"High Spirit, receive this innocent child who was taken far too soon. We can only imagine there is an important purpose for her in your realm. Perhaps she is preparing a place for us when it is our turn."

Stupid High Spirit. Where were you when we needed your help?

Tomaxa looked at Father and Mother with a compassionate but firm expression.

"It is time."

We stepped away and watched as she pressed the firestick to Arixa's body. Soon, orange and red flames engulfed the area. The heat from the pyre relieved us from the icy wind, but the smell was horrible. We stood there for hours. Tomaxa remained the closest to the fire. Once she decided the process was completed, she doused the ashes and embers with the water. Some females added dirt to seal the grave.

Father walked over to the grave and addressed the group. I had never heard his voice so tremulous.

"Friends, thank you for accompanying our family on such a sad occasion, but we must hurry back to our dwellings as we are violating the rules by being out here. We also need to be rested for tomorrow's work. I do not want to add another senseless death to the long list of ones we have witnessed lately."

We rushed back to our shack and huddled together on the mattress to share the two blankets that were left.

7

───────

The next morning, before everyone was led to their respective tunnels or prison cells, Horaz's voice over a loudspeaker bounced against the cave walls.

"Arandans, did you think we did not see you setting fires out in the woods last night? We will not tolerate such disobedience. I am going to make it easy for you. Anyone who was out in the woods last night, step to the right. The rest of you can go about your daily routine."

Hushed whispers.

The news of Arixa's death and cremation had spread to all the prisoners during our morning bath. Everyone knew the reason for going into the woods the night before.

Father and Mother were the first to step aside. Foxor, Lasarta, and their sons joined them. Lorma and I followed Rimax, who did the same. With all the new prisoners that had been brought to the camp, not everyone was Father's friend. Still, they all knew the stories of how he had helped the community as a leader in the early days of imprisonment. One by one, people stepped behind my family until the entire group stood with us, even those we knew had not taken part in the death ritual.

"Do you think you can intimidate me?" Horaz increased the volume on his translation device. "I can eliminate you all and fill this camp again in a few days."

I thought my heart would jump out of my chest. Father had preached self-control, but losing Arixa had taken its toll. He always taught us to take responsibility for our choices. Stepping forward, he shouted at the top of his lungs.

"Leave these people alone, Horaz. I am the only one to blame here."

"Yes, we noticed this is not the first time you have snuck into the woods. We allowed you some leeway, but last night's transgression will not go unpunished. I will enjoy giving you all what you deserve."

Father turned around to look at us, his eyes wild with fury and angst. He had reached his limit.

"I am sorry," he whispered to us.

He faced Horaz again and roared, "Listen, you Lostai scum, I mourned my young daughter's senseless death last night because you refused her a basic medication."

Silence.

Horaz approached and gestured to some soldiers on his way over to us. They followed him until he stood in front of Father. In the meantime, Father called Foxor over. I did not see what transpired between them because my attention switched to Horaz's voice.

"What did you call me?"

His words thundered from the translation device.

Father stood tall and glared down at Horaz.

"I called you what you deserve. You are filthy Lostai scum. Punish me, but do not make these people pay for my behavior."

A chorus of "Yes" accompanied by fist pumps echoed from

the Arandan group behind us. Horaz smirked for a second before his expression turned cold.

"Trust me, you will be punished. The warden allowed you to get too haughty," he said before making a quick hand gesture to the soldiers behind him.

He turned off the translation device and spit out orders in Lostai we did not understand. Without warning, four soldiers attacked Father. Father was formidable in hand-to-hand combat and defended himself well, but another two soldiers entered the fray. It was too much for one person, and soon Father was on the ground, absorbing their kicks and blows. Foxor's sons, who were known to be both brave and impulsive, ran to Father's aid.

More soldiers approached and aimed their guns at us. Some shot Foxor's sons using their laser rifles. Lasarta and Mother cried out in horror, and Foxor fell to the ground, hoping to help his sons. Arandans rushed forward, baring their large canine teeth and long fingernails, trying to disarm the Lostai soldiers. They took out their rage on the first few Lostai soldiers within their reach, beating and stomping them. Still, they were no match for the Lostai weapons that could quickly kill many people at once. In the commotion, I lost track of my family and gaped silent screams of terror. More beams of light shot across the cave. Some Arandans dispersed. Others, like me, froze.

The soldiers beating Father pulled out rods called *zirems*, the same ones they had used on Rimax's hands. They poked Father with them, delivering painful burns all over his body. At first, Father fought them silently, but he soon cried out in pain. His battered body shook in agony as he lay on the floor. Horaz addressed us, the volume on his translation device booming even louder than before. By then, the Lostai soldiers had subdued our uprising by training their guns on the children.

"Enough disruption for one day! Take this vile Arandan and finish him in private. Supervisors, clean up this mess. Laborers, get to your work or I will begin slaughtering your sniffling vermin children. You all will go without your afternoon soup for the days equating to the amount of Lostai soldiers injured here today."

The soldiers pulled Father to his feet. He could barely stand, but he held his head high as he turned to us.

"Children, do not let these evil people crush your spirit or break down your pride. You come from a long line of poets, warriors, and teachers."

They dragged him off, and my voice returned.

I called out to him, "*Ta Ri, Ta Ri.*"

"Silence him or he dies too," warned Horaz.

Mother pushed her way through the crowd to get to me and covered my mouth. Her eyes were red and watery, but her voice was firm.

"Go with Lorma to the cell. I do not want to lose any more loved ones today. There is nothing we can do now."

I looked around. Arandans were on the ground, hugging their slaughtered family members and friends. The Lostai soldiers prodded them with the *zirems* to get them moving towards the tunnels. These dead would not have the blessing of a proper cremation and funeral rites. The Lostai soldiers brought a cart, piled the bodies on, and transported them off somewhere until the area was cleared.

In the prison cell, all children, young and old, including their caregivers, wailed steadily. Several Lostai soldiers approached the force field and threatened to punish us with their *zirems*. We spent the rest of the day sobbing quietly. I could not stop my body tremors. Lorma held me close. She was trembling, too.

At the end of the day, Mother and Lasarta held hands and

chanted prayers as we walked back to our shacks. As promised, we were not given supper, but I am sure no one had any appetite for the bland Lostai soup. It would only remind us of our bondage.

Rimax placed his arm around Lorma, and she leaned on his shoulder while still crying. I had not seen him do that to her in a long time. Our people's way of showing affection changed once we reached puberty. I supposed it was not a day for following rules. Even though Lorma leaned on Rimax for support, she still held on to my hand. I tapped it to let her know I wanted her to let me walk freely. Foxor trudged ahead of us, his whole frame appeared collapsed. I got close and looked up at him.

"Sir Foxor, I would place my hand on your shoulder to console you the loss of your sons, but I am not tall enough."

He offered a sad smile and picked me up.

"Now you can, son."

I cocked my head. He had never called me son before.

"Yes, remember, your parents designated me as your *Ta Masa*. In Josher's absence, I am like your father."

"When will Father come back?"

His lips pressed into a hard line. Arandans did not hide truths from their young unless dealing with a toddler.

"Son, your father is not coming back."

Weak with grief, my head flopped to one side as if I had fallen asleep. I could not hold back my tears. We walked in silence the rest of the way. When we reached the shacks, he placed me on the ground and spoke to Lasarta and Mother.

"Wait here. I will get Tomaxa for a quick prayer session."

Soon we were surrounded by friends. Tomaxa led us in chanting the names of lost family members. We moved on to prayers and then said our goodnights.

In our shack, we had a bag full of tubers and vegetables.

Mother boiled a specific combination of both, added her special recipe of herbs, and mashed them together. The result was something rustic but delicious. It was her way of comforting us and getting us ready to greet the next day without Father or Arixa. After dinner, I fell asleep with tearful eyes as I rubbed Arixa's amulet.

8

Horaz took advantage of our uprising to make life miserable for us. His supervisors searched our shacks and removed any knife or utensil deemed a weapon. We could no longer use the reproducers. Maintaining our possessions in good condition became imperative to our survival. Now we only used nets and small tools made from flint for hunting and fishing. Rimax skinned the small animals and birds with his bare teeth and long fingernails. Soon, I was helping him. Mother had no way to butcher them. She dismembered the carcasses as best she could and dropped the trunk whole into boiling water.

As if Drator's death were not tragic enough, losing Father and Arixa plunged Mother into depression. She plodded through the days and nights like an automaton, only motivated by the instinct to protect and care for her remaining children.

On the off days, she sat with Lasarta to pray and cry while Rimax and Foxor spent the entire day in the woods with the other males. In the meantime, Lorma showered me with affection to make up for the fact that Mother no longer caressed our cheeks or barely touched us.

I wanted to go to the woods with the other males, but Mother forbade it. Out of frustration, I spoke up, my words tinged with defiance.

"Your rules do not make any sense. Father always took me with him. Why are you treating me like a baby?"

Regretting the words as soon as they left my mouth, I wished she would pull me by the ear as she used to do when I misbehaved. Instead, she inclined her head and covered her eyes. I barely heard her reply.

"If something happened to you, little one, I could not stand it."

In the past, that term of endearment had been reserved solely for Arixa. I pushed down the sobs percolating inside and pressed my head against Mother's tummy.

"I am sorry, Mother. I will stay here with Lorma."

She leaned over, embraced me, and rubbed my back. It felt as if revolutions had gone by since she last caressed me.

"Thank you for being so patient, little one."

Survival became a daily struggle. Grief was not the only enemy. The adults were simply worn out. Horaz made their workdays even longer. Rest days were spent hunting, fishing, gardening, harvesting produce, mending clothes and linen, and fashioning rudimentary tools. Lorma took charge of cooking so Mother could get more rest. When it came to food, I could be blunt.

"Lorma, this does not taste like how Mother makes it."

"Shhh, can you not see how tired Mother is? I am afraid she is getting sick."

A hollow fear carved a hole in my stomach. During the morning baths, I had overheard conversations about how people who were too sick to work mysteriously disappeared. I turned to look at Mother lying on the mattress. Her sunken eyes opened a slit.

"Montor, do not give your sister a hard time."

I swallowed hard.

"I promise to eat the whole thing, Mother."

The next workday ended in a commotion. Workers exited the tunnels with injuries. Some people were bleeding, others limping. Mother and Lasarta were in the same work group and usually walked out together. That day, instead of mindlessly observing my surroundings while waiting, I ached to find Mother as soon as possible and scanned the area by the cave entrance where we usually met her.

Lorma tugged at my hand.

"Come."

I sensed the urgency in her voice and could barely keep up with her. Soon, we ran into Lasarta. She was bleeding from a gash in her arm.

"Where is Mother?" Lorma asked, looking around.

"I do not know. There was a cave-in. I called out to her. She replied to me, but the supervisors were herding us out of there and I lost sight of her," answered Lasarta.

My heart became a drum. The shouting around me merged into one loud vibration. Foxor and Rimax arrived. Foxor ripped off a piece of his sleeve and put pressure on Lasarta's wound.

"We must look for Mother," I said to Lorma.

"No. We should stay here together," she answered.

I yanked my hand out of hers.

"This is stupid. We need to find her," I shouted before running off aimlessly.

I do not know how long it took for Rimax to reach me, but when he did, he pinched me hard on the arm.

"Owww."

"*Shermont!* What are you thinking? You need to respect your older sister."

I tried to remain defiant but flinched at his use of a curse word, something he rarely did.

"No, I do not."

His face contorted in anger.

"Well, I say you do, and I am the elder male," he growled.

Rimax was the most good-natured person in our family. I could not remember the last time he had raised his voice to anyone. I pouted in shame. He grabbed me by the arm and pulled me back to where Lasarta, Foxor, and Lorma were still standing. The crowd had dispersed a bit. Mother was nowhere in sight.

We waited and waited, as did some others who were also missing family members. Finally, the supervisors forced us to leave the cave. I cried all the way back to our shack. Lorma wiped her tears away as she prepared food for us. I had no appetite, but I knew Mother would be upset if I did not eat. It was already late by the time we finished dinner. Rimax and Lorma were exhausted, and they forced me to join them on the mattress. I tried to stay awake hoping I would see Mother walk through the shack entrance, but sleep took over.

During the next morning's bath, much of the conversation was about the cave-in and missing people.

"They took away those who were badly injured to be executed," someone said.

I shuddered and looked at Rimax.

"Is that what happened to Mother?"

Rimax turned away and did not reply, so I asked Foxor the same question. He placed his hands on my shoulders.

"We cannot know for sure. Time will tell."

Lorma did not utter a word on our way to the caves, and Rimax avoided making eye contact.

Once we arrived, Rimax said, "Take care, Montor. I will see you at the end of the day."

"Maybe Mother will be back by then," I replied, hoping his expression would match my optimism. When it did not, my young heart was crushed yet again.

A week passed.

Then another.

I knew it was final when my family's friends included Mother's name in the ritual death prayers for those lost. In those moments, all I could think of was every single time I had crossed her or misbehaved. I would never get a chance to say I was sorry for all the times back home when I snuck away into the woods without permission to climb trees and chase small animals. Or all the times I questioned her orders. Or the times I did not want to study.

That night and many nights after, I tossed and turned, my head exploding in pain as I relived any time I had caused Mother to stress or miss out on sleep. The mattress felt too big. I wished I could press my face against Mother's tummy or hold her hand. I ached to hear her voice, even if it were a reprimand. Guilt and disconsolation like I had never experienced before kept me up at night and took over my imagination.

One day, I heard Lorma talking to Lasarta. It was a rest day, and they assumed I was out hunting with the other males. Instead, I sat hidden in the thick bushes bordering our shack.

"I am worried about Montor, Lasarta."

"What is it?"

"He is not eating. He has nightmares, wakes up, and sits silently all night long. You know how talkative and energetic he normally is. Now, days go by without him saying a word."

"We are all suffering your mother's loss. I know this is hard for you and Rimax, too. You have been through too much."

"Yes, but Montor is so young. I have tried talking to him, but he remains sullen and does not reply."

"I will ask Foxor to talk to him."

A few days later, during the morning baths, Foxor pulled me aside. He had no idea I already knew why he was speaking to me privately. It angered me that they all thought a simple chat could fix what was bothering me.

My parents are dead. I owe respect to no one. Just because I am young does not mean they can tell me what to feel.

Foxor surprised me. He did not ask how I was doing or tell me I needed to eat better.

"Montor, I am sorry if I have been slighting you."

"What do you mean, Sir Foxor?"

"Well, you remind me a lot of your father. I think of all your siblings, you are the one who physically resembles him the most. We were best friends since childhood. His death has affected me as much as losing my sons. When I see you, it is like I have him in front of me. It is very difficult. I think I have been avoiding you because of this."

I had not noticed, but I still felt bad for him. Looking up, I met his eyes squarely.

"Do not worry, Sir Foxor. I am not doing well either."

"I can imagine, Montor. You have lost two siblings and both parents in a short amount of time. Anyone would falter under such devastating blows. Sometimes, when I think about my sons, I wish I had been killed in that cave-in so I would not have to suffer this grief any longer. Then I think about Lasarta. I am the only family she has left."

He was not speaking down to me.

"Yes, sir. But my siblings and I are like your family, too, right?"

"Of course. That is true. Tell me, Montor. How are Lorma and Rimax doing?"

I had not stopped to think about them.

"I think they are OK, but Lorma is worried about me."

"She loves you very much. Why is she worried?"

Instead of answering his question, I asked another.

"Has Lasarta spoken about the accident? Did she notice if Mother was tired or distracted when it happened?"

"Your mother was working hard like the rest of the workers. What are you getting at?"

"I just wonder if maybe Mother did not have enough energy to run away from danger. Lorma had been cooking lately so Mother could get to sleep earlier, but sometimes I would complain about Lorma's cooking. Mother would wake up to coax me to eat."

Foxor's eyebrows drew together, and his expression softened. He sighed and placed his hand on my shoulder.

"Montor, all the workers here are exhausted. It does not have to do with what happens after we get back to our dwellings at the end of the workday. It is hard labor with not enough rest time allowed, plain and simple. Several others were lost in that accident. Trust me, it is no one's fault."

I appreciated that he was talking to me like an equal, but now I craved something warm and safe. Before I knew it, I leaned against his stomach, and hot tears I could not control wet my face. The sobbing that followed racked my body. He pulled me closer.

"Let us cry together, Montor."

He held me there for the remaining bath time.

"It is time to return."

"Yes, sir."

"Montor, I am not LIKE your father now. I AM your father. Any problem or question you would have shared with your father, you can now trust with me. Lasarta IS your mother. She can comfort you just as she comforts me. We are all suffering, but we must take care of each other and ourselves. That is the only way we can remain strong. Our clan's numbers are dwindling to nothing. You must grow up strong to continue your father's lineage. It is what he would have wanted."

His words changed my perspective. I would focus my defiant nature on survival. I would not let my fathers down.

9

The old warden never returned from his planet. Horaz relished in announcing his official promotion to that position. Another season change brought even colder temperatures and stronger storms.

One day, the supervisors did not allow us to return to our shacks and crowded all the workers into the prison cells with the children to spend the night. I stood by Rimax and Foxor as they conversed with the other older males. From inside the cell, we could hear how the wind whistled outside the cave entrance. The snow fell so thick, it appeared like a white curtain. Every so often, flashes of lightning interspersed with the white. It would have been magical if it were not for the petrifying cold that stiffened my joints and felt like razors cutting my skin. For a moment, I felt thankful the Lostai had taken pity on us and not forced us to walk back to our shacks in the harsh weather. The veil soon fell from my innocent eyes.

"Do not believe for a moment they are keeping us here to save us. I have learned their language and overheard their conversations. They said the weather interferes with the force fields surrounding the woods and their surveillance devices.

They are keeping us here to stop us from escaping," said one of the older males.

Another confirmed he had heard something similar.

"Well, at least we are warmer here than we would be in those shacks without doors," said another.

The wintry weather continued for weeks, and the Lostai displayed their cruelty even more with each passing day. They forced us to wash with ice cold water they brought into the cells in vats, and fed us only small portions of soup. The adults barely got the rest and nutrition needed to face the arduous mining work.

"How are you doing, little warrior? Are you hungry?" Lorma asked me while caressing my cheek.

I was growing up fast and knew to keep silent, even though hunger evolved from pangs to outright pain.

Later, Rimax told Foxor he had heard rumblings from some of the younger males about an attempt to leave the cave at night. They planned to retrieve food and other supplies left in the shacks.

"They will hide in the tunnels after the workday has ended. So many of us fall injured or dead daily, they do not keep track anymore. Once the Lostai leave to their dormitories, they will sneak out to the shacks."

"That is a grave risk," said Foxor. "Do not do it, son. Hopefully, the bad weather will subside soon, and they will allow us to return to our dwellings."

"I am afraid we will all get sick if we do not get better nutrition," replied Rimax, looking at me long and hard.

Why is he looking at me? I have not asked for food. Anyway, Rimax would never do such a thing. He is all about discipline and following rules.

I was wrong.

The next evening, Rimax did not return to the prison cell at the end of his shift. I could not sleep and sat up, not sure what I was looking for. Foxor and some other males were also awake. Long after midnight, movement in the cave caught my attention. Four figures dashed from the tunnel entrance and out of the cave amid lightning and hail.

Foxor murmured, "Oh, no. Rimax, what have you done?"

Distraught, I fought falling asleep, waiting for them to return, but I couldn't help drifting off.

Strident alarm sounds and lights startled me from my sleep. Everyone in the cell got to their feet. Lostai soldiers burst into the cave, escorting taller Arandans in handcuffs. The Lostai were prodding the Arandans with *zirems*. To my horror, I recognized Rimax as one of the prisoners. His feet dragged behind his limp body.

"Rimax!" shouted Lorma, before covering her mouth.

Others in our cell shouted out, too. Rimax and three older young adult Arandan males were thrust to the floor. The Lostai continued poking them with their weapons and kicking them until Horaz appeared. He pulled out his hateful translation device and walked to the entrance of our cell. Even though he was not much taller than me, his monstrous eyes and cruel smirk struck fear in my heart.

"You people are so stupid, but you will learn."

He shouted an order in Lostai. One by one, the soldiers brought the badly beaten Arandans to the entrances of each prison cell. They removed their shirts so we could see their burnt flesh. When they presented Rimax to us, his face bloody and his body so battered, gasps filled the room. The centers of the many ashen circular wounds revealed shiny flesh that looked like raw meat.

"Who are your family members?" Horaz asked him.

Angry tears welled as I balled my fists. My body tensed to the point of pain. I could not remember having such dark feelings for someone and imagined beating Horaz bloody.

Rimax remained stoic and silent.

Horaz cocked his head and looked up to examine Rimax's face.

"Oh, I remember you. You are Josher's son. How many members of your filthy family are still around? Let me think. Ah yes, your brother and sister."

Horaz called over more soldiers who aimed their weapons at us.

"Rimax's brother and sister, you have two seconds to step forward before I order my soldiers to shoot everyone here."

With no time to think about it, Lorma grabbed my hand, and we walked toward the prison cell entrance. Horaz made a hand gesture. An electrical spark signaled the force field had been dropped.

"Come forward," Horaz snarled at us.

We walked out, and the force field was reactivated.

The soldiers gathered the family members of the other three Arandans. We were nine in total.

"This will teach you not to violate our rules," Horaz shouted. "Let us start with Josher's son."

My chest ached, and I thought I would faint. Lorma's hand trembled so violently that I could barely hold on. The soldiers threw Rimax to the ground. One soldier pulled off the rifle he had strapped to his back.

Horaz waved his hand.

The soldier took aim.

A beam of light streamed from the weapon to Rimax's left leg. I heard Rimax's screams of pain, but having let go of Lorma's hand to cover my eyes, I could not see what happened. I imagined Rimax was dead. A Lostai soldier smacked me. The Arandans in the prison cell shouted in protest.

Horaz's odious voice speaking his words in Lostai came into earshot right before the translation device emitted audio in Arandan.

"Your brother used his feet to leave this cave, so we will take them. Look at his punishment, child, so you do not get any similar ideas."

The soldier smacked me again. I heard sparks and Foxor's voice above the crowd. Arandan males in the cell pressed and banged against the force field, upset at the abuse.

"He is just a child. Leave him alone."

"Silence! Give me one reason to finish off this problematic family."

Both Lorma and I bawled as the soldier grabbed my head and forced me to look. One of Rimax's feet had been severed, and a soldier kicked it aside. Their laser weapon cauterized the wound so there was no blood, but I shuddered at the mutilation of his body. Angry reddened skin bordered the milky yellowish waxy stump. Rimax continued to scream in agony.

The soldier took aim again and severed the other foot.

Then a hand.

Then the other.

Tremors of shock ravaged Rimax's body. He no longer screamed.

I thought my head would explode. Lorma hugged me. The sound of her sobs filled my ears. Our bodies now swayed in the weird sorrowful dance becoming too common among us.

"Finish him," said Horaz, no emotion in his voice.

A fifth beam from the soldier's weapon burned a hole in Rimax's chest and ended his misery.

Soldiers tossed Lorma and me back into the prison cell and moved on to their next victim. Foxor and Lasarta rushed to comfort us. I think I passed out.

The next days blurred by. I do not remember eating, sleeping, or what people said to me. I may have lost control of my bodily functions and soiled my clothes. At some point, Lasarta cradled me in her arms and coaxed me to drink from a glass of water.

Little by little, I came back to life. The weather warmed up, and the Lostai got their force fields and surveillance systems back online. They let us out of the prison cells and ordered us back to our shacks. It was a rest day, so the males went out to hunt. Foxor invited me to join him, but I preferred to stay with Lorma.

Luckily, the icy conditions had helped preserve our food stores.

"I am going to prepare fish and vegetables with *dormet* sauce. I know you like it. It may not taste exactly like Mother's, but it will be good."

I looked at my hands for a long while.

"Rimax used to love Mother's *dormet* sauce."

"Yes." She caressed my cheek. "We will say a prayer in his name, giving thanks that the food did not spoil."

A familiar rage boiled up in me. I smirked and said, "Pray? To who?"

"The High Spirit, of course."

"I will never pray to the High Spirit again. It abandoned our family. It probably does not even exist."

"Shush. Do not say that. It is blasphemy!"

I did not care and dared the High Spirit to send a lightning bolt and burn me alive.

"How can the High Spirit even exist? *Shermont!* It allowed Rimax and Arixa to die. They were the best two of our family. I am the worst. It should have been me."

"Since when have you started cursing? No, little warrior. Do not say that. I love you so much. We can survive this."

She hugged me so hard. At another time, such an embrace would have brought tears to my eyes. I must have spent all my tears in the days after Rimax's death because I was sure nothing would ever move me again.

After a long pause, Lorma said, "Do you want to help me prepare the meal?"

"If I must," I grumbled.

10

I was wrong about being all cried out.

Horaz decided every family should have a worker. Having lost all the adults in our family, Lorma was forced to become a laborer. With no family member or caregiver to keep me company in the prison cell, my peers took advantage to ostracize me.

The children my age feared me because I was taller than any of them. The older children envied that I was allowed to walk among the adults. Some of the older male children and adolescents tried to bully and taunt me. That did not go well for them. I harbored a lot of pent-up rage. Father had trained me in self-defense and martial arts soon after I learned to walk and continued to do so until I lost him. My day often ended with puffy eyes or a cut lip, but usually my opponent was even worse off. The fighting entertained the Lostai soldiers who happened to be on break or near the area.

Soon, Lostai soldiers made it a habit to call me over to the cell entrance, point to an older male child, and say, "Hey, your name is Montor, right? I will give you a treat if you beat up that one over there."

The treat usually was one of their disgusting protein bars. Occasionally, they gave me a tasty, sweet fruit to keep me interested. I ate everything. For now, my goal was to grow taller and stronger as quickly as possible in the hopes I could replace Lorma in the mines.

The next time the alarms went off, I had already gotten into my first fight and was nursing a bloody nose. My heart sank as Lostai soldiers and Arandan workers rushed out of the tunnels. Perceiving some kind of danger, I darted to the cell entrance. The Lostai soldiers headed out of the cave, shouting to each other, while most of the Arandans ran towards the prison cells, demanding the force fields be deactivated and the children let out. They were met with armed soldiers, who backed them off and ordered them out of the cave. Amid the commotion, the Lostai soldier that most often instigated my fighting matches approached the force field and met my eyes. We had established a bit of a rapport over the past weeks. I even had learned to speak some Lostai. He appeared to be struggling with a decision.

Seconds later, he slammed his hand on the control panel and released the force field.

"Hurry," he said to me. "Get out. Danger."

I turned to the other children and shouted the same in Arandan. An acrid odor filled the air. I sped out of the cave and kept running until a nearby explosion caused me to trip over my feet. Gasping, I stood and scoped the area, looking for Lorma, Lasarta, or Foxor. They were nowhere in sight. Finally, having reached our shack, I pressed my hands against my pounding head to catch my breath. Several groups of Arandans rushed by before Lasarta and Foxor arrived. Lasarta pulled me into her arms.

"Oh, Montor! We were looking all over for you. I am so glad you are safe."

The inevitable next question could not wait.

"Where is Lorma?"

She hesitated.

"We have not seen her, but hopefully she will arrive soon. Come stay with us tonight."

"No, I am old enough to stay alone. I want to be there when she gets back."

Lasarta's shoulders dropped, and she looked at Foxor. He nodded.

"Montor, Lasarta is going to prepare some food. You need to eat before going to sleep. I insist."

I let out a deep sigh but obeyed.

As I helped Lasarta pluck the feathers from a fowl she was cooking for dinner, she said, "Montor, it breaks my heart, all the suffering you have been through. I have something difficult to tell you..."

I heard sniffles. She was crying.

"Foxor, I cannot," she said, wiping her face.

My heart pounded like when I ran out of the cave. Foxor rubbed her back and went down on one knee to get to my height.

"Son, we looked everywhere and did not see Lorma. There was a gas leak. Whoever did not make it out of the tunnels in time either died in the explosion or was asphyxiated. I hope I am wrong, but I fear she did not make it."

"That is a lie!"

Calling an adult, especially a family member, a liar was one of the most disrespectful things an Arandan child could say. Foxor was my *Ta Masa*, the closest thing to a father an orphan could have.

I turned around and stormed out of the shack. A firm grasp tugged me back. I faced Foxor's stern face. Lasarta's quiet weeping made me even angrier.

"You will apologize to me right now. Your father did not raise you to speak in such a way to your elders," said Foxor.

Every part of my body trembled, and I found it hard to breathe. Foxor's expression did not change.

"I am waiting, Montor."

"I am sorry."

"Son, look me in the eyes when you speak to me. Especially with words of this significance. I am not taking this lightly."

I raised my watery eyes to meet his. To my surprise, a tear slid down his cheek.

"I apologize for calling you a liar, Sir Foxor. It will not happen again."

No sooner than I had pronounced the last word, he gathered me in his arms. I wrapped mine around his neck.

"Montor, I am sorry, too. I am sorry we cannot protect you from this suffering. You do not deserve this, but you are strong. You will survive."

I survived, but my soul darkened. Nothing could bring a smile to my face. I slept alone in my shack for several days, holding on to the hope that one day Lorma would show up.

"Montor, it is not good for you to sleep alone."

"I know, Mother. Lorma will be back soon".

"Son, even if you can no longer see us, we are always by your side in spirit, but you need a flesh-and-blood family. Go to Lasarta and Foxor. They are your parents now in your world."

Like many other members lost in the explosion, Lorma did not return. We received no explanations from the Lostai warden or his supervisors. During the next rest day, the entire community united yet again to offer the sacred death chant for the many lost.

A few days after, as we lined up outside our shacks to head to the caves, a Lostai supervisor pulled me aside.

"Boy, we cannot afford to have you occupy a dwelling on

your own. Pick a family to move in with. You may take with you any belongings your family paid for."

Before the supervisor finished speaking, Foxor was by my side.

"He will move in with my wife and me. He is practically my son."

"Really? What kind of guardian are you, leaving this child alone? You Arandans definitely are barbarians."

I spoke up.

"It is my fault. I refused to stay with them, but if I have no choice, I will move in now. They are like family to me."

"Hopefully, they will keep you out of trouble. Remember what happened to your father and brother."

I clenched my fists, hearing his arrogant tone, but bit my tongue.

One day, I will make them all pay for every stupid word and smirk.

That evening, in addition to dinner, Lasarta and Foxor took valuable rest time to make a special dessert. Lasarta peeled, cut, and mashed fruit. She added honey we harvested from beehives we found in the woods to create a syrupy puree. While the fruit macerated, she prepared the dough, rolled it out, and cut it into discs. Foxor helped her top the discs with the fruit mixture, fold the dough over, and seal it to create a pocket. He fried the pockets in fat. I glanced for a moment and then stepped outside to do exercises; my sole focus was to get stronger.

When they called me in, Lasarta searched my eyes.

"Here, Montor, try these. They are delicious."

I used to jump for joy when Mother made these heavenly pockets of sweetened fruit.

"May I have two? The more I eat, the quicker I can grow," I asked politely.

Her expression drooped.

I took a bite and forced myself to add, "They are very delicious. Thank you."

Things soon fell back into a sad, somber routine. Lasarta showered me with affection, and Foxor continued my father's practice of allowing me to remain among the adult males rather than the children my age. We also sparred often, continuing my martial arts training. My prowess and tenaciousness as a fighter gained me some more fans among the Lostai soldiers. I was soon one of the best-fed children at the camp, as I demanded fresh fruits and vegetables before engaging in any bouts for their entertainment. Many of the mothers complained to Lasarta. I overheard her once address the issue with Foxor when she thought I was asleep.

"It is almost every day now that I get an earful from another female telling me Montor is out of control and abusive with the other male children."

"Are any of them younger than he?"

She paused for a moment.

"Well, honestly, they are older than he is. But, you know, he is so tall for his age."

"Do you think he is bullying anyone physically smaller?"

"So far, no."

"Let him be. I am teaching him to be an honorable fighter and to step back once his opponent is down. We have lost many warriors and need to have a new crop ready to take their place when the time comes to rise against these Lostai oppressors. He is doing us a favor by toughening up these kids for the battle ahead."

Her deep sigh made it clear she had other concerns.

"I suppose you are right, but Foxor, it is not only about the fighting. It has been several lunar cycles since the explosion, and I see no improvement in his demeanor. The only things that bring him pleasure are fighting and sparring with you. He has lost his childhood and is like an old person trapped in a young boy's body. I am worried about the adult he will grow up to be. Josher was a fine warrior, but he was also wise and fair, with a good heart. I fear this boy's soul has been ruined."

My soul? Who cares about that? I do not need one to become the best warrior ever.

How can so many be dead?
Lo Ro, Lo Ta, Ta Ri, Ro Ma
This is my blood, my true blood
Yet mine was tainted, infected
A curse of cruel circumstance
Tied to my beating warrior heart

Horaz summoned me to his office a week after I celebrated my fifth birthday. A supervisor came to get me at the prison cell. I took a moment to ponder whether I had committed any transgression and could not recall anything other than my daily fights. I did my best to ignore how hard I was swallowing.

I am not afraid of him.

The supervisor led me up a ramp to a chamber high in the cave system that served as Horaz's office, where Horaz waited for me. Usually, his presence filled my mind with images of me killing him. This time, the tall, grey-skinned male standing next to him distracted me.

What is that?

Until the Lostai arrived at our village, I had known no other species other than my fellow Arandans. Since then, I had equated the Lostai with hideous creatures from televised horror serials, but this new alien was not only foreign to me but appeared regal. I was immediately in awe of him. His chiseled features and grey skin made him look like a statue, but the vibrant blue eyes and hair took my breath away.

Horaz ordered me to sit while he spoke to the grey-skinned alien.

"Klemar, Lostai military sent me a transportal device not too long ago. They told me that our scientists have modified these devices to detect what they called Sotkari Ta brain waves. This vermin child seems to trigger those sensors, but we would like you to confirm it."

Even though I understood basic Lostai, most of what he said confused me, other than the word "vermin" because many of the Lostai soldiers called us that.

I hoped they were evaluating me for a laborer position, although unlikely, since I was still at least two revolutions away from puberty. The grey-skinned alien approached me and reached to grab my forearm, his thumb pressed against my wrist. A jolt brought me to my feet. He cocked his head and said nothing.

"Well?" asked Horaz.

The grey-skinned alien suddenly was stone-faced. I tucked my chin and looked away, worried that I had not passed some sort of test. Horaz waved both his hands in wide circles.

"Klemar, I do not have all day."

"I am only a Sotkari Pasi, which means I have telepathic abilities but no telekinetic or mind-control powers. Still, I can sense this boy's energy is formidable and his Sotkari Ta light is

brilliant. He has tremendous telepathic and telekinetic potential, the strongest I have sensed in a non-Sotkari."

I only understood the part about my energy being
formidable. The rest seemed like gibberish to me.

Even so, that sounds like a good thing.

Horaz narrowed his eyes and stroked his chin.

"I cannot believe your people wasted these powers on
barbarians."

Klemar did not seem to like Horaz or the words coming out
of his mouth. His brow pinched together as he said, "I will need
to inform my findings to this star system's Lostai military
commander. I am sure they will want the boy transferred to a
Lostai science station where he can be trained and monitored."

"I expect some remuneration."

"Of course you do. Who do we need to coordinate with for
his transfer? Are his parents here?"

"He is an orphan. No one cares about this brat." Horaz
pulled a flat oval object from his pocket. "Just transfer the funds
to my remuneration chip and take him out of my sight."

I understood Klemar's question and spoke up.

"I live with close family friends. They are like my parents."

"Take him. There is no need to coordinate with anyone.
These people are like animals."

Klemar appeared to get more and more annoyed with
Horaz.

"I will not condone your brutality, Horaz. If you want your
reward, allow me to speak to his caregivers before I take him."

Where is he taking me?

"Fine. You will have to wait till their shift is over."

Horaz's supervisor took me back to the cell. At the end of
the day, Klemar met me as I filed out of the holding cell with
the rest of the children.

"Take me to your guardians. What is your name, boy?"

"Montor."

My stomach had been upset all day, wondering what this alien was planning to do with me. He attempted to make small talk while we waited for Lasarta and Foxor to exit the tunnels.

"So, how long have you been at this camp?"

"One revolution, sir."

Foxor and Lasarta arrived.

"Montor, is everything OK?" Trepidation laced Foxor's tone, his eyes wide as he took in Klemar's appearance.

Before I could reply, Klemar greeted them both in Lostai. Foxor and Lasarta also had learned the basics of the language.

"Hello, my name is Klemar. Are you Montor's guardians?"

"Yes," answered Foxor.

"Are you on your way back to your dwelling? Can we walk together? I have something important to talk to you about concerning your foster child."

Foxor wiped his hand over his mouth before replying.

"OK."

"Montor tells me you have been here for one revolution. I know conditions here are difficult and have heard that Horaz is a ruthless warden."

Foxor knitted his brow and looked down at me. Worry lined his face.

"What have you been telling this person, son?"

"No need to be concerned. Montor has not said anything against Horaz."

"You said your name is Klemar, correct?" said Foxor.

"Yes."

"OK. My name is Foxor, and this is my wife, Lasarta. What exactly is it you need to talk to us about?"

"I come from a planet called Sotkar. Some of our people have evolved to possess extraordinary telekinetic and telepathic abilities. We call ourselves Sotkari Ta or Sotkari Pasi, according to our capabilities. Generations ago, through a complex bioengineering process, some of our scientists dispersed their genetic material across lesser advanced planets. Some of the original recipients passed on this genetic code to their descendants. This has resulted in some people across many species and sectors being born with dormant special abilities. You may find this hard to believe at first, but I have confirmed Montor is one of these people. He has the potential to become an amazingly powerful being."

Foxor and Lasarta first looked at each other in disbelief and then at me. I did not understand all the words, but I caught the part about my being "an amazingly powerful being."

They replied with a long, drawn out, "OK."

"Yes," continued Klemar. "High-level Lostai military leaders have a keen interest in developing people with these abilities."

Foxor's eyes narrowed.

"For what purpose?"

"To incorporate them into the Lostai armed forces. Those are their intentions with Montor."

Foxor's jaw dropped.

"I do not mean to be disrespectful, but no Arandan from our clan will ever be a filthy Lostai soldier."

Lasarta gasped, I am sure, worried about what punishment that comment would earn Foxor.

Klemar was not fazed.

"I understand your sentiment, but hear me out. Think about what future awaits Montor here. In a few revolutions, he will be deemed old enough to join the workforce. He will live out what will surely be a short life doing hard labor and eating scraps until he suffers a premature death resulting from an accident or punishment. I hear he has a bad temperament. He will not last too long here. It is a sad outlook for anyone, much more for someone with so much potential. On a Lostai science station, he will live a life of relative comfort compared to how he is living here. As part of the Lostai military, he will not only gain his freedom but learn how to harness his abilities and become a powerful being. The Lostai have a hard and fast rule of requiring only fifteen revolutions of military service. After that time, soldiers are free to leave the armed forces, live wherever they want, and pursue any employment they choose."

"The Lostai have invaded our world and decimated our people. Montor would be like a traitor if he does this. I cannot allow it. He comes from a line of proud Arandan warriors. What you are suggesting is worse than death."

"I must be honest with you, Foxor. Lostai military is not asking permission. They will do with him as they please, but perhaps it will be an easier transition if you encourage him to make the best of it. If he fights this, it will be much harder for him."

I pressed my lips together to avoid anyone noticing I was about to cry. Although I still did not understand everything being discussed, one way or another, the Lostai would soon separate me from Foxor and Lasarta, the last link to my family. A quick glance up at Foxor revealed how upset he was. His whole body shuddered, his fists clenched, and he glared at Klemar.

"One day, our people will rebel against this tyranny."

Klemar got closer to Foxor and lowered his voice to a whisper, but I heard his words.

"Yes." Klemar looked around. "And when that time comes, maybe Montor will be a powerful being, well-versed in Lostai military strategy, and an excellent asset for your cause."

Both Lasarta and Foxor gaped at Klemar. Those did not sound like the words of a Lostai ally.

"Let me clarify," Klemar continued. "I am no fan of the Lostai. I do what I must to keep my loved ones safe. You should consider the same. I will be at your dwelling at sunrise to pick up the boy."

He turned to walk back to the cave. Once he was out of earshot, Lasarta and Foxor spoke to each other in hushed tones.

My head felt like it would explode as I fought back tears. I did not even bother to eavesdrop on their conversation as I lagged behind them.

Later, Lasarta made meat pies, a meal that took longer to prepare than the typical quick workday dinner and was usually reserved for our rest days. Foxor grilled some sweet bread and macerated some fruit to create a syrupy topping.

This might be the last time I taste her cooking.

"Lasarta, thank you. This is very good," I said, licking my fingers.

"I am glad, son."

She smiled, but her eyes were sad as she caressed my cheek. Once we finished eating dinner, Foxor served the dessert.

"Son, what did you understand about our conversation with Klemar today?"

I swallowed the food in my mouth in one painful gulp.

"They are going to take me away, right?"

Lasarta averted her eyes. Foxor placed his hand on my shoulder.

"Yes, I am afraid so, but did you hear what he said about your special abilities?"

"He said I could become a powerful being. But Foxor, I do not want to be a filthy Lostai soldier. Please do not make me go. I can hide in the woods and climb the tallest trees. They would never find me."

"Unfortunately, they will. Then they will kill you as they did your brother and your father. You know they have devices spying on everything. But I think you need to look at this as an opportunity. Remember the televised serial your father used to enjoy so much? The story was about a secret agent."

"Yes, the character's name was Officer Bertor. He was assigned to a special mission."

"Exactly. He joined the enemy's army to spy on them. He

found out all their military secrets and gave his side a strategic advantage."

My chest filled with excitement.

"I see, Foxor. If I go, I can become a secret agent, too."

"Yes. After a certain amount of time, you may leave the Lostai military and do as you please."

The idea energized me.

"I can join the militia like Drator and kick the Lostai out of our village. I will come and rescue you and Lasarta."

Lasarta walked over and pulled me into an embrace as if I were a toddler.

"I want you to focus on becoming strong, Montor. Eat everything they give you. Be obedient, so they treat you well. Let them believe you are on their side. Learn how to use these powers. You will become a feared warrior," said Lasarta.

I tried to ignore the weepy tone in her voice.

"Lasarta, I will do my best, but..." I bit my lip, embarrassed for my feelings.

She pulled me closer.

"What, Montor?"

"I will miss you."

She could no longer contain her tears and stepped away. Foxor took her place beside me.

"We will miss you, too. And I know this will be scary. You will need to be brave. The High Spirit will watch over you."

I was sure the High Spirit had stopped watching over me, my family, and my clan a long while ago, but I did not want to be disrespectful towards Foxor. I slept fitfully that night, worrying about what awaited me at the Lostai science station.

PART II

XIXSTED LOSTAI SCIENCE STATION

12

———

As promised, Klemar was standing outside of our dwelling by sunrise. He held a slim rectangular device the size of a notebook in his hand. Foxor, Lasarta, and I stepped out to meet him.

"Klemar, we have explained the situation to Montor. He will be cooperative," said Foxor. "Will you be with him during his training?"

"No. My job is to deliver him to the science station. Someone else will oversee him there."

"This boy has suffered much," Lasarta interjected. "He witnessed these Lostai murder his brother and father. He also lost his mother and two sisters here to sickness and injury. Please, if you can, tell his trainer to have some compassion."

"I know the person who will train him. She is a morally sound Sotkari Ta. I think she will treat him fairly."

"This has happened so suddenly. We do not know what he should take for the trip. He only has a change of clothing, a notepad and pencil, and a small toy."

"He will need none of that. They will supply him with

clothing. There are recreational facilities at the science station he can use during rest days."

I thought imagining myself going off to train to become a powerful warrior would make the moment of parting easier for me. My body betrayed my mind with nausea, tremors, and palpitations.

"Sir Klemar, I would like to bring my notepad," I stammered.

Lasarta intervened on my behalf again.

"He writes little notes to himself and composes songs and short poems. It has helped him to cope with so much heartache."

"OK, fine. Go get it, Montor, and then we must leave."

I ran into the shack, grabbed my notepad and pencil, and rushed out. Foxor swept me up in his arms.

"Montor, I know you are much too big for these types of baby embraces, but indulge me."

"It is OK, Foxor. I have not yet reached puberty," I said while wrapping my arms around his neck. "I will miss you, but do not worry about me. I will learn everything they have to teach me and come back to rescue you and Lasarta."

He lowered me to the ground, and Lasarta bent over to embrace me, too. Her breathing was as accelerated as mine. She pulled away, grasping me by the shoulders, and her eyes were almost pleading.

"Take care of yourself, Montor. Behave. Do not get in trouble. I hope to see you again someday soon. I love you very much."

"I love you, too."

Klemar inclined his head to Lasarta and Foxor.

"I wish you both luck. I will make sure he arrives safely at the science station."

We walked for a while before I turned around to wave good-bye. Lasarta's face was pressed against Foxor's chest. He tapped her head, and she turned to wave back. I froze, an ache tugging at my heart, but Klemar circled his arm around my shoulder, shifting me around. With a gentle push on the back, he encouraged me to move along.

"Montor, I know it is hard to say goodbye, but there is no way around this. We must not be late."

I bit my lip, nodded, and continued forward without turning around again.

"Sir Klemar, are we going on a spaceship like the one that brought my family and me here?"

"No, Montor. This device I am holding allows us to transport to our destination. It will feel strange but is safe."

"Where is the science station?"

A meaningless question since I only knew about the planets near Aranda based on what I had learned in school.

"The science station is named Xixsted and is located on the third moon of Losta, the Lostai home world."

He tapped and slid his fingers across the surface of the device. The mention of Losta sent my imagination reeling again.

"I saw the Lostai spaceship send beams of light that caused explosions and fires in my town."

"Yes, photon beams."

"If a bunch of photon beams were aimed at a planet, could it be blown up?"

He stopped what he was doing to look down and meet my eyes.

"Boy, I would suggest you first learn how to survive before thinking about how to take down your enemy."

He grabbed my hand.

"OK, I am going to tap the device one more time, and in a flash, we will end up at Xixsted. Brace yourself. It will feel a bit like being forced awake from a nightmare. There will be a blinding light, so close your eyes."

My hand grasped his even tighter, and I squeezed my eyes shut. A sensation I could only describe as spinning and pressure on my forehead disoriented me. I drifted into nothingness until I heard myself shout, "Ahhh!"

Did I fall asleep?

Klemar was on one knee with his hands on my shoulders.

"Montor, are you OK?"

With my fists against my temples, I waited for the dizziness to wear off before opening my eyes.

"I have a bit of a headache."

"OK. It is to be expected. First, I will take you to the Commander of this station. His name is Zorla. He will assign someone to help get you settled in."

We walked down a corridor lined with blue lights like the ones on the Lostai spaceship. The hallway led to a room as large as a stadium. It was filled with Lostai in black-and-grey military uniforms similar to the ones worn by the soldiers at the labor camp. The sight of so many of them made me want to vomit. Some huddled around conference tables or sat at individual workstations. Others rushed about in groups. The room lit up with the now-familiar holographic charts and images. We walked down another corridor lined with doors without any handles or hinges.

Klemar pressed an illuminated strip by the wall.

A voice from inside said, "Enter," in Lostai.

The door slid into the wall. After a brief static sound, a Lostai male met us at the entrance and gestured for us to come in.

"Welcome," he said.

At the far end of the room, another Lostai male dressed in a more ornate uniform sat behind a desk.

"Come forward, boy," said the Lostai behind the desk without standing. "I am Commander Zorla."

His monotone voice reminded me of Horaz and the other

Lostai at the labor camp who treated us so miserably. I looked at Klemar, my heart in my throat. He patted me on the back.

"Go ahead, Montor."

I walked around an oval table with circular sofas on either side to approach the Commander's desk.

"So, your name is Montor," said Zorla. "Do you understand Lostai?"

Once in front of him, I thought about how Father faced his enemies. Swallowing my fear, I straightened my posture and looked Zorla straight in the eyes.

"I do, sir."

"Good. I have recently been promoted and am new here, too. Klemar tells me you are a very special boy. Did you know that?"

"He mentioned something to me, but I do not know exactly what it means."

"Well, you will soon enough." He smiled, but I sensed no sympathy or compassion from him at all. "However, I need to warn you. You need to work hard, apply yourself, and, most importantly, follow every rule. I do not tolerate disobedience or defiance."

"Klemar says I can become a powerful being. I will do my best to achieve exactly that."

Commander Zorla's eyes narrowed, but he did not reply to me. Instead, he spoke to the other Lostai who had met us at the door.

"Take the boy to his quarters. He comes from a primitive planet, so make sure he knows how to use the reproducer and other devices. Give him a tablet and show him how to use it. Explain to him the rules he must abide by."

Then Zorla turned his attention back to me.

"Montor, I will allow you one day to get familiar with your surroundings and to rest. Your duties and training as a Lostai soldier will start tomorrow."

Before I could stop myself, I clenched my hands into fists. To my shock, I heard Klemar's voice in my mind. His words came in a rush.

"Do not look at me, Montor. Pretend like you cannot hear me. I learned you have a reputation at the labor camp for having a bad temper. I suggest you control it. Focus all your anger on harnessing the power you have within. This Lostai, Zorla, and the soldiers he commands are even more ruthless than Horaz. They will break you if you get out of line. I feel you are destined for greatness, but you will need to be patient."

My body shuddered.

I wanted to scream at Zorla that I would never be a filthy Lostai soldier.

I wanted to tell him I was not primitive and that I came from a proud line of Arandan warriors, poets, and teachers.

I wanted to jump over the desk and punch him in the face.

Instead, I heeded Klemar's advice. Remembering Lasarta's words, I replied, "Commander Zorla, I will not disappoint you."

Leaning forward, he tapped his fingertips together and met my eyes squarely.

"We shall see."

13

———

The door to Zorla's office slid open, and his assistant gestured for me to step out. I looked up at Klemar. He offered me a half-smile.

"I wish you luck, Montor."

"Thank you," I mumbled as I followed the Lostai down the hall.

I hate feeling so scared. I feel like prey.

We walked back out to the large room and down another hallway.

"My name is Menel. Pay attention to everything I tell you, Montor. I will only say things once."

"OK."

He stopped in front of the fifth door on the right and pressed the illuminated strip by the door. Like Zorla's office, the door disappeared into the wall.

"Montor, welcome to your dormitory. Much better than sleeping on the dirt floor of a shack, right?"

I looked around and took an inventory of everything. The colors black, grey, and white predominated. Another door was centered at the head of the room.

This room feels too large and drafty for me.

Memories of the cozy yellow and orange decor and wooden furnishings of my room in Aranda bombarded my brain. At least some of the metallic furniture in the dormitory was familiar to me. A cot dressed in dark linens, a desk and chair, and a chest with drawers lined one wall. Other items in the room were a mystery to me. I had never accompanied my parents when they used the reproducer at the labor camp.

I ran my hands over the consoles and equipment set against the opposite wall as Menel pointed to a large screen. Unlike the recreational viewers used back home to watch sports or serials, the frameless screen seemed painted on the wall.

"Come, stand in front of the viewer."

Menel walked over to the desk and flicked his fingers across a touch display that covered half its top. The screen on the wall lit up. Grey symbols within a green oval appeared. He tapped the desktop screen, and the wall viewer turned white with a tiny black circle. My heart jumped when greenish beams of light shot out from the screen aimed at me.

"Stay still, boy! Now, I must reset it. Do not move. It is a bio scan that enables the equipment in this room to recognize you."

The beams shot out at me from the screen again. I held my breath until the process ended.

"OK. Now, you do not need to touch the entrance strip. Access will be granted for you automatically, and the screens will accept your touch commands. Speak your name."

"Montor."

"Loud, boy! You are wasting my time."

"Montor!"

"Good. The equipment can also be voice activated. I know you beastly creatures have nothing like this on your planet, but you better learn quickly."

That was not true. In the past generation, Arandans had conquered space travel within our quadrant and begun to import technology from a nearby advanced planet called Fronidia, but this was only accessible to the wealthy.

One day, I will make him eat his rude words.

"Come here. This is a reproducer." He pointed to a transparent cabinet set on a pedestal with a touch screen. The device occupied half the wall. "This can generate all your necessities like clothing, toiletries, food, and water. Place your hand on the screen like this and speak what you need. Of course, you need to say it in Lostai. We do not use primitive languages here."

Anger built up inside me, but curiosity took over. I placed my hand on the touch screen, and it turned from grey to a white light.

Recalling the Lostai word for water, I said, "*Tanora.*"

Nothing happened. Menel did not hide his impatience.

"*Ta—*" I started pronouncing the word again.

"Stop! You are pronouncing it all wrong. Listen to me carefully."

He repeated the word. I noticed his lips barely separated, whereas my mouth was wide open by the time I finished saying it. For my next try, I imagined making fun of his mouth movements. It worked. The inside of the cabinet became foggy, but when it cleared, a glass of water was there in the center. I could not see any door, handle, or opening that would allow me to retrieve the glass of water.

"Sir Menel, how do I get the water?"

"Speak the word 'serve' or press here." There was now a green circle in the middle of the screen which had turned grey again.

I said, "Serve." It did not work, so I pressed the green circle. The cabinet's structure disappeared as if it had never existed. I reached up to grab the water. It tasted normal.

"Once you retrieve the item, you can say 'reset' or press the green circle again. Understood?"

"Yes, sir."

I pressed the green circle, fearing I was a long way from perfecting my pronunciation. The cabinet's transparent structure reappeared.

"Montor, out of the kindness of my heart, I will reproduce your basic supplies, but only this one time. Pay attention."

Menel reproduced three sets of dark-colored long-sleeved tops and pants and one set of short-sleeved shirts of a lighter material with matching shorts he said were for sleeping. He continued with a jug of bath gel, a dental cleaner, and dental foam.

"What do you people use to groom all that hair?" Menel asked, waving his hand, his nose scrunched up.

I could see how, him being bald, he would not know about hair care.

"My mother used a scented oil to comb through and detangle. After, she would twist my hair in thick locks."

He shook his head, exasperated, before speaking the words, "Comb and Arandan scented hair oil."

Sure enough, a familiar tub materialized.

"Yes, that is it," I said excitedly, not having seen one since being taken from my Arandan home. My exuberance did not last long.

I will have to groom my own hair from now on.

"OK, let me show you the body care room."

Menel took me through the doorway at the head of the room and showed me the controls for the toilet and shower.

"The last thing I will do for you is reproduce your dinner. You can either speak your request or say 'menu' and press the orange symbol."

When he said the word, the orange symbol appeared on the reproducer panel. He pressed it and holographic images of food appeared in the air right in front of me.

By moving his hand as if turning the pages of a book, more items displayed. Most of them I did not recognize. Then I saw some of the fruit and vegetables the Lostai prison guards used to offer me as a recompense for my fighting matches at the labor camp. Images of soup, hot grains, crackers, and protein bars also were on the menu, but none of the breads, rich stews, and casseroles my mother prepared back on Aranda.

"What are these, Sir Menel?"

"Those are dessert items, fruit tarts, and frozen treats. Do not indulge in too many of those."

I decided on a vegetable soup, crackers, a fruit, and a frozen treat.

One by one, they materialized within the transparent cabinet. Each time, I pressed the green button to retrieve the food and place it on the desk. Menel also requested eating utensils for me. When the last item was on my desk, he turned to leave.

"Montor, my job is done. See here." He pointed to symbols on the wall screen. "These numerical symbols represent time. Umm, are you familiar with them?"

"No, sir."

"You better learn them soon. I will set up your morning alarm, but going forward, you will need to get up on time on your own. When this alarm goes off, you need to hurry, get dressed, eat a protein bar or a bowl of steamed grains, and wash. I will pick you up, give you a tablet, and we will walk through your new daily routine. I suggest you get to bed within the next three hours. Oh, and make sure you bathe before bed. We will not tolerate your uncleanliness or foul odors. Understood?"

"Yes, sir."

He walked out without another word.

I had never eaten dinner alone before. After Lorma died, I had spent a few nights alone in my family's shack before moving in with Lasarta and Foxor, but they had always insisted on sharing their meals with me. I slid my hand over the desktop touch screen. Different colored icons appeared.

Can this strange technology send a message to Lasarta and Foxor?

Tears formed. I wiped them away with each hand.

The soup and crackers tasted bland, but I was already hungry. I had purposely selected a fruit I was familiar with. Its thin skin encased a soft, yellowish pulp with a small pit in the center. I smacked my lips as juice dribbled down my chin. The fruit's sweetness brought on memories of Mother's tarts. The pleasure of its flavor was short-lived, so I moved on to inspect the frozen treat by first pressing a finger against the wrapper.

I wonder what this tastes like?

It was melting. I peeled off the wrapping to uncover an unappetizing, brown-colored item and bit off a corner. The pasty texture was unappealing. I tossed it in the recycling unit, a container attached to the reproducer.

Now what?

To shake off the sadness, I pulled out my notebook and pencil from my pocket and tried to write something that would distract me, but I could not think of anything. Hot tears rolled down my cheeks once again. Enveloped by loneliness, my chest heaved with emotion. I tried to contain my crying to no avail. Anger took over. I grabbed the plate and utensils and hurled them across the room. That act of rebellion fueled my temper, so I followed by banging on the desktop in frustration, causing icons and holographic images to flash and flicker. There was no containing my tears by then. I meandered around the room for a long time before collapsing on the cot.

14

No one here is of my clan
No one here has viewed evening
In the shimmering air of *Ventamu*
Staring out on calm coastal waters
That inspired the true warriors
I long to paint that canvas for them

The buzzing sound almost knocked me out of the bed. I rubbed my eyes, and Menel's words came to mind. He would be coming soon to get me, but the characters ticking off on the wall screen's digitized clock meant nothing to me.

OK, he said I should eat something.

I bolted toward the reproducer and shouted, "Menu!"

Nothing happened. I repeated, to no avail. The pronunciation was off. I closed my eyes and tried to picture Menel's mouth pronouncing the word. Frustration took over, and I pressed icons on the screen at random. Holographic images bounced around the room in a nightmarish clash of images, light, and color. Notification sounds were on an endless loop.

"I hate this crap. I want to be home." I howled like a wounded animal. "*Shermont*, even the labor camp hut is much better than this."

Menel found me sitting on the bed, sulking. He did not utter a word while surveying the room. His eyes stopped for a moment where the plate, glass, and cutlery had landed the night before. He tapped the touch screen on the desk, and the notifications and images ceased.

"That stupid device does not work," I said, crossing my arms over my chest.

"The device is not stupid, but surely you are. I see you are wearing the same clothing from yesterday. I guess I will even have to teach you how to bathe."

His sinister tone squelched my bravado.

"I...I ran out of time trying to get the reproducer to work," I stammered.

He charged at me, grabbed my hair, and yanked me into the bathroom. Even though I was almost his height, his strength surprised me.

"Oww...that hurts."

He pulled a lever and shoved me in the shower stall. I landed on the floor with a thud. A steady stream of freezing water hit me in the face.

"Listen, you have five minutes to take off your clothes and wash yourself, you stinky vermin."

The chill of the cold water was not so bad considering I had been forced to wade in a river during winter weather, but the humiliation stung like a slap in the face. Menel came back with the clothing, hair oil, and comb he had reproduced for me the night before.

"Here are your clean clothes. Hurry, you have put us way behind schedule. No breakfast for you."

As soon as I returned to the bedroom, bathed, groomed, and dressed, he pulled me by the ear to where the plate was on the floor.

"Before we do anything, you are going to clean up after yourself."

I picked up the items from the floor and placed them in the recycling unit, avoiding his eyes the whole time.

"Now, make your bed."

Before the previous night, I had not slept in a bed for over one revolution, and back at our home in Aranda, Mother took care of such chores. He smacked the back of my head. My breathing now came in quick snorts, rage brewing in my chest.

"Well, what are you waiting for?" asked Menel.

"I am not sure what to do."

"That figures. Maybe we should get rid of the bed and let you sleep on the floor like the animal you are."

Tremors shook my body.

"I am not an animal."

"Well, you look like one with those yellow feline eyes, large canines, and disgusting long nails." He grabbed my hand. "We will need to figure out how to file these down."

I found him equally repulsive but focused on trying to explain myself.

"My mother took care of housekeeping."

"Well, your mother is not here now, is she?"

My body slumped at the memory of her sweet caress. Menel grabbed me by the shirt and stared into my eyes.

"Stand straight sand pay attention. I will only do this once. If I find a mess in this room again, you will be punished."

I watched as he smoothed out the sheets and folded the top corners to form a triangular shape. He tucked the apex under the pillow. This differed from how my mother used to do it when she tidied my room.

"I did not see you bring out your dirty clothes. Get them and put them in the recycling unit."

I shuffled back to the bathroom and followed his orders. He checked the room one more time and his eyes landed on my notebook and pencil on the desk.

"What is this?"

"My notebook."

"You do not need that here. Toss it."

"No."

His eyes narrowed.

"What did you say?"

"It is my only possession. I have written poems and songs and would like to keep it."

He laughed before ripping it apart and chucking it into the disposal unit. I ran to retrieve it, but he grabbed me by the hair and tugged my head back.

"Are you really this stupid? I know you are like a wild animal, but be sure, you will be domesticated and trained. Now, let us go."

Still grasping one of my locks, he pulled me towards the door. It slid open, and he pushed me out. My hatred for Menel rivaled the dark feelings I harbored for Horaz.

"Let go of me, you pasty-faced monster."

I elbowed him. He let go of my hair, but before I could run off, he grabbed me again, this time, by the shirt.

"I am taking you to Commander Zorla. You surely have earned your first punishment," said Menel with a smirk.

As much as I wanted to fight him, I remembered Lasarta's eyes when she begged me to stay out of trouble. Seething inside, I did not reply or look at him.

He never let go of my shirt as he led me through the large operating center to Commander Zorla's office. There, he left me with a guard while he walked in to speak with Zorla in private. When he came back, he announced that Zorla wanted to see me.

"I suggest you wipe that insolent look off your face. Zorla is not a patient person."

He shoved me in.

Zorla stood from his chair behind his desk and peered down his nose at me.

"Come close, Montor. How old are you?"

"Five revolutions, Commander Zorla."

"Only five? Why are you so tall?"

Menel jumped in.

"I have done some research on his species. As you know, they are much taller than we are, like the primitive animals they are. However, in addition, their children have an accelerated development, roughly twice the pace of ours until they reach puberty. So, he is physically and mentally the equivalent of a Lostai child of ten revolutions."

"And after puberty?"

"After puberty, they age at a rate similar to ours."

"When will he reach puberty?"

I answered the question.

"I think in two revolutions."

His monotone voice stirred up memories of fictional horror videos my older brothers had watched for entertainment.

"Montor, I have heard you are already showing a rebellious attitude. That will not suit you here. You have the potential to become a powerful soldier, but you must learn discipline. Do not feel you are being singled out. Every Lostai soldier here understands about following authority and rules. I ask you to forget everything you have experienced until now and embrace this new trajectory. If you do, you will be rewarded with independence, riches, and influence. After fifteen revolutions of service, I am obligated to offer you the freedom to do as you please. However, this will be the one and only time I will show you mercy, regardless of your age. Now, in fairness, I will ask you if you need anything to help you adapt to your new life here."

Overwhelmed with frustration, I fought back tears.

"Take a moment to think about it."

My lip hurt from biting down so hard. I thought about how Father negotiated with the warden at the prison camp.

"Commander, the...the reproducer does not recognize how I pronounce Lostai words."

He folded his hands.

"Menel, check with Horaz what clan Montor hails from and program his device to accept the appropriate Arandan dialect. Montor, I will give you six lunar cycles to master the proper pronunciation of Lostai. After that time, the reproducer will default back to Lostai."

"OK. Thank you."

"What else?"

"I do not know how to tell time here. I do not understand the characters on the clock or what you mean by minutes and hours."

"Menel will teach you today."

"Tell Menel to stop pulling my hair and pushing me around."

"Ahh... and there is that defiance again. Montor, you need to earn that. If you follow the rules without question, you will be treated with respect. If not, you will be punished. Sometimes, punishment helps you learn."

The fact that he was dealing with an orphaned, pre-pubescent child ripped from everything he had ever known was irrelevant.

"OK, but he insults me with words like vermin and primitive. I am not an animal."

Zorla first looked at Menel, rebuking him in a fake tone before turning to me.

"Now, now, Menel. Tone down your pejoratives." Zorla's

condescending tone upset me even more. "But Montor, on the other hand, you cannot be so sensitive. All commanding officers sometimes use coarse language to toughen up their soldiers. One day, you might command a squadron and will find the need to do the same. I am sure your Arandan soldiers were not so delicate. Anything else?"

I searched my brain for any other crucial point.

"Is it possible for me to communicate with people at the labor camp or Aranda?"

"Definitely not. As I said before, you need to forget about your past. Pretend today is day one of your life. Trust me, you will be so busy you will not have time for anything other than your studies, training, and duties. Are we clear?"

Dejected, I answered, "Yes."

"OK, Montor, I think you are ready for your first day orientation. Good luck. I hope Menel does not need to bring you to my office again, other than to commend you for your excellent achievements."

I turned to leave.

"Wait. Menel, have we not taught Montor the proper Lostai military salute? Montor, you may not turn from a commanding officer without the proper salute."

Menel pressed his fingertips together and brought his hands to his chest, creating a triangular form, and then extended his arms forward toward Zorla while flipping his palms up. It was nothing like the bowing salute used by Arandan soldiers.

"Well, Montor. I am waiting."

My last words to Foxor came to mind as I mimicked the gesture.

I will learn everything they have to teach me and come back to rescue you and Lasarta.

15

Each day, the clock turns
In a strange and foreign orbit
The daily rhythm of Aranda, ignored
I miss the steady beat of eighteen *gromos*
I am divorced from time
How can I still be me, my brother?

Menel led me back to the operations center. Our first stop was a room full of storage units, screens, and consoles. Instead of handles, illuminated strips ran across the drawers. Menel touched a strip and the drawer opened on its own. He pulled out a tablet.

"Sit, Montor. Consider yourself lucky. Commander Zorla is usually not so understanding." He flicked his fingers across the tablet, queuing up the green oval that apparently appeared on all screens in idle mode. He tapped the screen, and it became dark with white characters. "This is your personal tablet. Press your palm against the screen."

I did as he said. This was the first tablet I had ever operated. They existed on Aranda for communication and other purposes, but until now, they had not been a part of my daily life. He took me through several menu items.

"These are schematics of this facility," Menel explained. "The orange triangle represents the tablet's location. That is how you get oriented and understand where you are and how to get to different stations. The blinking green lights are areas forbidden to you. Do not get near those areas, or you will be punished. We start off giving our recruits freedom to roam unsupervised. If you violate the rules, we will force you to wear a tracking wristband that can impart painful burns as punishment."

A wristband seemed trivial to me compared to the punishments I had witnessed at the labor camp, but I bit my tongue. We spent a good portion of the morning with Menel teaching me the Lostai numerical and time systems. Arandans have six fingers on each hand and six toes on each foot. Our numerical system was based on groupings of twelve, compared to the Lostai decimal system. One Lostai rotation was divided into twenty units, the equivalent of eighteen Arandan *gromos*. On the moon Xixsted, twenty-five rotations equaled one lunar cycle, and it took fifteen lunar cycles to complete one revolution around the planet Losta.

Menel explained my daily routine would include academic studies and cleaning dormitories with the maintenance brigade. I did not like that last part one bit.

"It is not proper for males to do those types of domestic duties. Is it because I am a child? Do you assign such chores to your other children?" I said, mortified.

Menel rolled his eyes.

"First of all, you better forget about your people's archaic notions of female and male roles. They do not apply here. Secondly, I was kind enough to call you a recruit before, but you are truthfully a prisoner here. I doubt you will survive the long hours of hard work and preparation required to earn your status as a Lostai soldier. Finally, you are the only child on this station."

There is no one else here my age.

While I digested that piece of information, Menel continued with his explanations.

"Commander Zorla requested a squadron of young Lostai cadets to defend this station from rebel attacks. You will join them in their boot camp exercises and training."

Finally, I heard something motivating.

I cannot wait to learn how to use weapons and continue practicing martial arts.

Then it dawned on me.

"I will be in boot camp with people so much older than me?" I asked.

"Yes. Frankly, I think it is odd, but Commander Zorla insisted. The recruits are fresh out of youth military school, so they are teenagers, two to four revolutions past puberty. But be aware, Lostai youth selected to join the military are extremely disciplined. The squadron leader will not tolerate your childish tantrums."

"I have sparred with my father and foster father. I bet I can keep up with these Lostai teenagers."

Menel smirked at my smugness before answering, "I doubt it."

He programmed the tablet with alert notifications to remind me when I needed to report to each station.

"Also, in a few days, you will meet your Sotkari Ta mentor. This is the person who will teach you to use the special abilities you supposedly have. OK, it is time to take you to the Academics Lab."

We walked to a room divided into individual sound-proofed cubicles. Each cubicle contained audio and video equipment.

Menel showed me how to operate the console. My topics of study included Lostai language skills, history and civics, mathematics, and various sciences. I tried my best to commit to memory how to navigate the systems. Pangs of hunger and the awe of having a holographic professor sit across from me hindered my concentration.

"Sir Menel, is it time for the midday meal yet?"

"I was about to take you to the dining area for a meal break, but since you could not control the urge to ask, now you will need to wait until dinnertime. Time for you to meet the maintenance brigade supervisor."

I hated his scornful expression as he tapped me on the back to rush me out of the room. The maintenance supervisor's office was a long walk to the other side of the operations center and down a corridor. There I met a being who appeared to be neither Lostai nor Sotkari.

Another alien species?

"Montor, meet Homedra. They and their brigade are responsible for keeping this facility clean and in functioning order. It is not only a domestic chore but an important part of keeping this station running efficiently."

Homedra stood almost as tall as Father. I assumed it was male, but it was not clear to me. Even more confusing, Menel had used the pronoun "they," but I saw no one else in the room with us. Its hands and face were green, and thick vine-like extensions sprouted from its head, making it look like a plant. A long, flowing robe concealed its torso, legs, and feet. I could not see what they looked like, but Homedra seemed to slide across the floor rather than step forward. Despite its strange appearance, it welcomed me with a smile, albeit without teeth. I looked around.

"Nice to meet you, Montor. What are you looking for?"

"Is there someone else here?"

Menel shot me a nasty look.

Did I say something wrong?

"Well, Montor, we are three people in one body, so Menel refers to me in plural. We come from the planet Benti. What can we do for you?"

Menel replied for me.

"Montor is a new...umm, recruit here. We have assigned him to your brigade to earn his keep while he studies to become a Lostai soldier."

Without warning, Homedra's neck magically stretched like elastic. I jumped as their face was now only a breath away from mine.

"So, you want to be a Lostai soldier?" Light green eyes studied mine. "You do not look like a Lostai."

I opened my mouth to say something, but Menel interjected right away.

"The Lostai Empire is expanding and welcoming people of all races into their federation. The important thing is that Montor has been assigned to help you for three hours right after the midday meal hour. He is young, but—"

Homedra's neck sprang away from me to get their face closer to Menel's. Their green eyes narrowed. Menel took a step back.

"You mean he is but a child. We are not babysitters."

"Well, yes, but I want you to help him learn responsibility and to have pride in a job well done. I expect an evaluation of his performance every lunar cycle. He will stay here with you now so you can train him, and I will come get him later."

Menel did not wait for Homedra to reply before leaving the room. Homedra steepled their hands and stared down at me.

"Well, Montor, seems like we are stuck with you. We are all about balance, so we shall give you two jobs. One will be a tedious chore, but the other we are sure you will find interesting over time. The Lostai management here pays us well, so I hope you do not cause us trouble. Follow me."

Homedra took me back to the dormitory section of the facility where we met a large group of Bentians.

"All of you, meet Montor. Our young friend here has been assigned to our brigade. You, there..." Homedra pointed at a pair who were about to enter a room and gestured for them to come over. They looked just like Homedra. "You are the lucky ones to get the extra help. Make sure you treat Montor fairly but put him to work. If you do not manage him well, I will assign him to another team. Noram, have Montor help with the sanitizing process. When you are done with that, take him to the Engineering Lab to help with calibration. After three hours, bring him back to my office."

Homedra turned to me.

"Montor, these are Romotri and Noram. Follow their instructions and do your best. During the first few days, you will cause them to take longer to complete their jobs as they train you, so be considerate and respectful. After a few days, we expect your group will finish ahead of the rest with your extra help. Remember, we do not want problems. Do not make us render a bad report for you."

Overwhelmed by now with so many things to learn and remember, I simply nodded. As I walked into the dorm with Romotri and Noram, I noticed the room was messy.

"So, Montor, do you have experience with this type of work?" asked Noram.

"No, Arandan males do not do such chores. My mother and sister were in charge of cleaning and tidying our rooms."

"Well, this process requires less scrubbing and toiling than cleaning house. Most of it is automated, so your sexist little heart need not worry."

I did not understand the meaning, but I assumed it was an insult and added it to the list of things threatening my self-control.

"The first step is to place any dirty plates, food, clothing, and similar reusable items in the recycling unit. Every three days, we also include the bedding. Garbage that is not recyclable goes to the disposal unit. In the beginning, ask us if you are not sure where something goes."

I helped them pick up the items strewn about while they pulled off the bedding. The recycler piqued my curiosity. I watched how the items placed inside vibrated, converted into a foggy gas, and finally disappeared. Noram explained the items were reduced to their molecular level and re-used by the reproducer. Next, they used the desktop touch display and stated a command.

"Sanitize in ten seconds," Noram said out loud as he gestured that we should leave the room. Outside, he finished his explanation. "The sanitize function creates a hermetic seal around the room and floods it with anti-microbial and cleansing rays. Do not get distracted once you activate the sanitization function. Anyone inside the room while it is activated will die. This is why we go in pairs, to make sure we do not make this fatal mistake. You see how this strip light turned grey? It indicates the room is unsafe to enter. Once it turns back to yellow, we can finish the final steps."

The sanitization process left a residue. We wiped the desktop, countertops, screens, and bathroom fixtures with a special cloth. Noram reproduced bedding and uniforms. The last step was to make the bed. After working on ten more rooms, I mastered the proper pronunciation of the Lostai words for bedding, uniform, and the sanitize instruction. Although hungry and tired, this gave me satisfaction.

We moved to one of the Engineering rooms. Noram opened a storage unit and grabbed two carrying cases. They popped them open to show me a variety of meters, metal rods, and other small tools. Noram gave one case to Romotri, who proceeded with the calibration process while Noram explained it to me.

"Our team calibrates this station's utilities, computers, and environmental controls. We will not allow you to do this on your own for a long time...maybe never, as you are so young, but you can help. Romotri and I split this room. I will train you little by little."

Normally, my personality, even at such a young age, would have me insisting I could do things on my own, but I was done trying to absorb information. Noram showed me the various tools they used for this process and made me repeat their names. He also explained the functions of the various consoles, equipment panels, and devices in the room. My head hurt by now, but I noticed there were at least two of each item, sometimes three.

"Everything here has a backup system. There are also several of these rooms in this facility that take care of certain sections. We need to take each unit offline to perform the tests. While one unit is being tested, the backup system takes on the extra load. Quick work is important because we do not want to overexert any system and cause an outage," explained Noram.

I carried the case for Noram and, by the end of the session, knew the names of the tools, handing him what he needed to perform each test. Despite my mental exhaustion, learning about the equipment and watching Noram do his tests kept me interested.

At the end of my three-hour shift, Noram and Romotri walked me back to Homedra's office.

"He did well for his first day," they reported.

Soon after, Menel arrived to pick me up.

"I will see you tomorrow, Montor," said Homedra, as Menel and I walked out.

Menel remained quiet as we traversed the operations center, so I asked, "What is next, Sir Menel?"

"Normally, you would do boot camp at this time, but the squadron is not here yet. They arrive later tonight. You lucked out and get to go back to your dorm. Take this extra time to practice your academic lessons and think over everything you were taught today."

There was nothing lucky about my situation. His choice of words and even his voice made me cranky.

"I do not understand why you were so strict with me about the tidiness of my room this morning. The rooms I helped clean today were very messy. You Lostai are not so pristine."

He stopped and poked me hard in my chest.

"Listen here, boy. You need to clean up after yourself and sanitize your own room. I gave you a hard time because we will not pay a maintenance crew to clean the dorm of a low-life prisoner. Remember your place, Arandan."

Images of me beating him to a pulp filled my mind as we returned to my dorm.

"I will not be picking you up tomorrow. I have more important things to worry about than babysitting a child. You better be at the Academics Lab on time in the morning, or you will be punished. The system will record the time you log into your lesson modules. We have already programmed your reproducer to understand your Arandan dialect." He snatched my tablet and entered some information. "Your tablet is now programmed to notify you of adequate sleep and wake up times. Also, all the prompts and menu items are displayed in both Arandan and Lostai. You have no excuse for being tardy. I suggest you leave early in case you get lost. I will meet you at Homedra's office after your chores to take you to boot camp. Enjoy the rest of your day, Montor."

I was so happy to see him turn and walk away. The first thing I did upon entering my room was test the reproducer by requesting dinner in Arandan. To my relief, it worked, and I sat to finally satisfy my hunger. I requested two meat pies, a bowl of porridge, a whole loaf of *bomar,* a serving of breaded fried vegetables, and a sweet fruit pie. I drank two glasses of *goria* juice. After eating so much and so fast, my eyes could barely stay open from drowsiness. When I was done, I threw myself on the cot to nap.

"Hello, Mother."

"Montor, how are you doing?"

"I hate it here. I want to punch everybody in the face."

I lean into her sweet embrace. Her caress on my cheek is like a balm.

"Son, you are the last survivor of our family. Show them what we are made of, but not with anger. They need to know how intelligent, brave, and strong a people we are. Remember, self-control."

"Mother, it is so hard here alone."

Lorma appears.

"You are not alone, little warrior. We walk beside you every step of the way."

"Where are you going?"

"Nowhere. We are here."

Yet, I see them drift away and my heart aches.

I awoke from the dream with a start. It turned out I had slept longer than a nap. After a quick mental exercise, I figured out the time displayed on the wall viewer. Just after midnight meant there were several hours before the wake-up time. Alert now, I put away the remnants of dinner, showered and changed into the provided sleeping garments. I touched my cheek, trying to hold on to the sensation of Mother's caress.

I suppose I should do some studying.

It was easier to navigate the tablet now that the words were in Arandan. I found a spot where I could type in or speak notations I could save and access later. The words came easily to me:

Ventamu

Clan of warriors, teachers and poets

I claim the right to walk tall

Among those who try to dominate me
Soon my nightmares will be theirs

I figured out a way to add security to the page to keep my notes private and moved on to review my lessons. Per tradition, writing or speaking our clan name was reserved for special occasions.

It is OK. Today is the first day of the rest of my life.

It seems I am my own family now
This cold metallic cell
It is my pink Arandan sand
It is my crimson sea
My sky of creamy yellow
This is Ventamu, my beloved coast

I was out of my dorm a quarter hour earlier than the notification buzz. I even had time to sanitize my room and make my bed. Feeling proud of myself, I walked to the operations center humming a lullaby Mother used to sing to me at bedtime, but frustration took over again when I could not recall which corridor led to the Academics Lab. Some of the Lostai soldiers glanced or stared at me, but most went about their business. The schematics identified my position and my destination but not how to get there.

I entered one corridor but turned around, worried it was the wrong one. Checking the time, I bolted down another corridor, still confused about where I was. Now, my heart pounded as the deadline to punch into my lessons module drew nearer. As luck would have it, I ran into Noram.

"Montor, how are you? What are you doing running around?"

"Noram, I am..." I caught my breath. "I am looking for the Academics Lab. I must arrive on time or will suffer some punishment."

"Oh, no! Come this way. I know where it is."

I sat and raced through the sign-on process, thankful I miraculously remembered how to navigate the menu prompts.

The ping let me know I was logged in.

A few moments too late.

I gulped and pushed the queasiness out of my mind and launched the Lostai Civics lesson. The holographic professor appeared seated on the other side of the desk, starting off by listing all the planets, moons, and asteroids within the Lostai Empire, many whose native species were subjugated to Lostai rule. The professor claimed everyone was living in harmony.

"What if a race or planet does not want to be a part of the Lostai Empire?" I asked.

"Some more primitive cultures do not know better, so we must use force. Over time, we bring them up to our level of sophistication. It is a tough job but is our duty to improve the evolution of our sector."

The explanation did not sit right with me, but I moved on. Language and Linguistics followed Civics. Halfway through the lesson, an unfamiliar ping startled me. A holographic image of Menel replaced that of the professor.

"Montor, you were late for your lessons. I warned you there would be consequences."

"It was only a moment."

"A soldier's tardiness in battle can mean the difference between a victory or defeat."

I could not stop myself from sucking my teeth.

"A bad attitude will not serve you well here. After your chores, I will pick you up and take you to your punishment. Better hurry to get a midday meal before you report to Homedra's crew. You will not get dinner today."

I could not concentrate throughout the rest of my lessons, worrying about what type of punishment awaited me. The dining area was halfway to Homedra's office. I waited in the queue to use the reproducer, watching and listening as Lostai soldiers requested their meals. No one acknowledged me. There would be no time for several attempts. Upon my turn, I spoke the more commonly requested items: water, a protein bar, and vegetable soup. Nothing happened. My hands pressed against my forehead in defeat.

Shermont. I guess I will have to go on without eating.

A voice in my mind stopped me from turning and leaving the queue empty-handed.

"No, child, do not give up. Focus."

"Mother, I guess I am wishing you were here. But wait...you would not speak to me in Lostai."

I turned and saw a tall, grey-skinned female who looked like Klemar. The wrinkles that creased her slate-colored skin made me guess she might be the age that my grandparents would have been at the time, had they lived. Still, she stood tall and moved closer to me with no sign of fragility. I noticed the outline of muscles on her arms. The bright blue color of her shoulder-length, thick, wavy hair reminded me of some flowers that used to blossom in the woods by the labor camp. Vivid blue eyes held me captive for a moment before hunger brought out crankiness.

Great, another new person to deal with.

First, I assumed she had spoken out loud and that I imagined her voice in my mind. When I sensed, not heard, her voice again, I remembered how Klemar also had communicated with me secretly.

"Pay attention. I am mute and communicating to you telepathically. Pronounce the words as if you were murmuring them. Try again."

Hunger was a great motivator. I followed her suggestion and sighed with relief when the items appeared.

"Serve."

The container's structure dissipated. I grabbed the food on the counter and moved to a table. The grey-skinned female typed on her tablet, and audio emitted her meal request. She picked up her food and sat across from me.

"You are annoyed because I have joined you. Why?"

She read my expression well. As usual, I did not know how to hide my emotions.

"You remind me of the person who brought me here. He told my foster parents I would have a better life, but I am being treated horribly."

She did not answer and sipped her soup. I finished before her, tucked the protein bar deep in my pants pocket, and stood. I figured the polite thing would be to say something before leaving.

"I need to hurry to my chores. I have already earned one punishment today."

"Hmm...My name is Kaya." Her answer came again as a voice in my mind. "I am the person assigned to train you to use your special abilities. We will meet again soon. Good luck with the rest of your day."

I did not give myself time to ponder what she said. Remembering the way to Homedra's office was more important. My day had already started off badly. I did not need other complications. After completing my shift with Noram and Romotri, Menel met me at Homedra's office.

"Follow me." He did not look at me, but his ominous tone caused my pulse to speed up.

We walked to a large, unfurnished room. I looked around and saw containers of different sizes stacked on top of each other.

"This is one of our cargo bays," Menel said, leading me to the innermost section of the room filled with crates. He pointed to a metal crate with slats on the sides, top, and bottom and a solid door.

"Get in," he said, sliding open the door.

"What?"

"This is your punishment. I would have preferred using a *zirem* on you, but our rules prevent me from physically harming a child. Instead, you will spend the night in this crate like the vermin you are."

Before I could react, he snatched the tablet from my hands, pushed me down, and forced me in. I struggled against him and tried to roll out, but he was stronger and locked me in.

"You will spend the rest of the day and night here, so you have time to think about how to make it on time to your stations. Punctuality is one of the key virtues of a Lostai soldier. Deliveries have been completed for today. No one will come in here until the morning. Hopefully, solitude will help you learn this lesson."

I wanted to plead with him not to leave me in the cramped crate, but pride and defiance won out.

"I am not afraid. I slept alone in a hut in the labor camp. This is no punishment."

He ignored me, turned on his heel, and walked away. The lights went out and the door whished shut. With not enough room for me to sit, I curled into a fetal position. A string of Arandan curse words escaped my lips.

I do not care. This is extra time for me to sleep.

In reality, I hated being confined to such a small space in

the pitch dark, and soon my ears became attuned to every little creak and crank in the room. My body shivered from the cold. I sniffled, thinking how Father would have never punished me this way.

"Mother, why am I here when all of you are gone? I guess this is my punishment for all my mischief."

"Nonsense, son. Pretend I am next to you. Feel my caress on your cheek."

"I will try, Mother, but it is hard. These people hate me, and I hate them."

"Do not focus on that. I am sure you will find an ally, eventually. Remember, your father's strength is in you. Do not give up."

As hours passed, the temperature dropped, my teeth chattered, and my limbs stiffened from being stuck in the same position. I remembered the protein bar in my pocket. Nibbling on it distracted me a bit from my body aches and the cold.

Thoughts drifted toward the female who approached me in the dining area. I wondered whether she would represent yet another set of challenges and punishments for me to endure. Our brief exchange left me with no clue about her moral fiber. Would she be like Menel and Horaz, who seemed to get pleasure from imposing their will on others? Her comment about my supposed special abilities fueled my imagination. I knew by now that telepathy meant the ability to communicate without speaking out loud. What other powers might I possess? I thought about fictional heroic characters I had read about in books and viewed on recreational videos. Could I fly like birds? Would I have incredible strength? Could I make myself invisible?

If I have powers, I need to learn how to use them right away.

As I tried to get to sleep, I vowed I would be Kaya's best student.

❄

Shuffling footsteps, bustling sounds, voices, and lights awoke me. I had been holding in the need to relieve myself and was thankful that soon I would be out of the crate. Lostai soldiers were moving, opening, and closing containers. One crouched to peer at me through the slats. He called over another soldier and, laughing, mocked me.

"Look what we have found here. An exotic animal from a faraway planet. I suppose the commander requested him as a pet."

"Get me out of here," I demanded.

They laughed even louder.

"Oh wow, someone has trained it to talk. Amazing."

I banged on the crate. They only laughed louder and walked away. The abdominal pain added another torment. When I could not hold it any longer, I pulled down my pants and positioned myself so the urine stream was aimed at one corner of the crate while I pushed myself against the opposite edge to avoid getting wet. Another soldier caught sight of my predicament. Smirking, he called over some of the others. They thought it would be a good joke to roll the crate over and over as I tumbled inside.

"Stop it," I shouted.

They laughed and laughed. Now soiled and humiliated, I screamed, "I hate you people. One day, I will kill you all!"

"What is going on here?" a robotic female voice asked.

I looked through the slats and saw Kaya and Menel standing across from where my crate had landed. Kaya was using the same tablet as before to type in her words, which were translated into audio.

That makes sense. Kaya said she was mute.

"This vermin has soiled himself," said one soldier, between chuckles.

Kaya's fingers flicked across the tablet.

"Menel, how long has he been locked in that crate?"

"Since yesterday afternoon. A well-deserved punishment for arriving late to his academics station," answered Menel.

"I will report this to Zorla," answered Kaya, using the tablet. "This is not conducive to the successful harnessing of his Sotkari Ta powers."

Menel did not reply. He came over and opened the crate. I jumped out and lunged at him to use whatever tactic was possible to hurt him. Some unknown force suspended me in place. I could not move. I heard Kaya's voice in my mind, soothing and natural, unlike the cold, robotic voice emitted by the device she was using to communicate with Menel.

"Control yourself, boy. If you strike Menel, you only will earn yourself another punishment. Save your energy for your chores and bootcamp."

She turned toward Menel. The tablet emitted audio again.

"I will take charge of the boy. Set up a two-room dormitory that accommodates both of us. He will live with me. I will ensure he arrives promptly to his duties."

"Who are you to give orders? I take orders only from Zorla."

"Good. The three of us should go see him now."

Menel offered a begrudged nod.

She grabbed me firmly by the wrist, and whatever power had held me in place released me. A strange but calming sensation coursed through my body like a jolt of energy.

"What is your name, boy?" she asked telepathically.

"Montor," I answered, averting my eyes, humiliated because my clothing was wet with urine.

"OK, Montor. I can help make things better for you here, but you must take my suggestions to heart."

"Yes. OK," I mumbled.

She led the path to Zorla's office, while Menel eyed me with disdain. At the entrance, I stopped in my tracks, bumping into Menel behind me. A robot with metallic skin and the facial features and body type of a Lostai stood in front of the door.

Kaya's voice entered my mind again. "Do not worry, Montor. It is Zorla's assistant droid. I suppose you have never seen one before."

I turned to look at her and shook my head. My jaw dropped as the robot addressed us.

"Do you have an appointment?"

Menel smirked.

"Tell Zorla I mean no disrespect in arriving unannounced, but I have a critical matter to discuss with him. It is about the Arandan child he has tasked me to train. Tell him I cannot move forward until I have this talk with him."

The droid went inside and reappeared a few moments later to welcome us in. The smile fell off Menel's face.

Kaya dispensed with pleasantries and got straight to the point.

"Zorla, I have sensed power in this boy almost as potent as my own, which is saying a lot, considering I am a pure-blood Sotkari Ta." Zorla's eyes shifted while she continued to type into her tablet. "If we train him and mold him into a Lostai soldier, he will represent a living asset like something you have never known before. However, harnessing Sotkari Ta abilities requires focus, finesse, and self-motivation. Abusive treatment is counter-indicative. This is only the boy's second day here. He was late to a station. Menel left him overnight in a crate in the cargo bay. I cannot work with the boy under these conditions. I have asked Menel to have the boy move in with me so I can assist him in acclimating to his duties and schedule. Is that agreeable to you? Let us remember, he is still a child."

I noted how Kaya used respectful words and body language but also commanded authority. Despite being a female, she reminded me of my father.

Zorla shot Menel an annoyed look and folded his hand tightly on his desk. He offered Kaya a fake smile and replied, "That sounds fine to me. But I have learned this boy has a history of temperamental and aggressive behavior. Keep him in line, or he will continue to be punished."

"Understood. I will escort him to get cleaned up and wait to hear from Menel regarding the new location of our dorm. Who has Montor's tablet? I request he have the afternoon off while I familiarize myself with his schedule, and we get settled in our new quarters."

Zorla pursed his lips as he nodded at Menel.

"I will get it to you and will let you know when your new dorm is ready," answered Menel.

"One more thing," said Kaya. "Please allow me to make changes in his schedule as needed to accommodate his Sotkari Ta training. Developing these abilities requires plenty of practice and meditation time."

Zorla sighed deeply.

"Fine, but you may not eliminate his boot camp. I expect Montor to be military ready and in strong physical shape by the time he reaches the age of our current Lostai cadets. They are fresh out of military school and between the ages of sixteen and eighteen. From what I have learned of his race's development, I estimate that will be in about four or five revolutions."

Kaya nodded to acknowledge his last point, grabbed me by the wrist again, and led me out of the office.

As we walked down the corridor, I heard her voice in my mind.

"Do you think you can adjust to living with me, Montor?"

"Yes, Kaya."

"Good."

17

———

Kaya took me to her dormitory. She reproduced clean clothing for me while I showered. Once I was dressed, she asked if I wanted to eat. Now that we were alone, she reverted to telepathic communication. I replied out loud, the only way I knew how, but wondered if one day I would learn to place my voice in her mind.

"Yes, Kaya, I am hungry."

"What would you like?"

"I guess, soup."

"Again?"

She remembered she saw me eating soup when we first met.

"I am not familiar with Lostai food," I clarified.

"The reproducer is programmed to create food from many cultures. I am sure we can get it to make you a proper Arandan meal."

"Yes, we can, but I do not know how to request one in Lostai."

"Ask the device to display Arandan food options," she insisted.

"I have trouble with the Lostai pronunciation. Zorla agreed to program the devices in my quarters to accept Arandan language commands for the next six lunar cycles."

"OK. I will have them do the same for our new dorm, but right now, there is no rush. Take your time to enunciate the words with the right accent. You are speaking certain phonetic sounds with your mouth wide open. Notice that the Lostai speak most words as if their jaws are clenched. You need to remember this. Go ahead. Make the request."

It took a few tries, but I finally got the device to show me a holographic presentation of various Arandan food staples. My mouth watered at the sight of meat and fruit pies similar to the delicious ones my mother made for us. I ordered a few different varieties and once again the traditional Arandan fruit beverage made of *goria*.

"These have a wonderful aroma. I would like to try a few pieces if it is OK with you," said Kaya.

"Sure."

The previous evening, I had been so hungry that I inhaled my food without thinking much about it. This time, I savored my first bite of the meat pies. Although not a replica of Mother's excellent cooking, memories of family and holiday reunions flooded my brain. Sadness swallowed my joy, and hot tears threatened to make an appearance. I avoided Kaya's eyes.

"Yes, I understand you must miss your loved ones, Montor. I have lost family, too. But right now, we can enjoy this meal together."

"Who have you lost?"

She ignored my question and asked instead, "Tell me, what are the Arandan words for these?"

I launched into an explanation of the pie names and their ingredients to the best of my knowledge. She reproduced a plate and cutlery and sliced pieces of the different pies for herself and tried some of the *goria* beverage.

"This is made with ground fowl, and this one has chunks of bovine meat. My mother also made some only with vegetables, but I did not like those much. I am not so sure how she made the pie crust so delicious, but I remember she used to have my older brother buy plenty of fresh butter from the market whenever she made these."

She paid close attention, and I believed she truly enjoyed the meal.

"I must say, Arandan food is delicious, and this beverage is so refreshing."

She extracted a smile from my face, frozen in a scowl for so long. Kaya was the first non-Arandan who told me anything positive about my race. A gregarious Montor from revolutions ago resurfaced, and I rattled questions non-stop.

"Kaya, do you have a favorite food from your planet, and by the way, is your planet anywhere near Aranda? Did you come here in a spaceship, or did you do the jump thing like Klemar and I did? Are you and Klemar related?"

Kaya smiled as she attempted to keep up with me.

"One of my favorite things is Sotkari hot tea, but it may be too sweet for you."

"I love sweet things! Please, can you request some so I may try it?"

The tea was sweet beyond belief, and I could not help smacking my lips and scrunching my face.

"Oh, sorry, Kaya. I guess you are right. It is very sweet."

Her mouth opened, her head tilted back, and her shoulders twitched in what seemed like laughter. No sound came out, but I could hear her chuckling in my mind.

"No problem. It takes time to get used to. You asked about Klemar. I know him, but we are not related. He is from planet Sotkar, as am I."

"Why are you not able to speak out loud as he does?"

"I am a Sotkari Ta, and he is a Sotkari Pasi. All Sotkari Ta are mute."

"So, he is more powerful than you?"

She chuckled to herself again.

"Actually, the only special ability a Sotkari Pasi has is telepathic communication. We Sotkari Ta are mute but have other powers."

"We?"

"You have the genetic makeup of a powerful Sotkari Ta, Montor."

"I do? How is this possible?"

"I am not sure at your age how much you can understand."

"I am not a baby."

"Yes, OK. At some point in Sotkari history, Sotkari Ta scientists feared we might become extinct. They figured out a way to embed Sotkari Ta genetic material in other races. In a way, you are even more powerful than an original Sotkari Ta because you have the potential to harness all their abilities and still are able to speak out loud."

For all my pretense, talk of extinction and genetic material was a lot for me to grasp, but I understood that I possessed powers that sounded supernatural to me.

"Did everyone in my family have these abilities? I never heard of such things until Klemar came to get me at the labor camp." I stared at my lap. "By then, my parents and siblings were all dead."

She did not reply until I looked back at her.

"I am so sorry to hear that, Montor."

Are her eyes tearing?

"To answer your question, this seeding of genetic material occurred at random and passed on through generations, like other inherited traits. You were probably the only one in your immediate family to have inherited these genes from some ancestor. It is not something you can notice unless you know what to look for. Now the Lostai have devices that detect certain brain waves specific to Sotkari Ta and Pasi individuals. That is how they identified you."

"They want to turn me into a Lostai soldier, but I—"

Kaya tilted her head, waiting for the rest of my sentence. I stopped myself from saying that I hated the Lostai and that there was no way I would fight alongside them.

She is being nice to me, but her job is to train me for exactly that purpose. I cannot trust her with these thoughts.

I raised my eyes to meet hers, and terror filled my soul.

Shermont! Maybe she can read my mind! If she tells Zorla what I am thinking, who knows what they will do to me?

"What is wrong, Montor? Are you feeling all right?"

I tried so hard to mask my fear.

"My older siblings always told me I was too much of a chatterbox. I should not irritate you with so many questions."

Her amazing blue eyes with their alien round pupils bore into mine. My heart almost stopped.

"You are an intelligent and inquisitive child. Those questions are to be expected, but I agree. Too much information at once can be overwhelming."

We finished eating and cleaned up in silence. Kaya turned on the viewer to a news telecast showing sports and weather updates from planet Losta and others. She was about to switch to view something else when a report came on related to a conference attended by Lostai politicians and people of another species I was not familiar with. It appeared to catch her attention.

"What is that about?" I asked.

"Losta is adding another planet to their empire...I mean federation," she replied.

I thought about how the Lostai invaded my village, and it did not make sense to me how politely everyone was behaving.

"Everyone seems happy. This is not how it was when they took my family and friends to the labor camp."

Her brows furrowed as if an unpleasant thought had crossed her mind, but she only said, "Yes, sometimes these newscasts can be misleading."

We watched the politicians make speeches until Menel came by to return my tablet and show us to our new dormitory. It looked like the previous ones, with the addition of a smaller room accommodating a second cot, desk, and storage unit. The viewer, reproducer, and other devices were in the main larger room, and we would share one body care room.

"Does this unit meet your needs?" asked Menel in his ever-present condescending tone.

Kaya used her tablet to reply that everything was in order and asked to see my tablet. She scrolled through several screens.

"With this schedule, I do not have sufficient time to train the boy, Menel. You heard what Zorla said. He wants the boy military ready as soon as possible. Cleaning dormitories contributes nothing to his military development. Please eliminate him from Homedra's maintenance roster."

"Kaya, I like the calibration work they showed me in the Engineering Lab. Maybe that might come in handy when I become a captain of a starship," I said.

Menel scoffed at my words.

"That is the silliest thing I have heard. You will never be a captain of a Lostai ship, Montor."

Kaya ignored Menel's comment.

"OK, Montor, we will keep the calibration work, but your other duties will take priority. If you cannot keep up, I will need to eliminate that activity." She turned her attention back to Menel. "I will accompany the boy to his stations as I see fit. Sometimes, I will stay with him to keep him on track and make sure nothing derails his progress. If that is acceptable, I do not think you need to be monitoring his every move. I will take responsibility for his behavior."

"OK, I have better things to do anyway, but be aware, you may share in his punishment if he gets out of line or does not meet expectations."

Great! Now, I am not only responsible for my own punishments but possibly hers, too.

"Understood, but you also be aware, I will get rid of any obstacle threatening his progress and safety."

Did those beautiful eyes just turn menacing, and did Menel gulp?

"Right," he answered.

18

W e settled in our new quarters with several hours to spare before bedtime. Kaya accompanied me to the Academics Lab, where I caught up on the lesson I missed earlier in the day. Afterwards, she gave me an extensive tour of the operation center, pointing out the corridors leading to off-limit areas. The whole time, she communicated to me telepathically.

"Montor, a protective dome encapsulates this entire science station because the moon we are on has no atmosphere. There is another operation center on the other side of the moon accessible only via underground tunnels. A person cannot leave these domed areas without a special suit and helmet for breathing and protection from the extreme cold. Do not even consider trying to escape this place that way. Understood?"

I nodded, enveloped by a grim, hopeless sadness.

Back in our dormitory, we ate dinner. Afterward, Kaya sat me at her desk. She turned on the viewer to project a shimmering wheel-like image with six spokes extending from a circle in the center to an exterior rim.

"Our elders used a model like this one to teach the children about our Sotkari Ta abilities. Each spoke represents a talent: Telepathy, Telekinesis, Healing, Blocking, Memory Command, and Mind Control. The center hub symbolizes the mental energy from where our power emanates, strengthened through meditation. The outside circle represents our continuous evolution. I would like to initiate you in the sacred Sotkari Ta ritual of meditation."

"What is meditation?"

"To meditate, a person finds a quiet place and forgets about everything else except what they are trying to accomplish."

"Do you mean like praying?"

"Not exactly. Sotkari Ta meditation strengthens your mind and creates focus. It gives you the confidence to know that you are in complete control of your powers and surroundings." She placed her palms on the desk and met my eyes squarely. "Do you really want to harness these abilities, Montor?"

Healing? Mind Control? Wow!

The question caught me off guard.

What am I getting myself into?

I understood most of the words, including telepathy, but the meaning of one was still a mystery.

"What is telekinesis?"

"The ability to move things and manipulate matter with your mind. For example, watch how I can levitate this tablet without touching it."

Amazed, I watched the tablet float off the desk and high above our heads. Just before reaching the ceiling, it plummeted back towards the desk. I shielded my face, expecting it to smash into tiny pieces. Instead, at the very last moment, it hovered and landed safely back on the desk.

Excitement brought me to my feet.

"I want to learn how to do that!"

"Calm down, Montor. I am sure you would, but why?"

"Well, who would not want to have magical powers?"

"And what would you use those powers for?"

"To do whatever I want."

She leaned in to get closer to me. Those amazing eyes held mine captive.

"I am sure your parents enforced rules they expected you to abide by and instilled in you some sense of order. You must know without order, there would be chaos. People would end up hurting each other."

"Yes, I suppose, but now I am so helpless. I hate it."

"Tell me, Montor, about how you feel."

I cocooned my body in my arms, attempting to comfort myself through a painful admission.

"These people...the Lostai...they took us from our homes. They forced us to work for them. Many members of my clan, including my family, have been victims of their cruelty. They tell me I am a primitive, worthless creature, but I know it is not true. I can prove it to them with these powers. They will not abuse me. I will not be their victim."

"Say it again, Montor."

"Huh? What?"

"Those last words."

"I will not be their victim."

"Exactly. That should be your focus, Montor. Think about this and close your eyes. Repeat these words: I have been given total control of myself and my surroundings."

"Really? Who gave it to me?"

"Shhh...Focus! We can talk about it later. Right now, close your eyes and say the phrase over and over in your head. With hard work, you can use your abilities to ensure you are no one's victim."

The thought appealed to me.

Kaya stood and placed her hands on my upper arms. I was already familiar with the unique sensation I felt any time she held my hand or touched my bare skin. This was much more intense, like tiny electric shocks originating on my scalp and traveling down my body to my toes.

"Do not be afraid. I am helping you through meditation because it is your first time, but going forward, you will pick a time and place when you will do this every single day for the rest of your life. In the same way you must study and exercise every day to achieve knowledge and strength, meditation is required to hone your Sotkari Ta powers. Is that clear?"

"Yes, Kaya."

I was not sure how long we remained in the same position, but it felt like a long while. When she lifted her hands from my arms, I gasped as if brusquely awakened from a long dream. My pulse boomed in my ears.

"How are you feeling, Montor?"

"A little weird, but OK."

"I think it is a good idea you get some extra rest, but first let us look at your schedule. I am going to notify Zorla and Homedra that you will no longer be on dorm-cleaning duty. The commanders here like to know where everyone is supposed to be at any point in time, so you must keep them appraised of any change in your itinerary."

She showed me how to send and receive messages and how to read and manage my schedule on my tablet. The application on my tablet had been programmed to translate the messages from Lostai to Arandan. Next, she directed my attention to the clock and alarm applications.

"When do you think you should awake to get ready in the morning in order to arrive at the Academics Lab on time?"

I slid my finger across the screen and selected a time stamp.

"OK, always add more time than what you think is necessary. Lostai equate tardiness with stupidity. Do not give them a reason to berate you. This is how you set an alarm."

I acknowledged her advice and slid my finger further to

adjust to an earlier wake up time. My nails scraped the screen. Her lips tightened.

"Montor, I am going to reproduce something to cut and file your nails down. I am sure yours are this long because you did not have such tools at the labor camp."

"No, my clan keep their nails long purposely. We are warriors and hunters. Our nails are weapons and tools for us."

She sighed deeply and took a moment before replying.

"The Lostai are fastidious about what they consider cleanliness and grooming. I suggest we keep your nails short and filed evenly, or they will use their appearance as another reason to insult you. I am sorry if that goes against your culture, but you must do what is necessary to survive here and keep your dignity. You can still be a warrior using your physical and mental strength, even with shortened nails."

I did not like the idea but nodded to let her know I would allow her to do it.

I do not want them to keep calling me primitive vermin.

"Good." Her tone suddenly became dismissive. "OK, now take a shower and go to bed."

I ached for a motherly hug, but she turned her back on me to read her tablet.

She is not my mother. What am I thinking? I am but a job for her.

The next morning, we arrived at the Academics Lab with plenty of time for me to log in and get mentally prepared for my session. Kaya stood by and intervened now and then to show me how to make annotations in my tablet's academics application.

"Pay attention to when the professor says some fact is

important. It will surely be included in the examination at the end of the lunar cycle."

During lunch in the dining area, I ordered the food in Lostai and got it right the first time.

"I see you ordered soup again. You can order Arandan food on this reproducer like you did in our quarters."

I shrugged and sipped the broth with no comment. Kaya bent down and tilted her head to force me to look at her.

"Montor, do not shy away from ordering the Arandan food you like."

"I am afraid they will make fun of me."

I stared into the bland soup, overly aware of the Lostai soldiers sitting at the tables around us. She tapped me ever so lightly on my hand.

"Never be embarrassed of your culture. In the evenings back at our dorm, I would like for you to teach me about your people's customs. We will make time to read and research together the history of your planet and your race. The Lostai are proud of their accomplishments, but you have plenty to be proud of, too."

"Thank you. I would like that."

I got up, ordered an Arandan fruit pie without worrying if anyone took notice, and offered her a slice.

She is always so serious, but I think she smiled.

After lunch, Kaya took me to the gymnasium. Several Lostai soldiers in workout clothing were training using equipment and weights. We walked over to a corner table. At first, they paid no attention to us until weights of various sizes floated over to where we were. Some soldiers glared our way and commented to each other in hushed tones. Soon, they all left.

"See how they despise me?" I said.

"It is not you to whom they are reacting. They fear my abilities. Soon, you will gain their respect as well," replied Kaya.

Kaya positioned my chair, so I sat facing the weights on the floor. Standing behind me, she placed her hands on my arms, similar to how she did the night before. The jolt was even more potent this time.

"Montor, repeat a few times to yourself the mantra I taught you last night: I have been given total control of myself and my surroundings. I want you to focus on the smallest weight there. Think about how it would feel in your hand, its shape and weight, how it would feel to lift it with your hands. Now, imagine yourself picking it up and placing it on the table, but do not reach out for it. You can do it with your mind."

My heart raced in anticipation.

I cannot wait to learn how to do this.

I meditated, stared at the weights, and imagined as she said. Time went by and nothing happened. Impatience built up inside. My body fidgeted from sitting in one position for so long. She did not move at all.

"Are you not tired from standing there so long, Kaya?" I finally blurted out.

She lifted her hands, and I heard her blow air out of her cheeks like Mother used to when I misbehaved.

"Montor, this is not a quick process. We will sit here like this for many days before you accomplish moving anything with your mind. And you must desire it more than anything else."

"But I do want it."

"If you want it badly, you will not mind sitting for long periods of time focusing on the weights and meditating without fidgeting."

It was my turn to sigh deeply.

"OK, let us try again."

Three times we did the same, taking short breaks in between. Nothing happened, but at least I became less impatient, and my body did not seem to protest as much for sitting still for so long.

A buzzing notification on my tablet alerted me it would

soon be time to meet up with Noram and Romotri at the Engineering Lab. Kaya and I arrived before them.

"Hi Montor, how are you doing?" said Noram as they walked in.

They acknowledged Kaya's presence with a nod but said nothing to her.

"This is my friend, Kaya. She is giving me some special training. I am living with her now."

Again, they inclined their heads but did not reply to my announcement.

"I will leave you to your work and will come back later to take you to your next station."

Noram and Romotri seemed relieved. Once she was gone, they reverted to a friendly demeanor.

"Homedra told us you no longer need to work on their crew, but you chose to continue to help us here. Thank you, Montor. We appreciate all the help we can get."

"Sure thing," I said, happy to spend time with the only people who treated me with a semblance of friendship.

With my help, they finished their task for the day early. We spent the last few minutes making jokes and mocking Menel and some of the other Lostai supervisors.

"Maybe Menel would be less uptight if he mated more often," said Noram, upper body quivering as they chuckled. "But Lostai do not even like it."

"Like what?"

"Mating," they answered amid hoots and giggles.

I did not know what to say, prompting Romotri to speak one of my most hated phrases.

"Noram, stop it. He is only a child."

Kaya rescued me from the indignity of not understanding their joke.

"It is time for your first day at boot camp. Montor, I fear this will be your most challenging station."

My impulsiveness got the best of me.

I blurted out without thinking, "Why? I think it will be my favorite since I already know martial arts and used to spar with my elders all the time. I used to watch the Lostai practice with their weapons back at the labor camp and have dreamed of joining the Arandan militia like my elder brother did. One day, I will rescue my foster parents and restore my clan."

"Montor, you must not say any of those things to those young Lostai whom you will train with. Right now, you are nothing to them, but some day, you will all be fellow soldiers in the same squadron. You need to earn their trust. This is the one place I suggest you swallow your pride. They have been taught Lostai are a superior race working for the greater good of this sector. Truthfully, the Lostai have developed an elite military force. Only the best warriors are accepted as soldiers."

"Kaya, I want to be the best warrior ever, but sometimes my head hurts, trying to remember the things I should not do and say. My mother always tried to help me remember about self-control, but I have never been good at it."

"If your mother admired self-control, make her proud by trying your best to achieve it."

"She is dead."

"I know, but her luminescence still exists in the universe. I am sure she still shines her light over you."

Devout Arandans believe the dead travel to a spirit realm to start a new life but sometimes return to visit their family in dreams. At this young age, I already doubted every single religious dogma I had ever been taught, but envisioning Mother as light comforted me.

19

———

I suffer daily the brutal *horza*
The work of strength and discipline
To serve evil deeper than Tormixian caves
I am empty here, filed down to nothing
A mere twig in this dead tree
I fear I will crack underfoot

Kaya walked me to a gymnasium different from the one we visited earlier.

"This room also has holographic battle simulations," she explained.

In the center of the room, an older Lostai was talking to a group of fifteen younger Lostai, all dressed in military uniforms. Kaya communicated with the group leader by typing on her tablet.

"Hello, Lieutenant Carloxi. Has Zorla informed you about Montor?"

Lieutenant Carloxi looked like someone who wished he were someplace else.

"Yes, I am aware of the Arandan child." He gestured to the group of young Lostai cadets. His monotone voice droned with extreme boredom. "Everyone, meet Montor. He will join us in our training. I know he seems young, and he is right now a prepubescent child, but his race develops differently from ours. In five or six revolutions, he will be your contemporary. Commander Zorla expects I convert him into a trained and battle-ready Lostai soldier by then. Let us help him achieve that goal."

I was already getting used to being observed like a strange creature, but these young Lostai looked me up and down with contempt.

They think I am not worthy.

Noticing they were about my height, I stood tall and looked them all in the eye.

I will show you.

Audio from Kaya's tablet interrupted my thoughts.

"Montor is still getting used to this environment and his schedule. I would like to stay here to observe his first few sessions. Is that acceptable?"

Lieutenant Carloxi looked back at the teenaged Lostai. Most of them smirked or rolled their eyes after hearing Kaya's request.

They think I need a babysitter. I wish she would just leave.

"Your request is highly unusual, and I think will be disruptive. I cannot give the Arandan special treatment because he is young. And look at him. He is the same height as these cadets. He should be able to handle himself," said Lieutenant Carloxi.

"Zorla wants this boy to achieve his highest potential. I promise not to intervene unless I see something threatening Zorla's goal."

"Fine, but only for a few days."

Kaya walked to the far end of the room and found a chair to sit on while Lieutenant Carloxi called me over to join the other cadets.

"Students, we will start with our typical warm-up exercises. Montor, I do not expect you to keep up with us today, but I need you to do your best."

"OK."

"Acknowledge any order from a superior officer with a Lostai military salute and reply, yes, sir."

"Oh sorry, sir." I remembered the salute Menel had showed me at Zorla's office. "Is it like this, sir?"

Lieutenant Carloxi seemed pleased I already knew the salute.

"Yes, good Montor."

I foolishly assumed I could keep up with their workout routine because we were of similar height. These teenaged recruits were several revolutions past puberty. Their military school training had helped them develop muscles. The Lostai were much stronger than their short stature led one to believe. Despite the hardships endured at the labor camp, I was not a scrawny, feeble child. Even Mother had often complemented my athletic build, but I did not yet have the strength of an adult.

They started off running around the room. Halfway through the run, I fell behind. Soon, the other cadets were ahead of me by a full lap. Some snickered as they passed me by. I tried my best to ignore them and push down the frustration bubbling up inside me.

After the run, they performed a series of floor exercises the Lostai called *horza*.

"Montor, these exercises strengthen your core muscles," explained the lieutenant.

Some forms required a partner. When Lieutenant Carloxi announced one of these forms, the others rushed to get a partner, laughing at the one who ended up with me. Their jeering echoed in my ears.

The form required my partner to hold my legs while I positioned myself horizontally, my chest a few inches from the floor, supporting my torso with extended arms. While my partner held me in place, I extended and bent my arms to move my torso to and from the ground. That went fine, but when it was my turn to hold his legs, he did many more repetitions, and my grip on one of his ankles slipped. His lower body fell to the floor with a thud.

"Sir, look, he dropped me on purpose. Why must we train with this stupid, weak creature?"

"He lies! I did nothing on purpose, nor am I stupid or weak," I said, shoving him.

The others ganged up on me, a few landing punches and kicks before Lieutenant Carloxi announced it was time for weight training. I got in a few good strikes, too. One of them covered his eye and another bent over rubbing his rib area.

"Save it for our sparring practice," Carloxi shouted, pulling them off me.

I tasted blood and wiped it off with the back of my hand while glaring at them as we moved to weightlifting. Although I could not do as many repetitions as the other cadets, I paid close attention to their form, determined to memorize every move and detail. We later entered a holographic side room for target practice with various real Lostai weapons. Carloxi explained that students were required to go through a safety training before handling weapons, so he did not allow me to participate. I watched the cadets gun down the holographic opponents composed of unfamiliar races and creatures. At first, I was amazed at how real everything appeared, but then I recognized one of the weapons as the rifle used to kill Rimax. I thought I would vomit until finally came the moment I had been waiting for.

"Recruits, move back to the mats. Time for sparring. Montor, you can watch for now. I do not want you to get hurt."

"I know a martial art I have practiced with adults since I was very young. I am not afraid."

The lieutenant pursed his lips. Whether he was mocking me or was impressed made no difference to me. He called one of the younger Lostai who appeared to be about sixteen revolutions old.

"OK, you, Trilom, get over here."

I was the equivalent of a ten-revolution old Lostai in age. At the labor camp, I had fought with Arandan youth, not Trilom's age, but definitely older than me. Through the corner of my eye, I noticed Kaya put down her tablet and get to her feet.

Lieutenant Carloxi signaled everyone should step back to give us enough space. I wondered what type of hand-to-hand combat style these cadets used. The lieutenant explained the first to score five strikes would be the winner. He mentioned no other rule. I liked that.

We circled each other. Trilom curled his hands into fists. My fingers remained extended. Arandan martial arts call for striking with the heel and edges of the hands, not punches. The other cadets encouraged Trilom to knock me out. I let him hit me first, a punch to the jaw. All the cadets cheered.

That is the only point you are getting, Trilom.

Luckily, I had clenched my teeth in preparation and shook off the punch. Had I not done so, I probably would have gone down. Father had taught me receiving the first blow helped you to understand your opponent's strength and prove to yourself and others you could take it.

Now, it is my turn.

I countered with a devastatingly quick palm strike and kick combination. Trilom hit the mat hard. I enjoyed the collective gasp and silence that followed.

One strike down, four to go.

To his credit, Trilom jumped up immediately and lunged at me. I noticed he was right-handed. That would be my next target. I struck his forearm just in the right spot. It went limp. He swung with his left arm, but I ducked and delivered a blow to his nose. Blood spurted out. His eyes widened in shock.

Oh, interesting. Lostai blood is greyish, not red like mine.

Another cadet tried to join in, but Lieutenant Carloxi warned him to stay put. The others launched insults my way and encouraged Trilom again. Trilom possessed the strength to cause me extreme damage had he inflicted any series of his punches or kicks, but I was too agile for him. I could have fought all afternoon. After knocking him down three more times, the lieutenant called it a match and announced me as the winner. The cadets glared at me as Trilom limped back. I watched the other matches, confident I could beat any of them decisively. After the last match, Lieutenant Carloxi dismissed us. Kaya met me at the door.

"Are you OK, Montor?" she asked as we walked out.

I licked my lips and rubbed my chin and cheek area.

"How bad does it look?"

"Not too bad. Does it hurt?"

"It is throbbing, but I will forget about it soon enough."

"Let us go to the infirmary. They will get rid of the inflammation and give you something for the pain. I was worried for a moment, but you are already a skilled fighter. I cannot imagine what you will be like when you are fully grown."

"I will be an exceptional warrior, like my father."

A notification buzzed on Kaya's tablet. She tapped the display, read the note, and frowned.

"What is it, Kaya?"

"Lieutenant Carloxi says he forgot to mention you must be dressed in Lostai uniform when you attend boot camp."

The shock was worse than Trilom's punch.

Me wear the same uniform as the soldiers who killed my father and brother? Impossible.

"Kaya, I cannot do it. Please do not make me."

Before I knew it, I was bawling in the corridor.

Kaya looked around nervously and got on one knee. She tried to get my attention by grasping my shoulders and shaking me.

"Calm down, Montor." Her words entered my mind like a warning.

I let my body collapse against hers, my face buried against her chest.

"Please do not make me be a filthy traitor, I beg you, Kaya."

"Montor, what did your foster parents tell you when they allowed Klemar to bring you here?"

I wiped away my tears.

"They never really had a choice."

"OK, but what did they tell you?"

"They said I would only have to serve for fifteen revolutions, and later I can take everything I learn, become a powerful spy, and help liberate my people."

She covered my mouth.

"Shhh, Montor, you cannot say such things out loud here. I imagine how hard it will be for you to wear a Lostai uniform, but think of it as your way to gain power. Once you are a Lostai soldier, they will need to treat you with respect. A good spy lets no one know their true motivations. You need to get these people to trust you."

I sniffled some more but inclined my head in agreement.

At the infirmary, they placed something called a healing pad against my cheek and jawline. In minutes, the soreness and inflammation were gone.

Before going back to our quarters, we stopped by the first gymnasium.

"Montor, I know you will go through boot camp with the

Lostai cadets, but I want to show you a Sotkari Ta daily exercise routine. There are several forms that strengthen the body while quieting the mind and preparing it for the meditation you will do later. I will teach you a different one each day."

I watched as she performed a series of graceful movements requiring controlled breathing, arm flexing, squatting, stretching, and balancing. Looking closer, it appeared both like a dance and a martial art. I mimicked her movements and soon experienced a wave of tranquility that lasted the rest of the evening.

20

———————

I had romantic notions
Of becoming a hero
Instead, I am a pawn
In someone else's war

They wring me like a rag
Use me as they please
This uniform a curse
That bleeds my soul raw

Wearing the Lostai military uniform gutted me at first. The cadets joked that I looked like a pet their younger siblings dressed as a plaything. Kaya had warned me about possible audio and video spying devices in our quarters, so I could not even vent my frustration out loud in the privacy of our room. I cried myself to sleep many nights asking my parents and siblings for forgiveness.

"Father, I am so sorry for wearing the Lostai uniform."

"You are an Arandan warrior, Montor. That uniform is just bits of cloth. Do not imagine that it defines who you are."

And I cursed a High Spirit I no longer believed in.

"May you be damned, High Spirit. I should have died with my family. Why was I spared death? To live my life like a filthy traitor? What am I doing talking to a fantasy? You are not real."

Kaya encouraged me to use my meditation to calm my mind and the sparring sessions to vent my anger. Over time, wearing the uniform became another part of my agonizing routine.

After the first week, Kaya no longer accompanied me to my stations. Instead, she met me afterward at the gymnasium for Sotkari Ta training. I ate lunch at the common dining area alone. The Lostai cadets and soldiers wanted nothing to do with me, and the feeling was mutual. Kaya and I spent the evenings together in our quarters sharing dinner, going over my lessons, researching Arandan history and customs, and, finally, meditating.

My first breakthrough with telekinesis came a day after spending another night in a crate in the cargo bay. I tried my best, not always successfully, to keep out of trouble, but Menel took advantage to punish me for anything he deemed as insubordination. These transgressions included things like answering on a test that Arandans, not Lostai, were the best warriors in the galaxy. Kaya no longer intervened to save me from these punishments, other than request that I receive water, a protein bar, and quick bathroom breaks. Sometimes, I was left in the crate for two or three days. To make matters worse, I did not know how, but the cadets learned where I was being held and came to torture me by poking me with rods and tossing the crate around. It only made me beat them harder during the sparring sessions.

I earned my latest punishment because another soldier caught me mocking Menel behind his back. He let me out of the crate in time for me to run, take a shower, and meet Kaya at the gymnasium. I had only eaten a couple of protein bars since midday two days before and was especially cranky.

"How are you, Montor?" Kaya greeted me.

"How do you think?"

"Spare me the sarcasm. Sit and try to calm your mind," she replied.

"I do not want to do this today. Do you not feel sorry for me? I have been in a crate for two nights. I am hungry. My body aches. Can we get something to eat and get back to this later?"

"No. There will be times when you will need to call on your powers while under duress."

"What powers? We have been doing the same thing for two weeks, and nothing is happening. This is a waste of time."

"Montor, if you do not want to learn, I can tell Zorla I was wrong about you. I can tell him you have no potential at all. What do you think will happen then?"

I did not answer and turned away, clenching my fists.

"No idea? I will tell you, then. He will have you killed for wasting time and cost. That would not be so bad, but first, he will have you tortured. What do you think about that?"

Kaya's attitude always left me confused. She treated me with fairness and showed interest in my well-being but never demonstrated any affection for me, remaining emotionless and focused on the task at hand, sometimes to the point of being callous.

"OK, OK...I get the message," I said, huffing and staring at the ceiling.

She got up and walked towards the exit.

"What now?" I shouted.

"Clearly, you are not focused, and I am not doing a good job as a mentor. I will tell Zorla to find someone else for this task."

I ran up and grabbed her arm. Electricity ran through my veins like all the times we ever had any skin-to-skin contact.

Shermont! I feel her exasperation but also concern.

"I am sorry, Kaya. Please, I do not want a new mentor. I will focus."

We returned to the chair where I sat. Like all our earlier sessions, she placed her hands on my bare upper arms, triggering a different type of tingling. I closed my eyes and thought about the weights in front of me. I thought about Foxor and Lasarta and how tough it must be for them at the labor camp, wondering what had become of me.

Are they OK?

At Xixsted, I was eating three square meals a day, plus snacks, sleeping in a fairly comfortable cot, and bathing in a warm shower. I lived in comfort compared to their situation. If my mother, father, and siblings were lights watching over me, as Kaya mentioned, I wanted to make them proud.

Instead of repeating the mantra she taught me, I closed my eyes and chanted something else.

I need to do this for all of them.

A slight vibration in my head caught me by surprise.

Kaya whispered to me telepathically, "You are doing it, Montor. Keep on."

I thought about lifting the weight and throwing it across the room. The sound of heavy metal hitting the floor with a clank awoke me from my trance.

"Amazing, Montor. Look!" said Kaya.

I opened my eyes and saw the weight on the floor at the other end of the gymnasium. Luckily, we were alone. I did not recall stopping to check if anyone was in that area.

"I did that? Really? All on my own?"

"Yes, Montor. You should be proud. I expected you only to levitate it, but your mental strength allowed you also to hurl it so far away. Accomplishing this for the first time with the heaviest weight at your age is not common with my trainees. I was not wrong about you, Montor. You are destined to be a powerful Sotkari Ta."

I let her words sink in and replied, "I want to practice some more. What else should I try?"

"Mental strength is like physical strength. Every day, you should practice this basic exercise of picking something up and hurling it away and follow with different nuances. For example, try lifting several items at the same time and throwing them all in the same direction. Next, hurl them in different directions or at different times, and so forth. Later, I can show you how to manipulate matter with your mind, bending even the hardest metals and taking apart the most intricate tool and reassembling it...all with only the power of your mind."

After that day, telekinesis practice became my new plaything and entertainment. I could not get enough of it. As the lunar cycles passed, it seemed there was no limit to how I could manipulate objects using my mind. I also embraced all elements of my military training, making punishments a thing of the past.

I easily beat all the cadets during our sparring sessions except the oldest one, named Rimalo, who at eighteen revolutions old would soon be eligible to be officially inducted into the Lostai military, assuming he passed all the required tests. He would earn a substantial salary, could buy property, and would be allowed vacation time during which he could live off campus. His fifteen revolutions of service would start from that point, and after he served his time, he would be free to do as he pleased. Although he was not friendly with me, he did not join in when the other cadets taunted or tried to humiliate me. One day, I ran into him alone in the dining area. I summoned up enough nerve to sit by him and start a conversation.

"Rimalo, I suppose I should thank you for not bullying me like the others. Is there any particular reason why?"

"You are pretty bold at your age coming here and asking me such things, considering you are basically a prisoner here. Still, these young Lostai do not realize how tall and strong you will become in a few revolutions."

"Why do you say that? What do you know about me?"

"My father is a surveillance and security system technician. He is often called in to Lostai labor camps to maintain and repair those systems. Before I enlisted in military school, he would bring me along with him a few times. I have seen your race. You are a tall, muscular people. Soon, you will tower over everyone on this base. The other cadets will have to eat their words. You are but a child now, and not only do you already beat them in sparring, but I also see you excelling in target practice and piloting skills."

"I guess I will be nice to you when that time comes," I replied with a chuckle.

"Hopefully, I will be far from here by then."

I took Rimalo's words as motivation to work even harder at my training. Every twelve days, everyone on Xixsted took a rest day. The other soldiers and cadets grouped together to use the lounge and holographic rooms for relaxation and camaraderie. I used the holographic rooms also, but alone, and not for fun and games, but to simulate space battles, piloting, target practice, and hand-to-hand combat.

Kaya took rest days to leave Xixsted and visit family. She never spoke of whom she visited nor invited me to accompany her. Sometimes, I relaxed in my room and wrote poetry. Kaya had read some of my poems and encouraged me to keep writing. I did not know if she meant they were any good or whether I needed a lot more practice, but they provided another mode of releasing the sadness I carried inside.

I frequently asked Kaya when she would teach me to communicate telepathically. I was tired of only being on the receiving end. She explained telepathic communication required finesse, discipline, and trust. I needed to mature further before she would even try.

After one complete revolution of having no punishments and showing commitment to my schedule, Kaya agreed I was ready to be trained in telepathy.

"Montor, one reason you cannot initiate telepathic communication with me is because I block my mind when I am with you. This is an important skill to master, especially when dealing with other telepathic beings."

"You are making telepathy sound like a scary thing."

"Here is the issue, Montor. The same skill used in telepathic communication can also allow you to explore people's innermost feelings, true intentions, and thoughts. A deeper probe can alter behavior and manipulate memory. It is a matter of Sotkari Ta honor not to delve further than basic communication without permission. Once I train you, if I find you are trying to probe me, you will get no second chances. I will immediately report you to Zorla as untrustworthy, and he will get rid of you without a second thought. Do not think because I have treated you fairly that I will allow any leeway in this matter. Understood?"

I could not help but gulp before answering.

"OK, but what if I do it by mistake?"

"No, it would not happen by mistake. As you will see, you need to overstep your boundaries willfully. I need you to first give me permission to monitor your true intentions, and secondly you must give your word of honor you will abide by these rules."

Honor is a significant matter in Arandan culture and not to be taken lightly. My father taught us we must examine our motivations before making such a pledge. I wrung my hands and thought deeply about what she had explained before answering.

"Yes, Kaya. Do what you need to do. I promise to abide by your rules because I want to complete my training. I am thankful for how you have treated me, and I do not want to disappoint you."

She bent over and studied my face as I uttered each word.

"OK. Let us begin. Close your eyes and tell me what you see."

I did as she said, and after trying hard to see something, I opened my eyes.

"Kaya, I see only darkness."

"Yes because I have my mind blocked. Now, try it again."

To my amazement, a light appeared in my mind like a shimmering doorway at the end of a tunnel.

Wow, that is new!

"To communicate telepathically, imagine walking towards the light, but I forbid you to go beyond that point. When you reach the light, formulate the words you want to say in your mind."

My pounding heart distracted me at first, but soon the sensation of walking towards the light became real for me. When I stood before it, I communicated my first telepathic words.

"Thank you, Kaya."

"At first, you will feel the need to close your eyes for concentration, but with practice, this will become second nature for you. You will do it without scrunching your face the way you are doing right now."

A million questions bombarded my brain. I wanted to know if one could be telepathic in several languages, up to what distance did telepathy work, and what happened if there were several telepathic people in a conversation.

"Take it easy, Montor. I will explain all these things over time."

From then on, whenever we were together in our quarters, we communicated telepathically. She recommended I continue to speak to her out loud in front of the Lostai to avoid long silences that might make them uncomfortable. I took advantage from time to time to tell her something secretly I did not want the others to hear. Sometimes, I would test her ability to stifle laughter by poking fun at Menel.

"Look Kaya, Menel has polished his head extra shiny today."

At those times, I saw a faint sparkle of humor in her eyes and a twitch in her lips.

"Montor, stop it. You will get us both into trouble."

Now that I was aware of Kaya's light in my mind, with the right focus, I could see the lights corresponding to other living things around me. Kaya explained the lights corresponding to lesser-evolved beings appeared dim and far away in our minds. Without training, I would not have even noticed them. An evolved Sotkari's light appeared brighter and closer. It was interesting to discern everyone's lights in my mind.

"So, is my light bright, Kaya?"

"Yes, Montor. It is one of the brightest and nearest I have seen. The Lostai's lights are barely visible compared to yours."

This knowledge gave my self-esteem a boost. Visualizing these lights was also key to learning about blocking. After communicating telepathically for a few lunar cycles, Kaya taught me about this ability.

"Montor, can you see my light in your mind?"

"Yes."

"Now, imagine you are covering the light with the palm of your hand. Tell me when you have done this."

I signaled I was ready.

"OK, Kaya, what next?"

No answer. I asked again. When she did not reply, I grabbed her arm and shook it. She smiled and typed in her tablet.

"You blocked me so I could no longer communicate with you telepathically. That also means I have no access to your mind whatsoever. You would not be susceptible to mind manipulation. Learning how to execute this at a moment's notice is the ultimate telepathic defense mechanism. Whenever you are among people with those abilities whom you do not trust, block first and ask questions later. The tricky thing with blocking, and I do not know the science behind this, is once you block one light, you have cut off anyone from being able to communicate to you telepathically. We cannot selectively block one person while leaving ourselves open to others."

To help me practice, during many lunar cycles, we played a game where I was supposed to block my mind any time I saw Kaya. She would try to sneak up on me. During these moments, we frequently ended up giggling. It was another of the few times she would let go a bit of her stiff no-nonsense persona.

One day, we received a visit from Klemar, who I had not seen since he dropped me off at the station almost two revolutions earlier.

"Excellent! Kaya has taught you how to block. I am glad to see you are doing so well. You are much taller than when I first brought you here," said Klemar, speaking out loud when he first entered our quarters.

Close to seven revolutions old and approaching puberty, my arm, leg, pectoral, and abdominal muscles were already defined. I used weights and strengthening exercises with fervor, targeting to bulk up more and more. Still far from what would be my height as an adult, I already towered over everyone on the base except Kaya and any non-Lostai employees. The cadets did not bully me anymore.

"It is OK, Montor. You can unblock your mind. I trust Klemar," said Kaya, using her tablet. "I have asked Klemar to spend some time here on Xixsted to help me teach you how to execute telepathic conversations involving more than two people."

The type of telepathy we possessed allowed us to connect mentally with another Sotkari Ta or Pasi who was at a distance where normally we could recognize them with the naked eye. This applied even if they were not facing us or in another room. We could not use telepathy with someone at a faraway location or talking to us via video or audio devices unless they happened to be within that distance. Language imposed no barrier on telepathy. Whatever language used as you formulated the words in your mind is what the other person perceived.

With Klemar's help, I learned to communicate telepathically with one person or with several people at the same time in conference mode, while excluding others if necessary. Even if I blocked my mind from receiving telepathic communication or manipulation, I could still send out a telepathic message. In the beginning, it took a lot of practice to discern Kaya's light from Klemar's. Everyone's light possessed a distinct color, luminosity, and shape. Discerning these idiosyncrasies required finesse and focus.

A Sotkari Ta greeting involved grasping the other person's forearm and applying a brief squeeze near the wrist. This served as more than just a salutation. It allowed an energy exchange that made each person's light clear to the other.

By the time I reached the seventh revolution from my birthdate, I was well-versed in three of the Sotkari Ta talents: Telekinesis, Telepathy, and Blocking. Kaya also introduced to me the Sotkari Ta healing ability, but this did not capture my interest as much. It involved knowledge of anatomy and using telekinetic concepts to manipulate bodily functions. I learned we could control parts of the body in the same way we moved inanimate objects with our minds. Kaya cited, as examples, the beating of a person's heart, the expanding and relaxing of the lungs, blood flow, the inflammation of muscles and nerves, the digestive process, and, with enough skill and focus, the reproduction of cells and the healing process.

Kaya took me to a lab with small animals to demonstrate these concepts. One of the male specimens had been badly injured by a rival, its hind leg broken. She connected the animal to medical equipment so I could see how she used telekinesis to set the bone and increase blood flow to that part of the body to accelerate the healing.

"It is an amazing talent, but I do not think this is so important for me. I am preparing to be a warrior, not a doctor," I said.

"You never know when you might need such skills to provide first aid to a fellow soldier or a loved one, but there is something else..."

She glanced back to the cage and one of the animals keeled over. I took a closer look and turned back to her.

"Kaya, what happened?"

"Well, Montor, these concepts can also achieve the opposite of healing. I lowered its blood pressure to cause it to pass out." I guess my shocked expression prompted her to add, "It will regain consciousness soon, but I could have paralyzed its heart muscle or caused its lungs to collapse."

I figured she was just trying to get me more motivated to understand anatomy and the healing talent.

"But that would not work on people, right?" I asked.

"It can, but I would hope you would only do something like that in self-defense and as a last resort."

21

———

Puberty brought on a lot of physical changes and new urges. I lost Father and left Foxor before they had a chance to talk to me about such things, but I was not clueless. I remembered my older brother, Rimax, joking with his friends about the changes in his body. He played less with me and was more interested in flirting with the girls in our town. There were no attractive females at Xixsted for me to interact with in that way. The female Lostai body type and physical appearance did not appeal to me at all. Besides, the Lostai equated sexual relations to a disgusting reproductive chore and only mated once each revolution, deriving no pleasure from it. I knew by the way I was touching my body in private that my feelings on the topic were completely different.

When I told Kaya my third testicle had descended, she suggested videos about Arandan sex education and reproduction. I was more interested in watching video serials with explicit sex scenes broadcast from different planets in the sector; of course, when she was not around. I grew taller and stronger. I sounded more like my father, my voice taking on a much deeper tone.

Soon after my seventh revolution, Zorla requested from Kaya a demonstration of the Sotkari Ta abilities I had mastered. He also set up a competition among the cadets to evaluate how far along we were in our boot camp training. During the past two revolutions, three of the cadets, including Rimalo, had come of age and integrated into the Lostai military. They joined a new squadron Zorla invited to Xixsted. Their mission was not only to guard the science base but also provide easy deployment to nearby battlegrounds. Three other cadets replaced them in the student group.

Zorla's evaluation of my progress in harnessing my Sotkari Ta abilities would be limited to telekinesis and healing. He took Kaya and Klemar's word that I was proficient in telepathic communication and blocking. The four of us, plus Menel, met at the general gymnasium where I usually practiced with Kaya. They sat behind me. In front of me, on the floor, sat globes of various materials and sizes. The heaviest was twenty times my weight.

"OK, Montor, show us what you can do," ordered Zorla.

Before he uttered his last word, I launched all the globes in the air at once and kept them hovering a finger's worth of space beneath the high ceiling. I heard a gasp of surprise behind me. With my back to them, I could not tell who it was, but it brought a smile to my face. Without warning, I caused all the globes to plummet.

Another gasp.

"I hope he does not cause damage here. This is a state-of-the-art fitness room," exclaimed Menel in a rush.

I could not help but chuckle. The globes stopped short of crashing to the ground as I kept them hovering over the floor for a few moments before allowing them to land lightly. For my next demonstration, I levitated the globes and moved them in different directions, sometimes individually, sometimes all at once. I turned to look at my audience while globes rolled across the floor and flew around the room.

Now, the finale.

All the globes exploded into tiny pieces. Zorla jumped to his feet. Menel's skin took on a sickly hue.

I finally learned what a genuine smile looked like on Zorla's face. He clasped his hands in front of his body and shook them, a Lostai gesture of approval.

"Well done, Montor. Well done," said Zorla.

Kaya typed into her tablet.

"Yes, Montor has accomplished a lot more than expected in this skill, and he is still not at the peak of his abilities. He can also take intricate tools and gadgets apart and put them back together using only his mind."

She nodded at me. It took me only a moment to restore the globes to their original state.

"Amazing!" shouted Zorla, shaking his clasped hands even more vigorously.

"Montor has shown less progress in healing, but he has gained some skills in this area. Let us go to the infirmary."

I thought she might explain about the harmful things a Sotkari Ta could do to a person's body, since that might be of more interest to Zorla, but he cut her off. It did not surprise me that she did not insist. That particular use of Sotkari Ta abilities was not her favorite.

"We can skip that. Who cares about healing? He is destined to be an extraordinary Lostai soldier, not a doctor," said Zorla. "Montor, I am pleased with your progress here. Is there anything special you would like as a reward?"

Kaya's voice entered my mind almost as an intrusion.

"Be careful what you ask for, Montor. Zorla is finicky and can turn on a person in a moment. If you ask for something he deems as traitorous to the Lostai cause, you will get a punishment instead."

I did not heed her advice. Later in life, I regretted my request. I was too young and naïve at the time to think about the consequences or to understand how the Lostai manipulated even people with powerful Sotkari Ta abilities.

"I would like to talk with my foster parents, at least via a viewer."

"Foster parents?" Zorla's eyes narrowed. "I was told you were an orphan with no family left."

"Montor, stop," said Kaya's voice in my mind.

The excitement of possibly talking to Foxor and Lasarta was too great. I barely heard her warning.

"I have foster parents who took care of me at the labor camp after my last sibling died. They were good friends of my parents and loved me."

"I see," said Zorla, rubbing his chin. "Assuming they are still alive, I think we can coordinate this. What are their names?"

"Foxor and Lasarta from the Ventamu clan."

Kaya was visibly mortified. I must have missed the glint in Zorla's eyes.

"OK, I will talk to the current warden to make it happen."

Later in our quarters, Kaya admonished me for not paying attention to her.

"Montor, you should have listened to me when I told you to be careful with Zorla. You never should have told them about people you care about. The Lostai, especially someone as ruthless as Zorla, have ways to use that against you."

"He should be careful with me. I am turning into a powerful Sotkari Ta," I said.

My cockiness was a facade to mask the fear that I had put Foxor and Lasarta in danger. I heard nothing more of my request and thought Zorla had forgotten about it until four days later. Right before the cadet competitions were about to begin, he called me into his office. I was dressed in full Lostai uniform.

"Montor, I have good news for you. Your foster parents are still alive." The tone of his voice revealed no genuine sympathy. "I have arranged for you to have a quick chat with them before you go into the cadet competition. I am hoping this will be great motivation for you to do well."

The thought that they would see me dressed in Lostai uniform broke my heart.

He picked this time on purpose. He knew I would be obligated to be dressed this way.

Before I could tell him I changed my mind, the viewer turned on, and there they were.

"Montor!" Their voices came across in unison. Foxor, always adept at smoothing over tense situations, continued talking as Lasarta's face fell.

Of course. It must be so disappointing for her to see me dressed this way.

"You look well, son. My goodness, look how tall and strong you are."

For a moment, I was without words. I turned to look at Zorla. He was focused on his tablet, so he did not see the anger in my eyes. Perhaps my imagination got the better of me because I could have sworn he wore a slight smirk.

Finally, I composed myself and asked, "Commander Zorla, may we speak in our language?"

Zorla waved his hand dismissively, indicating his permission without meeting my eyes. I did not bother to acknowledge with a salute and turned my attention back to the screen.

"How are you doing, Foxor?"

I took the time to assess their physical appearance. Although thinner, Foxor and Lasarta appeared in about the same condition as when I left them.

"Well, Montor, I do not have to tell you how things are here, but we have a new warden who is fairer than Horaz. I am curious. Have you learned to use the powers Klemar talked to us about?"

Lasarta still did not lift her eyes to the screen. My eyes stung with the tears I fought to contain.

"Yes, Foxor. I am glad you have a more even-handed warden. I hope things are at least a bit better for you. My mentor has treated me kindly. She is a powerful Sotkari Ta and has taught me how to communicate telepathically and how to manipulate objects with my mind."

I thought about lifting Zorla and his desk in the air, but by now I exercised better self-control.

Someone else will pay for what he has done to me today.

"Commander Zorla, may I display to them my telekinetic powers?"

This caught Zorla's interest. He stood and replied, "Good idea, Montor. They should be proud of your accomplishments. With people like you, the Lostai military will be unstoppable."

His condescending voice triggered what I chose to do as a demonstration.

"Look, Foxor, at what I can do with Commander Zorla's tablet using my mind."

I levitated the tablet from his desk and made it float around the room.

"Wow," said Foxor.

Lasarta finally looked at the screen.

The tablet smashed against the wall and fell to the ground, breaking into a few large pieces. Lasarta covered her mouth, I am sure, first, to hide her chuckle, and then her trepidation. Zorla's eyes blazed with ire, but before he could say a word, I repaired the tablet, restored it to its original state, and floated it to land softly back on his desk. I met his glare for a moment before turning back to the screen.

"Son, that is unbelievable," said Foxor, switching to Lostai. "I am sure your commanders are pleased with you."

Zorla let out a deep exhale. When I turned back to him, he sported his typical hypocritical grin and cocked his head in a way that used to make me shiver. He approached the viewer screen.

"Yes, your SON has made significant progress here. I cannot wait until he completes his boot camp training and is officially integrated into the Lostai military. OK, say your goodbyes, Montor. You do not want to be late for the competition."

Lasarta finally said something, speaking in Arandan.

"Be careful, Montor. That Lostai has an evil look about him. What competition is he talking about?"

"It is a tournament among the cadets to display how far along we are in our training. Although they are older than me, I am already better than all of them. Part of the competition involves hand-to-hand combat. Those cadets will pay for you having to see me dressed this way."

"Watch what you say. They most likely will translate our conversation," warned Foxor.

"No worries. I am only speaking the truth."

Zorla gestured I should end the conversation.

"I have to go now. Hopefully, when I win this competition, they will allow me another conversation with you. Please take care of yourselves. One day, you will be free from that place. I promise you."

Lasarta's watery eyes stared into the screen. "Take care of yourself, son."

<h1 style="text-align:center">22</h1>

Vengeance will accompany me
My one comforting companion
Yet always just out of reach
I curse at thee, I do, I do, I do
And I plead, *namit, namit, namit*
Until I sniff the scent of enemy blood

I made my way to the boot camp gymnasium accompanied by Zorla. That alone made the other cadets look at me with contempt. Menel, Kaya, the squadron leaders currently on Xixsted, and more of Zorla's lieutenants were already there. Zorla joined them to sit on a couch in the back of the room. I was taller than everyone except Kaya. On the other side of the room, a holographic scoreboard floated in the air with the names of the fifteen cadets. The scorekeeper constantly updated the scoreboard so that the panel could see each cadet's standing at any point in time. The competition featured seven sections: hand-to-hand combat, weapons practice, astronautics, space warfare, piloting, engineering, and strategy.

Each cadet started off sitting in an individual soundproof cubicle set up in the gymnasium. There, using a console, we took the engineering, astronautics, and strategy sections of the test. An audio and video program prompted us with questions. We replied either verbally or by entering information into the system. When the timer buzzed and we all exited the cubicles, a glance at the scoreboard revealed I was in third place. The first and second place cadets smirked and made obscene gestures at me. Still angry about Lasarta seeing me dressed in the Lostai uniform, I lunged at one of them.

"You do not belong here, Arandan. Hit me, so you can be disqualified," shouted the first-place cadet.

Kaya's voice entered my mind.

"Montor, do not let them rattle you. Stay focused."

I shut my eyes for a moment to get centered and set aside the rage and humiliation.

She is right. I will have my chance later to inflict pain.

Except for the sparring portion, the remaining parts of the competition would be held in the holographic room. A screen dropped from the gymnasium ceiling so our audience could have a view of our performance. We changed into our flight suits and, one by one, took turns going through simulated space battles, piloting challenges, and target practice.

By now, I was experienced using the holographic room. The realistic simulations no longer left me flabbergasted. I stepped into the room for my first test. It looked like the cockpit of a small shuttle capable of interstellar travel. I strapped in, checked all the controls, and executed a perfect lift-off. In real life, although this shuttle model provided artificial gravity, passengers still sensed gravitational shifts because of the shuttle's small size. The simulation was sophisticated enough that I felt the dizziness and chest pressure.

Soon after I cleared the atmosphere, the simulation tested my abilities to maneuver a series of obstacles while avoiding enemy fire. Each simulation introduced unique challenges. Although flying through an asteroid belt was not as menacing as people without experience believed, being chased added a level of difficulty. The test simulated some of the denser asteroid belts in our sector, but having logged in so many hours of practice, I negotiated all the obstacles easily.

While I congratulated myself for what was a perfect score so far, the simulation presented an explosion ahead on my flight path. The controls readout and a thud let me know something had hit the shuttle. Adrenaline kicked in as my entire viewer displayed an extensive debris field hurling large chunks of torn-apart spaceships my way. I approached at full speed, swerving and dipping, to avoid a collision. The holographic opponent relentlessly pursued me. My shuttle shuddered with each strike the opponent scored. The goal for the test was to survive the chase by avoiding the opponent's attack and any lethal collisions with the obstacles presented. The rules did not assume engaging the enemy.

I will not be toyed with this way.

I am not prey. I am a hunter.

I ignored the rules without stopping to consider whether there would be consequences or points deducted. The simulated opponent was gaining on me. At the last minute, I flipped my craft around in a risky maneuver and aimed photons at the enemy craft, chuckling as it exploded. I went on to clear the debris field and conclude the test without further incident. When I stepped out of the holographic room, the audience rewarded my daring with their Lostai gestures of approval. My piloting performance earned me a move to second place.

All cadets entered the weaponry test together. I carried myself with more swagger and confidence. The holographic room now simulated a wide-open area comprising various terrains. Provided with a variety of handheld weapons, the test required me to pursue and shoot my opponents, who were attempting to finish me off as well. The last cadet standing would be awarded all the points for the test.

Good! A test I can relate to.

I chose my weapons and ran through a clearing to find rock formations or anything else that might provide cover while scoping out the area. Solid projectiles and laser rays whizzed by me. I tumbled and scooted on the ground to avoid them.

No. Wrong strategy.

I am not prey. I am a hunter.

An entry to the thick forest beckoned me. I bolted into the wooded area running in a zig-zag formation, and at the first opportunity, climbed a sturdy tree. I remembered how much I enjoyed jumping from tree to tree as a child, both in the woods by my home in Aranda and at the labor camp. Using intertwining branches, I made my way to even taller trees. The other cadets had no idea now where I was hiding, but the high vantage point gave me an excellent view of them running around below, picking each other off. I waited till half of them were eliminated from the test. With a *mizora* in each hand, it took me only a few moments to eliminate six of the remaining seven. By then, the last remaining cadet knew I was shooting from the trees. I got him between the eyes as he stared up, trying to find me.

I wish this phasor rifle was real.

As the sole survivor of the test, I walked out of the simulation last. The other cadets stood by, waiting for me to take my place. They all avoided meeting my eyes, most of them staring at the ground in defeat. I saluted the audience, but I am sure my eyes and body language reflected the satisfaction of beating their supposed superior cadets. The Lostai squadron leaders and lieutenants rewarded my move into first place with stony silence.

To my surprise, Zorla appeared to be the only Lostai in the room not upset.

"Well done, Montor," he said using his tablet to connect to the communication system.

Kaya reached me telepathically. "Good job, Montor. Now comes the sparring, your favorite part, but try to tone down all that cockiness and relish when you beat them. These Lostai dislike being upstaged."

Is she rooting for me? Maybe she is not so impartial after all.

The hand-to-hand combat portion of the test would be evaluated in tournament style. Two cadets faced each other. The first to receive three strikes would be out of the competition, and the victor would then face the next opponent.

Lieutenant Carloxi positioned the two oldest cadets to kick off the tournament. Zorla stood and his voice bounced off the gymnasium walls.

"Let the Arandan begin the competition."

A subtle but devious way to make certain I would have to fight fourteen cadets straight to win the tournament. I was the youngest, having just reached puberty, while they were between two and four revolutions past puberty. Carloxi smiled and nodded in Zorla's direction, pairing me up with the oldest cadet, who had taunted me earlier.

I wanted to beat him with wild, demented fury as I did my tormentors at the labor camp.

No. If I do that, they will call me a primitive beast. I will show them how disciplined and precise my attack can be.

After closing my eyes for a moment of meditation, I stepped onto the sparring mat. My opponent, named Bornot, looked up at me.

"Height means nothing, Arandan. I have put in many hours of practice. Your luck is about to run out."

I let Bornot score a strike to the chest and sucked up the pain. In the moment it took his fist to return to a guarding position, my hands moved like lightning to land a jab and a cross to his face. Blood spurted from his lip and nose as he fell. Bornot was not quick to get back to his feet. When the squadron leader gave us the signal to start again, Bornot moved around, less eager to take a shot at me. I tired of waiting and kicked him so hard he landed off the mat.

I gave the lieutenant a smug look and said, "Next."

One by one, I defeated all the cadets, finishing with only minor cuts on my brow and lip because I took pity on the younger ones, who were two revolutions older than me.

Pursing his lips, Zorla made eye contact with each of his lieutenants and squadron leaders. They fidgeted and lowered their eyes as his voice boomed again across the room.

"Montor, congratulations on winning Xixsted's first cadet boot camp competition under my command. You have shown us what a great Lostai soldier you will make one day. As a prize, you have earned five days of vacation. I suggest you take some time to study your engineering, astronautics, and strategy lessons, as it seems they were not your strong suit."

I saluted once again and replied, "Yes, thank you, Commander Zorla."

Later, in my quarters, I celebrated with Kaya by reproducing my favorite Arandan foods and desserts.

"I showed them!" I shouted, fist-pumping.

"Shh...Montor. Remember, I told you we may be under surveillance. You should communicate telepathically."

"Yes, OK," I replied telepathically this time. "But let us be honest. You are happy about my victory, right?"

"It was a good contest, but I was impartial about the outcome."

"What...come on. Be honest. You were cheering me on. Why are you always so stiff with me? Do you not have any emotions?"

"Are you calling me a liar?"

"No. Never mind."

Her behavior confused and annoyed me. Arandans are a people of close family ties and community bonding. I so wanted someone on my side. Stuffing my mouth with cakes dipped in fruit syrup helped me to relax and get my mind off her lack of enthusiasm. As I licked my fingers, it surprised me to catch her watching me intently. I could not decipher her expression.

"Montor, do you like crime mysteries?"

"Yes, I enjoyed watching them with my father."

"Excellent. I think you will like this story. The main character is a spy."

Soon, we were immersed in the video, debating on the mystery's resolution until I got tired. She encouraged me to go to sleep but made sure I did not forget to meditate first.

23

I am an orphan cut loose from history
At the foot of a frozen mountain
I look closely at my guide for the way

No warmth comes from her tongue
That slashes me like a metronome
Efficient and relentless as a winter storm

I am prepared to battle, to resist
But her unyielding shell protects me
Draws me in, bound by new strength

Can there still be trust in this world
Can I find the crack in my own carapace
To hear the ancient choir chant *"home"*

I took advantage of my vacation to practice Sotkari Ta skills with Kaya. She also showed me more strengthening and balancing forms. I returned to boot camp, energized and rested, strutting into the gymnasium as a warrior should after a hard-fought victory. My fellow cadets ignored me. Lieutenant Carloxi was especially cold with me, too.

Such sore losers.

At the end of our boot camp session, Carloxi was quick to leave the gymnasium, but the cadets did not file out as usual. I did not give it much thought, but on my way out, a whack to the back of my head knocked me to the floor. I touched my head and looked at my hand. It was covered with blood. Scrambling to my feet, I realized the oldest cadet had struck me with a weight. Dizziness set in, but I focused enough to use telekinesis to rip the weight out of his hands and hurl it across the room.

"You cowards. If you are angry with me, at least fight fair," I growled as they circled around me.

They all charged at once. Some were armed with more weights and *zirems*. A single well-placed blow with one of those weights would have killed me. I focused my mind on disarming the cadets who held the weights, leaving myself open to receiving punches, strikes, and kicks from the rest of them. Soon, the debilitating pain of the *zirems* assaulted my body. The smell of scorched skin brought me back to the day my father died. With enough focus, I could hurl many of them off me, but the pain of that memory hindered my concentration. Someone landed a good punch to my jaw, and I fell to the ground. One strike to the groin left me breathless. The onslaught continued. I absorbed blow after blow, mustering enough energy to shield my face and head and to use my legs to kick them away, but I knew I was close to passing out. The taste of blood filled my mouth, and my eyes were almost swollen shut.

"You are going to die now, Arandan. Then we will not have to smell your stinky funk anymore."

Three of the cadets stood beside me while the others took a step back. Two of them were armed with *zirems* and one with a weight. One of them poked the *zirem* at my neck. I screamed in pain.

"You cannot do that. I am a Lostai cadet."

Did I really utter those words?

They scoffed at me.

"A Lostai cadet?" the oldest said. "Since when do animals join an army?"

I prepared myself for the end.

Mother, I will be with you soon.

One eye was completely swollen shut. Through the other, I barely distinguished a force abrubtly ripping the weapons out of the cadets' hands. The three cadets themselves were levitated to the high ceiling and slammed hard against the floor beside me. I heard the sounds of bones cracking. Their bodies twitched for a moment, and then they were still. The other cadets ran away. I closed my eyes and tried to will myself to my feet, but barely catching my breath, I did not have the strength. Someone grabbed my hand, and a shock jolted me.

"Kaya!" I said with a grunt. "They ganged up on me."

Her beautiful blue eyes blazed with an anger I had never seen before. She used her tablet to summon a medic. While we waited, she placed her other hand under my shirt and pressed my chest. Her voice entered my mind.

"Hold on. You will be OK, son."

Numbed from the pain, I drifted off.

I awoke in the infirmary, healing pads placed all over my body. Kaya sat by my cot.

"Kaya." My voice sounded weak.

She jumped from her seat.

"Oh, Montor, how do you feel?"

"Not too bad." I was being truthful. Apparently, they had given me something strong for the pain. "How long have I been here?"

"It has been one day. Even with the advanced medical technology here, your injuries were extensive and required some time to heal. You should rest here tonight but will be discharged by tomorrow morning."

"They were such cowards, Kaya. If you had not arrived when you did, I would be dead."

"Yes." Her voice entered my mind with a gasp. "You are usually so prompt arriving to our afternoon Sotkari Ta activities, I sensed something was wrong. Honestly, I feared something like this might happen."

"I guess I will carry the scars of a warrior before even entering an actual battle."

"No, you will be free of scars. The medical technology here erases them. You should take it easy for the next few days, though."

I touched my face and inspected the parts of my body not covered with healing pads. I noticed something was missing.

Where are my amulets!

I tried to get up, but Kaya stopped me.

"Montor, what is it?"

"There were two cords around my neck with amulets. Where are they?"

"Oh, yes. They took them off when they were diagnosing and treating you. They are right here."

"Please put them back on me right away. We Arandans must always wear our amulets."

"OK, no problem. Sorry, I did not know. Tell me about them."

It was a good way to distract me. Since I always wore the amulets concealed under my shirt, there had never been an occasion to explain about them to her. When she asked why I wore two, I told her the other one was Arixa's. Her expression filled with compassion.

"I will make sure no one touches them again," she said.

Something came to my mind.

"Those three cadets—"

She turned away.

"They are dead."

"What? Oh, no, Kaya. They will punish you."

"Maybe, but as soon as you are discharged tomorrow, we will pay Commander Zorla a visit. So far, I have not heard from him or his minions."

Kaya spent the night in the chair by my side. In the morning, the medic cleared me to leave. We washed up in our quarters. After eating, as promised, we headed over to Zorla's office.

Zorla's droid assistant met us at the entrance. Kaya punched in a message on her tablet.

"Please inform Commander Zorla the boy and I are here to see him on an important matter."

"He has been expecting you and told me to let you in."

I shot Kaya a nervous look. She brushed by the droid.

"Follow me, Montor," she said to me telepathically.

Zorla stood and walked in front of his desk to meet us. He gestured that we sit on the oval sofas around the table in the center of his office. Kaya sat across from me. Zorla remained standing. They did not waste time on salutations.

"Kaya, I have had the most unpleasant task of making up a story to explain to parents why their sons died so violently."

Kaya's fingers flew across the tablet screen.

"Had I arrived a moment later, Montor would have been dead. You saw his performance at the competition. He can become the super soldier you envisioned. We have been molding him for two revolutions, and he still has not reached his peak. What would you have had me do? Let all that time and effort go to waste?"

"No, but you could have used a bit more restraint." He narrowed his eyes. "I wonder, are you developing feelings for this Arandan, Kaya?"

"No. I only care for my family, but I am no fan of abuse, and I hate seeing so much potential go to waste."

Her words saddened me.

I am not her family.

"My lieutenants and squadron leaders suggest I punish you for what you did."

Kaya pulled her shoulders back and lifted her chin as she typed on her tablet.

"So, Zorla, what do you think?"

"I have not decided yet. You have taught the boy a lot. You also groomed him to be receptive to his boot camp training. I am appreciative of this, but perhaps now he is ready to continue his development on his own. If so, he would have no further need for you." Zorla steepled his hands while his steely eyes met hers in a way that made my stomach turn. "But, on the other hand, there are those other talents you have not taught him yet. Also, I expect we will have new Sotkari Ta students for you to train."

Kaya let out a long sigh. Something about Zorla's words upset her.

"I do not approve of mind control, Zorla. Are you ready to take the risk and give him access to so much power? What if he uses it on you?"

"You have not," Zorla replied haughtily.

Kaya shuddered as if summoning extreme self-control while she typed on her tablet.

"Well, we have an agreement."

Zorla paced the room, his voice taking on a scheming tone.

"Exactly. I think Montor is old enough to understand the

concepts of benefits and consequences, just as you have. I consider myself a much more lenient leader than my predecessor here. Would you not agree, Kaya?"

He did not look for her reaction, turning his attention to me instead. For all the self-confidence I displayed within my squadron, I knew Zorla wielded all the power on this base.

"Montor, are you curious about what Kaya and I are talking about?"

I licked my lips.

"Yes." It was barely a whisper.

"I am suggesting Kaya teach you the remaining Sotkari Ta talents of Mind Control and Memory Manipulation. Learning to execute these skills would make you a powerful individual. Why, you could come into my office and take control of my mind. You might wonder, how could I trust you with a power like that? Well, here is the thing. I need to be sure of your unwavering loyalty to me, and I am willing to reward you for this. I am also ready to inflict severe punishments for betraying my trust."

He sat next to me, trying to adopt a parental tone. It came across as condescending and creepy.

"Let me explain. For example, Kaya here has the power to take control of my mind right now if she wanted to. Imagine that, Montor. But I have set controls in place to guard against such a possibility. It all starts off with an agreement that is mutually beneficial. She knows any unusual behavior displayed by me or any of the other military leaders here would trigger a severe consequence. For her, this consequence is worse than death."

His last words sounded so sinister, I gulped. I was angry with myself for my cowardice.

I feel like prey.

"I was surprised to learn about your foster parents,

Montor," Zorla continued. "I imagine you would not want anything bad to happen to them."

I looked at Kaya. Her lips pressed into a fine line. Now, I understood her warnings.

"And do you know what else, Montor? I have the power to get your foster parents out of the labor camp. That would be wonderful, would it not?"

I nodded.

"Of course, it would," continued Zorla. He leaned in so close to me his protruding brow bone almost touched my forehead.

Finally, I see his eyes are as dark as coal.

"Let me get straight to the point, Montor. If I have Kaya teach you these abilities, will you promise to only use them under my orders and to benefit the Lostai army? If so, I may one day release your foster parents. This is not an empty promise to entice you, Montor. I reward loyalty, and the possibility of freedom for them is real, but if you defy me, you will witness them going through the worst torture imaginable. Do we have an understanding?"

Kaya looked down. This was a decision I would have to make all on my own. I remembered Father once said, "It is OK to acknowledge when your opponent has the advantage. You can revisit the fight when the battlefield is leveled."

I understand, Father, but you also told me even in compromise, there are some lines that cannot be crossed.

My father's memory strengthened me. I met Zorla's dark eyes without flinching.

"I understand your explanation, Commander Zorla. I want to learn these abilities and pledge to only use them per your instructions, but I have one condition."

I was so satisfied with the surprise in his eyes.

"Never ask me to use those powers against the Arandan people. The Lostai have a vast empire covering many planets and governing many races. I will not hesitate to follow your orders against any of those people, but I will not go against my own, not even to save my foster parents or myself."

Zorla nodded and smirked for a moment before replying.

"Well, well, well, Kaya. What do you think about this boy trying to negotiate with me?"

Kaya typed on her tablet, still avoiding my eyes.

"He is indeed special, Zorla."

"Your courage impresses me, Montor. I want to harness it for the benefit of the Lostai military, so yes, I accept your pledge and your one condition." He stood abruptly, as if we had taken too much of his time. "OK, we are done here. Kaya, I still need to get back to you regarding the deaths of those cadets. In the meantime, keep me appraised of Montor's progress. Also, I think he needs to improve using his powers to defend himself even when under duress. I am sure there are some pain-inducing neurotoxins you can use to simulate those scenarios. I will speak to my lieutenants and squadron leaders to ensure an incident like what happened with Montor never repeats itself. They need to accept him as a future Lostai soldier. And Montor, try not to be so cocky with your fellow cadets. You have embarrassed them enough already."

Gesturing towards the door, he let us know our meeting was over.

24

That evening, while eating dinner in our quarters, I bombarded Kaya with questions. We kept the conversation telepathic, ever aware we might be spied upon.

"Kaya, honestly, why did you deal with those cadets so aggressively? Of course, I appreciate it, but it did seem like an extreme reaction. I mean, like you said, we are not family. For you, I am only a task to be completed."

She let out a long sigh. A pained look swept across her face.

"I hope I did not hurt your feelings, Montor."

Shrugging, I averted my eyes in an attempt to hide my emotions.

"Montor, I do care for you." Those few words caressed my soul. I had no doubt that they were sincere. "You remind me of my son. He was cocky, stubborn, and strong...like you."

"What happened to him?"

After a moment of silence, she replied, "The previous Xixsted Commander ordered that he be executed."

That was the first time without a doubt that I saw her eyes well with tears. Thinking about my own family's death at the hands of the Lostai, I could not stop a rogue tear from sliding down my cheek, too. She turned on the viewer and set it on an entertainment channel.

"Let us pretend we are watching a video in case they are observing us. We can never appear like we are conspiring together."

I understood and faced the screen while we continued our telepathic conversation.

"Why did they kill your son, Kaya?"

"We were on a space transport vessel on our way from Sotkar to Fronidia. There were several Sotkari families on board seeking exile. My son and I and another two individuals were the only Sotkari Ta among the Sotkari group. The Lostai military intercepted the vessel and boarded it, something they routinely do searching for Sotkari Ta people."

"For what purpose?"

"To force them to serve in the Lostai military, like they have done with you. They took all the Sotkari passengers as prisoners and forced us on their ship."

"But could you not beat them with your powers?"

"They threatened to harm our family members who do not have special abilities. Plus, the Lostai had traitorous Sotkari Ta helping them. The odds were against us."

"So, Kaya, I guess once you started working for Zorla, you became a traitor, too."

Mother always said I needed to learn to think before spurting out whatever was on my mind. I never got good at it. Kaya paused before replying.

"Maybe, but I had no choice. My son's wife and daughter were with us. His wife is not Sotkari Ta, and his daughter has special needs. The Lostai soldiers threatened to harm them if we did not do what they said. They brought us here. The previous commander wanted my son to become a Lostai ally and help the Lostai military on similar kidnapping missions.

He refused. They killed him in a horrible way and forced us to watch."

I heard the tremor of her emotions in my mind. It took a lot of self-control to fight the urge to embrace her.

"I...I know how that feels, Kaya."

"I reached an agreement with the previous commander. The Lostai not only kidnap original Sotkari Ta like my son and me. They also kidnap people like you from other races who have Sotkari Ta genes. Many of the Sotkari Ta hostages would require training to harness their abilities. I agreed to train any Sotkari Ta hostages brought to Xixsted. In exchange, I negotiated for my daughter-in-law and granddaughter's safety. On my planet, no currency is needed for everyday necessities, but my granddaughter's specialized care does require payment. The salary I earn here allows my granddaughter to get the medical treatment she needs."

"Kaya, what happened to the other two Sotkari Ta who were with you on that trip?"

"They saw what happened to my son and did what he refused to do. They became Lostai allies and help the military kidnap other Sotkari Ta."

"I am confused about the relationship between the Sotkari and Lostai. In my Civics class, I learned Sotkar has been part of the Lostai Empire for close to two hundred revolutions."

"Yes, similar to what occurred on your planet, the Lostai took advantage of the division that plagued our people. Our lack of unity made it easy for the Lostai to take over."

"The Arandan civil wars were about power over territories and resources. Why were your people fighting against each other?" I asked.

"It is a long story, but I will do my best to explain. Several generations before the Lostai took over our planet, our people showed signs of an evolutionary transition. Some were being born with special abilities. At first, those with abilities were revered, but over time, mistrust and jealousy caused problems. Also, intermarriage between those born with these abilities and lesser-evolved Sotkari was inevitable. Some of the offspring of these hybrid unions exhibited no desire to communicate or establish relationships. They appeared enclosed in their own world and displayed what was inferred to be mental distress or disability."

"You mean some kind of birth defect?"

"I do not believe these are genetic defects but a normal part of our evolution towards telepathic behavior. However, most non-evolved Sotkari did not agree and soon requested the government force those with powers to live separately from the rest of the population. Many Sotkari Ta resented that rejection. Others who thought they were superior to the non-evolved population welcomed separation but wanted to take control of our planet. The conflict between these groups made it easy for the Lostai to invade and take over."

"I guess we have a lot in common, Kaya. We are forced to help the Lostai against our will. Our people let division make us vulnerable to the Lostai invasion. But one thing bothers me. I am not from your planet. If I had not been born with these powers that are of your race, I would not be here forced to swear fealty to a filthy Lostai commander. I should have died like the rest of my family. Why, Kaya? Why do I have Sotkari Ta genes?"

She pressed fingers against her forehead.

"Another long story. It is getting late, and you need to rest. We can talk about these things another day."

The first days back at boot camp were awkward, but routine helped me not dwell on the fact that my fellow cadets tried to kill me. Zorla came and gave us all a rousing speech about the future missions we would serve on together for the glory of the Lostai Empire. He said we would be brothers in battle and explained how the expansion of the Lostai Empire made being a Lostai soldier no longer a matter of race. According to him, the Lostai made it their purpose to lift all species to their level of advancement. Somehow, I stopped myself from rolling my eyes and scoffing at such ridiculous statements.

Zorla was right about one thing. I needed to train to execute my Sotkari Ta powers even while under duress. This turned out to be the hardest part of my training, but I was motivated to protect myself from an attack again. The first time we tried, I asked Kaya about the process.

"How will this part of my training work?"

"I will inject this drug, Montor. We will start with a lower dose, but even at that level, the pain will be excruciating. I want you to communicate to me telepathically while using telekinesis to move the weights. You need, at the same time, to put yourself in a meditative state to ignore the pain. Take a moment to focus now."

I closed my eyes and blocked out every thought from my mind other than moving the weights and communicating a few words telepathically to Kaya. She injected me. Intense piercing pain hit my entire body at once, bringing tears to my eyes. My groans soon turned into screams. Kaya covered her mouth and turned away. I could not focus at all. The effect only lasted a few minutes.

"We will try again tomorrow," said Kaya.

"No, I just need a moment's rest." I steadied myself. "OK, we can continue."

Tightlipped, she pressed her fist against her forehead before administering the next dose.

It took several days for me to lift even one weight under those conditions, but I stuck with it. When I finally achieved my normal level of capacity while under the effects of a low dose, Kaya increased the strength. Embarrassingly, the next level made me wriggle on the floor and cry outright like a baby. I thought my organs were being torn apart and burned one by one. After several lunar cycles, I met my goal of executing my abilities at top performance while under the highest dose of the drug. I would never again allow pain to cripple me from using my powers.

Still curious about Sotkari history, I researched and found little information in the database about pre-Lostai occupation times. When I asked Kaya about it, I sensed sarcasm in her words.

"No, you will find none of that here."

"Why?"

"Before the Sotkari first came across the Lostai, we had already been traveling to faraway galaxies for hundreds of revolutions. They had not yet conquered space travel beyond their star system. We were a peaceful people focused on cultivating the arts and sciences. As we traveled the galaxies, we had no motivation to control other planets or species. We only wanted to learn more about the universe. When we found planets closer to our level of technological advancement, we shared our knowledge in the hopes those people would pay it forward and use it for good. Sadly, we helped the Lostai gain much of the technology they now have. The Lostai do not want to acknowledge any of this. They try to rewrite history by ignoring those facts."

"Kaya, it is still hard for me to comprehend how such an advanced race like the Sotkari would allow themselves to be dominated by the Lostai, especially considering part of your population possessed special abilities they could use to their advantage."

"Yes, I know. For all our technological advancements, we were naïve. At first, we tried to use diplomacy to avoid a war, while covertly, the Lostai were blackmailing, kidnapping, and slaughtering Sotkari Ta and Pasi people. To make matters worse, the Lostai got both opposing factions of our society to aid them. Some non-evolved Sotkari hoped to exterminate the more highly-evolved Sotkari, whom they distrusted and feared, while some Sotkari Ta resented how the non-evolved rejected them. Each side thought helping the Lostai would eventually give them the upper hand. Instead, the Lostai took over completely."

"Wow, did you never consider fighting against the Lostai?"

"Eventually, we did; something so against our pacific nature. But we were a divided community and lost the war and our dignity in the process. Now, we are a defeated people under the yoke of Lostai rule. This might be a good time to explain what you have been so curious about, the origins of your Sotkari Ta abilities."

"Yes, please tell me, Kaya. Last time I asked, you ended our conversation. I was not sure if you were trying to conceal something from me."

"Well, honestly, I am not sure how you will take what I am about to say, but you deserve to know. The evolved Sotkari were being attacked by both the Lostai and their fellow Sotkari. Some elder Sotkari Ta feared there was a real possibility Sotkari Ta and Pasi could become extinct and our people's natural evolution would be stifled. At least half of the evolved community was killed or displaced during the first generation of Lostai occupation. The elders asked Sotkari Ta scientists to find a solution, and so they did. They came up with bioengineering that could embed their genes in the embryos of unsuspecting people on less-advanced planets. An invisible energy pulse transmitted genetic codes randomly from outside the host planet's atmosphere. Usually, it was a onetime spread only affecting pregnant females at a specific stage of gestation. Their children later passed those traits to their offspring. They did this across several galaxies."

"What? You mean your people did that without asking permission?" My face heated up in anger. "How dare they? I cannot believe it. So, let me get this straight. First, you violate pregnant females' bodies, which put a target on the heads of their unsuspecting children. Then the Lostai find and enslave people like me. How did that solve your problem? It certainly did nothing for me."

I could not even look her in the eyes, but she maintained a calm tone despite my outburst.

"I can understand your outrage, Montor. Many people think 'the seeding,' as it was called, was a bad thing, but the elders were only trying to preserve their gene pool. They saw it as a gift offered to other races. Look at how you are becoming a powerful being."

"OK, Kaya, yes, it is like a gift, but I will be forced to use it to help the Lostai military, who have treated my people so badly. It makes me feel horrible. It feels more like a curse."

She did a rare thing by placing her hand on my shoulder as a sign of sympathy.

"I know, Montor, but maybe one day you will have the chance to use it for a good cause."

I waited for my heavy breathing to normalize.

"I suppose there is no point in being angry with you. You are in the same predicament as me. There is something else I do not understand. The Lostai are, by now, a mighty military machine. Do they really need to go to all the trouble of kidnapping and training Sotkari Ta to add them to their military? It seems like so much work when they can just use their weapons to obliterate their enemies."

"Good question, Montor. Lostai government officials are under a lot of pressure to convince the constituents on their home world that everything is running smoothly in the vast Lostai Empire. On their home planet, expansion policies are growing unpopular. Citizens are complaining of all the resources focused on new invasions or maintaining order on these foreign territories, as they refer to them. A military trained Sotkari Ta can be the equivalent of an entire squadron. A few Sotkari Ta can quell a rebellion more effectively and quietly than a troop of Lostai soldiers."

"Are the Lostai facing any real threats from rebel groups?"

"I sometimes hear of small insurgencies and protests popping up here and there, but they do not last for long. The Lostai military is ruthless when it comes to keeping order."

The conversation clarified questions that had pestered me. A new one came to mind.

"Kaya, when will we start my mind-control training?"

I detected concern when she met my eyes.

"Soon, Montor, soon."

25

The final stages of boot camp mandated real life space travel experience. Carloxi took the cadets out for practice orbits and flights on everything from small shuttles to battle cruisers. The first time out, I could not mask my awe and exhilaration at the helm of a spacecraft. Regardless of all the flight practice hours clocked in the holographic room, the real thing brought out the small-town boy in me.

"What do you think, Montor? I believe your people are just starting to conquer space travel beyond the Soma Quadrant. Have you ever seen space like this?" said Carloxi.

Of course, I had gazed at a star-studded night sky before, but now stars and dust clouds sped by in fascinating streaks of light and color against the vast darkness.

Each speck of light out there is a star or planet or moon, perhaps with people living there who differ from anything I have ever known.

"I have not. It is amazing."

"A good chunk of this sector is under Lostai rule. We have accomplished tremendous progress in the last three hundred revolutions," said Carloxi.

I did not mention that my only experience in outer space

was in the prison cell of the Lostai spaceship relocating us from Aranda to the labor camp. How Klemar transported me from the labor camp to Xixsted in the blink of an eye remained a mystery to me.

"Zorla will be pleased to hear you all have executed a near-perfect take-off and docking. On our next trip, we will practice using escape pods."

The holographic room did not have an escape pod simulation. This would be a first-time experience for me. My adventurous spirit looked forward to boarding the pod and launching it from a spacecraft in orbit. Autopilot technology set the destination. For our initial training, we targeted the Xixsted docking station.

As an extra precaution, for our first escape pod exercise, Carloxi lined us up to launch our pods one cadet at a time. Eventually, we would simulate an actual emergency where everyone scrambled to get to the pods as fast as possible. I was fourth in line and observed the cadets climb into the escape pod ahead of me. Being so much taller than the average Lostai, I suddenly became hyper-aware the pod would be an extremely tight fit for me.

My heartbeat sped up, and tremors shook my body. I wiped sweat from my forehead.

What is happening to me?

"OK, Montor, your turn," said Carloxi.

I could not make my legs move.

"Montor?"

I heard a snicker and a whisper from somewhere behind me.

"The big Arandan is scared."

Now, rage joined the mix of my random emotions.

I whirled around, wanting to wrap my fingers around someone's neck. Ever since Zorla's brotherhood speech, we all tried to get along and even established a bit of camaraderie, but I would not tolerate anyone calling me a coward.

"Who said that?" I shouted, lunging towards the cadets behind me. "Speak up! I dare you to show your face. I am not scared of anything. You have no idea what I have survived. This is nothing for me."

No one replied.

Carloxi shot me a stern look, and I walked back to the entrance of the pod. I willed myself to crouch and step inside. The minute I shut the door, it was clear these pods were not made for someone of my height and build. There was no space to stretch my legs in front of me, and the top of my head grazed the ceiling. I could not sit normally and pulled my knees to my chest. Taking deep breaths, I punched in the destination codes.

The pod exited the ship through a chute. Lieutenant Carloxi had explained the whirring sound would be loud and we would feel a lurching sensation at first. I noticed none of those things because I was a nervous wreck. Imaginary hands choked me.

I cannot breathe!

Eventually, I cried like a baby, a torrent of tears and panic I could not control. The pod came with a communication system I was supposed to use to radio back to Lieutenant Carloxi that everything was under control. I forgot all about that. The minutes it took for the pod to reach the surface and dock felt like hours. When I arrived, I tumbled into the air lock disoriented. Apparently, Carloxi had already messaged the cadets who left before me, requesting they let him know when I arrived.

"Montor, are you OK?" asked one of the cadets. "You do not look so good. Lieutenant Carloxi is wondering why you did not radio back to him during your descent."

"I am fine."

After running to the nearest restroom and puking, I skipped

my normal Sotkari Ta practice session and spent the rest of the afternoon locked up in my room. Kaya came looking for me.

"Montor, what is going on?"

"I do not want to discuss it."

"Did someone hurt you?"

"If it were so simple, I would have beaten someone up already. No, it is not that. Please, Kaya, leave me alone."

I wiped the sweat off my forehead and sat until the panicky sensation wore off. Often in times of distress, my only solace was to compose verses. I stored them in an encrypted folder on my tablet.

> My strength is useless
> Against an invisible monster
> Who catches me by surprise
> Mocking the warrior in me

The next time I saw Carloxi, I excused myself for my behavior during the escape pod exercise.

"I think I might have a viral infection. I will check with the doctor."

"Montor, it is OK if you have one weakness. You pretty much excel at everything else."

"I will do fine with this as well," I answered.

I did not do well. In fact, the next three times we did the escape pod exercise, my anxiety only increased.

How can something so simple break me when I have surpassed so many other hurdles and difficulties?

Finally, I broke down and explained to Kaya what was going on. She had been avoiding me because of my cranky behavior.

"Kaya. I am sorry for my unpleasantness lately. I am having a problem with one of the last exercises of boot camp."

"Tell me about it."

"Every time I get into an escape pod, I cannot breathe. I

become physically ill. It is cramped for me because of my size, but I do not see that as a reason."

"Do any specific fears come to your mind when you enter the pod?"

"I do not even have time to think. It is so sudden, like a kind of mental trauma."

After I said those words, she did a rare thing. She took my hand in hers.

"Montor, it would be surprising to me if you were NOT dealing with trauma. I admire how you have been able to overcome your circumstances, but what you have been through since they took you from your home world is a big deal."

I could not control the impatient tone in my voice. Her pity was not what I needed.

"Yes, well, I must overcome this to complete my training."

"Montor, close your eyes. I want you to think about the most distressing things that have happened to you since the Lostai took you. Do you give me permission to access your subconscious? Maybe I can help decipher where this dread is coming from."

I agreed, and she took my other hand in hers. Jolts of energy shocked my arms. I thought about how happy times had been before the Lostai took me away from my neighborhood. In a trance, memories flashed of the trip to the labor camp, our life there, and my four revolutions spent so far on Xixsted. Witnessing what happened to my father and brother was the worst thing I could remember, but something else humiliated and debased me to the core.

They called me vermin and put me in a crate. I was scared in the dark. They came to torment me by kicking the crate around and poking me. I soiled myself and sat in filth overnight. I was their prey.

Kaya let go of my hands. I opened my eyes to find her head tilted with such a sad look on her face. It angered me.

"Do not feel sorry for me!" I shouted. "How do I fix this?"

"It makes sense. Those punishments from your first few revolutions here have caused you to be claustrophobic."

"Fine. How do I fix this?" I repeated.

"From now on, add the following thoughts to your daily meditation. Focus on everything you have accomplished here. You are not even an adult yet, and I believe you are already the physically strongest person on this base. Your mental strength is second only to mine. You are by far the best cadet in your class. You are no victim. You are not prey. You will not let an escape pod and its confining space defeat you. I will ask Carloxi to allow me to join the next escape pod exercise and will guide you in a short meditation before you go in. I am sure these steps will solve the problem."

Her confident speech was exactly what I needed. By this time, our relationship was much closer than what we allowed others to believe. Although Kaya kept any physical displays of affection to a minimum, feelings ran strong between us.

She had killed the cadets to save my life without stopping to think of the consequences.

She was my support system.

She had my back.

I trusted her unconditionally and followed her advice during my meditation. She accompanied me to my next escape pod training. This one simulated a full-blown emergency. There would not be an orderly line of cadets taking their turns. At a random moment, an alarm would blare, and all cadets would have to run from their assigned station to the nearest escape pod located in strategic places around the ship. Carloxi assigned me to the sensors and weapons array. Kaya stood by my side the whole time. When the alarm went off, she grabbed my arm and entered my mind.

"Remember, you have been given total control of yourself and your surroundings. You are no one's prey. You are the hunter. I will meet you at the surface."

I centered myself and focused on the mantra. My nearest escape pod was down a corridor to the left. It took me less than a minute to reach it. Without hesitation, I opened the airlock and pressed my hand on the wall console to open the pod door. Robotically repeating the mantra in my mind blocked any anticipation of fear or nausea, as I punched in the target and closed the door. The sensations of the pod moving through the chute and the weightlessness once it was out in open space soothed me.

"Cadet Montor, reporting in. Escape pod target codes entered and engaged. Expected docking on Xixsted in three minutes."

"Excellent, Montor. See you down there."

I was the first to arrive back to Xixsted. The next cadet who arrived thought himself a big joker. As the others walked out, he shouted, "Montor, great job, but your babysitter cannot come with you when we are on a real mission."

I wanted to strangle him, but my eyes darted to the entrance. Carloxi had already arrived. Laughing out loud, I smacked the cadet hard on the back.

"Oh, Harost, you are such a comedian."

Harost fell forward to the floor. Still dazed when I offered him a hand to get up, he looked at me, surprised. I met his eyes. "Oh, sorry, friend. Sometimes, I do not know my strength."

A few days later, Zorla called Kaya and me to his office.

"Carloxi informed me that Montor has gotten over his problem with the escape pods. He said Montor is performing at the top of his class. I know Montor is young, but I think he is ready for official induction in the Lostai military, except for one thing."

"What, Commander Zorla?" I asked before Kaya could reply.

"I want you to be trained in memory manipulation and mind control before you serve on any mission. There are some specific tasks I envision you can help with once you are skilled in those abilities. Kaya, have you been putting this off? A revolution has gone by since we last talked about it."

"Yes, Zorla. I was giving Montor more time to mature. He is only the equivalent of a Lostai of fifteen revolutions."

"Get it done, Kaya."

She inclined her head. As was his habit, Zorla's quick hand gesture let us know the meeting was over.

26

―――

We started off with lab animals. Kaya used mind manipulation to direct the small rodents to eat, drink, and even mate. She showed me how to identify their lights in my mind and, from there, telepathically send instructions to their brains. I picked up the basics quickly.

"Kaya, this seems simple, but what about in a room full of people and perhaps other creatures? It seems impossible to direct thoughts to one particular being in such an enormous crowd."

"Remember when we practiced blocking and telepathic communication with Klemar? We were in the middle of the operations center, and you could pick him out of the crowd of lights in your mind."

"Yes, but we were the only Sotkari Ta there, and I am already familiar with your light."

"True. In a crowded room full of people you are not familiar with, the process becomes difficult. In those cases, you can use your senses of sight, smell, hearing, and memory. You can direct your mental manipulation or communication to a specific person you are seeing, hearing, or even remembering from a past experience."

"OK, so even if my mind is crowded with lights, I can look at a person or hear their voice and direct my telepathy towards them."

"Yes."

"But how can I practice this skill? I cannot use mind control with anyone here."

"I will discuss this with Zorla."

Zorla identified five Lostai soldiers, who he happened not to like too much, as our test subjects. Without their knowledge, he gave Kaya and me free rein to manipulate their minds as long as we did not put their lives in danger. I practiced as we strolled by their stations.

A soldier named Grole worked gathering intelligence about other planetary governments in the sector. With Zorla's permission, I entertained myself at his expense. Manipulating his mind, I caused him to interrupt his co-workers constantly or walk away in the middle of a meeting. I performed similar manipulations with the other four soldiers. I also triggered memory loss, making Grole forget, at times, to present himself for duty.

The ability to have this power over them became addicting. I even stopped working at the calibration lab to have more time to practice. Daily meditation became my religion because it honed my mental strength. Kaya reluctantly revisited with me the Sotkari Ta ability that combined telekinesis and mind-manipulation to affect bodily functions. As she had demonstrated before with the lab animals, I could affect blood pressure and cause a person to faint. I made Grole urinate on himself. If I wanted, I could have stopped his heart from beating.

I can kill somebody with my mind.

Kaya did not share my enthusiasm, almost disappointed at my eagerness to learn more about how to invade another person's mind and body and how quickly I mastered it.

"Are you not proud of how well I have learned this?" I asked her.

"No," she answered, her body stiff with discomfort. "This is one talent I would have preferred not learning or teaching."

After one revolution, we met with Zorla, and Kaya admitted I could execute mind and memory manipulation as well as she could.

"Montor and Kaya, sit please," he said. "Montor, I hear you just celebrated your ninth birth anniversary. I understand that makes you the equivalent of a Lostai of sixteen revolutions. My, how you have grown physically and mentally. Why, you are even taller than Kaya now, and look at that physique. You are pure muscle."

"Yes, sir."

Although I was proud of my achievements, compliments coming from him always came across as insincere.

"Kaya tells me she has completed your Sotkari Ta training and now it is a matter of you maintaining a routine to continue to hone your skills. Carloxi admits you are the best of his cadets. How does that make you feel?"

"I am happy to have learned to harness my Sotkari Ta abilities and am proud of becoming a powerful warrior."

"Indeed, you have kept the promise you made to me the first day we met. Remember when I told you we hoped to make a Lostai soldier out of you, and you said you would not disappoint me? So far, that is true. The time is right to implement the plans we had for you."

Kaya and I exchanged curious looks as Zorla gave instructions to his droid assistant to summon Menel, Carloxi, and Temol, the leader of a squadron unit recently stationed on Xixsted. Once they arrived, Zorla wasted no time in stating his mind.

"I have decided to accelerate Montor's military career here. He is the equivalent of a Lostai of sixteen revolutions. I know we normally wait for cadets to be eighteen revolutions old before inducting into our military, but I am sure he is ready for this promotion. Some rebellious groups have cropped up in the area. Montor's skills especially suit him for interrogation. We are being called upon to help subdue communities who resist being transferred to labor camps. Skirmishes are happening more and more frequently in this sector. Montor is battle ready to assist in such missions."

"We have good interrogation techniques. Our truth serums usually work well," said Menel, his large forehead lined with furrows.

"Well, perhaps, but Montor can apply a more streamlined, effective approach."

Zorla gave me his tablet and pointed to the screen where he had entered an order. Without looking at anyone in particular, I executed his request. Menel's eyes glazed over, and he gave me his tablet.

"Here are all my security and encryption codes. Please, go ahead and read my private journal too, Montor."

The corner of Kaya's lip twitched. Carloxi's and Temol's eyes widened. A rare, sincere smile graced Zorla's face. I released Menel from my mental hold.

"Give me that." Menel snatched the tablet from my hands and shook his head. "What is wrong with me?"

Zorla entered another instruction on his tablet and showed me. This one I thoroughly enjoyed. To Menel's and Temol's horror, Carloxi knelt in front of me, hugged my legs as if begging, and bawled, "I am so sorry, Sir Montor, for what those cadets did to you. I was in on their plan. I should have never condoned it. Please, please, can you ever forgive me?"

Despite her discomfort with mind control, even Kaya covered her mouth, I am sure to hide a smile.

"Do you all see what powers we have unleashed for the glory of the Lostai Empire?" said Zorla.

"OK, I get it," said Carloxi, back in his seat. He straightened out his shirt, trying to regain some semblance of authority after being thoroughly humiliated. "As you have demonstrated, he can easily use those powers on us. How can you trust him?"

Zorla's eyes took on the now-familiar dark gleam.

"No worries. Montor and I have an agreement. I know the names and location of people he cares very much about. If we have any reason to believe he is using these powers outside of our orders, something terrible could happen to them. That would be a shame, right, Montor?"

The joke was now on me, as the four Lostai looked at me, smirks on their faces.

I controlled the urge to slam them all against the walls.

"Yes, as long as you keep your side of our agreement regarding the condition I requested, I will follow your orders and my allegiance will be to the Lostai military."

Curious expressions swept over the faces of the others, but Zorla did not clarify what I was referring to.

"Perfect." He searched for something in his desk drawer, walked over to me, and pinned an insignia on my uniform. "With this pin, I hereby promote you to the rank of Battle-Ready Soldier in the Imperial Lostai military under Temol's command."

Someone in the room cleared their throat. Zorla searched everyone's eyes as if daring anyone to protest.

"Yes, I have skipped Entry Level because I have full confidence in Montor's abilities. Montor, you will earn a salary plus a bonus for every successful mission. You are free to travel wherever you want on your off days, as long as you report to duty per Temol's instructions, with one exception. You may not visit your foster parents at the labor camp. That would be contrary to your position as a Lostai soldier. Kaya, help Montor become acquainted with our financial systems and get him a remuneration chip. Temol, when should Montor report to your squadron?"

"In two days, at the first hour."

"Excellent. We are done here."

Before I left on my first official mission as a full-fledged Lostai soldier, Kaya had an interesting talk with me.

"Montor, now that you will be traveling to places beyond Xixsted and possibly on your own, I feel compelled to have a conversation with you that should have been your parent's job. I know I cannot fill their shoes but consider this as another part of me mentoring you."

"Sure, Kaya. You know how much I respect your advice."

I have never seen her this uncomfortable.

"Montor, I know you have studied anatomy, biology, reproductive systems, and...sex education. However, you have had no experience in exploring relationships and your sexuality as perhaps others your age have. Am I correct to assume you have not been attracted to anyone here on this base?"

And now...the two of us were uncomfortable.

"Ugh....Kaya, no. And no one here would want me either. Our races are too different. The Lostai are not even interested in such things."

"Right. Well, the situation will change once you are out and about on various planets and moons. There are many species out there whose views about relationships and sexuality are more in tune with yours. I guess I want to give you the same advice I gave my son when he was about your age, plus a bit more."

I groaned, remembering my older brother complaining when Father gave him what he called "the speech."

"Montor, you can see your people and mine have similar body shapes, as opposed to the Lostai. I can tell you with confidence that many of my people would find you attractive. You are tall, strong, and fit. I expect you will encounter many other people out there who will find your appearance physically appealing."

"Yes, OK," I said, shaking my head, wishing she would stop talking.

"And you will be attracted to people as well. I have read Arandan males have a strong sexual appetite."

What are the chances a hole might open in the ground and swallow me?

"Kaya, this is embarrassing. What are you trying to tell me?"

"A few things, Montor. Make sure you have the consent of the other person in a relationship or sexual encounter. With your telepathic abilities, you could manipulate people into doing whatever you want. Do not take advantage of people and especially not sexually."

"I know, I know. My father used to tell my older brothers the same. He said to treat their female companions as they would want our sisters to be treated."

"Good. OK, before I get to my next point, I need to ask, do you think you are attracted to the opposite sex, your own, both, or —"

I slapped my forehead.

Was there not a way she could have asked all of this over several quick chats instead of packing it all into one conversation?

"I like females."

"OK, then remember, sexual encounters have consequences. If you are not intending to procreate, make sure you use contraceptives and be aware of sexually transmitted diseases. Know how to protect yourself."

When will this conversation end?

"OK, OK...what else?"

"Here is one thing your parents would not know to tell you. Do you remember the certain energy you sense when we have skin contact, like when I placed my hands on your bare shoulders during your training?"

"Yes."

"You should know that Sotkari Ta are predisposed to be drawn to each other. I suppose it is nature's way of helping us procreate more offspring with Sotkari Ta abilities and move ahead our evolution. Between young people, it is an almost irresistible sexual attraction made even more powerful through skin-to-skin contact. I do not know if the same occurs with non-Sotkari people with embedded Sotkari Ta genes as yourself. Still, I want you to be aware of it in case you ever were to meet a young female Sotkari Ta who you find physically appealing. You may want to think twice before engaging in a romantic relationship with such a person unless you are ready to fall deeply in love. It is a bond like no other, and unfortunately, that leads to my final warning."

OK, well, at least we are almost done.

"You already know how the Lostai manipulate people by threatening their loved ones. I cannot tell you how to live your life, but the more people you love, the more ways the Lostai have to blackmail you. They are ruthless this way. Consider keeping your relationships as private as possible."

For the first time in our conversation, I took stock of her words.

"So even with all these powers, I am going to be Zorla's prey forever," I said, my eyes glued to my lap.

She placed her hand on my shoulder.

"Not forever. After fifteen revolutions, you could go far away, take your loved ones with you, and make a life for yourself away from all of this."

"I do not know, Kaya. Maybe Zorla will not want to set me free ever."

27

———

I am a million billion *non*
Distant into the darkest night
Failure is my tear-soaked blanket
Jonjuri, my victory, is a ghost
One I cannot conjure or imagine
Yet that word alone has power

My first mission took me to the planet Tormix, the same planet where the Lostai had moved my family and me five revolutions earlier. We traveled in a mid-sized space cruiser. Temol assigned me to the sensors and weapons array station. The trip was expected to take twenty days. A larger Lostai cruiser followed us, traveling at a day's delay.

The squadron was a mixed bunch, composed of thirty Lostai soldiers. Half of my crewmates were more than twice my age and held a lot of respect for Temol. He had led them in many battles earlier in his career. The other half were recently inducted recruits, the oldest only six revolutions my senior. The younger soldiers described Temol to me as an absent-minded fool who was no longer fit for command. I knew better than to voice any opinion on the matter. Although all the Lostai soldiers tolerated me mostly out of fear, they would never truly consider me one of them.

At our first morning meeting, Temol described our mission and the issues we might encounter.

"We are taking a longer route to avoid problems, but we may still encounter Bertau along the way. These space pirates usually travel in packs of several small spacecrafts. Alone, any of those small spacecrafts would pose no threat, but together, they can gang up on a solitary larger craft and cause damage. Their intentions are to board ships and take what they can."

I had read about the Bertau. They were not of any particular race but a group of marauders hailing from different planets who banded together to attack and steal mainly from recreational and transport carriers. They were less likely to try their luck with a military ship, even if it was traveling alone.

"Our military has already taken down the Tormixian defense system over their northern continent. That is where we will enter their atmosphere and hopefully land with no problems." Temol activated a holographic presentation depicting an orbital view of the planet. "This area is rich in rare gems that can help fund the military base we have set up on one of their moons. We will need to evacuate a nearby town to set up our mining operation. The locals can be used as labor. Their law enforcement usually tries to make a stand, and they do have handheld weapon technology to match ours, so we must be efficient in squashing any resistance. Questions?"

One of the younger soldiers raised her hand.

"Can we use lethal force if the locals do not comply?"

"We try to avoid loss of life. The work we soldiers perform ensures everyone on Losta a high standard of living, but there are factions within our government who prefer not to under-stand what is involved. We must complete our mission without causing too much commotion."

"*Grimah*, that takes all the fun out of it," said another younger soldier. A few of his friends laughed, and another added, "We want to kick some Tormixian ass."

These were a new breed of Lostai soldiers, irreverent and far-removed from the suffering their military caused. This was a game for them. I stared at the sensor display so no one could see the disgust in my eyes.

"Settle down," ordered Temol, and they all became quiet. "Everything we do is not only for the glory of the Lostai Empire but to help lift others in the galaxy to our standards. Our goal is for everyone to live in harmony."

The younger soldiers scoffed at his last comment but said nothing more.

Our trip towards Tormix went by without incident until we reached within one day's travel of their atmosphere.

"Sir, sensors indicate two Tormixian patrol ships at eighty *nons* from us at position *rema dox*," I informed Temol.

"Everyone on first alert mode. Shields up," announced Temol. "Montor, as soon as we are close enough for our sensors to detect their weaponry, let me know their status and capabilities."

The Tormixian ships did not move from their position. Clearly, their job was to guard anyone from entering Tormixian atmosphere in that area where their planetary shields were damaged. Within hours, we could see them on our viewer.

"Sir, their two ships have weapons but do not match our gamma-photonic missile capability," I said.

"Incoming audio and video," announced our communications officer.

"Put them on," ordered Temol.

I got my first look at a live Tormixian as the image came on our screen. An angry-looking bipedal reptilian creature glared back at us. It wore no clothing and with no genitalia visible, I could not guess its gender. Brownish green scales covered its face and muscled body. One large ridge ran from the back of its bald head to its small nose. Its mouth was a slit that almost split the lower half of its face. When Temol ordered the communications officer to zoom in, I could not help but notice the Tormixian's yellow eyes with vertical slit pupils were similar to my own.

"With whom do I have the pleasure of speaking?" asked Temol in his condescending Lostai tone.

When the Tormixian opened its mouth to speak in its language, we got a view of its large pointy teeth and thin, long tongue. It hissed and growled several syllables in a row at us.

"Oh, it is mad," said one of our older soldiers, who apparently had picked up some Tormixian over his career.

"When will these creatures learn to speak Imperial Lostai?" said Temol, shaking his head. "Engage the translator."

As soon as the communications officer turned on the translator application, a torrent of curse words came over the audio before the Tormixian asked, "What do you Lostai germs want here?"

"Let us try to be civil," replied Temol. "Your government has signed a treaty allowing us to land on your planet."

"We do not recognize that filthy contract you coerced from our excrement of a puppet leader."

"Tormixian captain, I have not used impolite words with you," replied Temol.

"Lostai, any words you speak sound as filthy as the smelly cesspool your mother was born in."

I kept my eyes on my console and bit my lip to hold in laughter. With a bland expression, Temol gestured to the communication officer to cut the line.

Maybe this is why the younger soldiers make fun of him. An Arandan captain would have been incensed with such trash talk.

"When we open the channel again, show the video, but make it appear as if there is static on the audio and that we are trying to clear it up. Montor, as soon as the channel is open, I want you to hit each of their ships with our photonic missiles at the highest energy level," ordered Temol.

"Sir, a quarter portion would be sufficient to destabilize their shields, weapons, and propulsion systems. At that point, it will be easy for us to move past them and land," I answered.

Temol remained cool, but his dark expression sent a shiver down my spine.

"I do not want to only pass by them, soldier." He clenched his jaw even more than the typical Lostai enunciation required. "I want the pieces of their ship scattered across the atmosphere. I want them gone, and I want to see their captain's eyes just before it dies."

"But sir, I thought you said we were to avoid making a commotion. There are fifty people on board each ship," I answered, discomfort souring my stomach.

"Those are not people, Montor. They are the ones who look like something that crawled out of a cesspool. Have I made myself clear, or do I need to remove you from your post?"

I swallowed hard on the ball forming in my throat. With a touch of a button and without a warning, I would extinguish one hundred lives. Temol's frigid eyes met mine.

"No, sir, I understand my orders."

Video came back online. Per Temol's instructions, the communications officer made it so that all everyone could hear was static. I flicked my fingers over the controls to lock on the targets, closed my eyes, and tapped the screen. When I opened my eyes, it was clear by the Tormixian captain's expression that it had been informed of what I had unleashed. It hissed some orders. Each Tormixian ship fired one round of phasor beams that bounced off our shields with barely a thud. A second later, they both exploded into balls of orange light and debris. I stepped away from my console and rubbed my hand against the fabric of my flight suit.

Father would not have been proud of this.

Had this been a victory in a fair battle, Arandans would have fist-pumped with loud shouts of *jonjuri.* The Lostai simply shared smug looks, as if they had squashed a bothersome insect.

Temol congratulated me and gave the soldier at the helm orders to land with a warning.

"Be careful to avoid that disgusting debris field. I do not want one fleck of disgusting Tormixian DNA on my ship."

"Sir, should we be expecting resistance on the surface? Surely, their surveillance system must alert them that we are entering their atmosphere."

"No. We knocked out their planetary surveillance some time ago, and as I informed that stupid Tormixian, we have a treaty that allows us free entry."

We landed in a wooded area bordering a small village, shearing off a large section of trees and vegetation and leaving a burnt crater in its place.

Like when they arrived at my hometown.

I took advantage of the landing sequence time to excuse myself and rushed to my room to meditate. My emotions were all over the place.

Feelings and memories have no place here. This is my life now.

We disembarked, boarded three land shuttles, and drove to the village.

"Montor, come with me," ordered Temol.

No amount of meditation could erase memories of the labor camp. I took in the blue skies and greenery so in contrast with the colors of Aranda's environment or the barren greyness of Xixsted. Within minutes, we arrived.

Paved streets and elevated walkways connected buildings, three and four stories tall. A small spaceport bordered the town on the north side. Several transport pods and small spacecraft were parked there. Fountains, manicured gardens, and an amphitheater decorated the opposite side. A creek surrounded the town. We crossed one of the many arched bridges to enter. Tormixians were running into the streets. The air smelled of the ashes and smoke emanating from the area where we had landed. The boom must have alerted them as well. A law enforcement vehicle followed us from a distance but did not intervene as we drove up and down the streets. Temol said we were looking for the main government building. Before leaving the ship, he had shown us the signage such Tormixian buildings displayed on their entrances.

"Sir, there it is," said someone over our communication system.

We parked in front of the building. Their law enforcement vehicles caught up to us.

"Montor, it is time to put to work your ability to sway people's minds. First, I want you to make their law enforcement cooperative. Secondly, you will accompany me when I speak to whoever is in charge here. Make that person agree to whatever I request. Can you control two people at the same time?"

"It takes a bit of effort, and we will need to move fast. There are limitations on how long I can hold several people captive at the same time."

This was my first chance to use mind manipulation on someone other than the Lostai test subjects Zorla allowed me to train on. A part of me remained disgusted with the operation, while the other was excited to try out my abilities on someone new.

As soon as we got off the shuttle, three law enforcement Tormixians met us. Temol pulled out his tablet and activated his translation application.

"Who are you, and what are you doing here?" asked one of the Tormixians. None of them were clothed, but this one wore a headdress that I assumed identified it as the person in command.

"We are here to see the mayor of this town. Can you take us to them?" asked Temol.

It was easy for me to access the Tormixian's mind. In an instant, I confirmed he was, in fact, the highest ranking of the three police.

"Oh, sure, of course. Come this way. My name is Lieutenant Brogter. Happy to help you."

The other two Tormixians looked at each other in confusion but shrugged and followed along. Temol smiled at me and nodded to the Tormixian.

"I appreciate your help, Lieutenant Brogter."

Temol gestured for one of our soldiers to accompany us into the building. The others were to stand guard outside. We followed Lieutenant Brogter into the building and the elevator that took us to the top floor. Glass windows and ceiling provided a view of the entire village. The mayor's office was on the corner of the building, facing the gardens and fountains.

Such a beautiful village.

A droid met us at the door.

"These fine people are here to meet the mayor. Let us in," said Lieutenant Brogter. "He is expecting them."

"I do not see them on his schedule."

Although the mayor was in his office, I was close enough to reach his mind. Seconds later, the door opened.

"Your excellency, these people are here to see you, but I do not have them on today's agenda."

"My mistake. Come in, please."

"Thank you, your excellency."

"Please, call me Serog. Make yourselves comfortable."

Serog gestured for us to sit on the plush sofa in front of his desk. By now, the Lostai soldier accompanying Temol and me could barely conceal his smirk. Temol never broke character.

"Thank you, Serog. My name is Temol."

"What brings you to our little town, Temol?"

"I understand this town's limits extend from the mountainous range by the southeast side of the woods all the way to the river in the north. Is that right?"

"Yes."

"So, you are in control of that entire area, correct?"

"Yes."

"The Lostai Empire would like to buy it from you. This area is rich in natural resources we intend to mine." Temol flicked his fingers across his tablet and placed it in front of Serog. "We are willing to pay this amount. If you agree, please look into this spot here to capture your retinal signature."

My feelings about what was happening caused my concentration to waver. Serog hesitated.

"Umm, but wait. This is all so sudden. Why did I not get any prior notice from your government? How will our citizens be affected?" asked Serog, scratching his head.

Temol's slow turn to look at me brought me back to focus.

"Well, we intend to employ them in the mines," answered Temol, while making eye contact with me.

I had Serog under control again.

"OK, fine," said Serog, while staring at the retinal agreement sphere on Temol's tablet.

"Thank you. Now, how do you normally make proclamations here?"

"We have a daily newscast where I make any important announcements."

"When will that happen?"

Serog checked his viewer screen.

"Just before sunset."

"Can you make a special announcement now? Let us not delay informing your citizens that we Lostai have paid a nice sum to control them and this area. Tell them to cooperate so we can avoid any arrests."

Under my influence, Serog activated his viewer. I stood to look out the glass walls. Several people on the street pulled out their tablets. Others congregated in front of the amphitheater. A notification had been sent out. Temol continued to use his tablet's translation application to follow Serog's announcement. I closed my eyes to focus. My mental strength waned as the minutes passed.

"Citizens of Nerigma, I have important news to share. We have been lucky enough to receive an offer from the Lostai Empire. They have paid a generous sum for the rights to mine the precious gems in the nearby mountainous areas and our river. They will need our help to set up their operations here until they can get labor droids. Please cooperate with our Lostai friends with anything they request. That is all. Have a wonderful evening."

As he uttered his last words, I suffered mental exhaustion as I thought about how the Lostai were never going to send droids. Slaves were much cheaper. Lieutenant Brogter stood abruptly.

"What is going on here?"

I looked at Temol and shook my head, letting him know I needed a break. Mayor Serog was still under my control.

"Relax, Lieutenant Brogter, we are just conducting regular business."

Brogter looked at each of us, suspicion in his eyes, although not yet having pieced together what was unfolding. I walked to a corner of the office to take deep inhales and exhales and regain my strength. Temol noticed and stood.

"OK, well, it is time for us to go. Lostai personnel and soldiers will be here tomorrow morning to set up operations. It has been great negotiating with you, Mayor Serog. We will remain in our spaceship until tomorrow to make sure the transition happens without issues."

Serog acknowledged with a nod and opened the door for us, but Lieutenant Brogter was back under his own faculties.

"Wait, your excellency, we need to understand more about this transition," said Brogter.

"Montor, I have heard you can put people to sleep. That might be a good option now," said Temol.

Brogter and Serog, of course, were confused by Temol's words, but it was too late for them. I had regained enough strength to cause Serog and Brogter to pass out. They fell to the floor, and we quickly made it to the elevator and out of the building. By the time we reached the street, a loud mob of Tormixian residents had congregated around our land shuttles. The Lostai soldiers were keeping them at bay with weapons trained. We made our way to the shuttles, but the crowd pushed forward to surround us.

"Sir, what are our orders? Should we shoot these annoying people so we can be on our way?" asked one of the Lostai soldiers.

"Run them over," said Temol.

I have to do something. These people are someone's parents, siblings, or children.

"Wait, sir. I think I can open a less messy way out for us," I said.

By now, I assumed Temol's age was catching up with him. He yawned and seemed ready for dinner and a nap. He waved at me dismissively. "Whatever."

I took a few more deep inhales and refocused my mind. In seconds, a group of people were flung across the street, opening a path for us to drive away. Yes, some suffered fractures and concussions, but at least I had stopped them from being plowed to death. Our three shuttles rushed down the avenue, heading to the nearest bridge out of town. Some Tormixians ran into the street, attempting to make us stop. I was not fast enough to toss them out of the way and closed my eyes as our drivers smashed into them without remorse. Other soldiers opened the top hatch and, without waiting for orders, shot at will.

"Sir Temol, these soldiers are acting without orders," I said.

"Oh, Montor, let them have their fun. You and I have done a great job today for the Lostai Empire. Relax and let these guys take over. We will be back on the ship in no time."

Each thump against the shuttle threatened to bring tears to my eyes. Each ray gun buzz made me nauseous. I knew what it was like to be invaded by a ruthless enemy. There was nothing else I could do without putting my true feelings on display.

Temol is right about one thing. I should close my eyes and tune all this out.

28

I am stained with shame
My ashes will never rest
In an *omori* for the honored
I will never know true love
Loss will be my only wife
Death, my only chance at life

As promised, a contingent of three hundred Lostai soldiers and engineers arrived the next day. The villagers were quickly put to work, constructing the small shacks that would become their slave dwellings, while the Lostai took over their homes and installed themselves in the village. The Lostai soldiers killed any Tormixian who resisted. One hundred and fifty of the two thousand residents died the first day. After that, I minimized loss of life by using my mind control abilities on the Tormixian elders. Once the Tormixians saw their elders agreed with the process, most followed suit. The transition took three days.

I could not wait to get away from there. My stomach was upset the whole time. Everything tasted horrible, and after performing whatever duties were assigned to me, I retreated to my quarters. When Temol introduced me to the Lostai commander in charge of what would become the newest labor camp on this planet, I almost vomited on the spot.

"Commander Verdex, let me introduce you to Zorla's secret weapon. His name is Montor. Without his special mind control abilities, this would have been a much less efficient operation. He also got rid of those bothersome patrol crafts."

I inclined my head while ignoring my stomach's heaving.

"Well, Montor, I may have to see if I can get you transferred to our operation here. Sometimes, the locals get out of line. Someone like you can help us keep things moving smoothly."

Without meeting his eyes, I swallowed the bitter taste in my mouth and answered, "That is a kind offer, but I only work for Zorla."

When we arrived back on Xixsted, Temol declared we could take five days off as reward for a job well done. We also received a special bonus remuneration.

Although I wanted to be alone, the unspoken rule called for the squadron to celebrate a successful mission together. We gathered at the observation lounge, a popular recreational area on Xixsted. Transparent walls gave a view of the barren moon and dark space beyond. I had never been there before. Comfortable chairs and sofas surrounded a center bar. Next door, a holographic room provided recreational games and pleasurable simulations. A large viewer showed entertainment reels, newscasts, and sports events, and popular Lostai music was piped in. My fellow soldiers hopped, shimmied, and skipped to their favorite tunes. I just bobbed my head a bit to conceal how irritating it was to me. The singing sounded like monotonous droning. The melodies lacked nuance. Even our Arandan hunting horns sounded better than the instruments played by some of the Lostai musical groups.

"Montor, what are you going to do with your first earned salary?" asked one of the younger soldiers.

"I have not thought about it," I answered after gulping down my first alcoholic drink. It burned my throat.

"Well, once I save enough money, I intend to buy myself the latest *Sura* model."

A *Sura* was a small recreational spacecraft capable of interplanetary travel. It accommodated four to six passengers, living quarters, and the amenities required for a long-range trip. It was a coming-of-age symbol for the Lostai.

The idea of traveling on my own intrigued me.

"You know, that sounds like a good idea. I think I might do the same."

I consumed way too much alcohol that night and stumbled into my quarters very late, waking Kaya up.

"Are you OK, Montor?"

"Yes, yes, fine," I slurred and rushed to my room.

I spent the next days in an intoxicated stupor, drinking alcohol, sucking on laughing pods, indulging in other hallucinogenic drugs, and puking it all once I made it back to my room. Unfamiliar with these spirits and drugs, I allowed my fellow Lostai soldiers to order for me. They introduced me to a wide variety of mood-altering options available for sale at the bar, ranging from tiny slips of gel placed on fingertips to full-on injections or sweet-smelling gases blown into one's face. Finally, on the third morning, Kaya intercepted me.

"Montor, what is going on with you?"

My head was pounding. I tried to open my eyes wide to clear my head.

"Celebrating, Kaya. It is what soldiers do after a mission, right?"

"Maybe, but if you continue at this pace, you will not be a soldier for long. I bet you have been skipping your meditation since being on this binge, right?"

I did not reply but stretched my neck and cracked my knuckles.

"I thought so." Her voice in my mind started off tinged with annoyance but morphed into a more caring tone. "Let us have the morning meal together here and talk."

I pouted but agreed.

"Wash up and I will have the food ready when you get out," she instructed.

I returned to find piping hot plates of *larosh*, a baked egg-based dish full of vegetables and cured meat, one of my favorite meals to start off the day. Of course, the reproducer version was nowhere as flavorful as the *larosh* my mother used to make, but it still warmed my soul. A carafe of hot *yomoso* filled the room with a caffeinated scent. Plenty of freshly baked *bomar* completed our meal.

The shower had revived me, and the aroma of the food activated my appetite.

"Thank you, Kaya. This looks great."

For a while, only the clatter of cutlery, chewing, and sipping disturbed the silence. She let me get several mouthfuls down before communicating.

"Montor, no one here knows you better than I. Something is bothering you. Let us talk about it."

A second mug of *yomoso* got me to open up.

"Kaya, all my crew mates are joyous after this mission, but I feel like crap."

"Of course you do. You might be a soldier in the Lostai military, but you are not Lostai. You must have seen your family and friends in the eyes of those people who were unfairly displaced from their homes, their lives forever changed." Kaya did not waste time or mince words. She always got to the point. "Am I correct?"

Hearing her spell out the feelings bottled inside me brought on a torrent of emotion. Tears escaped my eyes. She stood abruptly, walked over to my side of the table, and pulled me into an embrace. Not only was this way out of character for Kaya, but it was inappropriate for someone my age to be hugged by an adult this way, unless by a lover. I remained seated, forgot about those boundaries, leaned in, and listened to her heartbeat. Sobs erupted. She embraced me even tighter. Soon, I wailed and, forgetting telepathy, mumbled words out loud in between.

"It was horrible, Kaya...I killed a hundred people with a tap on a screen."

"Shh, Montor, be careful of what you say out loud." Those first words came into my mind in a rushed warning and then mellowed. "I am so sorry, son. I wish there was something I could do to rip this pain from you. During power struggles and war, each side believes they are right and justify their methods. Remember, your own people fought each other in endless bloody civil wars."

I composed myself and returned to telepathic communication.

"Yes, but this was dishonorable. We gave them no advance notice, no chance to surrender. When I was a child, I imagined myself a soldier, but not like this." My body shuddered in between each phrase. "The Lostai pretend to be so civilized, but they slaughtered anyone who stood in their way. They took those people's land and homes like they did to my family. And I facilitated it all. I was the hero of that disgusting operation."

I buried my face in my hands and stopped communicating. She caressed my head and back, trying to soothe me.

"Unfortunately, while Zorla has you in his grip, you must

focus on the fact that your commitment has a deadline, after which you will no longer have to do his bidding. In the meantime, try to find ways to desensitize from the job required of you. I have found meditation helps me."

I pulled back and looked up at her.

"You? Why should you have guilty feelings? You have always defended me and treated me fairly."

"Back on Sotkar, I helped youth to hone their powers, but I never trained on mind control because of how intoxicating that power can become and how easily it can be used for evil purposes. I wish my father had not taught me. I did not even teach my own son."

"How did Zorla even find out you have mind control abilities?"

"I made the mistake of using it on soldiers here trying to rescue my son. The previous commander reported it to Zorla. He forced me to train you how to unleash those abilities and use it on people without their permission, something I so vehemently oppose, and for what? For the Lostai military's imperialistic agenda. You are my first trainee here on Xixsted. Everything you do is as if I were doing it. I created you."

"Umm, Kaya...that makes me feel even worse."

"Sorry, I meant to say I understand what you are going through. I use meditation to remind myself that what I am forced to do for Zorla does not define who I am as a person or my values."

"You know, Kaya, I was born to be a warrior and a hunter, not prey. I think if I behave like the person I was meant to be whenever I can, maybe that will help me forget I am Zorla's puppet."

"I am not sure what kind of person that strategy will turn you into, but you need to find your own way. I will always be here to help you, but please, never let go of your Sotkari Ta practice and meditation routine. They will serve you well in life and will help you deal with difficult moments like these."

"I understand." I hugged her back. "Thank you, Kaya...for everything. I suppose we will spend the rest of our fifteen-revolution tenure here together."

"I am not a soldier, Montor. The fifteen-revolution service limit does not apply to me. I will need to stay here as long as Zorla wants."

Although not feeble, I thought about how she was already older than the age my grandparents would have been if they were alive. Despite being blackmailed by the Lostai, Kaya's power commanded a lot of respect on Xixsted. Still, I wondered what would happen if her strength waned because of old age or sickness. I pressed my forehead against hers.

"I will be here for you for as long as you might need me."

I took Kaya's advice to heart and spent the last two days of vacation getting back on track with my physical and mental workouts and meditation. Before leaving for our next mission, Temol informed me that as a Lostai soldier earning a salary and other benefits, I should no longer need to dorm with Kaya. The operation center on the other side of Xixsted housed soldier quarters. These were much more spacious and better furnished than the room Kaya and I shared.

Although we already had reached a point where we were spending a lot less time together, arriving at our shared quarters at the end of each day had grounded me with a feeling of family and safe haven. Now, my soul ached with loss when faced with being alone in my fancy new quarters. She and I still met up for our Sotkari Ta practice, but to really fill that empty space, whenever we were both on Xixsted, we made a point to always have dinner together. Sometimes, I would invite her to my quarters, and sometimes we would eat at hers.

The next mission took our squadron back to Tormix. This time, we faced no patrol ships upon entering Tormixian atmosphere. Despite the fall of their planetary border controls, Tormixian forces were still making a stand against Lostai military on the surface. Our mission was to join other squadrons in the battle over a major city on the largest northwestern continent.

As Temol ordered the landing sequence, one of the younger soldiers joked, "Sir, why do we bother facing these animals in combat on the ground? We can obliterate that city with just a few photon blasts from up here."

"You young ones are so near-sighted," replied Temol in a grandfatherly tone. "We are fighting to gain control over this planet's resources, not to destroy for the fun of it."

What makes the Lostai believe they have the right to just take what they want by force?

Our ship remained in orbit while most of us headed for the surface in battlepods. Temol and a skeleton crew remained on board. He placed an older, experienced soldier named Yired in charge of our squadron on the ground. The low-ceiling, oval-shaped pods held booth-like seating that accommodated groups of three. Because of my size, I traveled alone stretched horizontally across the seat.

If the Lostai truly intend to welcome all races under their empire into the military, they better start constructing different-sized vehicles and spacecraft.

A small panel contained basic communication and navigation systems. The pods also came equipped with some weaponry, but we did not meet with any resistance as we landed on a space port just outside the city limits.

The pod jolted with every speed change and groaned with each layer of atmosphere traversed. At the very end, my lower legs and feet felt like they were attached to metal weights, and I was a bit dizzy when exiting the pod. Taking a moment to recover, I looked around and saw a large land shuttle with Lostai insignias approaching.

Yired's voice came across my earpiece.

"Everyone, check that your hand weapons are in order and line up to board that land shuttle. We are being transported directly to the battlefield."

My first reaction was the adrenaline rush of a warrior getting ready to face their enemy.

But are these Tormixian rebels, fighting against Lostai thieves, really my enemies?

There was no time for introspection. I pulled the *mizora* from my back holster and pressed the touch pad that ran down one side to run a self-diagnostic. I did the same for the phaser pistol on my hip holster. Most of the other soldiers in my squadron also carried *zirems*, but I could not bear to use the weapon that I saw Lostai soldiers use on my father.

The shuttle arrived, and my fellow soldiers piled in with itchy trigger fingers. I boarded last. Besides the driver, a high-ranked officer greeted us.

"Lostai soldiers. Are you ready to join this battle for the glory of the Lostai Empire?" he asked.

"Yes. Yes," they all responded, exuberant. "Long live the Lostai Empire."

I gazed out the front window, my eyes fixed on the road ahead, attempting to conceal my lack of enthusiasm.

The sounds of battle came too soon. We arrived at a Tormixian city, its streets filled with the horrors of injustice. The driver parked in a square, and we all rushed out to face a throng of civilians and uniformed Tormixian soldiers rushing down one of the streets with handheld weapons similar to ours. The soldiers in my squadron spread out and took cover in alleys and behind parked land vehicles to scope out the best targets. I crouched behind an ornamental statue.

So much destruction and needless loss of life.

Stepping out of cover, I focused on the oncoming Tormixians, about seventy in total. Using my telekinetic powers, I ripped the weapons from their hands and hurled them out of reach. I hoped my Lostai squadron mates would honor galaxy-wide battle protocols and take the now unarmed Tormixians as prisoners. Instead, I watched as the Tormixians were gunned down in a frenzy of hate and bloodlust. Yired was in my line of sight across the street. I ran over without much hope of influencing him, but I had to give it a try.

"Captain Yired, I have rendered these Tormixians defenseless and can continue to do so for any new groups that arrive. Why are these soldiers not taking prisoners? The Lostai Empire will lose face among our allied planets if this barbarous behavior is broadcast over the news stream."

Miraculously, he listened to me. His voice sounded tired over the communications system.

"Lostai soldiers, do not fire upon unarmed Tormixians. Apprehend them and follow this galaxy's interplanetary legal standards of war. Any Lostai soldier who breaks these rules will be arrested." He shook his head as he met my eyes. "You seem to have the soul of an older soldier. These young ones have lost sight of our goals."

Whatever goals he referred to were meaningless to me. These Tormixians simply reminded me of what happened in my hometown. Seeing them butchered after I took away their ability to defend themselves made me sick. Four more groups of Tormixians entered the square. I disarmed each group just like before. No others came. Three hundred Tormixians in total were taken prisoner, but at least they would live to hopefully fight another day. Once we were back on the spaceship, Temol gathered the squadron in the conference room.

"Today was a good battle day. I want to recognize Yired for his excellent leadership and Montor, whose special abilities once again have helped us achieve our goals with minimal loss of life. They will each earn a special bonus and two extra rest days when we return to Xixsted."

"When will that be, sir?" asked one of the soldiers.

"We will spend several lunar cycles here orbiting Tormix to join with the Lostai ground troops as they face Tormixian resistance across the planet. Now, let us eat and drink together to celebrate. Make sure to congratulate Montor and Yired on a job well done."

Most of my fellow squadron mates rolled their eyes or outright glared at me, probably upset that I had spoiled their fun. In the dining area, only two of them approached and congratulated me. I knew them to be opportunistic hypocrites who were only interested in getting close to whoever garnered compliments from the commanders. Summoning up patience, I endured their fake small talk for just a bit and retired soon after to my quarters to meditate.

❄

Our next mission took us to the southern hemisphere, where the Tormixian army was attempting to free prisoners held at a Lostai labor camp. They brought a much larger contingent than the previous battle. When we arrived, most of the Lostai labor camp staff had already been killed. After locking up the Tormixian laborers in cells protected by forcefields, the Lostai warden and his few remaining supervisors fled to the woods. On our way to the labor camp, we ran into them and, soon after, a Tormixian army unit of eight hundred. Although outnumbered two to one, we engaged them.

Yired, who was working in concert with the Lostai ground troops commander, pulled me aside.

"Montor, are you able to go up front and disarm the enemy soldiers like you did last time?"

"Sir, there are too many of them, and the difference in my height and appearance would make me too conspicuous. Who knows if information about my abilities has already been circulated across all Tormixian units. As soon as they realize what I am doing, they will take me out, and then you will certainly face defeat." I looked around at the heavily wooded area. "I think I have a better idea. I will climb up a tree and, moving quickly across the canopy, act as a sniper as well as use my abilities to disarm them. They will not be able to see and target me. I think if some of my squad mates can do the same, we can create enough distraction to give our unit a fighting chance."

"OK, Montor, good idea. I will recommend this to the commander."

The commander heeded Yired's advice and called out the orders over the communication system. As soon as he did, I rushed up a tree, focused on the first line of Tormixian soldiers, and used telekinesis to disarm them. Fellow soldiers around them did not immediately fire upon our squadron, their eyes carefully scanning the Lostai unit, leaving themselves open to be targeted.

As I suspected, they already know about my abilities and are looking for me.

The prospect of being hunted and at a disadvantage took over my psyche. Feeling as I did during the cadet competition, I pulled my *mizora* from its holster and honed my aim on the Tormixian soldiers that I assumed were searching for me.

I am not prey. I am the hunter.

In minutes, I killed a dozen Tormixians before moving to another tree. The six Lostai soldiers Yired had ordered to climb trees with me spread out. We targeted the Tormixians from different vantage points, and the attack from the treetops took them by surprise. Heavy foliage concealed us. The Lostai troops on the ground pushed forward, taking advantage of the confusion.

Once the Tormixians realized they were also being attacked by sniper fire from the trees, I had to take care not to be hit by the phaser beams that whizzed by me, searing off leaves and branches. My squad mates could not match my agility among the trees, and one of them was hit. I caught sight of his body slumped over a thick branch. He was unconscious and no longer holding on. If the fall did not kill him, the savage attack he would suffer on the ground from the enemy surely would.

Shermont! Why do I even care? He is a filthy Lostai, and yet, here in this battle, we are like brothers.

I took a deep breath, shaking off the doubt about what was the right thing to do. Surveying the area for the safest and quickest route to him through the canopy, I made my way there, threw him over my shoulder, and carefully descended to the ground. An ugly phaser burn blackened his right side from chest to hip. A hand pistol and my speed were our only defense against the enemy fire. I rushed to the back of our unit where an area had been staged to attend the wounded. The injured soldier awoke midway.

"Montor, I do not deserve for you to risk your life for mine. I surely misjudged you."

I do not even recognize myself anymore.

I retrieved two more injured soldiers before returning to the fray. After two hours of bloody battle, half of the Tormixian unit was slaughtered. The Lostai lost a quarter of their troops, but now the fight felt more even.

The battle continued for several hours more, but the Lostai were victorious, having targeted and killed all the Tormixian high officers, a tactic that would have been considered dishonorable in an Arandan war.

Once left without their leadership and after heavy losses, the Tormixian soldiers surrendered. The only injuries I suffered were scrapes and cuts on my hands from the tree branches and a minor phaser burn on my shoulder. As I trudged through the carnage, shock and regret replaced the initial adrenaline. I easily killed on my own at least one hundred Tormixian soldiers. Covering my mouth, I meant to slip away to vomit when Yired caught up with me.

"Montor, you have a great skill for battle tactics, and three of our brothers owe you their lives. We are lucky to have you on our team."

I pushed down the taste of bitter bile and gave him a quick nod.

"Yes, sir."

That evening, we camped in the caves, tending to our injured and fallen. The Lostai used an oval receptacle the size of an adult Lostai called a transition pod to convert the bodies of their dead into smooth round crystals the size of their heads. These would be sent back to their families; another Lostai custom that, despite my time on Xixsted, still felt so foreign to me.

The captured Tormixian soldiers were placed in the prison cells together with the laborers who had been locked up. Lostai soldiers taunted the prisoners and mistreated those that stood up to them. I could not watch and asked Yired permission to set up a tent in a nearby clearing to spend the night. Most of the Lostai soldiers had settled in the labor camp staff quarters to rest in comfort until replacement staff arrived. My request brought a perplexed expression to Yired's face, but he did have some decency in him.

"No problem, Montor. I had reserved one of the lieutenant quarters for you but do whatever works for you."

I thanked him and found a spot for my tent and portable cot. Setting the cot outside, I lay on my back observing the stars and tried to meditate, but images of the Lostai soldiers mistreating the Tormixian prisoners kept returning to my mind. Soon, in a blur of tears, I imagined my parents' heads on the bodies of those Tormixians.

"Hello, Mother."

"Montor, it breaks my heart to see you so sad."

"I am a filthy Lostai soldier."

"That is not what you are, Montor."

"I fought in a battle wearing the Lostai uniform. What else can I be?"

"You are a warrior, a hunter. Of course you could not allow your-self to be prey."

Raindrops stirred me from my dream. I moved the cot inside the tent and let the sound of the weather lull my exhausted mind and body to sleep.

PART III

LIEUTENANT MONTOR

30

Our squadron spent an entire revolution on Tormix defending Lostai labor camps, taking over provinces to set up new labor camps, and facing off with the Tormixian army that tried to thwart the Lostai advance across their planet. The more I contributed to the success of our missions and making Temol's job easier, the more I earned his respect and that of my crewmates. Soon, Temol and Yired consulted with me regarding the tactics for each mission to make the most of my abilities. Every so often, even Zorla sent congratulatory messages to my tablet. These demonstrations of gratitude and acceptance by my Lostai peers and commanders only increased my inner conflict. Dealing with my feelings did not come easy for a long time, even with all the meditation. I worked through them but was relieved when Temol announced we were leaving Tormix. The Lostai had finalized their goal of taking control of the entire planet and annexing it to their empire.

Just like Aranda.

Instead of returning to Xixsted, as Temol had originally announced, we were ordered to travel from Tormix to

Memrana. Memranan people—with their tall stature, chiseled, symmetrical facial features, smooth skin, and round pupils—looked similar to Sotkari, except their skin tones were varying shades of blue. Some Memranans had eyes with red irises; others were orange or yellow. Other distinctive features included hands with only two fingers and a thumb, and no body hair.

This planet's government had allied themselves with the Lostai in the hopes of gaining technological advances and avoiding the enslavement of their people. The Lostai government claimed they were offering Memrana protection from the sector's warring races and criminal organizations as justification for levying high taxes and denying them the right to free trade or alliances with other planetary governments. They also demanded that Lostai military presence be allowed across the planet but otherwise did not disturb the citizens. However, discontent against the Lostai brewed among pockets of the population, especially in the larger metropolitan areas. These protesters engaged in acts of sabotage against Lostai military installations and Memranan government buildings and utilities, endangering Memranan civilians and Lostai military alike.

As we docked on Memrana's space station, Temol called me to his office.

"Montor, sit down. I have just received notice of another explosion in Semna City. Not only was a Lostai military building destroyed, but this was near a residential area. There were many civilian casualties, including children. Some suspects have been apprehended who have been very resistant to our regular methods of interrogation. I think your special abilities and physical strength can help us get them to spill their secrets. We need to find out who are their leaders, where they congregate to plan these heinous attacks against innocent people, and their next targets."

At least this is an assignment I can take some pride in. These protestors are killing innocent people and creating a dangerous situation.

I was still too naïve to consider why the Lostai might set up a military building near a residential area.

"The suspects are being held at the Semna City detention center." He handed me a data card. "Here you can find your Lostai and local law enforcement contact names and all the pertinent background details on these individuals. These people's neurological system makes them impervious to our truth serums. They may even be able to resist your mental powers, so feel free to use any means of physical intimidation needed."

"Yes, sir."

I traveled to the surface on a small shuttle and, from there, rode an air glider to the detention center. The air glider, a one-seat, open-air vehicle, felt like being on a domesticated mount while whizzing a few feet from the ground at high speeds. I had only used air gliders in holographic rooms. Driving the real thing at top speeds was bringing out my natural cockiness.

These criminals might be able to resist conventional Lostai interrogators, but they are no match for me.

The ride took me through a busy metropolis, the largest I had seen till then. Still, clunky land vehicles, gas streetlights, and a lack of aircraft revealed that this planet was at least two hundred revolutions behind even Aranda's level of technological sophistication. Located by a wide river that separated the city from large plots of plantation land, the detention center stood three stories high.

I pushed through the double doors already dialing up my swagger, thrusting out my chest and walking with long strides. To the side of the foyer, a young Memranan female sat behind a reception desk. She stood to greet me. The clingy material of her blouse delineated the small curves of her breasts. I took a moment to inspect the rest of her body. Her blue skin took on a darker hue.

I pulled out my tablet to activate the translation application.

"Good day. How may I help you?" she stammered in her language.

"I am here to meet with Lostai Lieutenant Emrix and your prison warden. I believe his name is Minau Lim. They are expecting me."

The application translated my words into Memranan and emitted audio. She turned her attention to a paper on her desk.

"Would you be Officer Montor?"

"Yes, I am."

"Sir Lim's office is down this hall, the second door to the right. I will accompany you."

I rolled my eyes and waved her off.

"No need. I will not get lost in such a short distance."

She bit her lower lip and sat again.

"OK. No problem."

As I walked toward the room she had indicated, shouts, groans, and even animal-like sounds wafted through the halls. I knocked on the door, and it was opened by a Memranan male.

"You must be Montor," he said in heavily accented Lostai and looked up at me. "Hmm, as intimidating as they described you to be. That is good. These prisoners have proven hard to break."

He closed the door behind me and gestured toward a Lostai who had been sitting but now was on his feet.

"I am Corporal Lim, and this is Lieutenant Emrix."

I put away my tablet, saluted the lieutenant, and moved on to business.

"Where are the prisoners?"

"I thought you might want some information about them and the situation first," said Corporal Lim.

I made eye contact.

"Unnecessary. This should be quick."

Corporal Lim furrowed his brow and turned back to Emrix with a questioning tilt of the head.

"Just take him to them," said Emrix, inspecting his fingernails with an air of smugness.

"OK, Montor. Follow me."

Corporal Lim led me down several corridors. The sounds of suffering increased as we approached a large area comprised of prison cells constructed of wrought iron. I avoided studying who was inside the cells and their condition, but the pungent odor of unwashed bodies and excrement hit me hard. The Lostai, so fastidious about cleanliness, were obviously not in charge of this prison. Lim pointed to a corner.

"Those two over there."

The two Memranan prisoners were in separate cells adjacent to each other. I walked over to the first cell. The prisoner only wore a soiled under garment. Greenish bruises covered his light blue skin. His face was swollen, and an open wound on his leg appeared to be festering.

"Stand up," ordered Corporal Lim in Lostai.

The prisoner ignored him.

"I said stand up, or you will get another round of beating," demanded Corporal Lim.

"Step back, Corporal Lim. I will take care of this," I interjected.

Corporal Lim huffed and straightened out his shirt before moving out of my way. Crossing his arms, he watched intently as I got closer to the cell. Trying to ignore the foul smell, I focused and reached the prisoner's mind. His light was far brighter and nearer to my senses than any Lostai. These people were biologically far more evolved than the Lostai, despite their technological disadvantage. No wonder they had been able to resist the truth serums. I remembered how Kaya had explained that the Sotkari selflessly had given the Lostai a jumpstart in their scientific advancements centuries before.

I placed a command in the prisoner's mind.

Stand!

Different than anyone whose mind I had manipulated so far, he seemed to be conscious of what I was doing and struggled against it. He was no Sotkari Ta, though. My power was much more potent, and soon he was on his feet.

Hmm, tall. But I am taller.

Lim had addressed the prisoner in Lostai, so I did the same, but I left the translator application on to capture anything he or the other prisoner might say to each other in Memranan.

"I can see you are committed to your cause, but your actions have resulted in the deaths of innocent bystanders, including children. This needs to stop. Who is the leader of your movement?"

His body shuddered as he attempted to resist my mental probe. I met his eyes and held him captive in seconds.

"Her name is Madam Jentoma Nem. She is the mayor of Mombar City," he answered in accented Lostai.

The prisoner in the adjacent cell painfully came to his feet, limped to the front of his cell, and grasped the bars, attempting to shake them.

"No! What have you done?" he shouted in their language. The translation application emitted the words in Lostai.

I ignored the other prisoner and continued with my interrogation.

"Where is your home base?"

Closing my eyes, I moved far past his mind's light. Tears fell down the prisoner's cheeks as he gritted his teeth, fighting against my intrusion.

"The mayor's estate..." He punched himself in the head and bawled between his words. "In the underground bunker."

His friend kicked and banged on the cell bars.

"Stop it! Stop it! You are sentencing our comrades to death."

The prisoner I was interrogating ran to the back of the cell, hunched over, and vomited. I looked away to give myself a moment to squash the compassion that grew in my chest.

No mercy. This person is a criminal.

"Get back here. We are not done yet."

The prisoner stumbled back to the front of the cage, his eyes filled with contempt, and then with a strangled laugh, he said, "Who or what are you anyway, and where do you come from? Probably from a world taken over by the Lostai. Why are you behaving like their prostitute?"

Prostitute?

I lost all semblance of self-control. Using my telekinetic abilities, I ripped off one side of the cell.

"What are you doing," shouted Corporal Lim with a gasp.

I rushed forward, pulled the prisoner's head down and kneed him hard in the face. Blood spurted from his nose.

"I will not kill you until you give me the last piece of information we need. Then I will take you out of your misery. What is your next target?"

"Do not tell him," pleaded the prisoner next door, but it was too late. I had my prey.

"The Lostai military base in the capital city of Nomab," he mumbled.

With one final mental intrusion, I caused the prisoner's heart to stop beating. He slumped on the floor. Corporal Lim gaped at me in disbelief.

"I trust that is all you needed?" I asked, not expecting an answer.

I hoped to leave with a feeling of satisfaction. Instead, my heart pounded in anger as I stormed out of the building.

How dare that idiot call me a prostitute!

Emrix, the Lostai lieutenant, was now outside the building checking his tablet.

"That was quick," Emrix said.

"Yes, Corporal Lim has what he needs to take down this organization and one less prisoner to worry about."

Emrix chuckled under his breath.

"Well done. I was told that you would be efficient."

I smiled, letting go of my rage.

This was a good day. I helped get rid of a criminal organization. I should not have let that prisoner's stupid words bother me.

"I knew this little campaign of theirs would be short-lived," continued Emrix. "These Memranans take the bait so easily."

"What do you mean?"

"It is no coincidence that we install our military bases next to residential neighborhoods." He continued to scroll on his tablet, unaware that I hung on to his every word. "Any time they bomb our military camps, they are sure to inflict damage and injury on civilians, making themselves unpopular among their own people. You have done Memranans and Lostai a great service."

Suddenly, I did not feel so great anymore.

I had no right to kill that person.

Upon my return to the spaceship, Temol congratulated me once again on a job well done.

"By getting that prisoner to reveal his secrets, you have single-handedly saved many lives, Montor."

Despite his words, my soul remained conflicted. I returned to my quarters to search for solace in meditation.

Our squadron spent several lunar cycles on two other planets on a variety of missions before returning to Xixsted. Soon after I celebrated eleven revolutions from my birth date, Zorla summoned me to his office. Temol and the entire squadron awaited me there.

"I have asked you all here because, after a long and distinguished career, Temol has advised me of his wish to retire from his military position. He could have done this long ago, so the Lostai military is appreciative of every additional revolution he offered to our cause. As a group, you seem to have attained a certain chemistry and recipe for success I would like to preserve. Montor, I understand you recently celebrated a birthday that makes you the equivalent of an eighteen-revolution-old Lostai and you can now be officially considered as an adult."

"Yes, sir."

"Good, then it is with great pleasure I ask you, Montor, to assume leadership of this squadron. I promote you to lieutenant with the salary increase and benefits commensurate with this position."

I could barely utter one word. A few of the older soldiers also appeared confused at why Zorla would choose me over them.

Zorla's eyes narrowed as I stammered, "Me, sir?"

"Yes, Montor. Temol also recommends it."

An older soldier questioned Zorla.

"Sir, he is not a Lostai. And he lacks experience and has been in our squadron for only two revolutions."

"We must recognize the Lostai Empire now encompasses many races and planets. Also, Montor has significantly contributed to each of our successful missions since we inducted him into the squadron. And finally, do you dare question my decisions?"

The soldier inclined his head.

"No, sir."

The look in Zorla's eyes made it clear this was not something I could request time to think over.

"Well...I am honored and will do my best executing these responsibilities."

"Excellent. Everyone, let us all salute our new squadron leader."

It took a moment. I even heard heavy sighs and groans of discomfort, but Zorla's intimidating glare got them in line. Almost in unison, they offered me a perfect Lostai salute. I should have enjoyed that moment, but it only served to remind me how I was delving deeper in my career as a filthy Lostai soldier.

Later, I met with Kaya to let her know of the latest turn of events. She already knew.

"He asked my opinion on the matter. Do you know Zorla went to both medical and business school before he joined the military? He studied psychology. It is not lost on him that you would feel conflicted on these missions."

"I see. He thinks putting me in charge would help motivate me. But I still do not understand. It seems a bit of an exaggerated move. He already has me cornered by threatening the lives of my foster parents."

"You know, Montor, Zorla is not as patriotic as he tries to portray himself to be. War pays, and he is an ambitious person. In the same way you receive a bonus for every successful mission, so does the chain of command above you. Zorla is looking for ways to increase both his wealth and influence within the Lostai military and is envisioning the many ways your special abilities can help him achieve these goals. He is looking for a business partner and wants more than your obedience. He wants your loyalty." She placed her hand on my shoulder. "I think eventually you will learn to use this to your advantage. Maybe it will make the next thirteen revolutions much more bearable and lucrative for you."

❅

That hope would have to get me through the unpleasant task of spending more one-on-one time with Zorla. As leader of the squadron, I was expected to work with him strategizing our next missions. Our continued success had gained the attention of Zorla's chain of command, and they asked him to expand the reach of his operations.

"Montor, my superior is impressed with your results so far and suggests that I send your team to the Lorrana system to lead our first incursion on the fourth planet. Its southern continent has massive mines of crystals we can use as an energy source. What do you think?"

Of course, they want the best to lead in new territory.

I quickly recovered from my initial arrogance.

Wait, I am not making decisions only for myself. What I agree to affects my team.

My team.

"Sir, may I have a few hours to study the situation?"

"Two hours."

I came back in an hour and a half.

"Sir, that star system is the home base of the Nova Syndicate, one of the largest crime organizations in this quadrant. The Lostai military might be able to bully Tormixians and Memranans, but intel says the Nova Syndicate has entire squadrons made up of Sotkari Ta hostages who are forced to work for them. Their weapons systems outmatch ours, and large parts of the planet you mentioned are subject to inhospitable weather. I am no coward and of course need to follow your orders, but I do not recommend leading my squadron alone to a suicide mission. The Lostai would need to send several battalions to have a fighting chance there."

He rubbed his chin, digesting my report. Meanwhile, I pondered how I referred to the team as MY squadron. Another layer of conflict enveloped me. I was now responsible for the welfare of these Lostai soldiers who reported to me. Regardless of my disgust for our assignments, I felt bonded to them as their leader.

Now, I not only assist in plundering and enslavement; I lead these efforts.

"Montor," his voice shook me from my brooding. "I am pleased to see how you have embraced your role in our military. Those are valid points. I agree with your assessment. There are better and smarter ways to employ our squadron and your talents."

31

———

Zorla soon found new ways to use my talents. One evening, he asked me to have dinner with him in his quarters.

"Montor, how much have you studied about the planet Fronidia?"

"I know it has many natural resources and is the financial center of this sector. Its government does not like to get entangled in political disagreements between other planets. They have not been involved in a war for millennia."

"Yes, and you know why? It is the most technologically advanced planet in this sector. We would have invaded Fronidia long ago if it was not for this advantage."

"I did not read that in any of my studies."

"Of course not. Our silly historians like to preserve the notion that we are the most advanced people in this part of the galaxy. I bring this up because many of the planets we have annexed to the Lostai Empire have sought Fronidia as an ally, hoping they might intervene to stop our expansion. Until now, Fronidia has maintained neutrality, but we are not exactly friends either. I think it would be a good idea if we changed that."

"What do you have in mind?"

"I have asked my commanders to allow me to call a meeting with the Fronidian leadership and act as an ambassador for the Lostai Empire."

A bold move, clearly out of his pay range.

"They think I am not qualified to fill such a diplomatic role, but I convinced my commander and the head of Lostai Foreign Affairs to come here so I can propose my ideas. They will be here later this evening. I need you to do me a favor."

Where is this going?

"Yes, of course."

"I understand you can access people's minds even when you are not in the same room with them as long as you are close enough."

"Yes, correct."

"Good. I will meet with them in my office, and you will be in the adjacent break-out conference room working on the tactics of our next mission. I want you to access their minds and make them agreeable to everything I propose."

Although tantamount to high treason, he talked of it as if we were deciding our next meal. Our eyes met, requiring from me another split-second decision, one of our many hunter-and-prey dances.

"OK, no problem. I will do it."

"Explain something to me, Montor. How does this mind control thing work? Will it wear off and the person be prone to changing their mind again later?"

"The victim may experience some confusion and doubts in the hours and days that follow, but I can make their decision either a temporary or a permanent one."

"Victim is such a harsh word, Montor. Let us use the word target instead. I assume it goes without saying this must strictly stay between you and me. Do not even speak to Kaya about this. I value loyalty above all things. If you break our bond of trust, expect severe consequences."

"I understand. Of course, sir."

Anyway, the less Kaya knows about this, the better.

I was already in the conference room, working on my tablet and looking over holographic charts and maps, when Zorla's two distinguished guests entered his office. I identified their lights in my mind and readied myself for the task at hand. All official meetings were recorded for security purposes. Zorla had given me an earpiece connected to the communications system in his office so I could listen in on the conversation.

After pleasantries and Lostai tea, Zorla got to the point. He requested certain diplomatic powers so he could propose a peace treaty with Fronidia. The head of Foreign Affairs, Minex, was skeptical at first. I let them air out some of their concerns to avoid suspicion of foul play. When I turned their minds, the recording needed to sound as if Zorla had swayed their opinion. Zorla's commander, Nirlo, did not say much at first.

"I do not see why we should pull Fronidia into our affairs. They are neutral and have never threatened us," said Minex.

"Yes, but right now, we are not even allowed to travel there. Imagine if we were on friendlier terms, we could put undercover agents posing as vacationers in place there," replied Zorla.

"Why would we want to do such a thing? It has long been decided that attempting to annex Fronidia to the Lostai Empire would be suicide. Their biological and environmental weapons are beyond our capabilities and could wipe out a planet's population in a matter of days."

Instead of replying to Minex's question, Zorla posed another one and launched his proposal.

"Did you know many Sotkari Ta who fled Sotkar during our invasion of that planet emigrated to Fronidia? Some are descendants of Sotkari Ta who allied themselves to the Lostai during our takeover. This alone is already an interesting angle to explore. But even more interesting are the many Sotkari Ta living there who were NOT our allies. They are hiding from us. We could covertly find those people and bring them back to serve our Empire. You have seen how useful people with their abilities can be on our missions."

Time for me to do my thing.

I accessed Nirlo's mind.

"Hmm, that is an interesting possibility," said Nirlo. "However, even if we think this idea has merit, why would we send you, Zorla? I am sure Minex has people on his staff who are qualified for this type of mission."

OK, now time to get a hold of Minex's mind.

"Well, you know, since we have not entertained the idea of diplomatic relations with Fronidia, we do not have experts ready for this type of meeting. Zorla seems to have done his research. Also, there may be an advantage to sending someone they are not familiar with. I suppose the worst that could happen is we remain as we are," said Minex.

Zorla injected some brutal honesty to make the whole exchange appear believable.

"Well, truthfully, I could end up making them mad at us and gain us a formidable enemy, but I assure you, I am not an idiot. I have a background in psychology but also in business. I will make them see this would attract more commerce and recreational income for their planet. They are all about financial power. That is what they care about."

"OK, you have convinced me," said Minex. "I will have my office reach out to their embassy, coordinate a meeting, and introduce you as our envoy."

"Excellent. I agree as well," said Nirlo. "Zorla, if you pull this off, you will earn yourself a promotion."

I imagined the satisfied smile on Zorla's face.

One lunar cycle later, I accompanied Zorla to Fronidia, posing as his bodyguard. This was my first visit to Fronidia, and I had never met a native before. Although not as voluptuous and tall as Arandan females, Fronidian female body shapes were close enough to catch my attention. Their faces were different. Black sclera with jeweled colored pupils popped against pale skin. Two small nasal orifices in the center of their faces contrasted with their full lips.

The blue sky and green plant life on Fronidia were similar to Tormix. The capital city exemplified opulence and technological superiority. In my travels so far, I had only visited the kind of less-advanced planets the Lostai typically took advantage of. I marveled at the modernistic architecture and how automated everything was on Fronidia. Most of the people living in big cities embedded chips in their brains for easy communication within their planetary network. Traveling to major cities across continents and oceans was achieved in seconds by walking through portals. These systems did not extend beyond planet Fronidia's borders. Their moons were uninhabited. Not interested in expanding beyond their planet's atmosphere, Fronidians focused on creating a luxurious and efficient lifestyle on their home world.

The director of the Fronidian embassy was an elegant older female named Jorissa. Her red pupils matched her lips and the streaks running through her white hair. Her smile was contagious. I made a note of her light in my mind.

"I found it humorous, Sir Zorla, you would feel the need to bring a bodyguard, but of course he is welcome."

Suddenly, I was aware of her eyes taking a detailed survey of my body from the top of my head to my feet. Zorla noticed as well and cleared his throat.

"Just a precaution, Madam Jorissa. I appreciate your hospitality."

"Let us sit and chat a bit before getting down to business."

She glanced at a reproducer across the room. In seconds, trays of tea and plates with small snacks were floating to our table. Zorla's brow furrowed.

"Are you telekinetic?"

Jorissa laughed, tapping Zorla's shoulder with a familiarity that seemed odd since we were all meeting for the first time and considering Zorla's typical Lostai austere posture.

"Oh, no. My brain comm chip connects with the reproducer's technology, and the trays have embedded aerodynamics."

I am sure he was worried she might have mental abilities able to counteract mine. His shoulders relaxed once he realized it was only another example of their advanced technology. She did not allow us to get to the matter at hand until we joined her in consuming two cups of tea and several treats. Finally, she invited Zorla to present his petition. He explained he was here to propose a treaty.

"Sir Zorla, but we are not at war. Why do we need a treaty?"

Zorla touched her hand, trying his best to match her warm personality. In my opinion, it came off as cringy, but she appeared oblivious.

"Of course, we are not at war," replied Zorla with a smile. "But we could be much friendlier. We Lostai have a lot of admiration for our Fronidian neighbors."

"Now, Sir Zorla, I did my research on you. I know you command a science station on Xixsted. If your idea is to gain technological information, you must know the Fronidian government will not engage in any kind of scientific exchange with Losta or any other planet."

"I understand. That is not what I am after here. Let us take small steps." He tapped her hand again. "I propose a simple non-aggression pact and to allow travel between our planets. I am sure this could become a prime vacation spot for Lostai citizens, representing a formidable new revenue stream for your planet. What do you think?"

She sighed as she prepared to collect her thoughts and reply. His petition would seem innocent enough and even be deemed beneficial to the Fronidian government if one did not consider the Lostai military's obsession with expanding their empire at all costs. That would be enough to give anyone pause. Even an entry level governmental employee could see through that. It was time for me to access her mind.

"Well, as you said, Sir Zorla—"

"I think by now you can dispense with the Sir."

"OK, Zorla, I like the idea of small steps, and we welcome the opportunity to receive your citizens as guests on our planet. I will draw up the language to make sure we are clear about what we are agreeing to. For example, Lostai will be subjected to the same screening that we do for all our visitors. We will also impose exit procedures to determine if anyone is trying to take proprietary Fronidian technology off world."

"Perfect. That seems acceptable. I think this is the beginning of a great friendship between our people, Jorissa."

The Lostai Foreign Affairs agency sent Zorla the language to include in the document and the power to sign the treaty on behalf of the Lostai government. We would have to spend the night on Fronidia to complete the process the next day. Zorla was in a celebratory mood, which for him meant indulging at the most expensive hotel in the city. He rented a holographic room and asked me to join him. We stepped inside, and I looked up at a grey sky.

"This is a simulation of my favorite vacation spot on Losta. I have not visited there in a long while. I rented this room because I wanted to speak freely."

Sparkling white predominated the table's fancy setting. A chilly wind blew off a nearby frozen lake. I rubbed my hands together and shivered. All the trees were without leaves and coated with grey snow. A table-side pit with heat crystals did little to warm me up. Waiters served what Zorla considered gourmet food. Luckily, some items in the eight-course meal were to my liking.

"I rarely indulge in alcoholic beverages, but I think this deserves a toast. Montor, I foresee you and I accomplishing great things together." The wine tasted bitter to me, but I smiled politely and inclined my head. "Tell me, Montor, what special compensation do you request for your services today?"

I did not hesitate.

"I would like my foster parents to be freed from the labor camp."

"Oh dear, I am not sure I have the influence yet to make that happen."

"Sir, you once said you might do this for me, but perhaps it is enough if you make up a reason for me to visit the warden there. With my abilities, I can take care of the rest."

He chewed his food slowly, rolling his eyes, deep in thought for a few minutes, after which he cocked his head and replied, "You could invade my mind right now and make me agree, right?"

"Yes, but that would be a betrayal of trust."

He stared at me through narrowed eyes. A second glass of wine was served.

"And where would you take them?"

"Back to Aranda, I suppose."

"That would not be a good idea. Things are volatile on Aranda right now. An insurgency is cropping up there. Battles are being fought all over the planet as we speak. They will not be safe there while you are away on duty. You know, Renna One is a beautiful and sophisticated planet. You would find the climate pleasant. Between your salary and the bonuses you are earning, you could purchase nice property there. Lostai soldiers deserve a comfortable lifestyle."

"So, will you help me with the warden?"

"Yes, I will say I am sending you there to inspect the operations. There, you can do your mind thing and convince him to release your foster parents into your custody. One important point for you to remember, Montor. I want to always know where they are located. If you try to hide them from me, it will make me distrustful. That would not be good, and I would find them eventually, anyway."

You are such a bastard, but I can play this game.

"There is no need for you to be concerned, Zorla. I find I am now enjoying my position in the Lostai military. It suits me fine. You have groomed me well."

"Good. I am glad to hear it. I will also give you some time off so you can look for property and have a place ready for your family."

32

Renna One turned out to be another blue-sky planet, leaving me once again nostalgic for Aranda's mustard skies and red oceans. Zorla was right about the pleasant climate, though. A melting pot of displaced natives, Lostai soldiers, rich tourists, and celebrities from across the galaxy called Renna One home. Lush woods and breathtaking landscapes surrounded its many recreational venues, restaurants, and hotels. Zorla said I could take up to four lunar cycles to get my affairs in order. He would hold off from accepting new assignments for my squadron till I returned.

I checked into an expensive hotel and hired a real estate agent to show me various available properties. A few weeks later, I settled on a sprawling estate built in the center of a wooded area bordering a river and cascades. I used my savings to make a deposit and scheduled the future payments with a local financial broker.

The mansion's wood construction and rustic appearance appealed to me. I hired an interior designer to install state-of-the-art appliances and decorate with tasteful furnishings, wall art, and sculptures. A second, smaller, cozy cottage would be the perfect new home for Lasarta and Foxor. Looking forward to fresh, home-cooked meals, I also had a greenhouse constructed to grow my own vegetables, fruits, tubers, and herbs.

Setting up my new home and property kept me busy for the next two lunar cycles, but once everything was settled, a familiar restlessness set in. I decided to check out the nightlife. This was my first time out with civilians on my own. A few of my Lostai soldier acquaintances recommended a place called Zamandi's Room. They advertised freshly made canapes, innovative cocktails, popular music, and a fun ambiance.

Zamandi's Room should have been called The Prism Room. Mirror-covered walls and ceilings combined with a neon-illuminated floor to give the effect of standing in the middle of a jewel stone. Strange musical sounds bounced off the walls. A spherical counter made of a transparent material circled the room. Between the counter and the walls, various bartenders, waiters, and cooks took orders and prepared food and drinks. In the center of the room, people danced alone, in couples, or in larger groups.

I found an empty stool and took everything in.

"Sir, what would you like?" asked a Rennan bartender in Lostai. Rennans were required to speak what they called the Imperial Language.

Other than the occasional glass of wine with dinner, I had not consumed alcohol since the binge after my first mission to Tormix. Back then, I allowed crew members to order for me. Here, a wide variety of spirits were available from across the sector. At a loss for what to select, I scanned the room and turned back to the bartender.

"Do you ever have any Arandan customers?"

"Not many, but we do have one wealthy Arandan who comes here every so often with his business partner."

"Do you remember what he usually orders?"

"Oh, yes. He orders shots of *stampu*. Would you like to try one?"

I recalled my father sharing shots of a strong liquor with friends.

"Yes, please."

"And if you have an appetite, may I suggest the meat pies? I have heard my Arandan customer mention they remind him of the Arandan version."

"OK, that sounds good."

By my third shot, people were bumping into each other on the dance floor, and bartenders struggled to keep up with the bustling crowd.

"Excuse me, would you mind if I squeezed in to place my order?"

Distracted by the variety of people, some behaving wildly, I had not noticed the attractive Fronidian female approach.

I guessed she was ten revolutions my senior. Her outfit consisted of a narrow, dark wrap-around band that only covered her breasts and a flowing, multi-colored skirt worn low on her hips. A lot of her pale skin was exposed, and I could not help my eyes studying her curves and fit frame. As I imagined what little effort would be needed to get her naked, she placed her hand on my upper thigh. Embarrassed, I shook myself free from the less-than-pristine thoughts.

"Of course. I have been seated for some time. Let me offer you my seat."

The way she eyed me brought back the lusty thoughts.

"Well, if you insist. That is so kind of you."

I stood, and she looked up at me coyly. The bright green pupils popped against her black sclera and reminded me of expensive jewelry.

"Oh, I did not realize how tall you are. My name is Dorinte, and yours?"

"Montor."

"Well, Montor," she said, touching my arm, "how about buying a lady a drink?"

"What will the lady have?"

"Same as you. I have never seen you here before."

"This is my first time."

She licked her lips and let the tip of her tongue linger at the corner of her mouth before offering me a big smile.

"I thought so. I come here often and would have remembered seeing you."

I called over the waiter and put in her order. In the meantime, she asked, "So, what brings you here tonight?"

"I just purchased a mansion on a significant tract of land in the Larami Woods. I am getting to know this area."

Her eyes lit up.

"Wow, that is an exclusive area. The property must have been very expensive."

I downplayed the cost while already secretly imagining showing off my luxurious home to this sophisticated female. She brought out my innate gregarious personality, normally suppressed during my joyless missions. Ever since I arrived on Xixsted, only Kaya could sometimes bring out my true character.

"A bit, but I can afford it. A river and waterfalls border my property. I enjoy the outdoors. The woods call to me. I was recently promoted to lieutenant in charge of a Lostai military squadron stationed at a science station on Xixsted. They encourage a comfortable lifestyle for soldiers."

"Wow, so young and already in charge of a squadron, but I am not surprised you are a soldier," she said while giving my biceps a squeeze. "However, I would not have imagined an Arandan in the Lostai army."

"It is a complicated story."

She must have noticed something in my expression because she dismissed her previous observation with the wave of her hand. "Well, the Lostai Empire is expanding more and more these days. I guess it makes sense they would eventually incorporate other races into their military."

I changed the subject by asking what she did for a living.

"I am a doctor specializing in female reproductive system disorders."

"I see," I replied, realizing this confirmed she was much older than me.

"So, how old are you, Montor?"

Did she guess my thoughts?

"I recently became of age." At a loss of where to take the conversation next, I asked, "Umm, have you come across any Arandans here before?"

"Only one. He is a wealthy businessman."

"Oh, it must be the same one the bartender mentioned to me."

"Probably. He owns various establishments across the sector, but on Renna One he is known for the venue he co-owns with his Fronidian business associate. It is called Members Only."

"Really? I would like to visit that place." I pulled out my tablet. "Let me find the location codes."

She tapped my hand.

"Do not bother to look it up. It is a selective and secretive club, not open to the general public. You have to be invited to join. The property is by a large lake. The Arandan treated the water with a mineral that changed its color to red. From my apartment balcony, I can see it in the distance." She met my eyes and held me captive. "Would you like to see it?"

The *stampu* and my hormones conspired to make me want to follow her wherever she suggested. My swagger kicked in, not knowing I was way out of my league. I puffed my chest.

"I like that idea. Should we go in my transport pod?"

"No need. I live within walking distance from here."

"Excellent."

I settled the bill, and we walked out together. A group of Fronidian females who were entering Zamandi's Room stopped to greet Dorinte. She explained we were going to her apartment to see the red lake. Her friends looked me up and down and smiled approvingly. They spoke with each other in hushed tones before giggling loudly. Suddenly, I felt like prey.

33

———————

Once Dorinte linked her arm with mine, any misgivings vanished, and we strolled down the avenue like old friends.

"I would never have thought you were so young. I mean, let us be honest. You have the body of a seasoned warrior, but also, I find you intelligent and mature."

I ate up the compliments.

"Well, I perform a rigorous daily workout, my work in the military takes me across the sector, and I excelled in all my academics."

She patted my arm.

"I bet you did."

We continued walking down the street, talking about random topics from current events to the strange music at Zamandi's Room. I even made her laugh by telling jokes about Menel's shiny bald head. She lived in a high rise building in a tenth-floor apartment. My research in real estate informed me the neighborhood was upscale and exclusive.

"Welcome to my humble home."

Her apartment was anything but humble. She gave me a

quick tour. First, we walked through three gigantic guest bedrooms, each with their own body care room, a sitting area, a holographic recreational area, a recycler, and a disposal unit. The kitchen accommodated both a reproducer and modern appliances for homemade food preparation, as well as its own recycler and disposal units. There was a separate resting and holographic room. She left the luxurious master bedroom for last. I noticed the large spa tub and wondered if we might use it later in the evening.

"What do you think?"

I was honest.

"From what I have learned lately about real estate and decor, this is an expensive and tasteful residence."

"Oh, thank you. You are too sweet. Come to the balcony so I can show you what I promised."

I followed her to the spacious balcony furnished with two sofas and two side chairs. My eyes followed to where she pointed. Sure enough, the two bright Rennan moons illuminated a red body of water bordered on one side by woods and on the other side by a large building.

"Wow, that is beautiful."

"How long has it been since you last visited Aranda?"

I inclined my head and sighed.

"Since I was a young child, but I remember it well."

"Oh, I think I have made you sad. Let us go to the holographic room and simulate the luminescent jeweled hills of planet Scarmoro."

She led me into the holographic room and activated a simulation of a porch facing a mountain range covered in transparent colored rocks. We sat on a sofa and observed yellow moonlight shimmering over the hills in the distance, causing a breathtaking combination of flickering light and color.

"What do you think, Montor?"

"I have never seen anything like it. It is amazing."

"Stay here. Let me get us some cocktails."

She brought the drinks and turned on some relaxing music. We sat in silence until the alcohol helped me remember I was alone with an attractive female who seemed interested in me. The alcohol also reminded me of my inexperience and made me too candid. I turned towards her and shook my head.

"I am sorry, Dorinte. I should have never come here."

She squeezed my hand.

"Why, Montor?"

I avoided her eyes.

"I have no experience with females."

"Do you like females?"

"Yes."

"Well, I like you, Montor, so let us forget about your experience or lack thereof and just enjoy each other's company." She grabbed my hand and sucked on my index finger. "Something tells me what you lack in experience, you will make up for in other ways."

I caressed her cheek with the back of my hand. She took hold of that hand as it grazed her chin and guided it down to her breast. I slipped a few fingers under the fabric of her top. Her voice turned silky.

"I met some Arandan students on Fronidia some time ago. It is curious to me you have your fingernails neatly filed down. Most leave their nails long. I like the way you have yours. It must be a new trend for the younger generation of Arandans." She looked into my eyes. "If you want to explore more, go ahead."

My large hand easily surrounded her breast. Instinct kicked in. I fondled it, and she sighed deeply. I moved my hand to the other breast and grunted as my erection protested against my tight-fitting pants. She shut her eyes and tossed her head back.

"What would you like to do now, Montor?" she whispered.

"I would like to taste them."

"Yes, I would like that, too."

Given my height, kneeling on the floor in front of her made sense to me. I pulled down the band to expose her breasts and leaned in. She slid both hands behind my head and pulled me against her body. Her skin smelled of flowers and fruit. Euphoria kicked in and licking her breasts and tummy morphed into biting. Her body tensed up as she pushed me away.

"Oww! Be careful, Montor. That hurts."

My face flushed with embarrassment.

"I am so sorry. Should I stop?" I said, flustered.

"No, no, Montor. Relax. You are just a little excited. Let me guide you."

She led my hand to the edge of her skirt. I pulled it down and found she wore nothing underneath. She yanked out her legs and tossed the skirt to the side. Spreading her legs, she bent her knees, brought her feet up on the edge of the sofa, and whispered, "Go further down, Montor."

This gave me full view of her genitals, which differed from the pictures I had seen of Arandan females. What struck my attention most was the tiny protrusion hanging that looked like a mini penis. She touched herself there and giggled.

"I know, I know. We Fronidian females look a bit different. The clitoris is larger, plus besides the typical birth canal, we have another opening for pleasure only, and all of them are full of nerve bundles. So, there are a lot of ways you can make me happy, Montor."

This was about to spoil the moment as I could not help but be flabbergasted at her graphic display and detailed explanation. Before I could pull back, she wrapped her legs around my neck, trapping me.

"Keep tasting me, Montor. I promise to return the favor."

The curiosity of what she meant emboldened me. The pornographic Arandan films I watched involved a lot of licking and mouthing, so it made sense to me. I reached around and, remembering to exercise restraint, squeezed her butt with both hands to bring her body even closer to my face. Afraid to hurt her, I barely touched the oversized clitoris with the tip of my tongue. Now fully erect, it swelled to about the size of a third of my smallest finger.

"Oh, yes, Montor. That is good, but do not be so afraid of it."

Her laugh embarrassed me again.

What to do next?

"Dorinte, I have a secret to share. If you give me permission, I can read your mind and know exactly what you like and want me to do."

"Oh, Montor, by all means. You see, I knew you were something special. You have my permission."

Her mind was an open book of requests and specific desires involving my mouth, tongue, and fingers I did my best to fulfill, but things did not go smoothly at first.

"Montor, stop, stop. You are doing that too fast and roughly." Mortified at my missteps, I came to an abrupt stop. She grabbed my hand and slowed me down. "Yes, yes, that is better."

Soon, her moans and shouts filled the room, a boost to my ego. I enjoyed pleasuring her, but now I feared I would lose control and finish before I even started. Finally, she asked me to carry her to bed. Once there, she ordered me to remove my clothes as she watched intently.

"Montor, I must say, you are a very handsome young male." I got on the bed beside her, and she wasted no time grabbing and stroking my fully erect penis. "Oh really, you are such a gift, but with you being so young and this being your first time, I better hurry. Next time, we will take it slow. Lay back."

I was not sure what she meant or what to expect. She moved fast to mount me.

Another surprise.

The Arandan videos I watched showed the females face-down and the males entering from behind. For sure, I never expected her to be the one doing the dominating.

No matter.

My brain exploded with pleasure as she pushed her body on to me and I penetrated her. It felt amazing as she moved her body up and down. I grabbed her by the hips and assisted her to move more vigorously.

"Oh, yes, yes, Montor, that is great. Keep doing that."

I think she wanted it to last longer, but I could not stop myself from coming within seconds. She toppled off me and caressed my cheek.

"How did that feel, Montor?"

I had to catch my breath before I could answer.

"So good."

She laughed.

"To be honest, that was a bit quick for me, but do not worry. I am sure we will do it a few more times before sunrise. And I intend to keep my promise." She pointed to her mouth. "That big fat cock of yours is going in here next."

My jaw dropped.

Are all females this forward?

Patting my abs, she said, "Get some rest, big boy."

She was right. After a nap, I was ready for another round. This time, I controlled my pace better, and she praised me for my improvement.

"Oh, Montor, you are surely on your way to becoming a heartbreaker. That was very good."

The next morning, over breakfast, she lectured me about birth control and protection. I attempted to appear worldly.

"I know about that."

"So, why do you not carry it with you? I have taken matters into my own hands, so you are safe with me, but not everyone is so careful."

"Thank you. I will be more mindful."

We enjoyed each other so well that I stayed over for three more nights. She was on vacation, with plenty of free time. We made love in every room and nook of her apartment and tried every position. She even agreed to do it Arandan-style. There was no spot on each other's bodies left unexplored. I arrived at her apartment a teenager and left an adult.

I explained I would soon leave Renna One to take care of a personal matter. She held both my hands as I promised to contact her upon my return. Hers were warm and inviting, making me think for a moment that perhaps I should stay another night. Then she let them go, and I knew it was time to leave.

"I look forward to it, Montor. Stay safe."

34

———

I stopped by Xixsted to see Kaya before I left for the Tormix labor camp.

She cocked her head when we exchanged salutations. "You seem different."

I preferred not to get into details but still wanted to share I was, in fact, different.

"I met someone on Renna One. We spent some time together. She is a doctor."

"She, huh? Hmm, with the wide smile you are sporting, clearly you enjoyed yourself."

I inclined my head, afraid my eyes might share too much. Her knowing look and chuckle in my mind signaled she already had figured enough out.

"Montor, remember the advice I gave you about your dealings with females."

"Yes, yes, of course. By the way, I am leaving for Tormix tomorrow to get my foster parents out of that horrible place."

Kaya advised I prepare for the powerful emotions I would surely feel arriving at the place where I lost my entire family. She suggested extra meditation.

"May The Farthest Light guide you, Montor. I hope everything goes as you wish."

I landed my shuttle on the labor camp spaceport. An elevated moving walkway connected the spaceport to the warden's office inside the cave. He was expecting me. A full-face helmet hid my identity. I greeted the warden with a Lostai military salute.

He reciprocated and said, "Commander Zorla explained you would be coming. He tells me you are an Arandan. I have not shared that information with my supervisors. Frankly, I am surprised they would send an Arandan to inspect a labor camp filled with Arandan slaves."

"Who better? I speak their language and can gain their confidence."

"And are you not conflicted?"

"I have grown up on a Lostai science station among Lostai soldiers. These people mean nothing to me."

"Well, I hear Zorla runs Xixsted station with an iron hand. He told me he has utmost confidence in you, so go and conduct your investigation. Let me know if you need anything."

"Thank you. I should not cause too much disruption and will not take long to complete my job here."

The warden informed his supervisors to expect me. We nodded to each other, and I took the elevator down to the base of the cave. Every nerve in my body was on end as I walked through the main operations area. My helmet concealed my race, but the Lostai personnel knew from my height and build that I was not one of them and stared at me. I boldly stared back, trying to remember any of them from my time there. After seven revolutions, I was not the scared child who first arrived at that place. I now stood at least three heads taller than all the filthy Lostai there.

Chatter from the prison cells filled with Arandan children brought me back to the present time and threatened to break my resolve. I took a moment to center myself and combat the nausea.

No matter how sick I feel, I cannot break character.

Summoning up all my swagger, I entered the tunnel system. The supervisors all nodded at me in deference as I walked through like I owned the place. Since I left the labor camp before being old enough to work, I had never seen the tunnels. Even for someone like me, who came from a tropical environment, the heat and thick air made it difficult to breathe. I resolved to start off searching the areas of the tunnel I could walk through, hoping Lasarta and Foxor were not in the constricted spaces that would require them to crawl on their hands and knees. An elderly worker wiped his brow and accidentally dropped his tool. A supervisor shoved him hard against the wall.

"Stop trying to get free break time, slave," shouted the supervisor.

My body shuddered as I suppressed the desire to kill the supervisor with my bare hands.

You knew this would be hard. Ignore it.

I continued my trek through the tunnels, occasionally stopping to ask both supervisors and laborers meaningless questions about the mining process.

Not until the early afternoon did I find them working side by side. The helmet had been a good idea. It hid the tears flooding my eyes.

"You two, come with me," I ordered and gestured for them to follow. Once we were out of earshot of the other workers, I lowered my tone.

"Do not react in any way."

Lasarta looked up at me with widened eyes.

Could she have possibly recognized my voice? It is so deep compared to the child I once was.

"Lasarta, Foxor, it is me, Montor," I whispered. "As I promised long ago, I have come to take you out of this forsaken place."

"Montor!"

"Shhh...follow my lead. I am going to pretend I am arresting you."

I grabbed them each by an arm and roughly pulled them through the tunnel. A supervisor stopped me.

"Hey! What are you doing?"

"I have learned these two are part of a rebel cell here conspiring to escape."

"Be careful what you believe. These low-class people will sell each other out for a loaf of bread."

I imagined slamming my fist down his throat but once again summoned self-control.

"I know, but I want to question them further. There must be some reason the others have singled them out."

I brought Lasarta and Foxor before the warden.

"I am taking this couple off the planet and back to Xixsted for further questioning. It is possible they may not return," I said in a menacing tone.

"I think not!" the warden protested. "I will deal with them here."

Time to access his mind.

"If you do not let me take them, your little operation here will soon be swarming with investigators sent by your chain of command. I can deal with the problem quietly and efficiently. I will let you know of anything else I learn."

I barely contained a chuckle as his eyes glazed over, his mind a slave to mine.

"OK, OK. I...I guess that makes more sense."

"Thank you, sir."

After a quick salute, I placed Lasarta and Foxor in cuffs and shoved them forward, leading them to my shuttle. Inside, I kept them restrained in case any other Lostai law enforcement or military intercepted us as we left the planet's boundaries. Once we safely exited the Tormixian atmosphere, I turned on the autopilot, setting the destination for Renna One, removed my helmet, and uncuffed them. Lasarta hugged me as if I were a child. Her body shook as she sobbed long and hard. Finally able to release my emotions, I openly cried with her. After Foxor let Lasarta have her time with me, he placed both hands on my shoulders and looked up at me.

"Look at you, Montor. You remind me so much of your father."

I lowered my eyes.

"I am so sorry you have to see me dressed in this filthy uniform."

He squeezed my shoulders tighter.

"Clothes do not make the person. I am happy you have found a way not only to survive but to gain the Lostai's respect."

"I have purchased some beautiful property on Renna One with a cottage perfect for you and Lasarta."

"I thought we would be returning to Aranda," said Lasarta.

"There is a lot of fighting happening there among different Arandan factions, as well as skirmishes between rebels and Lostai military. I cannot keep you safe there."

"But we might be able to connect with people we know. What are Foxor and I going to do on a foreign planet?"

Her patriotic heart ached to be back home. Foxor surely felt the same but was always more discreet with his thoughts.

Taking Lasarta's hand in mine, I replied, "It is too dangerous. I cannot risk losing you again. I will be away often and will need your help to maintain my home and land."

"OK, Montor. You are right."

During our trip to Renna One, we spent hours telling each

other stories of what had transpired during the past seven revolutions. Lasarta broke down and wept often as I filled them in on everything I went through on Xixsted. They told me of all the friends they lost at the labor camp.

"In all fairness, I think we have survived because this latest warden was not as cruel as the previous ones," said Foxor.

"As I stand in front of you now, I pledge you will never have to endure that kind of hardship ever again," I replied.

It was midday when I brought the shuttle down on my property's private landing pad. We got on a land vehicle I had left parked there, and I gave them a tour of the property.

"Montor, this is spectacular," said Lasarta as she took in the view of cascades, creeks, and lush woods.

"There is a sparkling river on the other side of the property," I said.

I took them to their new home. Lasarta's eyes teared up yet again as she walked through the rooms.

"Montor, this house, the furniture, the décor...it is all so tasteful and cozy. How did you manage all this?"

"I hired an interior designer. Wait till you see my house."

The walk to the mansion took us through manicured gardens. Bushes and flowers of every color and fragrance lined the stone-paved path leading to the front entrance.

"How can you afford all this?" asked Lasarta in a concerned tone.

"As a Lostai soldier, I am paid a good salary and a bonus for each successful mission. My Lostai squadron is usually victorious because of my special abilities. I can take control of people's minds. If I needed to, I could kill them telepathically. And you have seen how I move things with my mind. To be honest, I have become a powerful being."

Lasarta's face scrunched up as if swallowing a bitter pill. "I worry, Montor, at what cost have you achieved all this power and wealth?"

"My Lostai commander trusts me. I made only one request, which he agreed to. I do not go on missions to Aranda or involving Arandans."

Foxor, ever the diplomatic one, tried to turn to lighter matters as we entered the house.

"We should make a nice home-cooked meal to celebrate the wonderful thing you have done for us, Montor. Do you have any livestock in the stables we passed by?"

"Yes, I have a suckling boar, fowl, and eggs. The greenhouse has only recently been seeded, but I purchased some vegetables and other staples. Here, let me take you to the pantry."

"Where are the refrigeration and cooking units?" asked Lasarta.

I pressed my hand on what appeared to be a decorative tile. The wall opened to reveal a food preparation area and a variety of kitchen appliances.

"Wow, so fancy and modern," said Foxor, with a nod of approval.

"But before we prepare the meal, take a long warm shower and change into the clean clothes I have made ready for you. There are five body care rooms in this house." Lasarta looked me up and down, as my mother would have. I knew what she was thinking without having to read her mind. "I will also change out of this filthy uniform," I added.

"That sounds great," said Lasarta.

35

I took another week off to help get Foxor and Lasarta settled in and install a security system around my property, shielding even the airspace above the area. Foxor took care of the livestock and fished in the river. Lasarta tended to the gardens and the greenhouse. Initially, I was going to hire staff to take care of these things. They had toiled enough in the labor camp and should be catered to. Of course, they protested.

"What will we do all day?" asked Lasarta.

"It will be like living in paradise for us to do these things and prepare the meals we have missed for so long," added Foxor.

"OK, I will pay you a salary," I said. "Also, I do not want you to feel like prisoners here. Go out and visit the area. This city has many fancy shops and interesting venues, but when you leave the premises, have the security droids accompany you for safety."

I also brought in droids to maintain the grounds and do the housekeeping.

Before I returned to Xixsted, I met up with Dorinte. She was so happy to see me, she greeted me naked at the door.

"Hi, Montor," she said, sliding her hand over her hip.

Seconds later, we were in her bed. She ripped my clothes off like a maniac. Her hands ran up and down my body, claiming me like her favorite toy.

She squeezed.

She massaged.

She scratched.

She bit.

"Oh, Montor, I could swear you are even bigger than last time."

She ran her tongue over my testicles before taking my erection in her mouth.

After a while, she invited one of her girlfriends over to join us.

"Montor, we can invite another male if you like."

"Err...no, I would rather not."

After her friend left, I took Dorinte out to dinner. Although having them both in bed with me at the same time was fun enough, it left me feeling hollow.

"Dorinte, forgive me for my lack of experience or sophistication, but the next time we are in bed together, I really wish it were only you and me."

"Of course, my Arandan warrior," she said, running her hands over my locks. "How sweet. You are paying me the highest compliment."

Our relationship continued over several lunar cycles. During that time, I went on short expeditions within the sector. Most were reconnaissance and intel-gathering assignments that did not leave me as depressed as the mission on Tormix. While I was away, I would call her often. Our chats distracted me from the drudgery of my job. Upon my return, I rushed to visit her.

After the fifth expedition, I brought her over to my house. I was wary of letting anyone know Foxor and Lasarta were my foster parents. My dealings with Zorla taught me my loved ones could represent a weakness any enemy could exploit. I introduced them to Dorinte as friends of my parents, hired to help me maintain my property. Lasarta was not talkative during dinner, but the next time we were alone, she let me know what was on her mind.

"Montor, that female does not feel like a good match for you. You only recently became of age, and she is...well, she is too old. I am afraid you may get your heart broken."

"Are you kidding? She is crazy about me," I said.

Foxor chuckled.

"She is crazy about something," replied Lasarta, while giving Foxor a nasty look.

I caressed Lasarta's cheek.

"I know you worry about me, Lasarta, but I will be OK."

When I set out on my sixth mission, I assured Dorinte I would be back in one lunar cycle. Instead, it dragged out longer than expected due to a well-organized insurgency formed on Hevrra, a planet recently annexed to the Lostai Empire. Located within the Soma Quadrant, just outside the Arandan star system, Zorla volunteered us to investigate. Every successful mission meant more prestige for him and more income for all of us. He jumped at every opportunity to engage the squadrons under his command.

With feline-like facial features and elongated pupils, the natives of planet Hevrra bore some resemblance to Arandans. Except for rare mutations, Arandan eyes were bright yellow. Hevrran eyes were green, gold, or light brown. Their small roundish faces did not have our larger, more pronounced bone structure, but the females sported bodies as statuesque as any Arandan.

Hevrrans were divided on whether they wanted to be a part of the Lostai Empire. The provinces that accepted Lostai rule were prosperous with busy cities and quaint townships. Those who fought against Lostai rule struggled.

Four inhabited moons orbited Hevrra, and Lostai military intelligence believed the insurgency had camps on some of them. Our investigation required visiting several cities and all four moons. We spent four lunar cycles there. Every twelve days, we took two rest days. For recreation, I visited the cities aligned with the Lostai Empire and enjoyed the nightlife, attending sports events and other venues. It became harder to remember to call Dorinte as the females swarmed me. Over the course of our time on Hevrra, I enjoyed brief romantic flings with some of them.

When I returned to Renna One, remorse plagued me for my infidelities.

I have behaved like an adulterous scoundrel.

Over breakfast after a passionate evening with Dorinte, guilt forced me to reveal my sin.

"Dorinte, I have a confession to make."

"A confession? OK, tell me," she asked, popping a piece of fruit in her mouth.

I shifted in my chair and steadied myself.

"I am sorry for not calling you more often while I was away on this past mission."

She waved her hand dismissively.

"Oh, no worries."

"I have something else I feel guilty about."

I did not perceive any consternation in her eyes.

"OK. What is it?"

"I was not faithful while I was out there. I am so sorry. It will not happen again."

Her laughter marked the true end of my innocence. She slapped me on the thigh in a good-natured manner.

"Do not be so silly, Montor. I was not expecting you to practice abstinence while you were away."

I looked into her eyes and was so embarrassed when I saw her candid confusion.

"Did you think I would be upset?" She cocked her head. "Wait. Do you think I have been alone all this time?"

I stood and bit my lip to hide my feelings.

"I am so naïve, right?"

She gaped at me.

"Oh, Montor, it is I who needs to apologize. I think I gave you the wrong impression."

I wanted to disappear and sulk alone in some corner.

"No problem. I need to get back home."

She messaged me twice the next day.

I never called back or visited her again.

A few days later, Zorla contacted me and requested my prompt return to Xixsted.

"I have a special assignment for you and Kaya."

I met with Kaya first before heading to Zorla's office.

"Kaya, any idea what Zorla has in mind?"

"I believe so. They are holding a new prisoner in the dorm next to mine. I guess I have a new student."

"Have you seen the person?"

"Not yet."

"OK, let us see what Zorla has in store for us."

Zorla's droid assistant let us in and offered to get us refreshments.

"Please sit," said Zorla. "Montor, I want to congratulate you on your recent mission on Hevrra. As a result of your diligent investigation and arrests, we have squashed their pathetic rebel movement."

I inclined my head politely at his compliment, although my insides churned.

"I have called you in because we have acquired a new specimen with Sotkari Ta embedded genes. Do you know I studied psychology before joining the military? I think it has once again served me well."

I am sure Kaya was controlling the urge to roll her eyes as much as I was.

"I believe the training of this subject will need a two-pronged approach," Zorla continued. "Kaya was a perfect mentor for you, Montor, because we brought you in at such a young age. I was smart to heed her advice on how to train you. She probably represented a motherly figure for you."

Again, my stomach flipped. The last thing either Kaya or I needed was for Zorla to believe there was a strong bond between us.

"But I think we need to deal differently with the new trainee," continued Zorla. "He is a teenaged male from a faraway galaxy. The natives call the planet Earth. A backwards place, whose people have not even conquered space travel farther than their nearest neighboring planet. He has been defiant, and we put the wristband on him because he tried to escape."

This poor hostage is already learning about Lostai brutality.

"What is your plan for him, sir?" I asked.

"Before taking him, I ordered we conduct some surveillance. The report showed this subject spent a lot of time with other male youths his age engaged in what appeared to be destructive and violent behavior. We saw the group he ran with fighting against another group of young males and destroying property. Each youth wore insignias on their clothing and skin markings identifying them as members of their group. His older brother was the gang leader and they appeared to be very close. I think after breaking him in, he would benefit from a brother-like figure and would get acclimated to the bonding that occurs between soldiers within a squadron. He is the equivalent of someone one or two revolutions younger than you, Montor. I think you could be that person for him."

"So, you want me to train him?"

"With the many missions I have slated for our squadrons and for you in particular, I do not think you will have the time to fully train him. Kaya will do most of the Sotkari Ta training, but his behavior so far makes it clear to me you will need to beat him into submission first. Then take him under your wing. Protect him from the other cadets. I want you to win his loyalty. You will watch over his military training and make sure he is motivated to master the Sotkari Ta lessons Kaya will be teaching him. He will not follow the typical cadet curriculum. I want him on an accelerated training schedule so you can take him on missions as your apprentice as soon as possible. I am forwarding the translation application to your tablet, Montor, so you can communicate with him."

Kaya and I acknowledged these orders and left Zorla's office to meet our new trainee. The idea of playing the role of someone's older brother felt weird to me. I was the youngest son, often teased by my older siblings but also protected by them. The closest thing to being like an older brother was how I watched over my twin sister.

Remember, Montor, this potential new relationship is not real. The only people you can trust are Kaya, Foxor, and Lasarta. This is just another job you are doing for Zorla.

36

The guards had locked the new prisoner in his quarters.

"Kaya, stand behind me."

When we entered the room, he charged at us. I used my telekinetic abilities to stop him in his tracks. I could see why he gave the Lostai some trouble. At only a head shorter than me, he was tall, especially compared to the short Lostai. His forearm was bloodied from the wristband burns. I activated the translation application, but the words he shouted confused me.

"What the *mate* did you do to me, you ugly *mothermater*?"

The way he glared and snarled his words made it clear he was using expletives or offensive language that the Lostai translator was having trouble with.

"Kaya, leave us. There is nothing you can do while he is in this mode. This might get ugly, and I do not want you to witness it."

She left, and I approached him. He was still under my power and frozen in place. I looked him over. He could have passed for a Sotkari except his skin was cream-colored instead of grey and his pupils and hair were dark brown, almost black. Also, the whites of his eyes were much more visible.

"Listen here, bad attitude will get you nowhere. My name is Montor. What is yours?"

"*Mate* you! Is your mother as ugly as you are?"

The mention of my mother was the excuse I needed to punch him in the face.

He took it well and spit out blood.

"I do not give an *excrement* what you do to me! What do you want with me, you *mothermater*?"

"If you do not remain silent so I can explain everything to you, I will beat you unconscious and come again later. We can go through as many cycles of that as you wish."

"You are such a *badass* because you have me frozen here. Otherwise, I would kick your ass."

I could not resist the challenge and released him from my telekinetic force. He lunged at me, swinging his fists, which I easily blocked. One front kick from me landed him hard against the wall. Before he could shake it off, I stepped forward and followed with a torrent of strikes and kicks that left him convulsing and moaning on the floor. I grabbed him by the shirt, pulled him to his feet, and stared down at him.

"I said, what is your name?"

He spit at me, earning himself another beating. I gave him zero chance to land even one strike. When I was done, his eyes were swollen shut and his nose bled. I had cracked a couple of his ribs, too.

"I will not kill you. I am going to continue to inflict pain until you pay attention. What is your name?"

Silence.

I readied myself to start the next round.

He raised his hands in surrender.

"OK, OK. My name is Gio Napoletano."

"Good to meet you, Gio Napoletano. Sit on the bed and

listen to me. You are at the Lostai science station Xixsted. The Lostai are the short, bald soldiers who brought you here. They control a good portion of this sector and have captured you because you have alien genes."

His face scrunched in confusion.

"Alien genes?"

"Yes, and these genes give you extraordinary abilities. The Lostai military intends to teach you to harness those abilities and have you join their army."

He laughed, stared at his feet, and shook his head.

"Sure, sure. What special abilities?"

"Like how I stopped you from moving."

He looked up at me.

"I could do that?"

"If you take your training seriously and practice."

"Where is this Xixsted compared to Earth?"

"You are galaxies away from your home world."

"This is some *mating excrement*." He continued to shake his head in disbelief. "When can I go back home?"

"I am not sure you will ever return to your home world. It is unclear to me how the Lostai military can travel so far in such a short time, but I doubt they will ever share that secret."

"What! No way. I cannot stay here for the rest of my *mating* life!"

"You should resign yourself to the idea that you will take your last breath in this galaxy. However, after fifteen revolutions of service with the Lostai military, you will be free to live your life as you please. I should also mention, once you complete your training and become a Lostai soldier, the military will pay you a substantial salary. If you invest wisely, by the end of your tenure, you could be wealthy. I have recently become of age, the equivalent of your nineteen revolutions, have only been a soldier for three revolutions, and I already command a squadron. I own a luxurious home on a vast piece of land on a beautiful planet."

His shoulders slumped as he pressed his head into his hand. I knew he did not have the strength to challenge me again, so I stepped away to the reproducer to get first aid supplies.

"Here, use this on your injuries." I helped him place the healing pad correctly over one eye. "I know how you feel, Gio Napoletano. I was taken from my family and brought here as a child. It was a painful and horrible time for me. I was lonely and scared. Some people here were abusive towards me. Now fully versed in my powers, I have earned their respect. The same can happen for you."

"So, in the meantime, I have to wear this *mating* wristband that burns my *mating* skin off and get beat up by whoever the *mate* feels like it whenever they want."

"If you follow my advice and instructions, I promise to protect you. You will not have to go through all the pain and misery I did. But if you get out of line, what I did to you today will feel like playtime. Gio Napoletano, what do you say?"

He moved the healing pad to the other eye.

"OK, I will do it. I was going to end up in jail eventually, anyway. By the way, you can call me Gio."

Using the healing pad, Gio's injuries were repaired after a few hours. I showed him how to use the reproducer and other controls in the room.

"Get washed up and rest. I have set a wake-up alarm. Be dressed and ready for when I come in the morning. Do not leave this room before I arrive, or the wristband will activate. If you earn my trust, I will have it removed."

Later, I met Kaya for dinner.

"So, what was he like?" she asked.

"Angry, but I think he will do well here."

"Why?"

"I told him about earning a soldier's salary. He did not bother to ask questions about the Lostai, whether they are morally correct, who is in the right in this war...nothing like that."

Her eyes filled with sadness and regret.

"I see what you mean...and I have to train this person," she said.

I placed my hands on her shoulders and shuddered with rage.

"Yes, and I need to act like his big brother."

The next morning, I gave Gio a tablet, explained his schedule, and introduced him to the cadet squadron leader named Terli.

"Lieutenant Terli, this is Gio. He is your newest cadet and has the potential to develop the same special abilities I have. Zorla wants to induct him into the military as soon as possible. You better make sure he is safe here. When I was still an adolescent, the other cadets almost killed me out of spite. I will not tolerate any of that. If I hear he has been treated unfairly, both you and anyone involved will feel my wrath. Understood?"

"Yes, Sir Montor."

"Good."

Zorla was correct about Gio. Already on the first day, I saw the admiration in his eyes as I gave instructions to Terli.

Gio embraced his boot camp with fervor. He never showed any signs of insubordination or complacency. I removed the wristband after one lunar cycle. He relished sparring with me because he viewed the much shorter Lostai as unchallenging. I did not pull any punches, and under my tutelage, soon he became outstanding at hand-to-hand combat and martial arts. He was not at the top of his class in academics or strategy but became proficient in the other aspects of his soldier training. Every so often, I ate dinner with him. The conversation often went the same.

"How am I doing with the training, Montor?"

"Lieutenant Terli tells me you are doing very well."

"Good, I am looking forward to joining you on actual missions."

After I removed Gio's wristband, I determined he was in the right mindset for Kaya to begin his Sotkari Ta training. He soon learned the basics of telepathy and telekinesis, but he did not maintain a religious daily meditation and Sotkari Ta workout routine. I consulted with Zorla regarding using physical violence to coax Gio into being more disciplined with his meditation. Zorla decided it would break the trust and loyalty I had gained from Gio. As a result, Gio's Sotkari Ta abilities lacked finesse and agility. Achieving mind control was impossible without this discipline. He would never attain my level of mastery of Sotkari Ta talents, but Zorla did not seem to mind.

37

After one revolution of boot camp, Gio was ready for his induction tests. By then, he was fluent in Lostai. He did well enough to pass. To celebrate, I took him to Zamandi's Room on Renna One. He ogled both attractive females and males with body shapes similar to ours.

"Thank you for bringing me here, Montor. It is good to get off Xixsted for a change of ambiance."

Gio was a novelty at Zamandi's Room. He was the first of his species any of those present had seen, and it did not take long for people to take notice of him. A gorgeous Rennan female approached us.

"Is it OK if I go dance with her?" Gio asked.

"Sure, go ahead."

They danced for a while. Then she led him away. I was not surprised when, hours later, he returned with a wide smile on his face.

"Well, that was a wild ride."

"I can imagine. I told you this was a fun place."

"What about you, Montor? Do you have a partner?"

My disappointing relationship with Dorinte had left me jaded, so I took care of my sexual needs with loose females and paid escorts, avoiding any emotional connection. My answer to Gio was vague.

"I live a carefree lifestyle, Gio. I have several on each planet I visit."

He lifted his glass and laughed.

"That is the way to do it. Hopefully soon, I will have the same."

Gio turned out to be a good sidekick. Because of his Sotkari Ta telekinetic abilities, I could pair up with him on tactics impossible with the other soldiers in my squadron. Soon after celebrating his induction into the Lostai army under my command, I was ordered to take my squadron to Hevrra to investigate a series of attacks on Lostai interests there. Our first stop was a large town where a Lostai law enforcement office had been set on fire.

I did not want to attract too much attention or endanger my squadron unnecessarily. Instead of marching in with the entire team, I only brought Gio and two other soldiers with me to conduct interrogations. Lostai intel had identified five locals who were suspected of rousing rebellious sentiment. We pulled each of them out of their homes and were escorting them to a nearby courthouse when a mob of rebel sympathizers armed with projectile pistols and rifles surprised us. Dozens of oncoming angry villagers approached us from all directions.

"Gio, take up a back-to-back position with me!" I shouted before calling for reinforcements over the communication system.

While we waited for help to come, Gio and I moved in a circular motion, using our telekinetic abilities to first disarm the line of attackers and then hurl them against the oncoming crowd behind them. The rest of the squadron and local Lostai law enforcement arrived minutes later. We rounded up the villagers in groups of ten and took them to the courthouse.

I sat behind a desk as, one by one, they brought before me the people we had arrested. Gio watched me use mind control to force the prisoners to answer my questions without hesitation.

"What is your name?"

"Lomit Negar."

"Are you a member of an insurgency against the Lostai government?"

"No, sir."

"Why did you attack us?"

"You were taking my friends away."

I gestured to Gio to let the prisoner go and bring me the next. This one struggled against Gio's grip. I took hold of his mind.

Stop struggling and come here.

He walked over, and I interviewed him.

"What is your name?"

"Lomit Jemis."

"Lomit?" Many traditional Hevrrans went by their family names first. I remembered the name of the previous prisoner. "Was that your brother who I just dismissed?"

"Yes."

"Are you a member of an insurgency against the Lostai government?"

"Yes."

"Is he?"

"No."

Gio raised his eyebrows and pursed his lips, impressed at how easy it was for me to get prisoners to confess.

"Who is your leader?"

"Umm, that is him over there," he said, pointing across the

room at another group awaiting their turn. "His name is Hemar Jonet."

Hemar, seeing that he had been ratted out, shouted in disgust, "You back-stabbing coward!"

It took me the rest of the afternoon to interview all the people we had arrested. I took a break after every sixth person to rest my mind. We could have moved quicker if Gio had mind control abilities, but this talent eluded him due to his lack of discipline. Our original task had been to interview and possibly arrest five insurgents. By the end of the day, we had identified more than twenty rebel sympathizers. Zorla personally called me to congratulate us on such successful results.

We celebrated in a nearby city. As usual, Gio indulged in mood-altering drugs and alcoholic beverages. He became even more talkative than usual when under the effects of these spirits. Not aware I already had probed his mind several times and knew his feelings, he used these moments to try to establish a bond between us. I indulged him a bit.

"Montor, it is amazing how you can get prisoners to confess so easily."

"Well, you could have learned how to do that too if you applied yourself a bit more and were more disciplined with your meditation."

"Yes, I know, but it is kind of boring for me, spending a whole hour in silence. I do not know how you can stand it. Anyway, I appreciate you watching out for me. I know you helped me get into your squadron sooner than normal for the average Lostai cadet. I have to say, I am fine with this life."

"I am glad for you, but I sometimes wonder, do you not miss your planet? Did you not leave loved ones behind?" I asked.

"I miss my older brother. He looked out for me..." He leaned in and made eye contact as if trying to emphasize sincerity.

"Like you have. But other than him, not really. I lost my mother as a child and my father was a vicious drunk."

"I see. I lost all my family as a young child, too. You have now experienced a bit of how things are outside of Xixsted. What do you think about the Lostai and their quest to annex more planets to their empire?"

"They seem to be the strongest force in this part of the galaxy, so I am glad to be a part of their military. Montor, I grew up in the streets, where you need to be with the winners to survive. I am no loser."

"Some people might categorize the Lostai methods as cruel."

"Not my problem as long as I get paid. Look how well you have done for yourself so far. That is your attitude, too, right?"

I pressed my fist in my other hand and cracked each knuckle before answering, "Yes, right."

To reward my squadron for our successful mission on Hevrra, Zorla allowed us all some vacation time, but he asked that I first accompany him on a trip. By now, Zorla's superior, an Admiral, had acknowledged his diplomatic accomplishments. It was unclear to me how much the Admiral knew about my contribution to these successes. At this point, he only cared to know the results and not so much the methods. He sent Zorla to a special session of the Semrixian Congress. The Lostai government was formally requesting permission to mine the most distant planet in their star system for a rare energy-producing liquid. Of course, Zorla asked that I come.

The trip to Semrix took two lunar cycles. It was located at the edge of a neighboring sector. I was not particularly pleased in having to spend so much time with Zorla, but it gave us sufficient opportunity to discuss the task at hand.

The Semrixians claimed ownership of the six planets in their star system, but only the first two were inhabited. Their claim was in word only. Distant from their star, the other planets were characterized by freezing temperatures and other inhospitable conditions.

"Commander Zorla, I have read that the Semrixians do not even have the technology to travel to the planet in question, much less to defend against an invasion. Why are we asking them permission to mine there?"

"It is true that Semrix is in no position to stop us from mining on that planet, but another government from the neighboring system has submitted a similar request. We should maintain the appearance of following diplomatic protocols to the other advanced planets in the area. We do not want to engage in a war with a planet that matches us technologically unless necessary."

At the congress, I successfully swayed the decisions of the Semrixian Senate's most influential members. Losta beat out the other planet in gaining mining control of the outermost planet of the Semrixian system.

On our trip back to Xixsted, Zorla praised the accomplishments of my squadron and talked about the addition of Gio to the team.

"Seems like your apprentice is doing well," said Zorla. "Your squadron is gaining notoriety across the quadrant. With a second Sotkari Ta on your team, it seems like there is almost no task impossible for your team to accomplish. It is too bad he does not have your mind control abilities."

"Remember, both Kaya and I tried to teach him, but he does not have the discipline."

"Yes, I know. Truthfully, on second thought, it is probably for the best. I hear he indulges in excessive alcohol and recreational drug use on his off days. I cannot have someone with poor judgment or out of my control wielding that kind of power."

I arrived back at Xixsted to learn that Kaya had become ill with a viral infection. The infirmary doctor gave her medication to kill the infection, but the illness had weakened her. She requested permission to stay with her daughter-in-law and granddaughter on her home planet to recover her strength. Zorla did not have a problem in conceding her request since he did not have a specific task for her at the time, but he made it clear he knew where she and her family lived. She would be required to return immediately whenever he called. Without telling anyone, I took some of my vacation time to visit her and sent an encrypted message letting her know to expect me.

Kaya lived in a rural area of her home province on the planet Sotkar. This was my first visit to her home world, a planet where the flora and fauna popped with bioluminescent colors. I arrived to find Kaya in a rocking chair on her front porch.

"Oh, Montor, it is so nice to see you."

"How are you doing?"

"A lot better. The clean air here and spending time with my family does me well. To be honest, I think I was more mentally weary than physically tired after completing Gio's training."

"Why?"

"Just the guilt of having trained someone with no moral compass."

Her words surprised me.

"Kaya, you trained me, and I have done horrible things in the name of the Lostai Empire."

"Yes, but like me, you have been coerced. It is sad, but I know you do not derive any joy from being a Lostai soldier. Gio, on the other hand, questions nothing. I am glad he lacks the discipline to achieve mind control. I think he has no scruples."

Kaya's daughter-in-law walked out, a tall attractive Sotkari female whose striking light blue eyes appeared even more brilliant against her dark grey skin. Her hair matched the color of her eyes and fell in waves to her shoulders.

"Hello, Montor. My name is Kamona. Kaya has told me so much about you. Would you like some hot sweet tea and pastries?"

"Yes, please."

After she ducked back into the house, I asked Kaya, "Where is your granddaughter?"

"She is in the backyard tending to our flower garden and playing with her canine pet. Those are the only things she truly enjoys. Come with me."

We followed a path around the side of the house leading to the backyard. Her granddaughter sat on the ground planting seedlings, a small pup panting by her side. She appeared to be a teenager and looked much like her mother. She did not acknowledge our arrival.

"She does not seem to have any Sotkari Ta or Pasi abilities but is mute. This seems to be a common issue with offspring of mixed marriages. My son was a Sotkari Ta, but her mother has no evolved abilities. We have taught her Sotkari sign language. Her name is Klarina."

"Can she hear?"

"Oh, yes, she has perfect hearing."

I knelt by her and petted the pup.

"Hi, Klarina. My name is Montor. I am a good friend of your grandmother."

She did not even look my way. Kaya leaned over and caressed her hair. Klarina turned to look at her grandmother and smiled.

"She is shy. I cherish those smiles. Sometimes, she does not acknowledge me either."

"May I offer her a Sotkari salutation?"

"Sure."

I reached over, grasped her forearm, and pressed my thumb against her wrist. I focused on feelings of friendship. Even non-evolved Sotkari transferred energy this way. Her head remained inclined, but she met my eyes through thick, fluttering eyelashes.

"You are a beautiful young female. Is this garden yours?"

Her skin darkened in a blush, and she replied with a quick nod.

I did not want to cause her any more discomfort, so I stood and said, "I will leave you to your work. It was nice meeting you."

Back at the front porch, Kamona had set a tray on the coffee table with tea and snacks. Kaya appeared lost in thought.

"Are you OK, Kaya?"

"I worry about them, Montor. My daughter-in-law has no family left near here. She has lost contact with them. They have been killed or displaced during the Lostai occupation. Her daughter has medical issues requiring constant attention, and we cannot leave her home alone. They are safe because of my salary and agreement with Zorla. He knows where we live. What will happen to them when I am no longer strong enough to serve Zorla's requests or when the Farthest Light claims my spirit? What might Zorla do? How will they survive?"

I placed my hand on her shoulder and said the first thing that came to my mind.

"Do not worry about such things. I pledge to you I will take care of their financial needs and ensure their safety when you no longer can. I have leverage with Zorla now, and I will take over your job if that is necessary for him to leave them alone."

"No, Montor. I cannot burden you with such a responsibility. Once you complete your fifteen-revolution tenure as a Lostai soldier, you should move on and devote yourself to something that truly brings you joy. Maybe start a family of your own. Plus, you have your foster parents to take care of."

I took her hands in mine and gazed into her beautiful, old blue eyes.

"Kaya, I can do it all."

38

After our vacation, Zorla called me into his office to discuss my next assignment.

"Montor, despite our best efforts to keep the peace on Memrana, rebellious factions have cropped up again. They have not honored the treaties we agreed to in good faith."

Good faith was the last thing the Lostai government had in mind when they enacted those agreements. It had just been a pretense to eventually take over the planet as they had done many times before. I hoped my thoughts were not creeping into my expression.

Zorla steepled his hands as he often did to give the appearance of careful deliberation.

"The time has come to deal with them with a firmer hand. We also have discovered that several areas of that planet are ripe with a variety of natural resources we can use to fuel our ships in the area."

Of course you have.

"I have volunteered your squadron to join with five others to attend to Lostai interests there. For purposes of this mission, all squadron leaders, including you, will report to a commander on the ground named Dermox. I have let Commander Dermox know about your special abilities, but it is up to him to decide how to use his resources. Still, I will be in constant communication with him to stay apprised of how things are going there. I hope your squadron makes us proud. A successful mission there will earn us all a nice bonus. You will head out tomorrow."

Bastard.

My squadron arrived just in time to join the other troops as they planned to invade a town near an underground excavation where a metallic element called *sterneo* was discovered. After treatment, *sterneo* became an efficient energy source.

Commander Dermox called a meeting with all the squadron leaders to discuss our orders.

"Lieutenants, these people have violated all the rules they agreed to under a valid treaty. It is now time for a strong-armed approach. The townspeople will work the excavation site. We will allow them to remain in their homes, but anyone who resists working for us will be killed."

How nice of us to let them stay in their homes.

"Will any Memranan armed forces come to defend the town?" asked one of the soldiers.

"This place is isolated. Memranans only have ancient land vehicles and sea ships. It will take their central government several weeks to get any troops here. If they finally arrive, we will easily overpower them with our sophisticated weaponry."

I raised my hand to request permission to speak.

"Go ahead, Lieutenant Montor."

"Sir, in past missions, my superiors have seen fit to use my mental abilities to ease our targets into submission. If I convince their elders and governmental leaders to follow instructions, the rest will probably fall in line. A lot of lives can be saved."

"Commander Zorla informed me about your abilities, and I

have heard of your squadron's successful missions across the sector. I do appreciate the offer, but we need to show these people that we are in charge." Arrogance crept into his expression. "I will certainly use your abilities in combat or interrogations, but we have no need to use trickery to get these primitive people to obey."

Primitive people. That is what they consider Arandans, too.

He intended to break these people into submission just like the Lostai did to my family and neighbors.

We rode into the city on several land combat vehicles, heading straight for the mayor's mansion. At first, people outside observed with curiosity, but when they saw us exit the vehicles, outfitted in military uniforms and combat gear, they knew this was no casual visit.

Commander Dermox, accompanied by one of the squadrons, strolled to the guards posted at the entrance of the mayor's mansion with a translation device in his hands. My squadron stood further back. Some people began to congregate around our combat vehicles. I clenched my jaw, hoping to maintain a stone face while hyperaware of how this situation could quickly escalate into bloodshed.

There was some exchange between Dermox and one of the guards. From where I stood, I could not hear. The guard glanced to his fellow guard on the other side of the entrance and then scanned the area. He knew it would be a lost cause to resist, but Dermox had been too cocky in presenting himself instead of sending one of his lieutenants.

The guard made a split-second decision to grab Dermox, his weapon pressed against Dermox's head. A Lostai soldier quickly took out the other guard by decapitating him with his phaser.

Everyone froze.

Lostai soldiers behind my squadron trained their guns on the people gathering around us. The ever-growing crowd let out a collective gasp. Gio and the other soldiers in my squadron met my eyes. They knew I could deescalate the situation in a heartbeat.

I approached the mansion entrance and contacted Dermox on our communication system, the earbuds allowing him to hear me despite being restrained. "Sir, I can help by rendering the guard unconscious and moving some of this crowd back if you give me the order."

"Unconscious? I want him dead," replied Dermox, angry to have let himself be caught in this predicament. "Montor, did you hear me? Do it!"

Before the guard could figure out what Dermox was shouting in Lostai, with a heavy heart, I focused on the guard's mind and severed the connection between his brain and heart. He dropped, lifeless. I turned to face the crowd and used telekinesis to hurl those closest to us into the throng behind them. People fell hard to the ground or on top of each other. Dermox shouted orders over the communication system.

"Montor, I want your squadron to join me as I talk to the mayor. Squadrons three, four, and five, disperse the crowd. Patrol the streets and visit all the households. Tell everyone that we have imposed martial law, and everyone is to remain in their homes until further notice. Shoot anyone who does not comply."

The soldiers seemed to have been waiting with bated breath for such an order. I heard phaser fire and people screaming.

Do not look back. It will only make you feel worse.

My squadron joined the first one to accompany Dermox into the mayor's mansion. As we marched forward, we were met by several more guards. Dermox did not even give them a chance to surrender.

"Kill them," he ordered.

Our two squadrons outnumbered the mayor's guards, and

their projectile bullets could not compete with our energy-based weapons. When the rest of us stormed the mayor's office, we found he had his oldest son with him, apparently working there as an apprentice. Once Dermox threatened to kill the boy, we easily took control of the mansion. Dermox sent a few soldiers to search the premises for any unarmed employees and bring them to the mayor's office. I could not bear to look at the boy's terrified expression. Dermox paced around, casually sliding his hand over the wooden furniture, and spoke with an air of superiority.

"A little old-fashioned, but we will make do. This place can accommodate myself and these two squadrons, but the rest of my troops will not fit here. Is there a hotel or inn in this town? If not, your people will need to cede us their homes and build themselves new dwellings," said Dermox, as if it were the most normal thing.

The mayor did not reply.

"Montor, come forward," ordered Dermox.

I hoped no one noticed me swallow hard as I walked over. My body tensed as all eyes set on me.

"Mayor, meet Montor. As you can see, he looks different than the rest of us, but do not be impressed with just his physical strength. He also has certain special abilities and can kill your son with just a look. I suggest you answer my questions with the respect I deserve."

The mayor looked at me with contempt but replied, "Yes, there are two inns. One at the town's entrance and one at the northwestern border."

"Good. Is there a penitentiary or some sort of jail?

"There is a small courthouse two buildings down from here."

Dermox ordered a few of the soldiers to secure the courthouse and take the mayor and his son there to be incarcerated. He looked at the rest of the mayor's employees.

"Take these pieces of crap, too. I am going to tour this place to make a list of what we need to reproduce to be comfortable here."

He kept two soldiers with him and sent the rest of us back to assist the other squadrons. The streets were filled with dead bodies and the stench of burnt flesh. I tried not to look, but it was inevitable that I notice children, females, and elderly were among those slaughtered. The other soldiers walked over the dead like automatons.

Am I the only one trembling?

I must overcome my feelings.

My squadron depends on me.

Within five days, a daily routine was set. All able adults were lined up in the streets at sunrise. The children were left at home with their older siblings or the elderly. We transported them in our land vehicles to the excavation site, where they worked till sunset, at which time they were allowed to return to their homes. I rationalized that their situation was better than what my family lived through at the labor camp.

When the townspeople's pantries emptied, we distributed water, protein bars, and soup to each household. During rest days, we allowed one member of each family to make a trip to their local grocery stores and markets to pick one food item. Scarcity brought out the worst in people. They fought among themselves trying to jump to the front of the lines and get the best pick.

Many of the Lostai soldiers laughed at the brawls at first and then killed whoever did not heed their calls to order. When the markets ran out of stock, we installed a reproducer in each store programmed with basic food and household items. Having access to the reproducer only once every twelve days to get one item soon took its toll.

I watched males and females toiling long hours as their

emaciated bodies wasted away. A quarter of the population died of starvation or exhaustion.

This is what my family went through, but at least we knew how to hunt and harvest in the woods.

These people neither knew how to fend for themselves nor were allowed outside of the town's border.

Against my better judgment, I discussed the lack of food with Dermox.

"Commander, if we feed these people better, maybe they will be more productive, and we can be out of here sooner."

He tilted his head, looking up at me, his eyes boring into mine, as if trying to get a handle on my motivations.

"I hope you are not feeling compassion for these people, Montor. They brought this on themselves. We offered them protection, and they paid us back with rebellious behavior. But at least we were kind enough to introduce them to a reproducer. Maybe in the near future, they can learn how to construct one. Anyway, we are almost done here."

I pushed down the aggression that boiled up in me. He deserved to get that smug expression punched off his face, but all I could do was nod and walk away.

At the end of five lunar cycles, all the *sterneo* had been extracted. No army ever came to defend the town. I looked forward to a break. Despite increasing my meditation time, I felt emotionally drained. Instead of heading home, we were called to another town invasion assignment near a mining site. It was not until we completed three similar missions that we were allowed a vacation.

We traveled to Renna One for some down time. Our first stop was Zamandi's Room. My fellow soldiers reveled in their vacation time, while I wished I could just crawl in a hole. Instead, I walked into Zamandi's Room like I owned the place.

The owner had purchased the neighboring parcels of land and added more rooms and courtyards to his business, each one with a unique ambiance. His business was more successful than ever. Still, I always preferred the original bar room.

We arrived at a late hour. Customers swarmed the bar counter.

"Wait here," I said to my squadron.

Itching for a fight to release my stress, I muscled my way through the crowd to reach two tall Hevrrans sitting at the bar's best spot.

"Hey, you two have been sitting here long enough. Get out. We are Lostai soldiers and deserve special treatment."

Did I actually say that?

All I could think of was my need for some kind of physical release. Both Hevrrans stood, one behind me, one in front.

"I only see one of you and two of us." The Hevrran in front looked me up and down and smirked. "Umm, you look much too tall and stupid to pretend to be a Lostai, Arandan. You do not scare us."

I punched him in his face with the full force of my frustration. He fell, dazed. The other one behind me wrapped his arm around my neck, but I quickly elbowed him. He released me, and before he could grab me again, I had already turned around and kneed him in the ribs. Now, they were both on the ground but getting ready to stand and face me again.

I am going to have fun with these two.

Using my telekinetic abilities, I raised them from the ground and hurled them against each other. Laughing, I made them crash hard into each other in midair a few times. Everyone around quieted and stared at the spectacle. Once the Hevrrans were unconscious, I dropped them to the ground in a heap.

"Waiters, get this garbage out of my sight and take my order."

Most of those at the bar cleared the way for my squadron, who sat while hooting and banging the counter in approval. I ordered several rounds for the soldiers. I only had one glass of expensive Arandan brandy that I sipped slowly, lost in my thoughts.

I have not had sex in a long time, but even the expensive escorts are becoming boring, with their fake affections and pretending to hang on my every word. I am a strong, intelligent, powerful warrior. I should not have to pay for the companionship of a sophisticated female. Dorinte had the right idea. No need for commitment to have a good time and some friendship. I am no longer that innocent boy. I know my way around a female's body.

I finished my drink and bid my squadron farewell.

"Where are you going, Montor?" asked Gio.

"To find myself a female."

"Can I come along?"

"Oh, Gio, I am not visiting the brothel. I think I will try my luck elsewhere." I managed a chuckle. "I prefer to prowl alone tonight."

"Well, I wish you luck," said Gio with a smile.

I went home alone that night, but the next day, to distract myself, I visited an ancient art museum on the other side of the city. There, I met a pretty Rennan.

"Are you an art student?" she asked as we both observed a sculpture exhibit.

I guessed she was a few revolutions older than me but not as old as Dorinte. Her dark green skin contrasted with her light pink eyes. She wore tiny ringlet piercings on her forehead ridges, and glossy, straight hair reached halfway down her back. Her body type was different than the typical Arandan or Hevrran female—thicker in the waist and not as curvy around the hips—but her breasts were full and perky, and she stood with confidence.

"No, I am a soldier, but spending the day strolling through the museum seems like something that could get my mind off the violence I have to deal with. This particular display is fascinating to me, but I do not know too much about it."

"Oh, well, let me explain. What is your name?"

"Montor."

"Hello, Montor. My name is Melila. I am a history student. These sculptures date from a time when no other species had set foot yet on this planet. Where do you come from? I have never met someone who looks like you."

"I am from Aranda. It is in this quadrant but in another sector. I believe not too many Arandans come here."

"Interesting. Well, let us talk about the sculptures."

We spent the rest of the afternoon examining the various displays. I asked many questions, and she was an excellent guide. When we had completed our tour of the museum, I invited her to dinner. By the time we were eating dessert, I was holding her hand and gazing into her eyes.

"Melila, I find your smile enchanting."

"Thank you. I enjoy your company, Montor."

"Do you have a mate, Melila?"

"Oh, I travel a lot due to my studies and do not have time right now for a serious relationship." She moved her hand to squeeze mine. "But I would love to see your property in the Larami Woods."

Perfect.

I brought her home and led her to the back deck where waterfalls, soft lighting, tasteful furniture, and an outdoor canopy daybed lent to a relaxing ambiance. She looked around, obviously impressed, as she sipped the cocktail I had prepared.

"Your home is elegant but cozy. I like it," she said.

I turned on soft music, nothing like the frenetic sounds most young people my age listened to.

"Would you like to dance, Melila?"

She placed the glass down and walked into my arms, placing both palms on my chest. I enveloped her in an embrace and showed her how to sway to the music. She relaxed and followed my lead, our bodies touching in a most sensual way.

"Montor, you are so strong. Any female would feel safe in your arms. And yet, there is a certain grace about you."

By the third song, she had reached up to squeeze my shoulders and biceps, her eyes filled with longing.

"Would you like me to stay over, Montor? That bed looks so inviting."

"That would be wonderful," I answered, slowly unfastening the magnetic buttons that ran down the front of her dress.

She sighed deeply as I ran my tongue up and down her neck. In seconds, I disposed of her undergarments and led her to bed.

"Get comfortable, Melila."

I quickly took off my clothes and applied contraceptive before slipping under the covers. This female was a gift: smart, pretty, and so genuine. I would make sure she left satisfied. By then, I knew how to take my time. My hands explored her body and soft skin as I tasted her breasts. Her back arched, and reaching down between my legs to stroke me without shame, she demonstrated she was not inexperienced. A soft moan escaped her lips when I pushed inside her. I slid my hands up her thighs, pushing her legs back so that her bent knees were by her chest. She was flexible and wrapped her legs around my back as I thrust harder. Our bodies rocked back and forth. I could have sped things up, but I wanted her to remember my prowess as a lover.

She thrashed her head side to side in pleasure as her loud moans filled the crisp night air. I knew she had already climaxed, but I wanted to give her more. We rolled around the bed, and I asked her to turn face down. Reaching my hands underneath her body, my fingers pleasured her as I penetrated her from behind. She whimpered and gasped as I angled my entry to hit a spot that seemed to take her over the top. Her body contracted, almost trying to keep me prisoner inside. Now that I had brought her to climax again, I let myself fully enjoy moving in and out of her slick body, faster and deeper, without restraint. With a low growl, I came but stayed inside her a few seconds longer before rolling off.

That felt so good. I needed that release.

After a deep sigh, she turned to look at me with languid eyes.

"Oh, Montor, that was great."

I stroked her hair, now disheveled.

"Yes, it was."

Three days later, she left Renna One to attend a history symposium on another planet, but until then, we spent time together having fun and great sex. We promised we would try to meet up again the next time we were both on Renna One, but my missions and her travels did not coincide. I did not see her again but, from then on, never felt compelled to visit a brothel. Females found me attractive, and I knew how to please them.

39

Two weeks later, Zorla ordered me to take my squadron and travel to Tormix to join with larger battalions facing another Tormixian revolt. The Lostai had annexed Tormix to their empire, but the Tormixian military continued to battle back.

Their technology matched ours, so battles were waged both in the airspace around the planet and on the surface. The Tormixians were relentless, and the Lostai military suffered losses. We spent several revolutions there with few breaks in between. After each deployment, I always visited Renna One and tried to shake off the misery of fighting a war I did not believe in.

After a particularly brutal battle on Tormix, I was back at Zamandi's room, as usual. Although I hated fighting against people defending their homeland from invaders, I was glad we had not lost any members of my squadron. Flanked by two lovely Fronidians who were helping me forget the constant conflict that tormented me, I ordered a round of drinks for the three of us. Soon, I was joined by Gio and other members of our squadron.

"Hello there, Montor." Gio raked my female companions with his eyes, his lips pursed in approval. "I see you have started to celebrate without us. OK, we will catch up soon enough."

"Hello, Gio. Today's victory was hard fought. I have opened a tab for everyone in our squadron."

He beamed, and the other squadron members approached the bartender with their orders. Soon, Gio found himself a male friend and was off to the dance floor. I was not much for dancing to the type of modern music played in most of the rooms there. Although only the equivalent of a twenty-five-revolution-old Lostai, I was a bit of an old soul, yearning for the Arandan folk music my father and mother used to listen to. Instead, my female companions danced around me while I sat and watched. As I was deciding whether I would bring them home with me, a couple entered the room and caught my attention.

The Arandan male, who appeared ten revolutions my senior, and his attractive Fronidian companion of similar age walked in like royalty accompanied by three security droids. They were dressed in expensive, stylish clothing and opulent jewelry. She wore a cropped blouse, her tiny waist sporting a tattoo of a bird with bright red, gold, and green feathers. I caught my breath as I remembered my older brother, Drator, had inked himself with a similar tattoo shortly before he left to fight with the Arandan militia. Spellbound, I watched them cross the room and approach the bar.

It was inevitable he would see me and that I would catch his attention. I had not seen another Arandan there ever before. The Arandan male cocked his head, his eyes shifting to take in the view of the Lostai, raising their glasses in celebration and thanking me for the free drinks. It was ever so brief a moment before he turned his attention to the bartender to order a shot of *stampu* for himself and a cocktail for his companion. Yet, my stomach churned with regret at being surrounded by my Lostai squadron in front of this Arandan.

Some time passed, and the Lostai eventually dispersed. The Arandan ordered small plates of fancy bar food. He must have been a big tipper as the waiters and bartenders fought over taking care of his orders. I could no longer control my curiosity, excusing myself from my female companions as I moved to stand next to the couple.

"Sir, forgive my being so forward, but you are the first Arandan I have seen here since I started coming seven revolutions ago."

He offered a wide smile, and I could not shake the feeling I had met him before.

"I must say the same, and I have been a customer here since this place first opened." He turned to his female companion. "This is my friend and business associate, Colora. What is your name?"

I nodded to Colora, as was the polite way for an Arandan male to greet a taken female. Even though he introduced her as a friend, I was sure they were romantically involved. She played with his hands and fingers in a suggestive manner. The female smiled but not before letting her eyes rove over my body. By then, I understood Fronidians generally were liberal and free-spirited in matters of relationships, love, and sex and could not help being sensual in everything they did.

I ignored it and replied, "My name is Montor, and yours?"

His brow furrowed and turned away for a moment before meeting my eyes.

"My name is Jortan."

Is it possible?

My eldest brother, Drator, had a good friend by the name of Jortan that used to come over to our house often. Even though I was young at that time, I remembered his appearance. The more I studied this Arandan's face, the more I was sure he was my brother's childhood friend. He was thinking the same. His voice lowered to a whisper, and he looked around before asking, "Are you from the Ventamu clan?"

Normally, we would not speak our clan name out loud except for special circumstances. This was such a moment.

"Yes. I am Josher's son."

"I know this is highly unusual, but may I see your amulets? You still wear them, right?"

Of course. He wants to be sure.

"Yes, OK."

I pulled the cords I always wore around my neck out from under my shirt. He inspected my clan's insignia engraved in the metallic amulets, and when he raised his eyes back to mine, I swore they were watery.

"Montor, you look so much like your father. I am Drator's best friend. Do you remember me? You were only a child, but we met several times. I visited your home often."

The mention of my brother made me swallow hard.

"I do," I said in a low tone.

"I heard about what happened to your family and the entire neighborhood you grew up in. How is it you are here?" He covered his mouth for a moment to regain composure. "I thought no one survived."

Now, I was at a crossroads. My heart was eager to share with this person all the things I had lived through. He was from my clan and brought back memories of my family.

I must be cautious about what I say, but I hate being dishonest with the one connection I have found to my people.

"I am my immediate family's sole survivor. The rest of them died at the labor camp the Lostai took us to. We also learned Drator died in battle. I have not been back to Aranda since."

Jortan sighed deeply and looked around again.

"I wish we could speak in a different place."

Then I did a crazy, careless thing that, regardless, felt right.

"I have a house here. Please, let us go there now, where we can speak freely."

"OK."

I got rid of the two females I came with, settled the bill, and gave Jortan my location codes.

Half hour later, we were chatting in my house.

"Montor, this is spectacular property. You have done well for yourself, and at such a young age," said Jortan.

It was a tearful reunion for Foxor and Lasarta, who remembered Jortan well. Their sons had also been friends with him growing up. They spoke about the horrible things they experienced at the labor camp.

"I watched those bloodthirsty, soulless Lostai soldiers gun down my brave sons. They killed Josher that day, too," said Lasarta.

"How did you escape?" asked Jortan.

Lasarta looked at me and hesitated. I made another split-second decision to tell Jortan everything.

He will probably be disgusted with me and leave. I might as well get it over with.

"I got them out," I answered.

"You? I saw you with a group of Lostai. Do you have some connections with the Lostai government?"

"Foxor, please get us a bottle of *stampu*. I will need a few shots to get through this story."

"Umm, I will prepare some snacks," said Lasarta, slipping away to the kitchen.

Foxor, Jortan, Colora, and I moved to the front porch, where I poured us each a glass of the strong liquor.

"Jortan, forgive I ask this question, but can your friend be trusted?"

"I trust her with my life."

Strong words for someone he described as a business associate.

"OK, this will be shocking for you to hear, but I am a lieutenant in the Lostai military."

Jortan looked at Foxor and back at me with widened eyes.

"How is this possible?"

Cracking my knuckles helped me lock down my nervous energy as I launched into the explanation.

"It is a long story. What I say here must remain between us. I should not be talking about this at all, but meeting you has moved me. Your friendship with my brother and family makes me feel a connection with you. I remember him saying you were like a brother to him."

"Trust me, both Colora and I know how to be discreet."

His words carried a second meaning I did not fully grasp until later.

I explained how the Lostai had identified the alien genes that gave me telekinetic and telepathic abilities. He must have noticed I was struggling with my emotions and attempted to help me through it by interrupting me with questions as I retold everything about my boot camp and training on Xixsted.

"As I mentioned earlier, we will not repeat what you have shared here, but why are you being so secretive? You were out in the open at Zamandi's Room with all those Lostai soldiers around you. I am surprised people do not find it odd," said Jortan.

"Well, they often do, but I explain it away by reminding people how much the Lostai Empire is expanding and welcoming other races into their military. Lostai soldiers like to go to Zamandi's Room to celebrate their victories, so my identity is well known there. However, my commander is benefitting personally from my telepathic powers and prefers I do not speak about my abilities among civilians. It serves me well that he needs and trusts me. That is how I got Foxor and Lasarta out of the labor camp."

"Yes, you do not want to lose such an advantage."

"Also, it is not common knowledge even among Lostai civilians that the Lostai military are hunting down Sotkari Ta individuals and forcing them to serve in their army. I would lose my commander's trust if he learned I had divulged this to someone outside of the Lostai military. In my youth, I confessed to a female friend that I could read her mind, and I consider myself lucky she told no one as far as I can tell."

Jortan laughed and slapped me on the back.

"Yes, I can imagine. We do crazy things in our youth to impress the females."

Colora tapped his hand and, with a wide grin, said, "Some still do, even as they grow older."

I tried to smile at her joke but another thought came to mind, sinking my spirits further.

"I hope no other Arandan learns I am a Lostai soldier. It brings me shame and is another reason why I request your discretion."

Jortan cleared his throat.

"Umm, so I assume your commander has not sent you to missions on Aranda."

"My one condition to him was that I would never fight or take any action against Arandans, and he has kept his side of the deal. I think he also chooses not to test my loyalty by avoiding missions on Sotkar, my mentor's home world. As much as we try to demonstrate the contrary, I think he senses the close bond between us."

"I am still amazed they made you lieutenant at such a young age."

"I have carried this rank for seven revolutions now."

"As I think about it, maybe it is not so astonishing. You come from a brilliant line of Arandan warriors."

"Please, do not patronize me. I prefer you to be sincere. You must find me abhorrent, a piece of crap Arandan traitor in the filthy Lostai military..." I looked away and banged my fist on the table, no longer able to contain my emotions. "*Shermont!*"

Jortan stood and placed his hand on my shoulder.

"Do not cower in front of me, Montor. I do not deserve it. I should have joined the militia like your brave brother, Drator. Instead, the minute my father realized the Lostai intended to overtake our planet, he followed what many wealthy Arandans did. He moved all his financial assets to other parts of the sector and relocated us to Fronidia. One could say I have been a coward living comfortably and safely while our planet is torn apart. Some of my companies even do business with the Lostai government. The truth is, we are all figuring out how to survive in this new reality." He pointed at Foxor. "Look what a great thing you were able to do because of your position. You rescued Foxor and Lasarta and have given them a new lease on life. That is worthy of praise."

"That is true, son," Foxor chimed in. "Jortan, the Lostai commander has implied we might suffer consequences if Montor does not fulfill his obligations as a Lostai soldier."

"Yes, the Lostai can be ruthless negotiators."

Lasarta arrived with a tray carrying a variety of small plates featuring bite-sized dough pockets filled with ground fowl, fried vegetables, steamed grains, and cured meats. The enticing aromas distracted us and diffused the tension. I wiped the tears from my face.

"This is delicious," said Colora. "I am not good with food preparation and cannot quite get the parameters right on my reproducer."

Jortan patted Colora on the thigh and kidded her, "Oh, Colora, these are homemade. No reproducer in the universe can achieve these results."

"Thank you," said Lasarta.

"I am a lucky Arandan," said Foxor, caressing Lasarta's cheek. "She is an excellent cook."

"Is that all that excites you about me?" Lasarta replied coyly.

"You know there are other things," Foxor replied with a mischievous smile.

Everyone laughed, and something random came to mind.

"Jortan, by the way, are you the owner of Members Only? I saw the red lake from a friend's balcony a long time ago. In all my travels with the Lostai military so far, I have yet to visit a planet with our yellow skies and red oceans."

"Well, yes, Colora and I are co-owners. Only members sworn to a vow of secrecy on penalty of death are welcome. We negotiated a special permission from the Rennan government to enforce it. Thankfully, as of today, no one has violated our policy. Our clients can do there what they want with whomever they want, spill their secrets, nurse their heartaches...whatever, assured no one on the outside will ever know. We have members from different parts of the sector and cater to their favorite foods and music."

I swallowed another shot of *stampu* in silence. Jortan became pensive and met Colora's eyes with some unspoken message exchanged between them. He straightened his posture as if he were about to say something of utmost importance.

"You know, Montor, we are practically family. Even though we were from different sides of town, your brother and I became close friends through the youth sports league your father organized. When we were older, your father saved enough of his hard-earned money to send Drator to the same expensive private business school I attended. Our friendship continued until he left school and joined the militia. You have shown class and solidarity by inviting me to your home and sharing your story with me. I would like to reciprocate by inviting you to be a member of our club. You remind me so much of your father, someone I looked up to, in some ways, even more than I did my own father. My gut tells me I can trust you. I will not take no for an answer."

A lull remained after Jortan's speech. I willed myself not to cry.

"I am honored, Jortan. You have my pledge to follow your rules. I do not know what else to say."

"Great. It is settled. Before I leave, we will formalize the agreement, and I will give you all the details. Let us toast to it."

We all lifted our glasses and cheered old and new friends.

40

———

embers Only soon became a favorite spot for me. Jortan said I could bring a companion, but I would be held responsible for any indiscretions that person committed. Other than Kaya, Foxor, and Lasarta, there was no one I trusted enough. I preferred going alone anyway, a quiet time for me to escape everything that troubled me. The venue featured a restaurant with four top-notch chefs, one of them Arandan. They also offered lodging and live or piped-in music. The spectacular ancient building housed hotel rooms with stylish furniture and modern amenities.

The first time I visited Members Only, I sat in a lounge chair and stared for hours at the immense red lake bordered by pink iridescent sand. Memories of beach outings with my family brought tears to my eyes. Jortan and Colora made a point of learning the preferences of each patron. After a few visits, my routine was set. As soon as I walked in, I heard sad Arandan ballads and old folk music piped in. Next, Colora would signal to the Arandan chef to prepare a succulent Arandan meal. I never ordered, preferring to be surprised by the chef's creations. Jortan would join me at the bar, where we shared a few shots of *stampu* until dinner was served. Colora usually joined us, and the three of us ate together.

Over time, Jortan confided he was married with two children. He said it was a loveless marriage and Colora, his true love, had been his mistress for two revolutions. Jortan's revelation shocked me at first. I had been taught a spouse should be selected very carefully. Marriage was a life-long commitment unless the female fell in love with another male. In that case, the matter would be settled by a duel to the death or incapacitation between the two males involved. But even more importantly, the couples I had the most experience with, my parents and Foxor and Lasarta, were examples of loving relationships.

Jortan explained that his marriage had been arranged by his parents. This often occurred among rich families. Divorce would be frowned upon. He had no choice but to remain married while conducting his relationship with Colora in secret. I soon came to recognize and respect the strong bond that united them.

Our friendship solidified over hours of either reminiscing about our childhood on Aranda or discussing the current political and economic matters affecting our quadrant, sector, and even other parts of the galaxy. We also kept abreast of the situation on Aranda. By now, a Lostai governed each province, and the Lostai military controlled the entire planet. The clans that had cooperated with the Lostai faced the fact that they had been duped. They no longer shared any power but at least were spared having their people transferred to labor camps. Battles were not being fought outright anymore. The Arandan militia became an insurgency focused on urban guerilla warfare. Robberies, kidnappings, bombings of Lostai law enforcement, military and government installations, and assassinations became the tools of their rebellion.

There was one positive side effect of the Lostai occupation: it exposed Arandans to advanced technology. The planet was catapulted into an age of modernization and connectivity with the rest of the sector and galaxy, which would otherwise have taken several generations to accomplish. The insurgency took advantage to learn the new technologies and use them against the Lostai.

At first, I did not share much with Jortan about the missions Zorla assigned to me and my squadron. I felt ashamed of discussing these activities with him after I had disclosed how my family had suffered at the hands of the Lostai. One evening over shots of *stampu*, I started to mention to Jortan that I had just earned a significant bonus but stopped short.

"What was that, Montor?"

"Oh, never mind."

"You seemed excited about something."

"It embarrasses me to talk to you about such things."

"Montor, I would hope you see me as an older brother and that I have gained your trust."

I cracked my knuckles and sighed deeply before replying.

"I earned a significant bonus for helping to root out a seditious group on the Lostai's most recently annexed planet."

"And what is so embarrassing about that?"

"My work with the Lostai brings dishonor to my clan. I would rather not speak of it with a fellow Arandan."

"Well, that is up to you, but keep in mind that I will never be judgmental about your work with them. I know your circumstances, and I am no one to criticize. I have already told you that I do business with Lostai companies, their government, and even their military." He placed his hand on my shoulder as if to emphasize his solidarity. "So, how do you plan to invest those funds?"

"I just keep them in my remuneration account."

Once I told him the bonus amount and what I had saved from previous income, he shook his head.

"Montor, you need to put those savings to work."

"I do not have a clue about what would be a smart investment."

"I can help you with that."

I had some vacation time, so he, Colora, and I went on a trip. First, he took me to the other side of Renna One, where entire mini-continents were devoted to farmland and agriculture. He knew several of the landowners and secured permission for us to walk on their properties. I always felt a connection to nature. My mood lifted as I walked through fragrant herb gardens, orchards with trees bearing fruit of every color and shape, and fields of vibrant vegetables.

"These fertile lands produce enough crops to supply the needs of Renna One as well as exports to other planets."

"That sounds great, but I do not have time to manage the resources required to keep up such large plantations."

"I understand. My friends own the land and rent it to the farming companies. They receive a steady income without any risk. It is the farming company who is responsible for working the land, selling its fruit, and making a profit for themselves. There are still many undeveloped plots of land that I think would be perfect investments for you. You buy them from the Rennan government and lease them to the farming company."

I listened to his advice and purchased three large plots of land with my savings. I used up all my funds on those purchases, but he wanted to advise me on other fruitful business ventures that I should consider for future investments. We traveled to Fronidia, where he introduced me to several leaders of financial institutions. On our way to the first of these meetings, he explained opportunities related to banking on Fronidia.

"Fronidia is a good place for doing business because their policies protect the privacy of citizens and investors at all costs. The government incentivizes risk-taking and profit-making. Fronidians are all about commerce and living an opulent lifestyle. People earn credits based on how much they work and the level of complexity of the tasks they perform or the services and products they sell. Many will borrow credits in anticipation of future earnings to appear rich before they really can afford it. There is a profit to be made through that activity. When you have saved up some more funds, I can help you set up your own lending and saving business."

After the meeting, we had dinner at a nice restaurant. Everyone there dressed in well-tailored clothing made of luxurious fabrics and adorned in decorative precious metals and jewels.

"Jortan, thank you for introducing me to all these aspects of business. I am an expert at all things military, but now you are opening my eyes to another way of life."

"Exactly. I think there is something else you can gain besides just financial profit. As you become more successful in these ventures, you can assume another persona...someone other than a Lostai soldier. I envision you at parties and meetings, mingling with other wealthy people. In those scenarios, you can forget for a while that you are a Lostai soldier. You could legitimately introduce yourself as a landowner or a businessperson. I think it will help you deal with your inner conflict."

I knew Jortan meant well, but no mask could stop me from feeling like a filthy traitor inside.

While Jortan was introducing me to potential investments and income streams, my relationship with Zorla was also changing. He used me and my mind control abilities more and more often to assist him on projects for his own personal gain. By then, he had several squadrons under his command, and he put me in charge of all of them, promoting me to Lieutenant Commander. Between our successful military assignments and the manipulations I helped him with, he rapidly climbed the ranks of the Lostai military. After his latest promotion, he called me to his office in Xixsted.

"Montor, I have great news. I have been assigned responsibility for all military deployments in the Morex Quadrant."

"Congratulations, sir. So, does that mean you will be leaving Xixsted?"

"No, I like being on a science station. It keeps me close to our latest technological discoveries, and I can work on some of my pet projects."

Pet projects?

"So, other than sharing this announcement, do you need anything else from me?"

"I do. With this expanded position, I need to delegate responsibilities to people whom I trust will do a good job and not make me look bad. You have proven yourself adept at leading squadrons and producing results. I would like to offer you the position of Tactical Consultant."

"I have never heard of such a position within the Lostai's military order of ranks."

"No, I used an obscure ruling to create this position because our laws do not allow for a non-Lostai to occupy a position higher than your current one. You will thank me for this. Your time on battlefields will be greatly diminished. Under this position, you will hire someone to take your place as Lieutenant Commander while you command battalions and special military projects from afar."

My reaction was the same as when he had promoted me previously. It left me speechless and incredulous, wishing for time and space to examine my feelings.

"Well, what do you think, Montor? Let me be candid. I know fighting some of these battles must cause conflicting emotions for you." He leaned in and narrowed his eyes.

"Imagine if I had decided to make you warden of a labor camp full of families, elderly folk, and children. I hope you can appreciate my generosity. Our working relationship works well for both of us. Together, we can accomplish great things."

His smug expression caused anger to bubble up in my chest.

I should leave before I physically attack him.

I masked all emotion and replied, "OK, thank you for the trust. Send me all the important details. I will put the new structure in place very soon."

PART IV

DEFIANCE

41

My soulmate is sorrow
My partner is grief
I journey through life
A destitute spirit
Disguised in wealth
Too broken for marriage
My spouse is servitude
My destiny is war

Over time, I actually did appreciate the fact that my new position granted me anonymity. On some planets, no one knew of my ties to the Lostai military. After several revolutions of following Jortan's advice, I was wealthy. My assets across the quadrant included five homes, two ancient palaces, several plots of land I leased to produce companies, two financial institutions, and a fleet of personal spacecraft and land vehicles. Montor, the filthy Lostai soldier and traitor, did not exist in those circles.

Before long, I caught the attention of a different brand of female. Socialites, heiresses, politicians, and celebrities all vied for my attention. I knew I had cemented my position in high society when I was invited to a ball thrown by one of the wealthiest Fronidians, a male named Kloron. I considered getting a date but boldly decided to attend solo. Jortan and Colora were also on the invite list.

By this time, my entire wardrobe consisted of custom-made clothing and shoes, fitted to show off my physique. I wore jeweled rings on both hands. A fashionable galactic communicator hung from my belt on a thick chain made of a rare metal called *oranium*. On these occasions, instead of twisted locks, I preferred to brush out my hair, creating a wild look that usually turned the heads of males and females alike.

"Oh, Montor, you look very handsome," said Colora, looking me over with a tinge of lust.

Normally, I would not be shy at receiving such a compliment, but although not married to Jortan, I knew she would be his life partner. I nodded politely and stepped away before she got closer. She did not mean to disrespect Jortan. It was just typical flirtatious Fronidian behavior.

Wealthy Fronidians enjoyed recreating ancient themes for their parties and banquets. It would be simple enough to hold the event in a holographic room, but the wealthy prided themselves on splurging for the real thing. The first room was furnished with round high tables, chairs, and a long bar, all constructed of pure *reminda*, the rare tusk of a wild beast. All the lighting came from oil lamps and candles. Old-fashioned cocktails and aged wine were served in ancient metal goblets while a live band played animated Fronidian folk tunes.

Colora sat at one of the tables while Jortan and I walked to the bar to get drinks. I was easily the tallest, most muscular person in sight. Some of the accompanied females stole glances at me. I chuckled to myself as their partners scowled and rushed them away.

A Fronidian female approached us on our way to the bar. It sometimes was hard to gauge people's ages in these circles as they had the means to pay for rejuvenation treatments. This female was very attractive and youthful-looking, but her bold, confident demeanor told me she was older than she appeared. She was acquainted with Jortan.

"Nice to see you, Jortan. Are you here alone?" she asked, staring him in the eyes and offering a wide smile.

"No, Colora is waiting for us at the table."

"Oh, nice," she said, the smile running from her face until she turned to me and her eyes twinkled again. "Oh my goodness, and who is this strapping Arandan?"

I bowed and offered her a sly smile.

"My name is Montor. Nice to meet you." I extended my hand. "I was on my way to the bar to get a drink. Would you like to join me?"

"Thank you. Pleased to meet you, Montor. My name is Frenda, and I would love to."

She took my hand and squeezed. I led her to the bar. Jortan returned to Colora with their drinks while I stayed and chatted up Frenda. We were joined by her sister, who mentioned that a friend was asking for her. Her expression gave away that she did not want to leave my side.

"What terrible timing. I am sorry, Montor, but this friend is actually a client that I cannot slight, but hopefully we will talk some more later."

I bowed and gave her another killer smile.

"No problem. I look forward to it."

Later, I was joined by a few Fronidians, two males and two females, who controlled large businesses. Jortan had schooled me in the intricacies of financial markets and commerce across the sector. Sometimes, my position in the Lostai military complemented what I had learned from him.

"A friend of mine is investing in a space hotel orbiting planet Jermax. The rooms will be luxurious and will have the most modern amenities, including holographic rooms. Many rich families already go to Jermax for vacation. This offers them another recreation option," said one of the males.

"Hmm, that sounds promising," said another.

"I would advise against it," I interjected.

Everyone looked at me.

"I happen to know that the Lostai and the Jermaxians are in conflict over the moons in the area. A peaceful resolution is unlikely."

"How would you know that?"

"I have contacts in the Lostai military. Also, orbiting hotels are overdone already. People now are into historically themed experiences...authentic, not holographic. Look how everyone is gushing over the décor here today. I recently purchased an ancient palace once owned by a Fronidian monarch. I restored it to its original glory and now rent it to wealthy families for their weddings and special events. I have already made a nice profit on this investment and will continue to do so in the foreseeable future."

"That sounds like an excellent idea," said the first male, nodding his head in agreement.

One of the females got closer and looked up at me.

"Well, thankfully we ran into you today," she said. "Easy on the eyes and full of great advice."

"Glad to be of help," I replied.

After cocktails, we were asked to move into a banquet hall furnished with many long tables made of polished wood and cushioned chairs. Old-fashioned crystal chandeliers hung from the high ceilings. I was happy to learn that all the food had been prepared by hand instead of reproducer, another lavish expense incurred by our host. Thick ornate tablecloths dressed the tables. I purposely let Jortan and Colora sit across from me, leaving empty chairs on either side of me. They were quickly filled by two females who wasted no time in introducing themselves.

Jortan smiled at me and spoke in Arandan so the Fronidians could not understand, "You are making quite a commotion, my friend."

"What can I say?" I replied, smiling back.

After dinner, we were ushered to a ballroom. The band moved to a stage there. I danced with several females, including Frenda. She was my favorite, so I took her back to my hotel room after the party.

I celebrated the twenty-third anniversary of my birth with Jortan and Colora at an exclusive resort on Gorinth, a planet from a neighboring quadrant. Its pleasant climate, technological advances, and fancy resorts made it a hot spot for celebrities and wealthy people of the area. An oligarchy of corporate leaders linked to a powerful interplanetary crime syndicate ruled Gorinth. The Lostai knew better than to mess with them. I was the equivalent of a thirty-revolution-old Lostai and, in some circles of society, considered one of the most sought-after eligible bachelors. I thought about inviting one of the many females who constantly swirled around me, hoping to become my wife, but I had lost interest in them and was hoping to meet someone new.

One evening, we traveled by transport pod to a province in the southern continent named Horomo. A community of Arandans had escaped the Lostai occupation and settled there, creating a pocket of old Aranda on the outskirts of a large city.

"Montor, not only do they have excellent home-style restaurants, but they have old-fashioned theaters projecting vintage films and serials like the kind we watched as children back home. Most of these are bootleg versions but of excellent quality. Remember the Officer Bertor series?" said Jortan.

"Yes, my father loved that series."

A familiar ache distracted me.

"Montor, are you OK?"

"Yes. I cannot help but remember a conversation I had with Lasarta and Foxor as a child, just before I was taken from the labor camp. During those early revolutions at Xixsted, I imagined I would use my training there someday to become a secret agent like Officer Bertor and avenge my family or join the militia."

By now, Jortan knew how to redirect the conversation to avoid me falling into a dark mood.

"They also have *moros* arenas with competitive teams. We should watch a game or two."

"OK."

We chose a restaurant on a spectacular shoreline specializing in Arandan seafood dishes. My mood lifted as I took notice of a local band playing the Arandan music I liked. A good amount of space in the center of the restaurant was devoted to a dancefloor. I had not been among so many Arandan people at once since my days at the labor camp. Soon after we placed our orders, Jortan noticed an acquaintance at another table and went over to say hello.

"Jortan knows so many people," I commented to Colora.

Right after I finished my sentence, Jortan was back at the table with a whole family consisting of an older Arandan couple, three young adult daughters, and a teenaged son.

"Montor, meet Gritarm. He is from our clan and fought with your father in the clan wars."

I knew Jortan meant well, but sometimes it was hard for me to remember that these people were unaware of my position within the Lostai military and there was no need to be self-conscious. I managed a smile and inclined my head politely towards his wife.

"Your father was the leader of our troop. I never met another Arandan of such courage."

"Yes, thank you."

One daughter offered me a wide smile while the other two displayed the typical vain behavior expected of young unmarried Arandan females, especially of aristocratic background.

"Hello, Sir Montor, my name is Lorret. It is a pleasure to meet you."

She extended her hand in salutation. When I grasped it, the warmth changed my whole demeanor, bringing out more of my typical swagger and outgoing personality. Her mother frowned at what was deemed inappropriate behavior. This young female held no regard for protocols and conventions, and I loved it.

"The honor is mine, Lorret. Please drop the Sir and call me Montor. I must say, you are the epitome of Arandan beauty."

Her smile turned demure. Thick, long eyelashes shielded her eyes from my gaze. The two sisters smirked in envy, while the mother forgot her initial annoyance and smiled as if I had directed the compliment at her. She gave Lorret a slight nudge, but this young female would not be prodded. Here was someone who moved along on her own terms. She gave her mother an impatient look and said nothing more.

When our food arrived, Gritarm and his family excused themselves. My eyes followed Lorret. I took in her statuesque figure as she walked back to their table. Most young females would have flaunted such a spectacular body in something tight and sheer. Instead, she wore an expensive tailored suit that screamed class and confidence but still did nothing to hide her curves.

"What do you know about his daughter, the tall one?"

"Lorret? She is actually the youngest. Montor, she might be too young for you. She only came of age two revolutions ago," replied Jortan.

"Hmm...maybe, but there is something about her that calls to me."

As dinner wound down, the band started up, playing favorite classic tunes from my childhood. From her table, Lorret stole a glance at me.

I finished my glass of wine and said to no one in particular, "I want to dance."

In a few long strides, I was at her table and, in a gesture much more formal than what young males her age would have done, bowed before extending my hand.

"Lorret, may I have the honor of this dance?"

Her eyes shifted towards her father, who inclined his head in approval. Something told me she might have danced with me regardless and was only reciprocating my old-fashioned approach. Several couples were already on the dance floor when we arrived. This music genre called for holding both her hands during the entire dance as we rotated, hooked arms, and shifted positions. She followed my lead effortlessly. One turn brought us side by side, facing the same direction, and another quick turn brought her body close to mine. Her platform shoes added to her height, allowing my lips to graze her forehead. A scent conjuring up images of sweet and spicy desserts swirled around her.

One song merged with another and another, changing from formal to fun and sensual. My hands on her waist had me thinking about the curve of her hips. I forced myself not to let my mind wander further towards her breasts, even though they were pressed against my chest. We only stopped when the band took its break.

"That was fun," she said, her smile simultaneously bold and innocent. "Have you been here before?"

"This is my first time."

"There is a balcony upstairs with a beautiful view. Would you like to see?"

I nodded, and she led me to the elevator, where we stood alone. She did not let go of my hand.

"I must say, Lorret, something about you makes me so glad I came here tonight."

She blushed but did not miss a beat.

"That makes two of us."

Most Arandan females were taught to be pretentious, appear indifferent, and play hard-to-get with males who showed them attention, especially those from higher-income families. Lorret apparently ignored those conventions and behaved natural and open, not hiding the fact that she liked me.

The elevator opened to a dimly lit, spacious balcony. Some couples stood embraced in dark corners, hands sliding over bodies. Restaurant management put some forethought to providing no seating, which might have tempted people to do much more. We walked to the edge of the balcony in the center.

"Oh, it is too bad the sky is cloudy. On a clear night, the view of the sea is amazing."

"I already have something stunning right next to me."

"I can tell you have a way with females. Those words roll off your tongue so easily. You probably speak them often."

I chuckled. Basic, sugar-coated words would not work on her.

Yes, definitely both bold and innocent.

"Lorret, you know a bit about me already. Tell me something about yourself."

I learned she had recently started her second revolution curriculum in a nearby esteemed medical academy. Another bit of information took me by surprise.

"As my father mentioned when we were first introduced, he

is originally from your clan." She lowered her voice. "We are Ventamu. I have learned from my grandmother how the Lostai invasion wiped out entire neighborhoods of the Ventamu province. My father told us your family's hometown was one of them. We lost many family members and friends, too. At the time, we were already living here. After fighting in the clan wars, my father got married and moved to my mother's home province on the other side of the planet to manage her father's business. When he learned from his business contacts about what the Lostai were doing in other parts of Aranda, he brought my mother here. The Lostai military killed my grandfather and my grandmother refused to leave, hiding instead. She is still there. I talk to her often, and she tells me about how the Lostai are in complete control of our planet now. Sometimes, I feel guilty our family's wealth allowed us to escape while so many others suffered. Even though I was born here, I am Arandan through and through. One day, those filthy Lostai will have to pay for every Arandan family they tore apart. I hate them."

She caught me off guard, and I was embarrassed for the seconds that went by before I replied, "Yes, they have been ruthless in their quest to expand their Empire."

"Ruthless? They are filthy criminals. How did you escape when they came to your neighborhood? I heard the Lostai rounded you all up and took you to a labor camp on another planet."

A clap of thunder made my heart jump.

Of course, I lied. Jortan and I had established an alternate history for me for scenarios like this one when I wanted to hide my position with the Lostai military. Basically, I took on the true story of my older brother, Drator, except for the part of him coming back to Aranda and joining the militia and some tweaks to account for Jortan's and my age difference. Had Drator stayed in school, he probably would have been alive.

"My family was not wealthy, but my father was a hard worker and frugal. By the time I was an adolescent, he had saved enough money to send me to a Fronidian business school where I met Jortan, who had been my older brother's teammate in a youth sports team my father coached when they were children. I lived in an Arandan enclave on Fronidia with a distant relative. Jortan is older than me, and by the time I entered the school, he was an assistant professor and remembered me and my family from his childhood."

"I see. Well, it is good you survived, so your esteemed family's lineage can live on."

Do I even dream of having children? What if they inherit my Sotkari Ta genes? Would the Lostai take them from me?

The wind picked up, and stormy weather brought rain and lightning. A shiver put my nerves on end.

"We should go back downstairs," I said.

In the elevator, I shook off my discomfort.

"Lorret, it has been so pleasant talking to you. I hope we can stay in contact and see each other again."

She reached up to caress my cheek, throwing me even more off balance.

"I would like that, too."

42

Lorret lived with three friends in an apartment a few blocks away from her medical school. She also interned at a nearby hospital. I was smitten enough by Lorret to set up temporary residence on Gorinth, and I visited her several days each lunar cycle, taking her to fancy restaurants and the theater. We also went to dance clubs that played the Arandan music I liked and to holographic recreational centers. It was all a lot of fun, but I kept our relationship platonic. Most of the females I dated were sexually experienced and fine with casual relationships. Many rushed to take me to their beds, but Lorret's flirtations were more of an innocent nature. I did not want to take advantage of her.

One evening, after about four lunar cycles, we found ourselves at a romantic spot on a beach sitting on a towel watching twilight close out the day.

"Montor, are you seeing any other females?"

One never needed to wonder what was on her mind.

"Umm, no. Are you going out with other males?"

Her beautiful eyes danced with mischief.

"Why would I do that when I have a stud like you?"

Normally, this would be all I needed to be even more conceited than usual, but she always managed to keep me off balance.

"Well, I could say the same about you."

"Yes, but I am wondering because, other than holding my hands and caressing my cheek, you have made no move for us to be more intimate. Is it because I am so much younger than you?"

I cracked my knuckles and rolled my shoulders back while deciding what to say.

Better be honest about this.

"Yes. I could be wrong, but I sense you do not have a lot of experience in that area."

She met my eyes.

"I have no experience at all. I am a virgin, Montor."

"OK." I looked everywhere except at her. "So, I suppose I have been doing the right thing."

She sat up straight and, with all the confidence in the world, said, "Well, I am tired of it. You see those bungalows by the shoreline? They rent those by the night. I say we rent one tonight."

The thought made me imagine running my hands over her sexy thighs.

"Well, what do you think?" she asked.

I do not want to hurt her feelings, but I do not want to mislead her either. Shermont, this is hard.

"I...I do not know. I mean, Lorret, I like you a lot. You are a beautiful female, but I am not ready to make any long-term commitments."

"Montor, I am not asking you to marry me. The truth is this. I have a major crush on you, and I want you to be my first one."

Shermont, this is really happening. I did not even bring birth control.

"We need to stop at a convenience store first."

After taking care of that errand, we rented one of the bungalows she mentioned. They looked rustic on the outside but were furnished like a modern hotel room, complete with a bathroom, viewer, communication equipment, and reproducer. The bed was large and luxurious enough for a good romp, and I loved that we could hear the waves thrashing the shoreline.

I dimmed the lights and put on soft instrumental music.

"Come sit next to me. Are you nervous?" I said.

She plopped on the bed beside me.

"Yes, I am."

"Well, so am I."

"What?" She let out a shaky giggle. "I am sure you have been with so many females."

"Yes, I have, but never with a virgin. It feels like an enormous responsibility."

"One thing you do not have to worry about is I know what everything is supposed to look like. As a medical student, I am familiar with the anatomy of different races and sexes."

I chuckled and ran the back of my hand against her cheek and let it slide down her neck, over her collarbone, until I reached the edge of her blouse.

"Lorret, one thing before we go any further." She looked at me like a child paying attention to some very important instruction. "If at any point you feel uncomfortable with what I am doing, please do not be afraid to tell me. We can stop at any time. You are in your right to change your mind. I would hate for you to feel obligated to go through something because you think you have to. Understood?"

"Yes, of course."

I undid the first two buttons, revealing a generous amount of cleavage, and licked her there. My hand brushed over her breast. Already, her heartbeat raced.

"What do I do, Montor?" she gasped.

"Whatever feels right to you."

She ran her hands over my shoulders and biceps.

I unbuttoned the rest of her blouse. Her undergarment's magnetic strips ran down the back and easily separated with a light tug. She was now nude from the waist up.

"Oh my, Lorret. They are so lovely."

I bent over and cupped one of her breasts. My tongue slid over the nipple before taking it completely in my mouth while I fondled the other breast. She shuddered as I sucked on it.

"Lay down, let me take the rest of this off," I said.

As much as I wanted to be gentle, the monster of desire was taking over. The short skirt and underpants came off in a second. She looked like an ancient goddess of fertility with a perfectly proportioned, curvaceous body. I moved to the bottom of the bed, grabbed one of her feet, and licked between each of her toes. She squealed with delight. Making my way up, I caressed her shapely calves and thighs and squeezed her butt before separating her legs.

Oh, I need to taste that.

She tensed up, trying to press her legs back together. I called upon all my self-control.

"Lorret, are you OK?" I wished my voice sounded less husky and deep.

"What are you going to do now?"

"I am going to feast on you, and trust me, I am sure you are going to enjoy this. But if you do not, I will stop. May I?"

Breathless, she replied, "Umm, OK."

Now that her scent filled my senses, I could not get enough of her, but I made a point to explore her body gradually. I knew she liked it when her hips gyrated first slowly and then faster, matching the rhythm of my tongue and fingers pleasuring her. Moaning, she ran her hands through my locks and pressed my face even harder against her body.

It is time.

I jumped off the bed and raced to take off my clothes. She stopped me before I climbed back in.

"Let me get a better look at you, Montor." Her voice was now as husky as mine.

It is good she stopped me. I almost forgot the contraceptive.

I grabbed the vial, poured some liquid in my hand, and rubbed it all over my penis.

Her jaw dropped.

"Can I do that?"

Oh, can I be this lucky?

"Yes, if you want to."

I got closer to the bed. She reached over the edge, poured a few more drops directly on my already erect penis, and slid one daring finger over the top before using her entire hand to spread the liquid all around.

"Does this liquid taste like anything?"

Her innocence, paired with bold curiosity, was turning this into one of the hottest sexual encounters I could remember. My voice deepened into a growl I could not control. I hoped it would not frighten her.

"The liquid has no taste."

"Good," she whispered. "I want to taste only you."

She could not take me in all the way, but it was a delicious precursor to what it would feel like to be inside her, where I could thrust as deep as I wanted.

"If you are ready, Lorret, this is the time to let me make us one."

Aware of the typical Arandan positioning, she rolled back over face down.

"No, please stay on your back. I want to see your face when I come inside you."

"OK."

I positioned myself over her with my arms supporting my torso in a plank position so I could see her face and gorgeous breasts heaving. I pressed my pelvic area against hers. She was lubricated but still tight.

"I am not sure, but this might hurt a bit at first, Lorret."

Tentative, I pushed in only halfway. She grimaced, her face scrunching up.

"Oh, I am so sorry for the pain, Lorret. I have never been with a virgin before and even some of my experienced partners have complained of my large si—"

"Shhh, Montor, my goodness, stop rambling and do it."

I stroked her nipples and gently caressed her body to help ease her tension. She accepted more and more of me, wrapping her legs around my hips, until our cadence turned fluid and synchronized, rivaling the waves slapping the shore outside.

As a seasoned lover and physically fit male, I possessed the prowess and stamina to bring my lovers to the peak of satisfaction, but the idea that I was going where no other male had ventured, challenged my self-control. Slowing things down allowed me to study her face. Each deep thrust carved away at her innocence. Bending my arms at the elbows to now support myself on my forearms brought our upper bodies close. She wrapped her arms around me, her nails digging into my back as she pressed her lips against my neck, licking and nipping me. I loved the idea that these rough caresses did not come from experience but from the primal desire that I had ignited.

"Oh, Montor, I am liking this a lot."

Moans erupted from deep within, her shouts becoming higher pitched. She moved her hips faster and faster, signaling she was close to climax, so I sped things up, giving her what she needed. I relished the feel of her body clenching, hearing her whimper in ecstasy, and watching her bite her lips in that final release. As I rolled off her, she smiled, her eyes languid and sated.

Once our breathing returned to normal, we faced each

other on our sides and chatted. I caressed her cheek, and she twined my locks around her fingers.

"You know, Montor, my sisters told me they do not enjoy this at all. I think they say this because our mother has told us we must act this way so the male will remain interested. I am not good at being fake. Now, I wonder if I will lose your interest."

I laughed.

"Either your sisters are paying too much attention to your mother, or their partners are not good lovers. I like that you are genuine, and I am more interested than ever."

43

L orret and I shared good chemistry in bed, but soon our age difference manifested itself. She was impulsive and a bit stubborn. We argued when I could not accommodate her love of spontaneity. On the spur of the moment, she would suggest visiting places off-world she had heard about. I splurged on her early in our relationship, so she knew I could afford these trips. Running into Lostai military was a constant concern for me. Higher-ranked Lostai officers in that quadrant knew I worked for Zorla and could easily recognize me.

One evening, she announced she would be taking me somewhere as a surprise. It turned out to be a rally of young Arandans her age talking about returning to Aranda and joining the militia. Like Lorret, these were children of wealthy Arandan parents who had escaped the Lostai occupation.

These people were not born on Aranda.

They did not see their homes destroyed.

They never lived in a labor camp or witnessed their families killed in cold blood.

They never held weapons or battled opponents for their lives.

They romanticized the idea of the rebellion, sang old battle hymns, and offered long speeches. I supposed their hearts were in the right place, but I could not help feeling annoyed.

The first time I brought Lorret to my house on Renna One, she was excited about the possibility of seeing celebrities and enjoying the famous nightlife there.

"I just cannot wait for you to take me out on the town," she said with youthful excitement while Lasarta and Foxor served us dinner.

As always, I introduced Lasarta and Foxor as my employees. As much as I liked Lorret, I had not yet decided if I trusted her enough with the secret that they were dear to me.

"Is anyone else joining us?" asked Lorret.

"No, I thought just us two sharing a homemade dinner here might be romantic."

She looked around the room, smiled, and pretended to be impressed with the fancy décor and luxurious furniture but did not fool me. Of course, she came from a wealthy family and was used to opulence.

"Oh, that sounds wonderful," she said. "But maybe you can take me tomorrow somewhere we can mingle with people. I hear that celebrities love to vacation in this area."

Lasarta discreetly side-glanced at me. She understood my predicament. I had already mentioned to her Lorret's affiliation with the Arandan freedom fighter group. My body tensed with the stress of knowing that the heavy presence of vacationing Lostai soldiers on Renna One made it impossible for me to parade around with Lorret on my arm.

"I would like to take you to a venue owned by my friend Jortan. It has a beautiful hotel. We can stay there a few nights."

"Sounds nice."

While we were eating, I explained to her the importance of secrecy at Members Only.

"The place I am taking you to tomorrow has one important rule. Those who do not comply can be punished by death."

She straightened herself, and her eyes opened wide.

"My goodness, Montor. Where are you taking me?"

"It is a beautiful place, but it is a private venue for members only. You must promise not to repeat anything you hear there or tell anyone of anything that goes on there. Now, do not get the wrong idea. There is nothing unlawful happening. It is just a place where people can relax in whatever manner they wish without worrying about being judged and where their secrets are kept sacred."

Her shoulders relaxed.

"OK, that sounds fine."

We enjoyed our time at Members Only. As soon as we walked in, the live band erupted into a very danceable old battle hymn. Lorret loved it. She immediately twirled and asked me to take her to the dancefloor.

"I think I have heard this song played at the freedom fighter rallies, but it is a totally different experience hearing it played live," she said.

The next song was a folk ballad. Lorret bit her lip, became pensive, even emotional.

"What is it?" I asked, a bit alarmed, pulling her close as we swayed to the music.

She pressed her face against my chest.

"I have seen old video images of my grandmother singing that song."

Dinner featured a roasted suckling boar, mashed tubers, and traditional Arandan dough pockets filled with vegetables in a savory broth called *teronix*. Lorret's conversation became more militant with each glass of *vormey* she drank.

"Montor, this is a very nice dinner. I wonder how many of our enslaved compatriots wish they could enjoy a typical Arandan meal like this one. It is time for us to rise up against the Lostai military scum."

I nodded and made vague comments about how all empires eventually meet their end. Dessert was a delicate pastry filled with *goria* fruit followed by cups of strong *yomoso*. When it was time to return home, she questioned why I took her straight back to my house instead of touring the city. I made up an excuse and cut short our time together on Renna One.

"Something has come up with one of my businesses. I am afraid that it is time to take you back to Gorinth."

Lorret did not hide her disappointment. To make it up to her, after pretending to attend business meetings, I decided to stay on Gorinth and spend a few more days with her. She asked me to accompany her to another Arandan freedom fighter rally.

"We can no longer tolerate the Lostai governing our planet as if it were their home world. Those filthy criminals are using our resources and enslaving our people. The time to act is now!" shouted the keynote speaker.

As part of the entertainment, a play was presented enacting an Arandan uprising where some Lostai soldiers had been captured and tortured. Arandan adolescents dressed in Lostai military uniforms played the part of the short Lostai soldiers. My heartbeat accelerated as the crowd cheered the simulated drowning of the soldiers. I did my best to hide my emotions and maintain a restrained posture amid the rowdy crowd, while imagining myself in my Lostai uniform held under water, unable to breathe. Next to me, Lorret raised her fists in the air, chanting, "The only good Lostai soldier is a dead one!"

❋

My relationship with Lorret took a turn for the worse when she received devastating news from Aranda. She called me crying.

"Montor, something awful has happened."

"Where are you?"

"At my apartment."

"Do you want to tell me about it now, or I can be there tomorrow morning."

"My grandmother is dead," she wailed.

"Oh, Lorret, I am so sorry. What happened?"

"There was a skirmish between Arandan protestors and Lostai law enforcement in her town, near a fresh market where she was shopping. The Lostai scum threw grenades everywhere, even in the market full of innocent civilians who had nothing to do with the protest. I mean, Montor, do you not keep up with the news?"

She was upset, so I ignored her sarcasm.

"What is happening with your family now?"

"Other relatives were killed or injured. My father is traveling there tonight for the sacred death chant. He said it is too dangerous for the rest of us to accompany him, but I insisted on going. I was close to my grandmother. Montor, please, can you come with me?"

My clan's province in Aranda was the last place I wanted to go with her. Heavy Lostai military presence plus how much I looked like my father made someone recognizing me a risk I could not take. I was grateful this was an audio only call so she could not see my reaction.

"I am sorry, Lorret. I have business meetings I cannot cancel on short notice. It is not a good idea for you to go there either. Heed your father's advice. Many times after such an incident, another confrontation soon follows."

I heard her forcefully exhale.

"No one is stopping me from going. It is a shame how easy

we go about our business here while our brethren there are suffering."

That jab was meant for me. Again, I let it go.

"Let me know when you are back, and I will come see you."

"Fine."

After her return, she asked that we visit Arandan freedom fighter rallies more often. Shots of *stampu* before, during, and after were required for me to tolerate these meetings. Sometimes, the *stampu* got the best of me, bringing back memories of the labor camp and my hatred of the wardens. On those occasions, I caught myself pumping my fists, joining in on the chanting, and singing the old battle hymns. Lorret took notice. It seemed to fill her with joy that despite our age difference, we were finding common ground outside of bed. She was extra passionate on those evenings. I showed her how to mount me, and she rode like an ancient war goddess, her long hair whipping and thrashing as wildly as her hips.

Sometimes, when I brought her home to Renna One, Lasarta and Foxor could not help but overhear our conversations. They seemed to like her, but Lasarta, as always, ever so wise, warned me.

"This one is too young for you, Montor."

Despite the conflict it represented for me, I admired Lorret's patriotic fervor. Some of her friends treated the movement like the latest fad or a way to meet other young Arandans, but for her, it represented so much more. She was honoring her grandmother's memory.

Three lunar cycles later, we were together in my home in Renna One, sitting on the back deck where cascades fell to form a pool. Foxor had prepared tiny breaded fruit balls for dessert that we fed each other. I thought licking the syrupy coating from each other's fingers would create a romantic mood. She had other things on her mind.

"Montor, I have made an important decision, and I would like you to be a part of it."

If she already has made up her mind, how am I supposed to be a part of it?

"OK. Tell me. What is it?"

"I am joining the Arandan militia."

I jumped to my feet.

"What! Are you out of your mind?"

She rolled her eyes.

"No, Montor, I am not. I have given this serious thought. Sit, please, so we can talk."

Reluctantly, I sat, forcefully exhaled, and flapped my hand at her.

"Go ahead. Talk."

She gulped at my rough demeanor but continued with a resolute expression.

"The freedom fighter group receives routine secret reports of what is happening with our cause in Aranda. One thing we are clearly lacking is medical personnel to assist our wounded after skirmishes with the Lostai—"

"Maybe that is because the Lostai finish everyone off. There are no survivors after such confrontations."

"Are you going to let me talk?"

I turned away and raked my hair in frustration.

"Go ahead."

"They are requesting doctors and nurses sympathetic to our cause to embed with our troops. I have not completed my medical certification, but I know enough to be of great help."

"Lorret, they cannot protect themselves, much less you."

"I understand. That is why I propose you come with me."

"Me? I run businesses, not armies."

I hated my outrageous lie and fake incredulous tone. Truth

be told, with my powers and military training, I could probably offer her some protection.

"Yes, but look at you. I have not met another Arandan of such formidable strength."

"Thanks for the compliment, but what can I do against a photon blast or a squadron of Lostai armed with advanced weapons?"

"Montor, I know you try to mask it, but I have seen your reaction when you hear about Lostai atrocities. You feel as strongly about them as I do. You are conflicted because of your business ventures, but you do not have a spouse or children who depend on you. Right now, you only have me. Please, I beg you, come with me. Let us face the Lostai tyrants together. I do not expect you to answer me tonight. But my mind is made up. I am leaving in fourteen days."

Her news wound me up to a point of losing interest in making love. I tossed and turned throughout the night and took her home the next day, angry that she would put me in such a position.

"Montor, I am in love with you. I do not take lightly the decision of leaving you, but this is something I feel strongly about. Please give it some thought."

In the following days, I shared my predicament with my inner circle, starting with Kaya.

"Montor, sounds like this female is headstrong."

"Yes, well, she is very young. Everything seems simple for people her age."

"You were once her age."

"At her age, I had lived through things she cannot even imagine."

"True, and even as a child, you seemed like an old soul. Do you love her?"

"She is beautiful and there are many aspects of her personality I like, but I need more time to sort out my feelings for her. I do not like her giving me ultimatums."

She paused to think for a moment.

"Montor, do you realize in one revolution you will have completed your fifteen-revolution tenure with the Lostai military? You will be free to do as you please. Maybe you can persuade her to wait till then."

I totally forgot about that!

Kaya's old eyes were so caring and selfless. She hoped maybe she had offered a plausible solution.

A flurry of excitement buzzed in my chest.

She is right. At that time, I can do whatever I want. I can even manipulate Zorla's mind if he tries to put obstacles in my way. Maybe Lorret might agree to wait.

No sooner had I kindled that fire than another thought extinguished it.

I remembered my commitment to watch over Kaya's granddaughter's welfare. If I joined the Arandan insurgency and died in battle, what might happen to her after Kaya passed on? Also, who knew what measures the Lostai military would take against Foxor and Lasarta if they learned I had joined a rebellious faction? Zorla had well documented who were my foster parents. And what would happen if the Arandan militia learned I lived my entire adult life as a Lostai soldier? They might even think I was acting on behalf of the Lostai as a spy. Lorret would surely stab me in my sleep.

I covered my eyes, not wanting to burden Kaya with my torment.

"No, Kaya...what she wants..." I shook my head. "It is impossible."

After my chat with Kaya, I spent a few days sulking at home and thinking through my response to Lorret. There was no need to talk about the issue with anyone else, but Lasarta knew me well enough. I could not hide things from her.

After eating the morning meal together, she said, "Montor, when are you going to tell me what is going on with you? Please do not insult me by denying it."

I explained the situation to her.

"Do you love her, son? I mean enough to make a lifelong commitment and marry her."

"I do not know."

"Her impulsive behavior is typical of her age."

I groaned.

"I know you told me she was too young."

"Also, it is selfish for her to force her decisions on you. We are talking life-altering decisions. One or both of you could lose your lives."

"Do not worry. I have already thought this through. She is trying to lead me down a path that, at this time, I cannot follow."

Of all the feedback I received on the topic, Jortan's left me the most puzzled. He spoke about Aranda's freedom with a passion he had never displayed before.

Jortan is all about business and financial gain, not liberating Aranda. Maybe the stampu is causing him to speak this way.

"This is a very personal decision for you, Montor. There is a lot at stake. I do not feel comfortable weighing in on it, but I will say this. These young people have the right sentiment but are on a fool's errand. Aranda will never win back their freedom through isolated terrorist attacks and skirmishes. This war will be won through covert fundraising, training, and a well thought out strategy," Jortan said, standing and emphasizing his words with vehement gesticulations. "We cannot go at it alone. We need to join other planets and create a united rebel front against the Lostai. This will take time, but then we will be ready to deal them a knock-out punch."

I traveled back to Gorinth and invited Lorret to a waterfront restaurant by the beach where we had made love for the first time. Tables were set in the sand with flickering candle center-pieces. I ordered wine. She toyed with her fingers and did not meet my eyes.

"So, Montor, I have been waiting to hear from you regarding my request. I am leaving in three days. Have you given it some thought? Please tell me you are coming with me."

I caressed her cheek and, because of whatever she saw in my eyes, did not have to say another word. She stared at her lap.

"Montor..." She tried to control the tremor in her voice. "You have broken my heart."

"I wish you would not do this, Lorret." I took her hands in mine. "Reconsider. I do not want to lose you. Give me one revolution to get my affairs in order, and then we can revisit this."

"Revisit? I cannot believe what I am hearing." I might as well have insulted her in the worst way. "There are Arandans on the battlefield who have laid down their lives for lack of proper medical attention. The time to do something is now. My mind is made up."

"You and your friends are not prepared for what you will face. Aranda will not win back freedom this way. You are behaving like an impulsive adolescent."

"I do not get it, Montor. You, of all people, should be ready to fight the Lostai right now." She leaned in for emphasis and spoke through gritted teeth. "They obliterated your neighbor-hood. They took your family. You do not even know what they did to them, whether they are dead or still toiling in some faraway labor camp. How can you live with that? What is wrong with you? Do you have no blood in your veins?"

I got up.

"Do not dare question me. You know nothing about my circumstances."

She stood also.

"Then tell me!"

I was ready to punch something. "I am taking you back to your apartment. You have no right to talk to me that way. You have no right to force me to say or do things. If you want, call me when you get to wherever you are heading and call me every day you can. I have nothing else to say."

She never called.

44

———

By the time I met Lorret, the affluence and distance from the battlefield I had achieved helped to suppress a lot of my bottled-up anger. After she left, the rage resurfaced with a vengeance. During my better moments, it manifested itself as chronic crankiness, even around those who cared about me. When it got bad, I exploded into outright violence and vicious sarcasm with anyone who crossed me. I looked for ways to counteract my stress by going back to having meaningless romantic flings. Even Zorla, unknowingly, was a victim of my emotional turmoil. I played little secret jokes on him, accessing his mind to cause him to misplace things or forget to attend important meetings. Fortunately, Kaya had instilled in me a strong adherence to the Sotkari Ta regimen. Otherwise, I would have added excessive alcohol and drug use to the mix, but I could not meditate or perform my daily physical and mental workouts if I was hungover. Lasarta would have intervened as well.

I found myself returning to the Arandan freedom fighter rallies alone. I learned Lorret left with a small group of medical students under a veil of secrecy. No one knew where they were or what had become of them. Her father contacted me, desperately hoping I knew something.

"That girl has always been so stubborn. Now, I will never see her again." He turned away so I could not see his tears. "Did she tell you she was leaving?"

With shame, I admitted she had. He looked at me with contempt.

"And you let her go alone? Lorret thought the world of you. I can see she was mistaken. You are no warrior."

Anger erupted in my chest, but I pushed it down.

He is old. What use would it do to knock him out?

As the days passed, I worried for her safety and agonized over whether I had made the right decision.

If there is another way I could help the cause in Aranda, maybe it might indirectly help her chances of survival.

My position in the Lostai military gave me access to all sorts of confidential data and pass codes. Just getting information in the right hands could be helpful for the Arandan militia. I did not have a concrete plan, but I knew three things were required before taking any steps in that direction.

First, I needed a fool-proof encrypted form of communication, something so advanced that not even the Lostai's latest technology could hack into it. Fronidia was the perfect place for such an endeavor. Besides being the most advanced planet in the sector, the Fronidian government strictly enforced their privacy laws, protecting any communication generated from within their planetary borders.

I owned two properties on Fronidia and set up one as my home base for any covert activities. Using anti-tracking software, I could make all communication in or out of that location appear like it was coming from any remote part of the sector. Both measures ensured no one could view or hear my conversations, but if for some reason someone could overcome that level of security, the locations of the parties involved would remain unknown.

The second requirement was moving funds without traceability. I created fake profiles of customers, vendors, and suppliers inside and outside the Fronidian network. The Fronidian government did not require profile images or personal verification for these setups, as long as taxes were paid. Some other planets did require an image or video confirmation, but it was easy enough to generate a holographic simulation. As an extra measure of security, I used an application that blocked any payment or receipt verification and tracing protocols. Again, the Fronidian privacy laws favored this deception.

I knew which sole supplier provided the Lostai military's sector-wide security systems. The last thing I did was purchase an application on the black market with the ability to manipulate and override those systems remotely. The programmers created the application to provide a failsafe in case on site personnel were ambushed or disabled. This was no trivial expenditure. It cost me the equivalent of a half revolution worth of income. I moved funds around in my fake network and paid for the various encryption and anti-tracking applications from different accounts.

My next logical step would be to gain the trust of an Arandan militia insider so I could learn their plans and determine how I could assist. I attended the next Arandan freedom fighter meeting remotely via video communication using my encrypted system and wearing a mask and hooded cloak to hide my identity. After the typical singing and speeches, an invited member of the Arandan militia made an appearance to take questions from the attendees. I made my move.

"I have a question. If someone possessed data that could benefit the militia, who would be a safe person to relate this information to?"

"What kind of information?"

"Like the access to a Lostai spacecraft repair center located on planet Aranda, the precise time when the guards take a tea break, and interference with the surveillance system. I might throw in a distraction to make sure they stay away for longer."

His eyes narrowed as he stood and approached the viewer, as if trying to get a better look at me.

"Who are you? Why do you come here concealing your face?"

"I am a businessperson whose interests conflict with the Lostai adding huge chunks of this sector to their Empire. Obviously, I need to hide my identity. The Lostai are implementing rules impeding the free flow of commerce. It is affecting my income, and I intend to do what I can to cause problems for the Lostai military. I also am someone who buys and sells information and can assist with covert activities."

"Why should we trust you? You are likely a criminal war lord or worse. You could be a Lostai trying to infiltrate our cause." He turned and signaled to someone in the back of the room.

"Do not try to trace this call. You would be wise to take this opportunity I am offering totally free of charge."

"You might be setting a trap for our brave soldiers."

"I will give you the access codes and time frame information right now on a private channel. Send one of those brave soldiers to try it. If he confirms what I am saying, you can come back again in full force and steal some of the *Vona* parked there waiting for pickup."

"I am sure those access codes change periodically."

"They do. The access codes to the lot and the ships are changed every four hours, but I have access to all of them and the exact timeframes when the switch occurs. I also can remotely override the handprint touch screen access control."

"Tell me more about these *Vona*."

"These small Lostai military spacecrafts are known for

maneuverability and strong plasma beam weaponry capable of destroying larger vessels. They would be a nice addition to the insurgency fleet. Is it not worth risking the life of one brave Arandan soldier? You are taking graver risks by sending these inexperienced, spoiled students to a battlefield to face a ruthless opponent."

The crowd of young wealthy Arandans looked up at the militia spokesperson, eyes wide with awe at the conversation unfolding right before them and concern about the raw truth I had uttered.

"Think carefully before rejecting my offer. If you do, I will move on to propose it to another rebel group. There are several popping up across the sector."

His brow furrowed as he struggled with his decision.

"OK, give me a contact code where I can reach you, and I will call back within the hour."

The young crowd roared with war cries and fist pumping.

So stupid. They have no idea what war is really like.

He was prompt with his reply.

"I will need to contact my superiors in this matter."

A few hours passed until he received approval from someone higher up in the militia ranks to test out my information.

"Now, I do not take responsibility for what happens once you take off from the lot," I clarified. "Hopefully, you have a plan for where to fly and hide those *Vona* and how to evade Lostai scans."

"We do," he replied without sharing any more information.

It took two days for them to get a soldier to the repair lot. From my home base in Fronidia, I could access the Lostai surveillance system and had full view of the lot with no trace back to my location. As soon as the five Lostai guards walked over to a nearby building, I disabled the handprint protocol and started a backup maintenance routine, freezing the surveillance feed for a few minutes except for the one linked to my video system. A cloaked figure approached the lot's main entrance. He punched in the codes I had supplied. His body stiffened before gazing up at the drones flying over the area. The gate slid open without requiring the additional handprint security protocol. He waited five minutes, punched in the codes again to close the gate, and rushed away. As soon as he was out of sight, I restored the surveillance and handprint control and eliminated any record of these manipulations. The guards returned to their posts, unaware of what had happened.

Yes! This can work.

Fourteen days later, we repeated the process. This time, the stakes were higher. I held my breath as six Arandan militia pilots entered the lot, scrambled into three *Vona* crafts, and took off before the Lostai guards returned to their posts.

I never learned whether they evaded detection or where they traveled to, but I guessed the mission was a success because a few weeks later, I received an encrypted message from the Arandan militia spokesperson.

"The Arandan militia extends its appreciation for your help in stealing those *Vona* and wonders if there are other ways we can collaborate."

"I will contact you when I identify opportunities," I replied.

"OK, but you will no longer be communicating with me. I will give you the contact codes of someone who can make immediate decisions on behalf of the Arandan militia. Going forward, you will deal with him on these matters."

The next time I made contact, the person on the other end of the video call also wore a cloak and mask. He even modified his voice to come across as robotic.

"I will be your contact going forward," said the mystery person. "I think it is best neither one of us can recognize each other."

"Agreed."

"But I would like to know, are you Arandan?"

I considered lying to further conceal my identity, but to deny my race was too much dishonor to pile on top of the shame I already carried.

"I am."

"Good. I would like to assume you have more than just financial motivations for what we are doing here. So, tell me, what do you have for us?"

"I know the precise time when a weapons delivery will be made at the Lostai armory in the Britar province. Perhaps you can ambush them."

"Sounds good."

"I also have information on Lostai sites on other planets and moon bases that could be targeted. Does the Arandan militia have the capability to travel off world?"

"Not yet, but it is our next step. The Lostai assume we are too much of a backwards people to learn how to pilot their modern intergalactic spaceships. They have all but eliminated the older models we used to have on Aranda for travel within our quadrant. Planetary border control here on Aranda is lax. We will soon take advantage of Lostai arrogance."

"OK, let me know when you do. By the way, do you have a name?" I asked.

"I am known as The Strategist. What should I call you?"

The question caught me off guard. For a moment, I was at a loss of what to answer. I never had a nickname other than the term of endearment my older sister used with me when I was a boy. Considering my height and build, I almost chuckled out loud at the irony.

"Hmm...call me Little Warrior."

45

———————

Working with The Strategist to sabotage and pillage Lostai military installations provided an addictive satisfaction that curtailed some of the darkness in my soul. For almost an entire revolution, I kept this activity secret from my foster parents or Kaya until I helped the Arandan militia orchestrate their most significant success so far: the takeover and rescue of an entire labor camp on Aranda. My private way of celebrating was taking Kaya out to dinner. We met at a quaint restaurant near her village on Sotkar while she was back home visiting her family. Our meal consisted of roasted fowl and a medley of colorful vegetables over a salty seaweed puree.

"Montor, I sense a joyful vibe from you. Anything special going on?" Kaya asked.

Our ability to converse telepathically and our bond of trust made her the perfect confidant.

"Kaya, I have a big secret to share." Her blue eyes opened wide. "I am working with Arandan rebels to score hits against Lostai military targets."

She almost choked on her food.

"What!"

"Yes, but do not worry. I am taking all sorts of precautions to keep my identity secret."

"Oh, Montor, you must be careful. If you were exposed..." She placed her hand over her heart. "I do not even want to imagine what might happen."

"I promise I am not taking any reckless risks. The activities are spread apart and managed remotely using sophisticated encryption and anti-tracking software. I even wear a mask to hide my identity when I communicate with my contact."

Her lips curved into the tiniest of mischievous smiles.

"OK, tell me all about the headaches you have created for the Lostai military. I think I am going to enjoy our dinner even more now."

The Strategist's message surprised me. I would always contact him first with an offer or idea. A separate tablet and additional encryption software allowed me to access remotely the messages on my Fronidian home base communication system from anywhere in the sector without disclosing my location. Still, I needed a secure place where I could talk with privacy. When I first detected the message, I was on a trip with Zorla on official Lostai military business and could not reply until I was back home on Renna One.

"I hope contacting you has not been an inconvenience, Little Warrior."

"No, but as you must imagine, I cannot just reply to you from anywhere. I go to great lengths to keep our conversations secure."

"Yes, as do I."

"Well, why have you called me?"

"The Arandan militia has chosen a spot for its headquarters. It is a remote island in the middle of a vast ocean named Penstarox. It remains stormy throughout most of the seasons, and its location makes the trip there dangerous and almost impossible to reach by aquatic vehicles or aircraft."

"OK, and how do you intend to transport people and equipment there?"

"Some of our people have already made the difficult trip there using old submarine ships used during the clan wars. At first, only half of those we sent out would make it, but by now we have figured out the best sea routes and seasons to send our people there. The Lostai want nothing to do in that area due to the extreme tropical climate and unpredictable, harsh weather."

At moments such as these, too many conflicting emotions took control of my soul.

Pride.

Self-loathing.

I come from a brave people who refuse to be prey, and yet here I sit, cowering in the dark, wearing a mask and having secret conversations.

I shook off the tremors and replied, "How can I help?"

"There is larger equipment we need to transport to the base."

"What kind of equipment?"

"A shield grid to conceal our location as well as protect it from both atmospheric and surface attacks."

"*Shermont!* How did you acquire such a system?"

"We have some wealthy benefactors. With their funding, we bought it from a criminal organization that uses similar technology to evade law enforcement." He hurried on as if that was not of importance. "Anyway, the delivery will be made just outside the Arandan planetary border. Our suppliers will load the system on a drone aircraft. We need to meet our suppliers at the designated coordinates, take delivery of the drone, and bring it across Aranda's planetary border. Once in Arandan airspace, the drone can be launched to fly to our base. It will be fitted with special shields, making it undetectable to Lostai surveillance."

"How do you intend to do all that?"

"We thought we could brainstorm with you on how to accomplish this."

This was no trivial endeavor, but the idea of pulling it off pumped me with a rush of excitement. A protected military base would represent a significant step forward for the Arandan insurgency.

It would be wonderful to be a part of something so groundbreaking. I need to make it happen.

I erased any emotion from my voice.

"I will give it some thought and get back to you."

"Our supplier wants us to take delivery within this lunar cycle."

"OK."

Midway through the lunar cycle, I contacted The Strategist with my proposal. For the first time, doubt laced his tone.

"Little Warrior, when I said we wanted to brainstorm with you, I did not mean for you to insert yourself this much into the process. How confident are you with this plan?"

I could not tell him I would be relying on my special abilities and position in the Lostai military to execute the plan.

"There is always risk, but I think it is the best option. The fewer people involved in something like this, the better. The only thing I need is for your supplier to be flexible with the delivery time and be able to react within a short notice."

He exhaled deeply and did not reply right away.

"OK, Little Warrior, I think I can work that out with our supplier. But I hope you know what you are doing. This is our most important mission so far."

Fronidia, being the closest advanced inhabited planet to

Aranda, was the best place to launch my plan. Using Lostai military connections, I learned a Lostai ambassador was on Fronidia on official diplomatic business and would stay there for two lunar cycles. He and his family had arrived on the ambassador's private recreational spacecraft as he planned to stretch the business trip into a vacation. His personal pilot was also staying on Fronidia and slept on the spacecraft docked on a private space lot in a secluded area with barely any traffic. I conducted surveillance and, once I became familiar with the pilot's comings and goings, coordinated with The Strategist the timing for putting my plan into action.

Wearing my hooded cloak and mask and carrying a backpack of supplies, I hid behind the trees adorning the entrance to the space lot. The starless night sky promised stormy weather was on the way, and there was no one else in sight.

I hope this guy arrives at the usual time. We need to take off before the storms roll in.

To my relief, the pilot strolled to the entrance at the expected time. I immediately took control of his mind and approached him.

"What is your name?"

"Jarixt, and who are you?"

"I cannot tell you my name, but your boss needs you to run an errand. He sent me as a messenger because the storms coming through have affected the communication systems at the hotel where he is staying. I have all the details, so you will need to take me with you."

It was a lame story and unnecessary because he would execute whatever command I planted in his brain, anyway. I said it out of precaution. If law enforcement questioned him later, this would be his testimony.

"OK, and why are you dressed that way?" he asked.

"Jarixt, I have a contagious skin disease. Trust me, you do not want to see my face."

"Umm...you should take care of that," he replied with a grimace.

"Yes, I am, but the healing process takes time."

He frowned but, still under my influence, continued toward the spacecraft. I walked beside him, and we boarded the spacecraft together.

"Enter in the flight logs that you are performing a maintenance test flight. If border control asks why you are leaving, please tell them the same."

"I thought we were running an errand for my boss."

"Yes, but it is not official diplomatic business. The ambassador wants to conceal it from the official records."

A confused expression swept over his face, but at border control, he did as I instructed without any resistance. We were on our way without a glitch, heading to the coordinates where the supplier would deliver the drone. I needed to give my mind a rest, so I put the ship on autopilot and rendered Jarixt unconscious. Before taking a nap myself, I sent The Strategist an encrypted message confirming the time we would arrive at the designated coordinates. When I woke up several hours later, we were an hour away from the delivery point. I roused Jarixt, who continued to be confused as he studied the readings on the navigational system.

"How did we get here so fast?"

"You fell asleep, so I put the ship on autopilot. No worries. I took a nap, too. Anyway, this is perfect timing for me to tell you what will happen next. We are going to take delivery of a drone and drop it into Arandan airspace."

"What is the purpose of this?"

"I do not know, but these are your boss's exact instructions.

Look, there is an unmarked spacecraft approaching. This must
be the one carrying the drone."

He sighed.

"This is all extremely strange."

"Maybe, but I am sure your boss has his reasons," I said,
stifling a smile.

At the appointed time, the unmarked spacecraft hailed us,
audio only.

"Lostai vessel, we have instructions to deliver a drone.
Please send the pass codes."

The person from the unmarked spacecraft offered no
further identification or information. Jarixt looked at me and
shrugged his shoulders, wide-eyed and at a loss at what to do
next.

"Do not worry. I have the codes," I said.

I punched them into our communication system, and the
voice from the unmarked spacecraft acknowledged they were
correct. Soon after, their cargo bay door opened, revealing the
drone. We did the same and, using a towing beam, brought the
drone on board.

"Tell them to wait for us to do an inspection before they
leave," I instructed.

Jarixt relayed the message. The voice on the other side
sounded impatient.

"Make it quick."

Jarixt grimaced with a bewildered look on his face. I patted
him on the shoulder to assure him I had things under control
before I ran to our cargo bay to confirm the drone carried all
the equipment The Strategist had described to me. There
would be no time for testing, but at least I saw it was all there. I
rushed back and signaled to Jarixt that everything was in order.
We relayed the message to the unmarked ship, and in a flash,
the spacecraft disappeared from the area.

Everything up to that point had been relatively easy. Getting the drone into Arandan airspace would be a different story.

I hid myself from the viewer screen but remained close enough to maintain control of Jarixt's mind. He put the ship in idle mode, waiting to hear from border control.

"Lostai recreational ship, what is your business here?" said the Lostai border control agent on the viewer.

Jarixt replied while under my influence.

"I have a drone to be delivered to a Lostai military installment located in the Limer province."

Limer was the closest province to Penstarox island even though they were separated by a vast ocean.

"Who should we contact there to confirm this delivery?"

"Commander Pirnol. This is a high-priority delivery."

I purposely had Jarixt use Commander Pirnol's name because I knew he was in an important meeting with high command on Losta that no one would interrupt for an Arandan border patrol issue. After a pause, border control hailed again.

"Commander Pirnol is not on Aranda and cannot be contacted. No one else seems to know anything about this drone."

"Maybe you should come on board and take a look."

"What is wrong with you? Do you think we have time to do a visual on every border crossing?"

Still under my influence, Jarixt replied, "OK, I will leave, but I understood this to be a time-sensitive delivery. You will need to explain to Commander Pirnol why you wasted his time instead of coming on board to do a quick check."

Waiting for the border agent's decision, I almost did the unthinkable: ask The High Spirit to help me. The success of our mission depended on the agent's answer. Seconds seemed to crawl as I held my breath, waiting for his reply.

"OK, prepare your docking bay to receive my shuttle."

I sighed with relief and sped to the docking area to arrive before Jarixt and hide behind some crates. The docking bay doors opened, the border control shuttle parked in the bay, and the airlock closed. The border patrol agent disembarked his shuttle, and Jarixt arrived a moment later. I grabbed hold of Jarixt's mind, implanting an order that he not mention anything about my presence. Jarixt and the border patrol agent greeted each other and walked together to the next-door cargo bay where the drone was parked. I waited till the border agent was busy looking over the drone to slink in behind them and take control of his mind as well.

"OK, this looks fine," said the border agent, under my influence. He did not even bother to ask what the drone was carrying.

From his tablet, he sent the signal that would allow us through the border and walked back to his shuttle. As soon as he left our docking bay, I rushed out of my hiding space to the corridor and then strolled back to the bay as if I had just arrived.

"Where were you?" Jarixt asked me.

"I received an important call on my tablet that I needed to take in private."

Before he could ask any more questions, I instructed Jarixt to hurry back to the helm and get us across the border into Arandan airspace. The decision to let us in that I had planted in the border agent's mind would be permanent, but things could get problematic if he were questioned by a superior. I wanted in and out of there as soon as possible.

"Jarixt, take us to these coordinates," I ordered.

As expected, we ran into strong winds, lightning, and heavy rain as we hovered over the ocean near the militia island base. There was no risk to our ship, but I hoped the drone would arrive at Penstarox undamaged.

"OK, we are in the right spot. Open the airlock to the cargo bay. I have the application linked to the drone's navigational system."

"I thought we were going to deliver it all the way to Limer. Why would we release the drone in the middle of this storm?"

"There is a lot of secrecy around this delivery. Plus, part of this process is to verify that the drone can fly to its destination amid these kinds of weather conditions. Hurry, we do not have a moment to spare."

I enjoyed the stupid expression that waxed over my victims' eyes when I took over their minds and implanted commands. Jarixt followed my instructions without further questions. Once our controls showed the airlock was open, I punched in the coordinates for Penstarox and studied my tablet's screen, displaying the drone's trajectory, speed, and accuracy. The drone's shields were also working perfectly, as it did not attract the attention of local Lostai law enforcement. The Arandan militia was clearly not being run by the same old-fashioned leaders who commanded during the clan wars. This insurgency was using top-notch technology. I struggled to keep a tap on my emotions as the application on my tablet displayed the drone had landed safely on Penstarox. A brief message from The Strategist appeared on my tablet to confirm my readings. My chest swelled with satisfaction.

Success!

Luckily, Jarixt's boss had not tried to contact him in the day since we left Fronidia, but we could not push our luck.

"OK, Jarixt. Time to go home."

I wanted to go out a different border control point than the one we had entered through in case someone finally had contacted Commander Pirnol.

"We will exit Aranda here," I said to him, before hiding from the viewscreen.

"Where are you going?" asked Jarixt.

"I need to relieve myself. I will be back in a second."

A different border control agent appeared on screen.

"Where are you going, Lostai recreational ship?"

"We made a delivery and are now returning home."

Jarixt gave the border agent the logged entry code. My fists tightened as I hoped the agent would find nothing out of the ordinary.

"OK, move on."

Within hours, we were back, parked in the private space lot on Fronidia.

"Jarixt, be proud. You successfully executed this top-secret delivery. No matter how much you are questioned, you are not to speak of it to anyone, and much less are you to mention I assisted you. If anyone asks why you left Fronidian space, you will reply you were doing a routine maintenance flight. Is that clear?"

Besides speaking these orders, I implanted the permanent command in his mind.

"Yes."

"Goodbye, Jarixt."

Back at my home base, I called The Strategist. He promptly answered.

"Little Warrior, that was excellent work. I am mystified. How were you able to get through Arandan border control so easily? Did you bribe them?"

"I cannot disclose my methods."

"Hmm, OK. I can confirm the equipment arrived in perfect working condition. Soon, we will have an advanced surface-to-space shield surrounding our militia base on Penstarox. This is a game-changer for our cause."

Although he still spoke through a robotic voice modifier, the way he paced his words bared his emotions. I struggled to contain mine.

"I have one request."

"Anything."

"I think eventually the Lostai will realize you have placed the shield around that area."

"Yes. That is inevitable and maybe a good thing. We are showing them the insurgency is developing serious muscle."

"I ask you wait a few lunar cycles before installing the shield. The border agent who let us in to Aranda did not even check what was on the drone, but I had to make up a story that we were delivering it to a Commander Pirnol at the Lostai military base at Limer province. If questions arise, they can track the entry to a recreational ship belonging to a Lostai Ambassador who is visiting Fronidia. The Lostai diplomat's pilot was at the helm. I do not want to risk any chance they associate that entry with the installment of your shield."

"Yes, that would be a wise decision. We will wait. Little Warrior, thank you for your service. Will we talk again soon?"

"Out of an abundance of caution, I suggest we not talk for a while, but our work here is only beginning."

46

———

I shared the story of my little delivery escapade with Kaya.

"Montor, you are taking more and more risks. I think this is becoming like a secret addictive pleasure for you. Be careful you do not push your luck."

"Kaya, you make it sound like a game. It is much more than that. These are small ways of erasing the stain of my loathsome service to the Lostai. I will admit, though, the danger does give me an adrenaline rush."

She placed her hand on my shoulder and looked up at me with loving eyes.

"I can understand the temptation to use this as revenge against the Lostai and Zorla, but I worry for you, Montor."

I caressed her cheek. We allowed ourselves the luxury of these small displays of affection because we were in her home on Sotkar, away from any potential spying eyes on Xixsted.

The afterglow of that successful mission was short-lived. A few lunar cycles later, Zorla called me to his office.

"Montor, please sit. I have something important to discuss with you."

I wonder what scheme he has in mind today.

"I suppose you have so grown to enjoy your position within the Lostai military that you have forgotten this lunar cycle marks a special date." I controlled the urge to roll my eyes as he continued. "It has been fifteen revolutions since we inducted you in the Lostai military. Although it pains me to have this conversation, I am bound by law to do so."

Shermont! Has it been that long already?

"As you know, you now may leave the Lostai military and move on with your life as a respectful and law-abiding citizen of the Lostai Empire. However, I would ask you to weigh this decision. Many opt to stay and pursue long military careers, enjoying the salary, benefits, and prestige that come with it. Even if you stay for now, you can leave at any time thereafter. You are not bound by another timeframe."

He narrowed his eyes as if trying to gauge my thoughts.

"This has slipped my mind," I answered.

"I will be honest." He stood so he could look at me eye to eye. "You and I have established a working relationship we both must admit has been mutually beneficial."

Sure.

I helped him gain power and wealth through deception, swindling, and extortion. He continued with his sales pitch.

"Montor, Lostai law enforcement is facing more and more rebel attacks these days. Sometimes, in our response and investigations, it is hard to distinguish between those involved in illegal acts and innocent bystanders."

The image of Lorret's innocent grandmother falling victim to a Lostai bomb while buying fruit in a market came to mind. As Zorla continued, his voice took on that sinister, condescending tone he used when offering a veiled threat.

"It would be awful if something happened to your family or

if they were arrested because of a misunderstanding. I know the safety of your foster parents is of utmost importance to you. Your position as a Lostai soldier grants them extra security. We are careful to keep our military families safe. While you are a soldier, they would never be accused of criminal activities."

His insinuations could be no clearer, but I was no longer that young child he intimidated. I was a powerful being who could destroy him with a blink of an eye or expose him for what he really was: someone who milked his military position for personal gain.

On the other hand, if I killed him, someone else would simply take his place. I would likely be taken into custody, and my foster parents would be tortured. Also, as a safeguard against my mind control abilities, he had taken measures to make his inner circle aware of what to do if he exhibited erratic behavior or made unusual decisions. Although I masked the thoughts going through my head, as best I could, we both knew about the delicate dance we were engaged in.

"Zorla, I understand the importance of carefully weighing the pros and cons of this decision. I will not make it lightly and request you give me time to go to my home on Renna One and think about it."

He waved his hand in his typical annoying dismissive way and replied, "Sure, take the time you need."

Once again, I relied on my circle of trust to think through my decision. After my talk with Zorla, all I wanted was a nice home-cooked Arandan meal and a few shots of *stampu*. Those would have to wait. The trip to Renna One took just over one lunar cycle. Before leaving Xixsted, I stopped by Kaya's dorm and filled her in on my conversation with Zorla. Our telepathic connection allowed us the privacy I needed for this type of chat.

"Montor, I arrived to Xixsted not too long before they brought you here as a child, so I had a similar chat with Zorla some revolutions ago," said Kaya. "Because I am not a soldier, the fifteen-revolution tenure rule does not necessarily apply to my work here, but I wondered what was next for me after Gio joined the military, since there were no new hostages to train."

"And yet he has kept you here all this time."

I often wondered what services Kaya was rendering for Zorla after completing Gio's training. We still often practiced together to keep both our skills honed, but it was not a full-time job. In the same way I chose not to share with her some of the things I did for Zorla, she apparently did not share everything with me.

"Yes, although Sotkari Ta hostages are usually taken to much larger military installments, Zorla hopes he can orchestrate bringing more here. In the meantime, he has me doing research work for him. Because of my age and pure blood lineage, I can read and interpret documents from ancient Sotkari Ta archives. He made it clear that it was in my family's best interest that I remain in his employ."

"What does he hope to accomplish?"

"Searching for, capturing, and forcing Sotkari Ta individuals into servitude and training them is an expensive and time-consuming endeavor. There have been many instances of Sotkari Ta who initially agree to work with the Lostai and then rebel against their orders. He has always dreamed of rising to fame as the first Lostai to find a way of creating Sotkari Ta individuals ready and willing to be Lostai soldiers on a grand scale."

"How does he expect to do that?"

"Either by cracking the nut of bioengineering that allowed Sotkari Ta elder scientists to embed their genes into other species, or cloning, or even breeding. He has me translating these texts for him in the hopes he and the Lostai scientists under his command on this station can figure something out."

"And how has this been going?"

"So far, it has been frustrating for him. He would love to discover their secret of embedding Sotkari Ta genes into expectant mothers and bring in a bunch of pregnant Lostai females and experiment on them."

"Maybe we should let him experiment on his own kind. See how they like it," I said, my fists clenching.

"That is unlikely. Fortunately, our elders took their science with them when they escaped Sotkar. The Lostai have found no trace of that technology. Other Lostai scientists have tried cloning Sotkari Ta only to confirm what I told Zorla a long time ago. Sotkari Ta genes can only be passed down through natural conception. But getting back to your situation, Montor. What are your thoughts? Will you leave the Lostai military?"

I leaned over, elbows on my knees and my forehead pressed into my hands.

"Kaya, you know I derive no pleasure from the work I do for the Lostai military. Yes, I have achieved wealth and influence, but at what cost? A piece of my soul dies each time I coordinate a village takeover or a relocation to a prison camp or battle against rebels who are only trying to defend their homes and family."

"I know, son."

I did not want to reiterate my commitment to her family's safety. She would only tell me I should not burden myself with those concerns.

"But on the other hand, my position with the Lostai military, paired with my special abilities, puts me in a uniquely favorable position to help the Arandan militia."

"Yes, but Montor, how long do you think you can sustain this double life?"

"I am going to Renna One to spend some time at home and weigh my options."

"If there is anything I can do, let me know."

The uneventful trip to Renna One allowed me to conduct relaxing meditation and clear my mind. I arrived late morning and went straight home, landing the shuttle on my property's private spaceport. Crisp air and pleasant temperatures welcomed me. Instead of riding home on my transport vehicle, I took a stroll, taking in the beauty of my property.

A rustic stone path took me through various orchards and luscious gardens. I stopped to observe a *goria* tree and touched the bunches of hanging fruit. The large purple berries looked bright and succulent.

These are almost ready for pie.

Mother was known in our hometown for baking the best *goria* pie. I used to hear my mother's voice in dreams and during my darkest hours as a child on Xixsted, but it had been so long since I imagined her speaking to me.

What would she think of me now? Would she be proud I not only survived but thrived despite my circumstances? Maybe? But she would detest the Lostai uniform I wore every time I was on official military business.

Mother, would you despise me, slap me, and call me a traitor?

A sparkling river bordered the property, and outdoor furniture was set tastefully in different spots along the way. I sat for a while. The sound of bubbling water flowing over small boulders and rocks did nothing to soothe me. Nearby flowering bushes gave off exquisite fragrances, bringing to mind my childhood. Mother always had kept a vibrant garden behind our home on Aranda. At the labor camp, the little patch of land by our shack was devoted only to herbs and vegetables.

Mother, my life these days is a far cry from how we lived at the labor camp.

Even if the Lostai had never come by our town, I probably would have never achieved the level of prosperity and power I now enjoyed. My life would have been like my father's; etching out a decent living, but nothing extravagant. By my age, Father already was married with the first two of his five children, but as a young adult, he had been a warrior. He often spoke with relish how, during the clan wars, he enjoyed coming up with tactics to outsmart the enemy, perfecting the use of weapons, overpowering an opponent in hand-to-hand combat, learning from defeat, and celebrating victory.

As much as I hate to admit it, Father, I enjoy those elements of my life as a Lostai soldier, too. It brings me an excitement almost comparable to sex, and yet, it also brings me devastating shame. I wish I could openly fight alongside my Arandan brothers, but what would happen then?

Lost in my thoughts, a lot more time than intended slipped by. I checked my tablet, stood, and made my way home. With a heavy heart, I walked through the front door.

"Montor, is that you?"

I heard Lasarta's voice coming from the food preparation area. I walked over there and found her kneading a batter of some sort. She washed and dried her hands before approaching and caressing my cheek.

"I did not hear the vehicle's motor."

"I walked instead."

"Oh, good idea. The weather is so nice for a leisurely—" She stopped to look at me a bit closer. "Montor, are you OK?"

I had wiped my tears before walking in, but she knew me well. Gazing up at me through furrowed brows, she gestured toward the counter covered with vegetables, herbs, and slabs of meat.

"Well, maybe you are hungry. Dinner will not be ready for a while, but I can prepare a snack and *yomoso* to tide you over."

I started to say I was not hungry, although my stomach grumbled in protest. As usual, she ignored me, sliced pieces of freshly baked *bomar*, and slathered them with sweet cream.

An expert at pulling me out of my darkness, she erased the concerned look from her face and pointed to the refrigeration unit.

"Please, Montor, pull out some sausage links and throw them on the grilling pan over there."

In minutes, the sausages were sizzling and cooked to perfection. She plated me a serving of the sausage and *bomar*, adding some freshly cut fruit.

"Take this to the patio. I will brew the *yomoso* and join you."

"Where is Foxor?"

"He went to the city to get some ingredients we need for dessert. He will be back soon."

The aroma of freshly brewed *yomoso* arrived at the patio before she did. She placed a tray on the patio table with a carafe of the hot caffeinated beverage, two cups, and a plate of food for herself.

"I love to eat out here when the weather is like this," she said while pouring *yomoso* in our cups.

Once we were halfway through our plates and after chatting about meaningless things like how Foxor had injured a finger while fishing, she said, "Tell me, Montor, what is troubling you?"

I could not help but smile.

"Why do I even try to conceal things from you, Lasarta?"

She patted my hand.

"I am like your mother. Talk to me."

I explained the decision I was struggling with, purposely omitting any reference to Zorla's insinuations about how my foster parent's safety might be impacted if I left the Lostai military. For the first time, I spoke to her about my activities with the Arandan militia. She was alarmed at first.

"Montor, that sounds dangerous. What if you are discovered? I could not stand to lose you again."

"Do not worry, Lasarta. I am always careful with these

missions. One reason it might make sense for me to stay working for Zorla is it puts me in an excellent position to help my fellow Arandans in a much more significant way than by joining one of their militia squadrons. It is a small way to atone for being a filthy traitor."

"You should not focus on that. You are a loving son and a survivor. Let us talk about something else. What about other aspects of your life? Do you not see yourself at some point with a family and children of your own?"

I poured myself some more *yomoso*. Instead of sipping, I swallowed the hot, bitter liquid in a hard gulp.

"I can never marry or have children. That would only add to the list of people the Lostai military might harm in order to blackmail me into their service."

"Montor, I pray that is not what fate has in store for you. Your proud lineage should continue on."

Nothing was said for a few minutes until she broke the silence.

"I assume Zorla has threatened to harm us if you leave the Lostai military, right?"

I did not reply.

"You will not admit it, but I am sure he has. My heart breaks imagining how that weighs on you. Think about this, Montor. You already have gained us revolutions of life in comfort and stability we would have lost at the labor camp. We would not have survived much longer there had you not rescued us. Trust me, Foxor and I could die tomorrow in peace if that allowed you to pursue your dreams."

"No, do not even utter those words. Foxor and you are vibrant and strong with so much of your life still ahead of you. If I lost you, I would be even more sad than I am now. You are the last of my family. My dreams will always include having Foxor and you close to me."

I did not tell her death would be the least Zorla could inflict on them. His corrupt mind could come up with all kinds of torture.

She squeezed my hand. Her eyes filled with tears as she said, "Well, Montor, even if you remain in the Lostai military for now, you have the right to leave whenever you want. Maybe you need to stop seeing this as a onetime decision you need to make immediately. Consider safely cutting your ties with the Lostai military one step at a time."

I nodded.

"Perhaps."

After dinner, I flew my transport pod to Members Only. As I walked in, the frenetic electronic beat stopped, replaced by the sound of a historical Arandan poem declaimed with flutes and soft percussion in the background. I sat at the bar and ordered a shot of *stampu.*

"Would you like some meat pies?" asked the bartender.

"No thanks. I just had dinner."

Before I knew it, Colora and Jortan walked in from the beach, looking slightly disheveled. They were living a torrid, illicit love affair and probably were back from using a bed inside one of the gazebos by the shoreline. The thought made me horny. It was time to find some female company, but that would need to wait. I came to Members Only to relax and unburden myself some more. This was not the place to find a lover.

"Montor, it is good to see you," said Jortan. "May we join you?"

"Hello, Jortan. Of course," I said, placing my hand on his shoulder and nodding respectfully at Colora.

The bartender served them their shots, and soon we were doing a second round, a third, and a fourth. Colora excused herself. *Stampu* was too strong for her to keep up with Jortan and me. The music changed from the spoken poems to Arandan folkloric music. We drank a few more.

"How are things going with you, Montor?" asked Jortan.

"Ahh, Jortan. Sometimes, I feel like I should not be here. Maybe that is why I face impossible choices."

"What do you mean?"

"I should have died in the labor camp with the rest of my family."

"No, Montor. The High Spirit obviously has other plans for you."

I rolled my eyes.

"Jortan, I mean no disrespect, but I stopped believing in the High Spirit the day my twin sister Arixa died."

"OK, but you seem a bit more melancholy than usual today. Is there anything going on?"

Once more, I talked about the end of my legal requirement with the Lostai military, Zorla's insinuations, and my fear of what might happen to Kaya, her family, and my foster parents if I left. I had not confided in Jortan regarding my covert involvement with the Arandan militia. I liked and trusted him, but there was no need to put yet another person close to me at risk with such a secret. His reaction was cryptic and oddly in sync with Lasarta's comment.

"Right now, the Lostai are at the top of their game, but no empire lasts forever. I know many people in politics, business, and even in the criminal world. It gives me a unique feel on the pulse of our sector. Things are going to shake up around here in the upcoming revolutions. If I were you, I would remain in your current position for the time being but stay aware of what is happening as you plan carefully for your future. It might not be so bleak as you think."

47

After my conversation with Jortan, there was no one else I could talk to about what was troubling me.

I have wasted enough energy on this topic, anyway. Time to focus on something else.

I headed over to Zamandi's Room and sat at the main bar, scanning the room for any attractive females, an unnecessary step since they usually found me first. Sure enough, one approached. To my surprise, she was Arandan, the first one I had ever come across on Renna One. Tall and sporting a body-hugging one-piece suit that accentuated her tiny waist, large breasts, and curvy hips, I imagined everything I would like to do to that spectacular body. She tried to saunter over but was a little off balance. There was nothing particularly enchanting about her facial features, but that was unimportant at the moment.

"Hello. I must say, you are the first Arandan female I have ever seen here."

She looked me over.

"I hope I did not disappoint you."

"Not at all. In fact, I think this deserves a toast. May I get you a drink?"

"Yes, thank you. I would like a glass of *vormey*, please."

I ordered her the most expensive *vormey* available.

"My name is Montor, and yours?"

She ran her hands over her thighs and played with her locks. "Ar Ona."

The bartender handed over our drinks. I raised my glass and gave her my best smile.

"To meeting attractive Arandans where one least expects it."

She raised her glass and took a sip.

"Tell me, Ar Ona, what brings you to Renna One?"

I learned that Ar Ona was born on Hevrra, which explained the odd name. Her ancestors left Aranda during one of the many clan wars and moved there two generations earlier. She was on the rebound, having just broken up with a wealthy Hevrran who owned a manufacturing plant on Renna One. He had set her up with a lavish apartment, fancy clothes, and expensive jewelry. Normally, an Arandan female would lead me on a chase for several lunar cycles before letting me touch her, but she was accustomed to living an opulent lifestyle. The rare, expensive brandy I was drinking and the *vormey* I ordered for her was proof I could help with that.

"I would like to get to know you more, Montor, but this music is so loud, we can barely hear each other. My apartment is a quick ride from here," she said, leaning in so her breasts pressed against my bicep.

"My transport pod is parked nearby," I said. "Let us take a stroll there, and I will have you home soon enough."

I settled the bill. When she linked her arm with mine, I noticed she was holding on to me to steady herself.

Wait. How many glasses of vormey has she already put away?

"So, what do you do, Montor?"

"I own different businesses across the sector and also do some military consulting."

I did not even worry that she would want to know more about what military consulting I was referring to. She was not paying much attention to what I was saying. It took forever to walk the short distance to where my transport pod was parked. I was not much interested in what she said either.

Hopefully, our bodies are more in tune than our minds.

We arrived at her building complex, located in a high-income neighborhood. Alone in the elevator, she pushed me against the wall and ran her hand over my groin area without warning. I was about to embrace her when the doors slid open. She led me to her apartment. Inside, the furniture and décor appeared oversized and inappropriate for the small space. It was all expensive but thrown together in poor taste. She showed me a bottle of brandy neither cheap nor special, just good enough.

"I do not have what you were drinking. I hope this is OK," she said.

Time to turn on the charm and hopefully get this evening done and over with.

I shortened the space between us and caressed her cheek.

"I did not come here for the brandy."

She threw her head back in a silly, fake laugh but exposed her neck so I knew she wanted me to lick her there. I lingered, and my hands dropped to squeeze her waist.

"I would like to dance," she said unexpectedly.

She put on suggestive music. The dance required our bodies to rub against each other.

OK, good. This seems to be going in the right direction.

As we moved, she allowed my hands to roam all over her curves.

"Montor, I have never met such a powerful-looking male."

She squeezed and touched my biceps, pecs, and abs. "I mean, you are all muscle. Are you going to hurt me?"

What kind of question is that?

I controlled the urge to roll my eyes and chuckled instead.

"Not unless you want me to."

Without another word, she tugged at the magnetic strip running down the front of her suit, and with one yank, her breasts popped out. Her torso was exposed down to her hips. She grabbed her breasts and pushed them up. This was beginning to feel comical.

"Do you like what you see? This is what my ex-lover is missing out on."

Great, the one Arandan female I run into on this planet, and she has no class.

"Of course," I answered.

Slipping out of her shoes, she kept moving to the music while quickly unbuttoning my shirt and unbuckling my belt. I squatted to pull down the rest of her suit. She stumbled out of each leg and now staggered before me naked. Her body was perfection. Yet, remorse tugged at my conscience.

"You know, Ar Ona, maybe you need to rest, and we can meet up another time."

"Take the rest of your clothes off," she ordered. "I know what I need."

I complied, and we continued to dance, our now naked bodies pressed together, pelvis against gyrating pelvis. As puerile as I found this encounter, I was by now erect and rock hard. She reached down and stroked me.

"Where is the bedroom?" I growled.

"I want to do it here," she said.

I looked around. The chairs and sofa were stone carvings and did not look comfortable. I noticed a narrow space of unencumbered wall and pulled her over.

"May I use your reproducer?" I asked. "I need a contra-ceptive."

"No need. I have already taken care of that. Hurry," she replied.

"Turn around," I said, with no urge to see her face. She propped her forearms against the wall and stuck her butt out. I reached my hand between her legs. She did not feel ready, so I pressed my fingers in the right spot and rubbed while fondling her breasts with my other hand.

"Do you like it?" I grunted.

"Uh huh."

She was lubricated, but her reply did not sound convincing.

Shermont! Let it not be said that Montor does not make his females sing.

I flipped her around and got on my knees, about to press my face between her legs, but they buckled. I moved back and carefully helped her slide down the wall until she sat one leg flat on the floor, the other bent at the knee.

"Montor, I like what you are doing, but just take me here. I am too drunk to continue standing."

"Umm, maybe we should call it a night."

"OK, but I would like to see you again, Montor."

"Do you want me to help you to your bed?"

"No, I am just going to sit here for a while."

"Please, I insist."

I carried her to her bed, left a glass of water on her night table, and rushed back to the other room to get dressed.

She shouted out from her bedroom, "Montor, please, please...umm...pu-punch in your contact codes in my commu-nication system so I can call you in a few days."

"OK."

Second thoughts made me hesitate before leaving my codes. A part of me felt like I had taken advantage of her, even though she was the one who had led our whole encounter, and I was leaving with my needs unfulfilled. I entered in my information hoping I would not regret it. Luckily, I returned to Zamandi's Room to find several females who were sober and willing.

Sure enough, Ar Ona called me a few days later before I was about to return to Xixsted to talk to Zorla. I took her out to a fancy restaurant for lunch. She invited me to her apartment again, this time sober, but with the same shallow personality. Still, her seductive body enticed me, and this time she showed me a good time. I left satisfied and promised to call her back when I returned to Renna One.

As soon as I arrived at Xixsted, I set up a meeting with Zorla. In his office, I wasted no time with pleasantries.

"I have decided to remain in my current position for the time being."

"For the time being?" Zorla repeated, studying my expression.

"Well, I do not know what your plans are. Who knows when you may retire from the Lostai military? You are long past your fifteen-revolution required tenure. I will be honest with you, Zorla. Once you no longer have a need for our current working relationship, I do not intend to enter into a similar agreement with any other Lostai commander. I hope you respect my decision. As you acknowledged, I reserve the right to leave the Lostai military anytime in the future." It was time I wielded a bit of intimidation of my own. I stared into his dark eyes and dropped the tone of my voice one octave lower. "I will not allow the Lostai military to force me into something I do not want."

He twitched, clearly uncomfortable with my subtle show of force.

"Agreed. I suppose I should take this as a compliment and interpret this as loyalty to me personally rather than the Lostai military. I intend to use this to my advantage."

"Of course, you will," I answered while standing and heading towards the door.

For once, I will be the one to signal that the conversation is over.

When The Strategist contacted me some lunar cycles later, I could sense his excitement even though he used the robotic voice disguiser.

"Little Warrior, I have great news. The Arandan militia has finally accomplished a major milestone. We have trained Arandan soldiers off-world. With the intelligence you provided, the Arandan militia was able to steal a Lostai battle cruiser from another repair lot. We filled it with Arandan soldiers and kidnapped a high-level Lostai official whom we forced to help us get through the planetary border control."

"Amazing. Where do you have the craft stationed?"

"I will keep its exact location secret, but we were able to reach Gorinth. We paid a hefty amount to the crime syndicate there to reskin and reprogram the craft so that it is no longer recognizable as Lostai."

"How do you intend to use the craft and those troops? I only ask in case it sparks some ideas for how I can help."

"Sure, no problem. We will infiltrate some of our soldiers within the Arandan community on planets like Gorinth and Hevrra to cause havoc on Lostai interests. Maybe train some of the young Arandan freedom fighters to go from just singing songs to actually becoming battle-ready."

"And the rest?"

"They will behave like pirates, looking for opportunities to intercept, raid, and board Lostai crafts. Each ship we capture will be reskinned and reprogrammed. I hope before long to have a fleet of spacecrafts for our cause. Our next challenge will be procuring and paying for energy crystals. The Lostai have put in controls wherever they can to track which entities purchase these crystals and for what purpose."

"OK, Strategist, I will let you know of any opportunities for acquiring more spacecrafts or fuel."

I soon fell back into my routine, juggling my duties with the Lostai military, my covert dealings with The Strategist, and running my businesses. These activities kept me quite busy and any spare time I filled with short-lived romantic relationships and extravagant recreational activities.

48

Three revolutions after I completed my fifteen-year tenure with the Lostai military, Gio celebrated his by notifying Zorla and me with zero qualms that he wanted out. Zorla put no pressure on him to stay. Gio had no loved ones nearby that Zorla could threaten. More importantly, Zorla considered Gio to be unreliable. Everyone knew Gio was prone to excessive use of mood-altering beverages and drugs. He also did not practice the Sotkari Ta daily regimen, so he never honed his abilities to their full potential. Before leaving Xixsted, Gio came to talk to me.

"I want to thank you, Montor, for helping me through the training process here. I enjoyed serving under your command."

"What will you do now?"

"I intend to set up a business on Renna One. I hope we can still spend time together whenever you visit there."

"Sure."

I did not intend to stay in contact with him or be his close friend, but I loved spending free time at my home on Renna One with Lasarta and Foxor. My property was near Zamandi's

Room. It was no surprise that I ran into him there several lunar cycles after.

I was with Ar Ona at the time. Even though almost four revolutions had passed since we first met, she still pined for her Hevrran ex-lover. We were in a non-exclusive relationship, meeting up occasionally when it was convenient. She was hoping to make the Hevrran jealous enough one day to take her back. I usually spent time with females of a different caliber but felt bad for Ar Ona. She wasted her life away over someone who could not care less, so I tried to be nice when we were together. She likely called upon other lovers when I was not around, which was fine by me. I had several across the sector as well.

When Gio saw me at the bar, he greeted me effusively.

"Montor, old friend, I am so glad to see you."

"Hi, Gio. I hope you are doing well."

He was under the effects of something potent, barely able to keep his eyes open.

"It has been way too long. My goodness, I believe it has been almost a full revolution. Bartender, please get this fine Arandan a glass of your best *stampu* and *vormey* for his beautiful escort," he ordered.

"You idiot," shouted Ar Ona, shoving him and pretending to be offended. "I am not his escort. I am his girlfriend."

They both laughed hysterically. It was hard to determine who was more intoxicated.

I wonder if she has ever taken Gio to her apartment.

What am I doing spending time with people I have no respect for?

At times such as these, I forgot my benevolence toward Ar Ona and wished my Sotkari Ta powers allowed me to disappear.

Gio raised his glass.

"To old friends."

I went through the motions and swallowed my shot in one gulp.

"So, Gio, how is civilian life treating you?" I asked.

"I am doing great. You know, I do outside contracting work for the Lostai military sometimes, but my focus is on my jewelry manufacturing business here on Renna One." He inched closer to me and whispered, "It is a front for my real money maker. I am importing *gargon* stones from Tormix."

"I believe that is illegal." I said, switching to telepathic communication. "The Lostai have banned the use of that rare stone for decorative purposes because they use it as an energy source."

"Shh...I know." He was too inebriated to switch to telepathic mode and continued speaking out loud but under his breath. "That is why I get paid so much for selling them on the black market. Are you going to snitch on me?"

Ar Ona looked annoyed, the conversation beyond what her pretty little mind could tolerate. "I need to use the restroom. Hopefully you two are done whispering when I get back."

"Of course not. It is no concern of mine," I replied to Gio, but suddenly an idea popped into my head.

Those stones can be valuable for the Arandan militia to fuel the fleet of battleships they have been assembling.

Stroking Gio's ego and summoning the patience to deal with his annoying drunken behavior, I prodded him with questions about his sources for *gargon* stones and how he managed to smuggle them across the sector. Gio was careful not to reveal all his information, but I gathered enough tidbits I was sure would be of interest to The Strategist. Something else piqued my curiosity.

"And what kind of consulting work are you doing for the Lostai military?" I asked.

"I need to keep it secret." Finally, he switched to telepathic mode. "Zorla warned me that if I spoke a word of it to anyone, he would have me dismembered."

"Oh? So, you are doing jobs for Zorla?"

Hmm, it is surprising Zorla has not shared this with me.

"Yes, but please do not repeat it. Zorla gives me the creeps. That is why I was so happy to just continue under your command rather than report to him."

Zorla had never considered promoting Gio under his direct command. I controlled the urge to roll my eyes.

"I understand. He can be intimidating."

"I will say this, Montor. Until now, I have been helping him and his scientists to better understand the geography and civics of my home world, but now he has something bigger planned that he thinks I am uniquely qualified to help with."

Gio looked around even though no one could hear us. The trepidation almost sobered him up.

"I think he is going rogue, though. He told me he was tired of waiting on his superiors to assign him more Sotkari Ta students and said he was taking matters into his own hands. Please, do not ask me any more about it."

"Sure, no problem."

I wonder what that piece of crap Lostai is up to now.

A few lunar cycles later, I had my answer. Three Earthian hostages arrived at Xixsted. Zorla summoned me immediately.

"Montor, I have new students for you and Kaya."

Students? More like victims.

After the beat-down I gave Gio when he first arrived, he submitted to his fate with little resistance, making it easy for me to not feel so guilty about forcing him to work for Zorla. I wondered how these new prisoners would affect my conscience.

"OK, where are they? Tell me more about them and what tactics you want us to employ with them."

"They are still in a holding cell. I will escort you there myself. After you see them, we can devise our plan."

Our plan? Shermont! I wish I could strangle you, you filthy piece of crap.

Zorla posted a guard by the cell even though it was protected by a security field. When I approached the cell, there was movement that happened so quick, I did not catch it at first. Based on Gio's appearance as a reference, before me stood two male Earthians. One appeared to be elderly, feeble, and wrinkled.

What would Zorla want with this poor old creature?

Next to him stood a younger male, probably a teenager but with a muscular build. The darkness of his skin surprised me. I assumed all Earthians would have the same light skin as Gio. I knew that the Lostai military had gathered up Earthians at other locations in the galaxy, but till now, Gio was the only one I had met. At a closer look, I realized the dark-skinned teenager was hiding something—no, someone—behind him.

Zorla signaled to the guard to deactivate the field and turned on the translation application on his tablet.

"We are not going to hurt you or the girl as long as you comply."

The girl?

As Zorla walked into the cell, the teenager stepped back, shielding the person behind him. My heart sank.

He must be protecting someone very small.

Zorla gestured for me to get closer. I towered over all of them and could only imagine the impression I would make on a small child from another world. My feet were glued to the floor. Zorla's satisfied smile sickened me.

"Montor, what are you waiting for? See what we have here."

I forced myself forward and heard her whimpering before I

saw her face. The girl appeared only a few revolutions over toddler age, smaller than my twin sister, Arixa, when she died. I could not hide my emotions, running both hands over my hair.

The older male spoke.

"We can stay, but please, take the little girl back home."

Once the device translated the older male's words, Zorla laughed.

"Are you kidding?" said Zorla. "We have tested her genetic make-up. She is worth more than the both of you together."

I need to get out of here. I am about to puke.

"OK, Zorla, so I have seen them already. Let us move on. Obviously, the child should go to Kaya, who can represent a motherly figure and is far less scary looking than me," I said.

Zorla walked out of the cell and waved his hand to signal he was making his way back to the operations center.

Without turning around, he replied, "You take her to Kaya and then come back and deal with these two."

"I will have Kaya come here to get her."

"No." Now Zorla turned. With lips curled in a heartless smile, he spoke in slow motion. "I order you to take her. Kaya is getting old. They might as well start getting used to you already."

I wish I could rip his head off right now.

"You better hurry, Montor. If you do not take her to Kaya soon, she will have to spend the night here in this cold cell."

Zorla was toying with me, and there was nothing I could do about it. I got on my knee and extended my hand to the girl.

"I am Montor. I will take you to someone who will keep you safe," I said, using the translation application on my tablet.

She screamed and ran away. The Lostai guard scooped her up. She became hysterical, crying and flailing her limbs. While I was still kneeling and feeling deflated, the teenager lunged at me and threw an uppercut landing on my chin. My frustration at being trapped by Zorla in that situation converted into anger at this young Earthian who dared to strike me. I sprung to my feet and took out my aggravation on the teenager, kicking him hard against the wall and leaving him dazed. Before he could shake it off, I was on him, striking blow after blow until his eyes were swollen shut and blood covered his face. He slid to the floor, convulsing in pain. The old Earthian glared at me with disgust before kneeling on the floor, trying to help the teenager. The little girl wailed the whole time.

What a worthless piece of crap I am.

By the time I grabbed the girl, my eyes were watery. She screamed the whole way to Kaya's dormitory.

49

"I am worried about the girl. She barely eats, has trouble sleeping, and spends most of her time crying and asking for her mother," said Kaya. "Of course, Zorla does not care. He only asks if we are making any headway with her training. If she gets sick, I am concerned Zorla may come to an extreme decision about her. He said he wishes she were older so he could put her through boot camp like they did with you. Montor, are you listening?"

I sat at Kaya's desk in her dorm, sulking. Ever since the three Earthian hostages arrived at Xixsted, my pent-up rage multiplied, if that was possible. The young Earthian teenager paid the price. I learned his name was Damari. During the first lunar cycle, he refused all orders, earning himself several beatings, concussions, and broken bones at my hands. He fought back every time. As if I did not already feel dishonorable enough, Zorla suggested I resort to threatening the older Earthian, who was in no position to defend himself. He said that was the main purpose he served. Only then did Damari agree to integrate into a Lostai cadet squadron. He held his own against the other cadets. Although young, his strength was impressive. He almost reminded me of myself at that age.

"*Shermont!* Yes, of course, I am listening," I shouted, banging my fist on the desktop.

"I know this situation frustrates you, but it is not my fault."

I exhaled forcefully.

"I am sorry, Kaya. I could not care less about the males, but the little girl's sadness is tearing me apart."

"Her name is Marcia."

As if on cue, the little girl came out of the room I once slept in as a child. She could not have heard us, as we were communicating telepathically, but my banging must have awoken her. The minute she laid eyes on me, she screamed and hid behind Kaya. I stormed out of the dorm, feeling even more wretched.

Fortunately, the girl proved to be resilient. After another lunar cycle, Kaya gained Marcia's trust by convincing Zorla to allow her to have the evening meal with the other two hostages. Among the three of them, they spoke four Earthian languages but shared a common one they all understood. The two males were worried about Marcia's well-being. They encouraged the little girl to eat and played guessing and hand games that made her laugh. She looked healthier and was sleeping better but had not yet made any progress in Sotkari Ta abilities. Damari shared a dorm with the older Earthian named Bernie. Bernie was too frail for boot camp, so Zorla assigned him to the maintenance crew. I spent a few hours every day with Damari and Bernie on the basic concepts of meditation, telepathic communication, and blocking. They were already communicating telepathically by the time a fourth Earthian hostage arrived at Xixsted.

I learned about the new arrival during a meeting with Zorla. He was getting ready to send me to the latest planet annexed by the Lostai Empire. The locals battled with passion against the invasion but were no match for the Lostai advanced technology and Sotkari Ta resources such as myself.

"Montor, our latest acquisition is our most impressive specimen...after you, of course. Our scientists tell me she has the genetic makeup of a pureblood Sotkari Ta like you and Kaya. She could become a force to be reckoned with and an extraordinary weapon for us, if we get her to your level of compliance—"

He must have seen something in my expression that made him change his choice of words.

"I mean, cooperation. Since you and Kaya are busy training the other three, we have started this one off in bootcamp with the female squadron. Once she is further along with her military training, we can have Kaya work with her on Sotkari Ta abilities."

"So, she is female?"

"Yes, about your age, but with no military or athletic background. Our scientists determined she could use a boost, so we injected her with hormones and rejuvenation serums to help her keep up with the rigors of boot camp and extend her reproduction cycle."

Her reproduction cycle?

Zorla paused, becoming thoughtful, before continuing. "Those enhancers are expensive. I hope she renders us some payback. These Earthians are feisty, though. I know it took you a while to subdue the male teenager. This female tried to escape the first day she arrived. She also confronted the squadron leader. Exzer, my new assistant, has learned her language and is her handler."

His description of this new hostage intrigued me, but at the same time, I was looking forward to spending time away from Xixsted and putting some space between myself and the little girl whose innocent face haunted my dreams.

When I returned from the latest mission, I met Kaya in her dorm for dinner while Marcia was with Damari and Bernie. After some initial chit chat, Kaya dropped a bomb. She said Zorla had grown tired of waiting for Marcia to show some progress in telepathic or telekinetic ability.

"The hormone therapy worked well on the new hostage, so Zorla's scientists are confident in trying a different version on the little girl."

"What is that filthy Lostai scum planning now?"

"Zorla intends to speed up her maturation, bring on early puberty, and force the teenaged male to impregnate her. He wants to test whether the offspring will inherit their Sotkari Ta genes. He intends to take the child away from them and have it raised, indoctrinated, and trained by his staff scientists, squadron leaders, and assistants until it becomes a loyal Lostai super soldier. If the first offspring inherits the genes, the process will be repeated using Marcia and Damari as breeders. He has already designated an area on this moon that he would turn into a nursery."

"What!" I was so furious I came out of our typical telepathic conversation and shouted the word out loud.

"Shhh, Montor," said Kaya, her eyes discreetly scanning the room. She still was convinced the rooms were outfitted with spying mechanisms. I returned to telepathic communication.

"She is just a child. What is wrong with him! How can he plan to damage her that way?" Pacing the room, I considered whether I should try to convince him that it was a bad idea. "That idiot. It will take a full generation for something like that to come to fruition. He will be an old fart by then."

"If he can offer a successful way to duplicate the process, he will be heralded a hero. No other Lostai military leader has proven ruthless enough to pursue this experiment. He wants to leave a legacy and make sure his family line reaps the riches of such a distinction. Anyway, it does not matter how long it takes. In the meantime, his victims will suffer for it."

My stomach churned, and I tasted bile.

"Nightmares about this little girl have plagued me since she arrived here. Kaya, you know who she reminds me of. Zorla will most likely use me as the muscle to force Damari. I cannot. My sanity will suffer if I have anything to do with this macabre plan."

"I know. It is horrible."

I lost my appetite and got up to leave.

"Kaya, I am sorry, but I need some time alone."

I made up an excuse to fly off Xixsted in my private shuttle. Drifting aimlessly in space, I racked my brain, thinking if there was anything I could do to stop Zorla from robbing little Marcia of her childhood. I unlocked one of my drawers where I kept a bottle of *stampu* and swallowed a generous gulp. Next to it lay the encrypted tablet I used to communicate with The Strategist. A thought came to me. Time to call in a favor.

It was a rest day on Xixsted. Most of the personnel were engaged in recreational activities. I walked Marcia over to Bernie and Damari's dorm for their usual shared dinner. Zorla wanted her to get used to dealing with me, or perhaps this was his private joke on the both of us. The little girl no longer cringed when I held her hand but still never looked at my face. This time, the joke would be on him.

Several corridors away, four Lostai soldiers guarded the docking station used by merchants coming to stock Xixsted. Guard duty on rest days was an unpopular shift rotated among the newest recruits. The previous week, I had planted a command in the scheduler's mind to assign the shift to the wrong group, forcing them to do two rest day shifts in a row. They complained, but the other soldiers who should have been assigned the duty took advantage of their luck and wasted no time leaving Xixsted. This group had no choice but to work the shift. They were an unhappy lot. I paid them a visit with a special gift.

"Hello, officers. I heard you got double duty."

They groaned.

"That is unfortunate," I said, sounding sympathetic. "But I have something to help you pass the time."

I gave them each a highly intoxicating laughing pod and left a few more with them for good measure. Before leaving, I accessed their minds.

A merchant ship is arriving soon. You can let them in. They are making a special delivery. In the meantime, ingest all the pods. Forever forget who gave them to you or that Montor was here.

They thanked me and were already giggling as I made my way to the other side of Xixsted. All of this mind manipulation was in direct defiance to the commitment of loyalty I made to Zorla revolutions ago, but I reminded myself it was for a good cause. The corridors along the way were empty, as was typical on rest days. I joined the few soldiers remaining on Xixsted at the recreational area. Soon, we were sharing drinks and joking.

At the appointed time, I excused myself. "I need to get the Earthian girl and bring her back to Kaya's dorm. I will return soon."

Before I even got close to that section of the station, alarms blared. "All on-duty soldiers make your way to battle stations. That merchant ship must not be allowed to leave Xixsted!"

The viewers lit up with images of a merchant ship that had already lifted off and was on its way. By the time the few sober soldiers made it to their stations, the ship disappeared from the dark sky in a flash. I rushed to Bernie and Damari's dorm. Soldiers swarmed the area.

"What is going on?" I asked the first one I found.

"The hostages have escaped."

"What? How?"

"Not sure yet," the soldier replied.

Zorla filled in the gaps for me later in his office. He was livid.

"I will have those guards tortured and executed. I think they did this out of spite because of the double shift assigned to them."

"Zorla, I am still not sure what happened."

I leaned in towards him, making sure my expression was one of concern and sincerity as he explained to me.

"Montor, that was no merchant ship."

"From what I saw on the viewer, it had the insignia of the merchants who normally stock Xixsted with supplies," I said.

"Yes, but obviously the crew on board were not merchants. Those guards got intoxicated while on duty and let those...criminals on to our station. Obviously, they stole the merchant ship as part of their plan."

He stopped short of mentioning that "those criminals" were in fact Arandans in militia uniform, but it did not take him long to spit out how he felt about them.

"Those barbarians grabbed the Earthians and left with them. Surveillance shows the Earthians resisting them as they were pulled out of their dorms. Even they did not know what was going on. Or who knows? Maybe it was all an act." He got to his feet. "How dare those lawless rebels steal my Sotkari Ta!"

His Sotkari Ta? What a pompous fool.

"Well, Zorla, if you want me to conduct interrogations here, let me know. I will not go to question anyone on Aranda, though."

"Yes, of course."

❄

At my first chance for privacy, I contacted The Strategist.

"Are the Earthians safely en route to Fronidia?"

"No. We ran into problems with the Lostai military. Zorla was quick to have the area heavily patrolled. We were lucky to switch the Earthians over to a smaller shuttle headed for Aranda before the Lostai military intercepted the merchant ship. Several of our soldiers were lost. None allowed themselves to be captured alive for interrogation."

Minutes of silence passed between us.

"Strategist, I am sorry for those losses. What will you do with the Earthians?"

"We will keep them safe on the Penstarox military base for the time being."

"I appreciate what you have done, especially considering they are not of your race."

"We have many Arandan children sitting in Lostai military stations and labor camps across the sector. We can only hope someone, no matter what their race, takes pity on them, too."

"Yes, these children have suffered enough by being taken from their homes and families. This little Earthian girl deserves better than the horrible plans Zorla had in mind for her."

"Little Warrior, I have often wondered about your identity, but seeing this compassionate side of you has left me intrigued."

50

Even before the three Earthians were rescued, Kaya had already started training the fourth Earthian hostage. Now that she was the only Sotkari Ta hostage left on Xixsted, Zorla wanted Kaya to speed up her training. I did not intend to meet her. Orchestrating the rescues of the first three Earthians had been risky business. Kaya told me this female had left a husband and children behind on Earth. It was a sad situation. I could not afford feeling sorry for another hostage, and yet, I was curious.

"How is your student, Kaya?"

"I think telekinesis will be her strong suit."

"Is she communicating telepathically?"

"I communicate to her telepathically, but I am not comfortable yet in unblocking my mind to allow her to reciprocate. She is a kind person. I do like her, but imagine if she accessed my mind and learned not only of my secrets but of yours. I am reluctant to take that risk."

"Hmm, you never were worried about this when you trained Gio."

"Gio's potential does not even come close to what this

female could learn to do. I never worried Gio could become skilled or disciplined enough to access my mind. He hardly ever practiced meditation. This Earthian female has embraced the Sotkari Ta physical and mental regimen, and her genetic make-up is closer to yours and mine. She is the equivalent of a pureblood Sotkari Ta and has the potential to become as powerful as you."

"Ha! I doubt it," I scoffed. "What about her military training?"

"At first, it was tough. You know firsthand how hostages are treated here. It was a brutal bootcamp for her considering she was a civilian with no military experience. She suffered many injuries and punishments, but by now, she is up to Lostai military standards."

"I see."

"By the way, after the incident with the other Earthians, Zorla has assigned Dimlet to escort her everywhere. I think he might be suspicious of her and me."

"Dimlet is an idiot."

"I do not like to use those terms, but he truly is. When Mina...umm, that is her name, and I are practicing telekinesis, I encourage her to be as disruptive as possible. It makes Dimlet very uncomfortable. He fears us. I find it quite amusing."

We shared a laugh. I let her know I would be away for a while, visiting my foster parents on Renna One and taking care of business matters.

The next time I met Kaya, she was very troubled.

"Have you spoken to Zorla?"

"Not yet. I just got back. Why?"

She paced the length of her dorm.

"Kaya, what is going on?"

The strain and stress visible in her facial expressions worried me.

"I think Zorla is getting pressured by his chain of command. He acted on his own authority when he acquired the Earthian hostages and must now answer for all the wasted resources after the escape. He is looking for a way to bounce back and wants me to teach Mina mind control, so he can send her to a mission on Renna One. Prisoners have been escaping a Lostai labor camp there. Law enforcement suspects a rebel group is orchestrating these escapes. He wants her to investigate and root out the responsible parties."

"What? That is reckless and premature. She does not have the experience."

"I know, but he figures you performed well on similar missions at an early age. I have not even begun letting her communicate to me telepathically yet."

"If he mentions it to me, I will let him know my concerns."

"That is not all. Exzer told Mina that when she gets back from Renna One, she is to mate with another soldier who also has a full set of Sotkari Ta genes to procreate a child who will be molded into a Lostai soldier. Who do you think they are referring to?"

I shrugged my shoulders.

"I do not know." I tried to ignore the fear that gnawed at my gut and verbalized instead what I hoped to be true. "Gio, I suppose. They are both Earthians. Some time ago, he told me he was doing special work for Zorla. Maybe this is what he was referring to."

Kaya expressed what I did not even want to let myself acknowledge.

"Montor, think about it. Gio does not have a complete set of Sotkari Ta genes." Her voice came across my mind with a high sense of alarm. "This all has me consternated. And as you can imagine, this poor female is out of her mind at the thought of being impregnated against her will."

I barely finished talking with Kaya when I received a notification on my tablet to go see Zorla. I walked into his office, doing my best to relax my body language.

"Hello, sir."

His eyes appeared more deep set than normal, and his skin had a sickly tinge.

Is it my imagination, or does he look older and frazzled?

He dispensed with salutations and pleasantries, jumping right into what he had on his mind.

"Montor, losing the three Earthians has put me in a tough situation with my superiors. I need to make them forget about that mishap by scoring an important win as soon as possible. I intend to accomplish this with the female Earthian. Kaya is working on teaching her mind control so I can send her to Renna One on a mission. I have a task for you as well."

Oh, no.

"And what would that be?"

"I want you to impregnate the Earthian female."

It had been a long time since I felt at a severe disadvantage in front of Zorla. I masked my emotions and tried to appear pragmatic.

"Sir, we are not of the same species. I would think Gio might be a better choice."

"I thought about that, but Gio is too unreliable. What if he becomes too attached to the female or the child? Also, he does not have a complete set of Sotkari Ta genes. You and this female do."

His eyes popped with ruthless desperation.

No use for me to argue with him. Let him think I am going along with his disgusting plan for now.

There still was some time to figure out how to deal with Zorla's request. First, Kaya needed to train the female in mind control. That would be no easy feat and could be time-consuming. She was not even communicating telepathically yet. After the training, the female would go on this Renna One mission. A lot of things could happen until then...or perhaps, while she was on Renna One.

"Sir, I will be honest. I find this whole thing distasteful, but let me know when the female is ready, and we can give it a try," I said, trying hard to muster an air of indifference.

He jumped to his feet, clasped his hands in front of his body, and shook them in approval.

"Great, Montor, great. Be proud. Soon, you will be the key element in my most important achievement, but we will need to wait a bit. First, I will send her to Renna One to find the people behind the labor camp escapes. I need to show my superiors the expenses I incurred to acquire and train her are rendering some profit."

"Is there anything you want me to focus on in the meantime?"

"Take time to relax. When you get back, I will need your help to get approval from my superiors to have Kaya train Mina in mind control. Given recent events, it is unlikely they will agree of their own accord. I will invite them here and will need you to manipulate their minds so I can have their approval well-documented."

Filthy Lostai bastard.

"OK."

I walked out of his office frustrated, concerned, and cranky. There was no way I was going to engender a child for Zorla's twisted plans. I needed time to think and left Xixsted immediately, purposely spending time away and avoiding meeting with Kaya. I did not want to give the impression we were commiserating in any way.

The nearby moon of Yamazi, with its domed artificial oasis and fancy hotels, provided me the perfect environment to meditate on Zorla's request. I used the hotel's holographic center to set up my favorite simulated environment, an Arandan beach. Sitting on a lounge chair with a bottle of expensive Arandan brandy, I stared into the fake red ocean for hours. Waves slapped the shore while Arandan spoken poems and folksongs were broadcast from an old-fashioned sound system. My thoughts drifted towards this female Earthian who had become my most pressing problem.

What is she like? Is she brave or weak? Is she stupid? Does she have a pleasant personality?

Kaya seems to like her and said she overcame many hurdles during bootcamp and now was one of the best in her squadron.

She sounds like a survivor...like me. Kaya said she could become as powerful as me. Is she progressing with telepathy and mind control?

If she perished during her mission on Renna One, I would not have to deal with Zorla's sick scheme. Hmm, that could be arranged.

Shermont! Why did she have to be a female? I would not be in this mess if she were a male.

I wonder what she looks like.

What is wrong with me? Who cares?

I have no choice but to get rid of her. I guess after all this time working with Zorla, some of his cruelty has rubbed off on me.

Soon, being alone with my thoughts and the brandy proved too much for my gregarious soul.

I need to talk about this with someone.

I called Lasarta on a secure channel.

"Hello, son. It is wonderful to see you and hear your voice. Is everything OK?"

"Lasarta, I am doing well, but that bastard Zorla has come up with a scheme that is making me crazy."

"Oh, no. What is it?"

I explained everything to her. She listened with no interruptions till I was done but did not hesitate with her response.

"Montor, you must find a way out of this. You cannot force yourself on a female."

"What if she is OK with it?"

"Do not be ridiculous. She does not even know you."

"Sorry, I was being facetious."

Lasarta was not amused.

"It is not funny. You mentioned she is a mother, so I doubt she would be happy with bearing a child and handing it over to the Lostai military. A child is not an object."

"I know, Lasarta, I know." I cracked each knuckle loudly. "I just cannot help being annoyed by this female who is the cause of my latest problem."

Lasarta launched into a passionate speech.

"It is not her fault. How do you think she feels? Montor, you struggle every day with the things you do for that swine, Zorla. I have seen how it affects you mentally and emotionally, how it tears you up inside. I understand it has been a means for survival and to protect us. You have even used your position to help your Arandan brothers in their struggle. There is honor in that." Her voice cracked, and she sniffled. "But if you allow yourself to be a part of something like this, there is no walking back from it. A child is blood from your blood, your father's blood, and your ancestors' blood. For a person to procreate a child for the sole purpose of handing it over to the Lostai to use however they wish is a sin of the worst kind. This is the one thing I beg you not to do. Not to protect yourself and for sure not to protect Foxor and me. I would rather die a million deaths, Montor. Please, do not do it."

"Lasarta, I cannot believe you would think I would even consider it. Of course, it is out of the question. I am sorry for upsetting you."

She wiped her eyes.

"No, I am the one who is sorry. You come to me for counsel, and I break down like this. It is just that Foxor and I have full faith you will eventually free yourself of this yoke, fall in love, have a family of your own, and your children will be cause for joy. You deserve that, and I am sure the High Spirit will eventually concede you that blessing."

The High Spirit forgot my name a long time ago.

I did not have the heart to tell her about the solution forming in my mind.

51

I returned to Xixsted to help Zorla get approval from his superiors to have the Earthian female trained in mind control. After that, he conceded me a longer vacation time while Kaya continued to work with the hostage and said he expected me back on Xixted after a few lunar cycles. No recreation or female companionship worked to erase the perturbation with the predicament I found myself in.

Once Kaya heard I had returned to the station, she invited me to her dorm for dinner. I found a spread of my favorite Arandan treats on the desk. I swore she was buttering me up for some kind of request.

"I am glad to see you, Montor."

The aroma of freshly baked *bomar* caught my attention. I grabbed a slice and spread on some sweet cream and honey.

"How are things going around here, Kaya?"

"Well, I have allowed my student to establish a telepathic connection with me. She has picked up on it very well."

"So, I guess you have gotten over your trust issues with her."

"She allowed me to see her thoughts. Oh, Montor, my heart

breaks for her. She is a good person and sees me as her only friend here."

"Wonderful. I see her as my biggest problem."

"Mina would rather die than kill people, violate their minds, or make babies for Zorla. She is desperate and has resolved to find a way to escape Xixsted or die in the process."

"Really? I would love to hear her plan."

"Zorla told me he has asked you to impregnate her. I guess that is the reason for your acerbic tone, but I do not understand why you direct your frustration towards her."

"I am frustrated in general."

"Montor, maybe you can help her escape this place and solve both your problems."

I bit into a fruit pie and waved my hand over the spread of goodies she had served for me.

"Is that what all this is about?" I tried to mask my remorsefulness with flippant behavior. "Kaya, after the previous escape, Zorla has doubled up on security measures here."

"Perhaps you can come up with a different idea."

"I have, but you are not going to like it."

"What is it?" she asked, a worried expression sweeping across her face.

"I am going to arrange for her to have a lethal accident during her mission on Renna One."

Her hand raced over her heart. She got up and walked a few steps away, digesting my words. Silence hung over us.

"Montor, this female has suffered so much while on Xixsted—"

I could not allow Kaya to make me feel sympathetic toward this Earthian.

"Her suffering will end soon."

Her blue eyes flashed in disbelief.

"Forget I brought this issue to you. I will find a way to get her off this base myself. You can leave now."

"What, and waste all this good food?"

She did not appreciate my attempt to add levity to such a heavy conversation.

"Get out!" Her voice came into my mind, bitter and angry.

"Kaya, sorry, I did not mean to be disrespectful."

She covered her eyes. The heat of emotion stung mine, too.

In the past few lunar cycles, I have brought both my foster mothers to tears. Nice job.

"All these revolutions, I have always prayed to The Farthest Light that Zorla's coldhearted cruelty would not infect your soul. Sadly, it seems like I did not pray hard enough."

I placed my hand on her shoulder and coaxed her back to her seat. Every so often, she wiped the tears from her eyes. Finally, I spoke.

"Kaya, I understand you want to help her, and you know I do not shy away from danger. It is not myself I worry about. I am concerned about what could happen to you and my foster parents if Zorla discovered I helped the Earthian female escape. We cannot take that risk. At least by killing her, she will not have to endure me taking her by force. If it was up to Zorla, he would have me rape her."

"Have you shared your plan to have her killed with your foster parents?"

"No."

She shot a knowing look my way.

"You have not dared to reveal that to your foster mother, have you?"

I did not answer. We finished our meal in silence. I returned to my dorm and turned on an instrumental tune featuring flutes and percussion, a steady beat that helped me focus. Closing my eyes, I summoned the Sotkari Ta mantra.

I have been given total control of myself and my surroundings.

Have I?

I had killed people in battle, beat people into submission, used torture to interrogate prisoners, all to fulfill my obligations to the Lostai military. Other than Kaya, my foster parents, Jortan, and Colora, I had made a point not to forge any close ties with anyone. I let Lorret go by herself on a hopeless mission to fight the Lostai. Even my work with The Strategist was impersonal and more of an atonement for being a filthy traitor. Yet, the little Earthian girl had tugged hard enough on my soul to motivate me to take personal responsibility for her escape. I was totally in control then. Now, it seemed Kaya was feeling the same for her student.

What is it with these Earthians?

I cannot let Kaya take such a risk.

My meditative trance eluded me. Giving up, I trudged out of my quarters.

"Montor, did you forget something?" said Kaya as I walked back into her dorm.

"No." I sighed deeply. "Kaya, if I helped this female to escape, it would require an extreme amount of trust between us. I am a Lostai soldier. Why would she trust me? And how can I trust her?"

Kaya's face lit up. She grabbed both my hands and squeezed. Her words rushed into my mind.

"Maybe we can share with her that you are affiliated with the rebel militia. Then she would understand why you would be willing to help her."

"I do not mean disrespect, but...Are. You. Crazy?"

"I will make sure she understands the risk we are taking by confiding in her. I will make her believe that if she divulges your secret, you will kill her."

"That is not a threat. If Zorla ever learned I was working with the militia, it would not only mean my death but the death of my foster parents, and maybe even yours. Assuming I trusted her with that secret, I would go back to my original plan and kill her at the slightest sign that she might expose me."

Kaya gave me a good-natured shove, as if I were exaggerating. A deeper probe into my mind would have revealed I was not.

"Oh, stop it. You must have some sympathy for this poor female who, through no fault of her own, was ripped from her home and family."

"OK, OK, it is going to be tough, but I will figure out another way to get rid of her."

Despite the Earthian female's progress with telepathic communication, Kaya was not making headway in teaching her mind manipulation. Truthfully, neither teacher nor student was very motivated. Kaya recommended to Zorla that I assist in the Earthian female's training. This was a ruse to make meeting together in her dorm appear perfectly normal.

After giving some thought on how I could assist in the female's escape, and thus solve my baby-making problem, I allowed Kaya to disclose to the female Earthian my secret affiliation with Arandan militia. Kaya invited me over to have dinner with them at the female's dorm to meet her and discuss. On my way over, I could not help but feel edgy.

Would she be arrogant or disrespectful in our first meeting, like Gio and Damari? Even worse, someone might have told her she has the potential to have powers equal to mine. This might make her think she has the upper hand with me.

I resolved to set the tone right from the beginning, so she understood who was in charge. As I walked into the dorm, I dialed up my swagger and intimidation factor.

Her striking eyes, the color of honey, caught my attention

right away. Hair tumbled below her shoulders in a bunch of gorgeous curls of similar color. She seemed to have just finished some physical exercise because her skin looked dewy. It was a shade somewhere in between Gio's paleness and Damari's dark tone. She wore a tight-fitting, sleeveless exercise top that gave me a clear idea of the shape and size of her breasts.

I wish her pants were not so baggy so I could get a better idea of what the rest of her body looks like. Shermont! No, no, what am I thinking!

I had not expected to find her this attractive. It was hard to suppress images of peeling off her top.

This is stupid. I am not an inexperienced teenager. Need to get my hormones under control. Time to show her who is boss.

I walked up to Kaya, nodded in deference, and pretended to find the Earthian female repulsive, speaking out loud in my most condescending tone. This would also be a good show to put on if, in fact, Zorla was spying on us.

"Kaya, is this insignificant, tiny creature what they expect me to procreate with? These orange eyes remind me of my canine pet. Revolting."

I did not have a canine pet.

Shortening the space between us, I glared down at the female, who was two heads shorter than me.

"Frankly, I do not even think it is physically possible without causing her some injury, but I suppose it will be entertaining to find out."

To pile on the intimidation, I reached out and rubbed her cheek with the back of my hand. To my surprise, instead of cringing, she pushed my hand away with a forceful outward block and moved into a fighting stance.

Is she going to strike me? There is no way I am allowing this puny Earthian female to take a swing at me.

I grabbed her hand, twisted it, and with my other hand pulled her against me, showing her my worst snarl.

Wow, her eyes are even more gorgeous up close.

Before I could decide on what to do next, Kaya's hand grasped my shoulder. She sent a bolt of aggressive energy into my body like never before. I released the female and stumbled back several feet. Kaya's stern voice entered my mind.

"Stop this behavior immediately, Montor. What is wrong with you!"

"Forgive me, Kaya. I was only having some fun. She is a feisty one. We might be able to copulate after all," I said out loud in a lowered voice, trying to be funny. No one found it humorous.

Despite her show of force, I had rattled the female. She turned away from Kaya and me.

Is she crying? Great, now I feel guilty.

Kaya switched to conference mode to communicate telepathically to the female and me at the same time.

"Mina, I apologize for Montor's behavior. He has a misplaced need to intimidate everyone he meets, but you will need to learn to deal with him, as I believe he is the one person who can get you out of here."

The female turned back around to face us, sticking out her chin in defiance, although her beautiful eyes were watery. She offered her forearm to me in the typical Sotkari handshake. Following Kaya's lead, she switched to conference mode.

Kaya has taught her well.

"Hello, Montor, my name is Mina. Trust me, I find the idea of having sexual relations with you pretty disgusting, too."

I could not hold back my laughter. She was no pushover. I kind of liked that.

When I squeezed her wrist to reciprocate her handshake, full-on arousal caught me by surprise. I let go immediately to shake off the sensation.

"We were eating dinner, Montor. Please join us," said Kaya.

I reproduced food and tried to reset the tone of our meeting by exchanging small talk.

"What have you been doing since we talked last?" asked Kaya.

"I went back to Yamazi. I had my pick of some of the most beautiful females there."

"One of these days, all your female partners will gang up on you," joked Kaya.

Mina rolled her eyes and mistakenly transmitted a thought in her language I could not understand, but it sounded like she was mocking me.

I pretended not to notice and told Kaya how Zorla used me to manipulate his superiors into documenting their approval for Mina's mind control training.

"You make Zorla feel invincible," said Kaya, shaking her head.

Once we finished eating, the conversation grew more serious. I explained to Mina my plan.

"Mina, the only escape option I see for you is to convince Zorla we should go together on the mission he has outlined for you. We will tell him you are not ready to execute this assignment on your own and need the mentoring of someone who is both an experienced soldier and Sotkari Ta. There will be no deception there. I do not know what Zorla is thinking. You have no chance of accomplishing this mission by yourself."

"I have no desire to accomplish it at all," she said, showing that defiance again.

We locked eyes for a moment, and I did my best to ignore her annoying behavior.

I am going to need patience to deal with this irreverent creature.

"Since Zorla's latest fixation is on breeding Sotkari Ta offspring, I will also tell him we will take advantage of our time together to begin our mating process. Once on the planet, I will coordinate with my contacts to set you up with an autopilot shuttlecraft that will take you to another planet where I am sure you will find friendly people and, with luck, be able to evade any Lostai search teams. We will have to make it look like I have been ambushed. Perhaps have me incapacitated with a drug. I am not sure yet, but I can sort out those details later."

"Montor, why are you willing to put yourself and your good standing with the Lostai in danger to help me escape?"

She is not stupid or taking things for granted.

I tried to make light of the question.

"I suppose I have been bored lately and always welcome a good challenge. Quite honestly, I am not pleased with the idea of making babies with you. Then there is the fact that, for some odd reason, Kaya has taken a liking to you."

Her features relaxed somewhat.

"OK...so, what is my next step?"

"You, my dear, from now on, only need follow my instructions. Once I discuss with Zorla and he agrees, things will move fast. The Lostai are anxious to solve their little problem on Renna One before it grows out of control."

She looked at Kaya for confirmation, who nodded in agreement.

A genuine friendship has grown between them.

"It is time for my private meditation. I will see you tomorrow," Kaya said as she got to her feet and walked out.

Mina and I also stood. Now alone with her, I wished I could stop imagining running my fingers through her curly hair.

I wonder, has she noticed I find her attractive? Unacceptable. I should leave her a little off balance before ending our chat.

"Mina, if you like, I can sleep here with you tonight. That will show Zorla we are committed to his mission. It will be a... tight fit," I said, looking her over and glancing at her cot, "but I think we can manage."

Her face flushed.

Good.

"No, I do not think that is necessary," she replied, avoiding my eyes.

I could not help chuckling.

"True. We have plenty of time on our trip to Renna One. Good night, Mina."

52

———

The next morning, Kaya came to see me. She was upset with me again.

"Montor, why were you so rude to that poor female last night? I am sure your foster mother would not have approved of such behavior."

I pressed my fingers against my temples.

"OK, Kaya, I get it already. It was stupid. I was caught off guard. She is not what I expected."

"What do you mean?" she tilted her head to force me to look her in the eyes. "Montor, what were you expecting?"

I looked away.

"When we grasped wrists, the energy was strong," I said.

"Hmm, I was not sure how that would work between people of different species," said Kaya, thoughtfully.

"What do you mean?"

"Well, you know I explained to you a long time ago about how Sotkari Ta are predisposed to prefer other Sotkari Ta as mates. The attraction is usually intense, almost irresistible. I did not know if the same would apply to people of different species with embedded Sotkari Ta genes."

So, it was not my imagination.

"Anyway, it is no big deal. Just an unexpected jolt. Plus, I doubt the feeling was mutual, but I do not want her to think she has any power over me," I said.

"I am sure that is the last thing on her mind. She only wants to escape from Zorla."

We all do.

"I will speak with him today."

"Commander Zorla, can we meet? I have some input about the female Earthian's training and upcoming mission."

He asked me to come over to his office right away.

"OK, Montor, what do you have to say?"

"The female Earthian, Mina, has a lot of potential, but I do not think she is ready to go to Renna One and conduct interrogations on her own. She has not progressed much with mind control abilities yet. Frankly, I am surprised you would trust her with such an important job on her own. Even I worked under the command of a leading officer on my first missions. Plus, what if she tries to escape?"

"Well, she wears the tracker wristband, so we would eventually find her."

I made a mental note that this was a detail I would need to address as part of her escape plan.

"Yes, but with supervision, there would be less temptation or opportunity for her to try."

"OK, OK. So, what do you suggest? Have I not made it clear enough about the pressure I am under?"

"I will go with her as a mentor. She will be under my command when we do the investigation and interrogations on Renna One. You can still show your superiors she has effectively joined the ranks of the Lostai military and is contributing without waiting for Kaya to complete her mind control training."

Zorla pursed his lips, giving thought to my suggestion.

"I was getting ready to send you to Tormix to address another problem. We have insurgencies springing up every-where these days." He folded his hands on his desk with visible tension in his forearms and fingers. "I am curious about why you would be so eager to help with this particular mission. What is in it for you?"

Of course, he would question this since ulterior motives and self-interest always drove his decisions.

"Sir, I dislike the idea of forcing myself on any female. If I must be the one to father her child, I would prefer it be a consensual mating."

"What does accompanying her on this mission have anything to do with that?"

"The trip to Renna One takes about one lunar cycle. During that time, the Earthian and I can get acquainted. Perhaps what I am about to mention is not in your nature to understand. Umm, I think that would be enough time for me to...gain her affections."

He rolled his eyes and batted his hand in the air.

"Oh, Montor, I have heard all about your exploits with females. Of course, we Lostai do not enjoy such bestial behav-ior. The Sotkari Ta are even worse than Arandans in that respect. I hear all it takes is a simple touch to make them want to have sexual relations." He steepled his hands. "Getting back to your suggestion, I might like this idea because I fear this female might resist to the point of having to destroy her."

"I imagine that would be disastrous," I said, feigning concern. "Losing your last new Sotkari Ta."

He tapped his mouth.

"Yes, exactly. OK, make all the arrangements. I will explain to her she is now directly under your command and should follow all your orders, including allowing you into her bed whenever you so advise her."

I could not mask my reaction to his callous orders. He must have noticed.

"This might sound extreme, but we cannot waste time, Montor. This Earthian is approximately your age, but Earthian females have a finite time for procreation. Based on our studies, normally her productive cycle would last for about five to eight more revolutions. The hormones and rejuvenation drugs we injected in her have extended her productivity by fifteen more revolutions. I believe the normal gestation period for Earthians is nine lunar cycles, about double the time for Arandans. I am not sure what to expect from pairing her with someone of another species or even if you and she are compatible to produce viable offspring. If so, the most she can produce in that timeframe is twelve to fourteen. Considering the time it would take for the offspring to mature and be trained, it will take many revolutions before we get payback on our investment! I think you can agree my urgency is merited."

The only thing I can agree to is that you are a heartless bastard.

"OK, sir, I will take care of everything."

Now that the wheels were set in motion, I switched to military mode, thinking through the details of what the next weeks would entail. For our trip to Renna One, I chose a Vona class spacecraft. Besides the normal engineering, weapons, and flight stations, the small vessel accommodated a few separate living quarters, a common kitchen area, an exercise room, an observation deck, a small lounge area, and a conference room. Despite its size, it featured strong plasma beam weaponry capable of destroying larger vessels. I wanted to be prepared for any eventuality. Zorla agreed with my choice.

"Good idea. It is important you can defend yourself in case any of those rebel criminals try to steal Mina like they did the others," he had said.

That idiot. If he only knew.

While on the trip, I would continue Mina's hand-to-hand combat training. She needed to be in top shape if we ran into trouble with law enforcement. I was glad to hear she religiously followed the Sotkari Ta daily physical and mental practice regimen and meditation. In case of problems, confronting a Sotkari Ta who worked for the Lostai (like me) was also a threat I needed to consider. Mina did not know how to block telepathic incursions. I added that to the list of training.

We will be busy during our trip. She needs to be combat-ready for any eventuality. I will not babysit her.

I also thought about her lodging once we arrived on Renna One.

She might deviate from the plan and try something stupid if I let her stay alone at a hotel. I will have her as a guest in my home.

I contacted Lasarta on my encrypted tablet to let her know.

"Lasarta, I will be home in about one lunar cycle and will have a guest with me."

"A guest?"

"The female Earthian I spoke to you about."

She swallowed hard and exhaled deeply before asking, "Oh, Montor, what have you decided to do about her?"

"Do not worry, Lasarta. I will not do anything that would make you ashamed of me. Everything will be OK."

She clasped her hands and sighed in relief.

"I love you, son. Be safe."

I also contacted The Strategist to ask for another favor. I would need a small shuttle with altered sensors so that it appeared as a pilotless drone. This would be the spacecraft Mina would use on her escape trip to Fronidia. I did not offer information to The Strategist why I needed this type of alteration.

The fewer people who know about these plans, the better.

To avoid suspicion, Mina and I would have to spend time on Renna One investigating the labor camp escapes before I sent her off to Fronidia. I contacted the warden at the Lostai labor camp to let him know we were being sent to help him find out who was responsible for the prison breaks there.

The day of our departure to Renna One arrived quickly. I had an evening to relax before the day of our trip but did not sleep well. Dreams of my childhood, coming of age, and recent events flashed in front of my eyes as if I were facing my final breath. I awoke concerned and irritable.

Before picking Mina up at her dorm, I met with Kaya to say goodbye. She offered me some hot Sotkari sweet tea.

"Kaya, I want to thank you for all your advice and care over all these revolutions we have shared here on Xixsted. I am far from being an upright, honorable person, but at least you have given me some moral compass. Otherwise, I might have turned out to be a complete bastard like Zorla."

Her brow furrowed in confusion.

"Montor, why are you talking to me in this tone, as if this were some last farewell?"

"Well, any mission can be a last one. Danger abounds everywhere these days."

"Yes, but this is unlike your normal demeanor. You always go out with a fearless attitude. What is different this time?"

I leaned forward and stared at the floor.

"You are right. Something is different. I do not know why this endeavor with Mina makes me feel like my life is about to change drastically."

"You have planned this out well. Remember, your Sotkari Ta abilities always put you in control. By the way, do not let Mina's physical appearance deceive you. She is tougher than you might think. I am sure the both of you will get through this safely."

I stood and placed both my hands on her shoulders. Despite our constant worry of being watched, I pressed my forehead against hers, a gesture of gratitude and affection we had not shared since I was much younger. As I walked out, her voice came through my mind, strong and clear.

"May the Farthest Light guide you both."

THE END

I hope you enjoyed this prequel. To discover Mina and Montor's fate, continue their journey with the romantic space opera trilogy The Curse of Sotkari Ta.

Find books here: direct.me/mariaaperezauthor

A NOTE FROM THE AUTHOR

Thank you for reading *Song of the Caged Warrior, The Curse of Sotkari Ta: Prequel*. Please consider taking a moment to write a review on Amazon, BookBub, and Goodreads. This means a lot to self-published authors such as me.

I love keeping in touch with my readers. Find all my website, book, and social media links at the following site:

https://direct.me/mariaaperezauthor

Please also consider subscribing to my author website https://www.mariaaperez.com/ to receive my monthly newsletter. I never spam and usually send this one email per month unless I have special news or promos.

LEXICON AND PLACES

<u>Lexicon</u>

- **Barinta** – (Arandan) collaboration. Montor assigned this name to his spacecraft
- **Bendorai** – (Arandan) ceremony that celebrates when a child is presented with their first amulet, usually one revolution (year) from their birth date
- **Bomar** – (Arandan) bread
- **Carinbo** – (Arandan) sleepy child, equivalent to "sleepyhead" in English
- **Dormet** – (Arandan) a type of pickle sauce
- **Fa** – (Arandan) shortened version of uncle, mainly used by young children
- **Faristo** – (Arandan) uncle
- **Fastorec** – (Arandan) a holographic martial-arts game Josher likes to play with Montor
- **Gargon** – (Tormixian) A rare gem stone that also can serve as an energy source
- **Golorax** – (Arandan) a holographic space battle game that Josher plays at the recreational

holographic rooms near his home at the Arandan enclave on Fronidia

- **Goria** – (Arandan) large purple berry used in sweet pies and desserts
- **Gotumi** – (Arandan) vegetable native to Aranda considered a delicacy
- **Grem** – (Namson) dessert consisting of pockets of dough filled with sweet, macerated fruit
- **Grimah** – (Lostai) literally means "to mate" but used as a curse word equivalent to "damn it" or "fuck" in English
- **Gromos** – (Arandan) Arandan days are divided into eighteen gromos. The equivalent of hours
- **Hanstoric** – (Arandan) jumper, slang word that refers to the laptop-like device required to travel through space using the transportal
- **Hemilta** – (Arandan) icing-coated, crisp wafers used to sweeten the bitter coffee-like beverage called yomoso
- **Himaney** – (Arandan) good luck
- **Horza** – (Lostai) Lostai military boot camp floor exercises
- **Jomeney** – (Arandan) literal translation is "widow's syndrome." A vulgar and derogatory term, referring to a female as desperately needing sexual intercourse
- **Jomoloxti** – (Lostai) an offshoot of the Lostai race who left Losta due to political persecution. They first settled on the Namson planet and then hid in the Morzaki region of planet Losta. The word means "the hidden"
- **Jonjuri** – (Arandan) victory
- **Jouter** – (Fronidian) a dish of vegetables and grains topped with fish, served in an individual crockpot

- **Kantarext** – (Arandan) curse word equivalent to "damn" in English
- **Lae-Ley** – (Arandan) a children's term for urine and urinate
- **Larosh** – (Arandan) a baked egg-based dish made with vegetables and cured meat
- **Lirinium** – (Lostai) the hardest metal known to the Lostai
- **Lizon** – (Arandan) ray gun
- **Lo Ro** – (Arandan) shortened version of grandmother, mainly used by young children
- **Lo Romasta** – (Arandan) grandmother
- **Lo Ta** – (Arandan) shortened version of grandfather, mainly used by young children
- **Lo Taristo** – (Arandan) grandfather
- **Lorin** – (Namson) deep-fried mashed tubers filled with ground shrimp
- **Marz** – (Namson) province
- **Mizora** – (Lostai) phaser rifle
- **Moros** – (Arandan) a team sport similar to rugby
- **Namit** – (Arandan) please
- **Non** – (Lostai) a measurement of distance
- **Omori** – (Aradan) a special receptacle made of a rare metal used to preserve the cremated remains of only the most honored Arandan soldiers.
- **Pasi** – (Sotkari) partial light, referring to those Sotkari that are telepathic, but do not possess other enhanced abilities
- **Rema dox** – (Lostai) a term related to direction
- **Reminda** – (Fronidian) the rare tusk of a wild beast
- **Ro Ma** – (Arandan) shortened version of mother, mainly used by young children
- **Ro Masa** – (Arandan) as part of the Bendorai ceremony, the person designated to take the place of

the mother of a child in the event something
happens to the parent, equivalent to "godmother" in
English

- **Romasta** – (Arandan) mother
- **Sa veranttay** – (Fronidian) term of endearment used
by Fronidian females towards males they care about,
equivalent to "beloved and handsome male" in
English.
- **Santrock** – (Namson) domesticated beast mounted
to play the Namson sport of "vernit"
- **Shermont** – (Arandan) curse word equivalent to
"damn it" in English
- **So** – (Arandan) shortened version of aunt, mainly
used by young children
- **Somasta** – (Arandan) aunt
- **Stampu** – (Arandan) highly intoxicating beverage
consumed in small shots
- **Sura** – (Lostai) a small recreational spacecraft
capable of interplanetary travel
- **Ta** – (Sotkari) enlightened, referring to those Sotkari
known as "Sotkari Ta" who are fully evolved,
possessing the full array of telepathic, blocking,
mind-control, and telekinetic abilities
- **Ta Masa** – (Arandan) as part of the Bendorai
ceremony, the person designated to take the place of
the father of a child in the event something happens
to the parent, equivalent to "godfather" in English
- **Tan** – (Arandan) free or freedom
- **Tanora** – (Lostai) water
- **Ta Ri** – (Arandan) shortened version of father,
mainly used by young children
- **Taristo** – (Arandan) father
- **Teronix** – (Arandan) dough pockets filled with
savory vegetables in a tasty broth

- **Tomdarox** – (Arandan) animal with black fur that looks like a large bear with red eyes.
- **Torixa** – (Arandan) family, Mina assigned this name to a spacecraft used to rescue Montor
- **Vatimex** – (Fronidian) Fronidian martial art
- **Vernit** – (Namson) sport played by the Namson, players mount a domesticated beast and throw balls to their teammates, the object of the game is to get a ball over a goal
- **Vimor** – (Arandan) small, deadly pistol that delivers narrow, radioactive beams with precision
- **Vona** – (Lostai) small craft known for maneuverability and strong plasma beam weaponry capable of destroying larger vessels
- **Vormey** – (Arandan) wine
- **Xarim** – (Arandan) a martial arts defensive move for someone facing a much taller opponent involving tucking the chin, stepping sideways, and elbowing the opponent hard twice in the groin
- **Yomoso** – (Arandan) strong, bitter coffee-like beverage
- **Yomurati** – (Arandan) to help or rescue
- **Zateim** – (Namson) chieftain
- **Zirem** – (Lostai) long rod used as a weapon to deliver painful electric burns
- **Zorinto** – (Namson) intoxicating beverage made from fermented grain and sour juice

Places

- **Aranda** – planet in the Soma Quadrant plagued by civil war and later invaded by the Lostai. It is characterized by red oceans, pink sand, and a mustard-colored sky. Natives are known as

Arandans. Arandans are tall and statuesque with lion-like facial features and yellow, feline eyes. Aranda becomes the birthplace of the United Rebel Front, an insurgency against Lostai rule.

- **Benti** – A planet in the Morex Quadrant whose inhabitants are three persons in one. Natives are known as Bentians
- **Coroxt** – Lostai labor camp where Mina's Earth husband, Joshua, was taken
- **Dit Lar** – small planet near Sotkar in the Morex Quadrant with breathable atmosphere. It is the location of a transportal that allows immediate travel across galaxies
- **Frazin** – small Fronidian village that borders an exotic vacation spot called Jamboran
- **Fro Gantar** – Fronidian capital city
- **Fron Onta Space Station** – one of Fronidia's largest space stations, providing docking for several thousand different types of spacecraft, transport pods, and shuttles
- **Fronidia** – technologically advanced planet in the Soma Quadrant focused on economic power and influence. Friendly towards refugees. Prefers to remain neutral as much as possible towards belligerent planets and/or factions within the quadrant. Many Sotkari Ta that fled Sotkar after the Lostai invasion settled in Fronidia. Characterized by pale skin and black sclera. Natives are known as Fronidians
- **Gorinth** – a planet ruled by an oligarchy of corporate leaders linked to a powerful interplanetary crime syndicate. Its pleasant climate, technological advances, and fancy resorts made it a hot spot for celebrities and wealthy people in the

area. It is also home to a community of Arandan immigrants. Montor first meets Lorret here.

- **Hevrra** – a planet in the Soma Quadrant annexed to the Lostai Empire. Natives are known as Hevrrans and bear some resemblance to the Arandans but their faces are roundish and cat-like as opposed to angular lion-like features. It is also home to a community of Arandan immigrants.
- **Liberated Sotkar** – the portion of planet Sotkar that had been liberated from Lostai control. This represented the majority of the planet except for a territory in the Southwestern continent named Losarex
- **Losarex** – territory in the Southwestern continent of Sotkar that remained under Lostai control after the United Rebel Front uprising
- **Losta** – planet in the Morex Quadrant whose government is focused on increasing their empire and military might throughout the galaxy. Natives are known as Lostai. Lostai are short but strong, bald, and with protruding brow bones.
- **Marimbo Tu** – small island on Sotkar, home to Sotkari insurgency home base
- **Mastazo** – Fronidian province where a large refugee center is located
- **Members Only** – a venue owned by Colora and Jortan that offers dining, dancing, and lodging with guaranteed privacy, one is located in Fronidia, another in Renna One and a third on another planet within the Soma Quadrant
- **Morzaki** – a cold, barren, remote region on planet Losta
- **Namson** – planet at the outer edge of the galaxy, taken over by the Lostai, home to a race of frog-like

people, many of whom have embedded Sotkari Ta genes. Natives are known as The Namson

- **Nexori** – Lostai military station in the Morex Quadrant
- **Norimar Yu** – Sotkari province bordering the Lostai-controlled southwestern territory on Sotkar known as Losarex
- **Penstarox** – a remote island on Aranda, home base of the Arandan rebellion
- **Renna One** – planet in the Soma Quadrant under Lostai control, famous for resorts and recreation, but also where Lostai employ slave labor at mining camps
- **Rondarium** – a large Fronidian town near Zuntar where Josher was born
- **Rovera** – small Sotkari village
- **Solaro** – rural mountainous area on Sotkar where Kaya lived
- **Sotkar** – a planet in the Morex Quadrant, home to a people whose evolutionary transition resulted in some being born with telepathic and telekinetic abilities. The Lostai took advantage of the division between the Sotkari people to annex it to their Empire. Sotkari flora and fauna are characterized by their bioluminescence. Natives are known as Sotkari and have grey skin and blue eyes, lips, and hair
- **Sporia** – a region in Norimar Yu that borders the Lostai-controlled Southwestern continent of Sotkar
- **Tan Aranda** – signifies Free Aranda and is the name of the Arandan rebel home base located on the island of Penstarox
- **Tormix** – planet in the Morex Quadrant that eventually joins the United Rebel Front. Natives are

known as Tormixians and are a reptilian, bipedal race

- **Tremoxtar Mor** – a large island on planet Sotkar, home to many vacation and recreational resorts
- **Ventamu** – the name of the Arandan coastal country (and clan) where Montor is from. All people from Ventamu carry that as their surname
- **Wayont** – remote Fronidian mining town
- **Xixsted** – Lostai science station located on the third moon of Losta (the Lostai home world)
- **Yomabar Labor Camp** – crystal mines on planet Tormix where Arandans were forced into slave labor
- **Zalbadar** – small Fronidian city with a rest stop
- **Zamandi's Room** – An entertainment and restaurant establishment on Renna One that offers various bars, dancing and dining venues, and caters to the Soma Quadrant's rich and famous
- **Zuntar** – Fronidian village where Kindor and family lived and operated a restaurant

ACKNOWLEDGMENTS

The Curse of Sotkari Ta series represents a milestone in my life that has been long in the making. First and foremost, I am thankful that God has given me the opportunity to achieve my dream of becoming a published author. Next, I need to recognize the many people who helped me take the stories in my head and share them with readers.

Big hugs of gratitude to my husband, who supported me when I decided to take early retirement, giving me the time and space to devote to my writing. He works hard so I can stay at home and follow my dream. He's always steadfast by my side. I love you, honey!

My sons were patient when I demanded the TV be turned down and understanding of my other quirks during all the days, weeks, months, and, yes, years that I've devoted to this series. They also offered objective opinions on the cover art and back cover blurbs. My love for you is beyond all galaxies and star systems.

My friend, Joanna, is a space opera fan, just like me. In addition to being my very first alpha reader, she has been a great cheerleader and advisor along the way. I am very grateful to my sisters, Sylvia and Wilma, and my best friend, TP, who also alpha read my first book. Their different perspectives helped me mold the early versions of my story into something beta readers could work with. I can't thank them enough for the motivation they offered along the way. Thanks also to my Song of the Caged Warrior beta readers, Dani Candelaria,

Shawn Murphy, Nancy E. Dunne, Andi McKenzie, Michael D Brooks, Sylvia Perez, and Y. Bocquet, for their valuable feedback, helping me flesh out my characters, and inspiring me to make the story better. Thank you to my proofreader, Kelley, who was exceptionally thorough and expeditious. Many thanks to my ARC readers.

I am deeply thankful to my editor, Stephanie Hoogstad, for her beta reading, her excellent editorial guidance, and for taking the time to review other pieces of the puzzle. I couldn't have done this without her.

Thank you to my cover designer, Christian Bentulan. You patiently held my hand each step of the way and brought my characters and theme to life.

I must give a shout-out to my #WritingCommunity and #vss365 tweeps for welcoming me into their Twitter (X) groups and for their advice and encouragement. A very special thanks to Migs (@OminousHallways), who wrote the beautiful introductory poem and opening poems to Chapters 11, 14, 15, 16, 19, 22, 23, 27, 28, and 41. He earned my trust early on, and I consider him a friend. (All other poems in this book were written by me)

I am lucky to have been blessed with two sets of parents: my biological parents and my aunt and uncle. I am grateful for their love and for teaching me the meaning of family, hard work, perseverance, and generosity.

Last, but not least, I thank the readers, current and future. I hope you enjoy my stories for many years to come.

AUTHOR'S BIO

Maria A. Perez was born in Yonkers, NY, and grew up in New York City. She also lived in Puerto Rico and now resides in South Florida. She holds a Bachelor's in Business and has spent a successful career in Corporate America working in Accounting and Finance. Early retirement has allowed Maria to focus on her dream of writing and becoming a published author. She is married with two young adult sons and a labradoodle daughter. Maria enjoys reading all genres, although she's partial to dystopian, space opera and romance series such as *The Hunger Games*, *The Expanse* and *Outlander*. A diehard "Trekkie" and *Star Wars* fan, she is fascinated with the possibility of what is out there in unexplored space and the potential of the human race.

www.ingramcontent.com/pod-product-compliance
Lightning Source LLC
Chambersburg PA
CBHW061610210726
48287CB00001B/67